THEIR SHATTERED HEARTS

ANGIE COLE

Copyright © 2024 by Angie Cole

All rights reserved.

Published by Cardinal Creek Publishing

No part of this publication may be reproduced, distributed, or transmitted in any form or by any means, including photocopying, recording, or other electronic or mechanical methods, without the prior written permission of the publisher, except in the case of brief quotations embodied in reviews, fan-made graphics, and certain other noncommercial uses permitted by copyright law.

Cole, Angie

Their Shattered Hearts, Angie Cole

Issued in print and electronic formats

ISBN 979-8-9900600-1-2 (Paperback)

ISBN 979-8-9900600-0-5 (ebook)

The story, all names, characters, and incidents portrayed in this production are fictitious. No identification with actual persons (living or deceased), places, buildings, and products is intended or should be inferred.

Content Warning

There are a couple of scenes of sexual harassment in this book in the form of unwanted public touching. If you'd like to skip these scenes, they are in chapters 37 and 50

For my dear grandfather, my hero.
Oliver Cole USMC
World War II
1922-2002

CHAPTER 1

Will Deluca nervously stepped into the Cattle Trail Café. The heavy wooden door creaked shut behind him. He dreaded these weekly family breakfasts because they reminded him of what he'd lost with his wife's passing. Despite his inner turmoil, the café was warm and inviting. Pictures of western icons lined the walls. The red leather booths had people chowing down on pancakes covered in sweet syrup, fried eggs, biscuits, and gravy, giving off a homey vibe. Will peered out the large picture window and surveyed Main Street. The boutiques, antique shops, and quilt store brought back bittersweet memories of old-time Texas. His mother, Liz, emerged from the crowd and approached him, reminding him of all he'd gained and lost in life.

He greeted her with a hug. "Good morning, Momma."

"Good morning. You look tired." She furrowed her brow. "Are you sleeping?"

"Let's eat. I'm starving," Will said, ignoring her question.

Liz scoffed. "So that's how it is. You're ignoring me."

"Yup." Will strode toward the table, where his kids, Eva and Caden, were seated.

Ten-year-old Eva dashed over and hugged him tightly. She had her mother's stunning beauty, from her sapphire-blue eyes to her long blonde hair and a smile brighter than Texas sunshine. "Daddy, I'm so glad you're here! I missed you."

"I missed you more, even though I saw you yesterday before I went to work," he said, ruffling her hair.

Someone tapped his arm. He looked down and saw a smaller eight-year-old version of himself. Caden scowled. "You're late."

"Yes, I am." Will knelt to his eye level. "Remember, the time I'm supposed to get off work must be flexible because I'm a firefighter."

Caden's face turned red, his fists clenching up at his sides. "You can't plan things if you are late."

Will let out a long, audible breath, struggling to explain the unpredictability of his job. Shelly, his wife, naturally connected with Caden, who was diagnosed with autism six years ago. Will thought she would be the one to help their son understand the complexities of life, but now, he had to impart wisdom on the gray areas that even he didn't understand. He could never connect with his son like Shelly had, but he would try.

"No matter how hard you plan and prepare, sometimes life's most dangerous moments can come without warning," Will said, hoping his words might make their way into Caden's mind.

"Not for the person who started the fire," Caden said.

Will suppressed a laugh. "This is true. I'm sorry I was late, Caden." He took a deep breath. "Do you smell pancakes?" Will ruffled Caden's hair.

"Yes, I do." He shook his head. "Grandma, he does that to you too."

"What, darlin'?"

"Change the subject."

"He does," Liz said with a laugh.

Will sat between his two children with his mom at the head of the table, a spot she'd taken five years earlier when his father unexpectedly died of a heart attack while working on fences at his ranch. Liz appeared much younger than her sixty years. Despite her silver hair, she wore a chic bob and was always dressed to impress. She wore capri jeans, an Aztec-print button-down shirt, and brown booties.

His younger sister, Kati, sat across the table with his best friend, Jon Clemmons.

"Was it busy last night?" Jon asked with a smirk.

Will narrowed his eyes. "You're worse than the rookies. Now you've jinxed them for the day."

Jon shook his head. "Come on, you know that's not true. It only applies at the station."

"I disagree," Kati chimed in, looking at Jon. "You've likely jinxed the emergency room too."

Jon pointed at Kati and Will. "You two have issues with superstition."

A chestnut-haired waitress approached the table, smiling. "Good morning." She turned her attention to Will. "Hey, Will. I haven't seen you in a while." Her eyes lingered on his face, and her lips curled into a smirk.

Will clenched his jaw to mask his agitation. "I'm here almost every week with my family. And how long have you worked here?" His eyes traveled to the menu. He was frustrated by the bold flirtation. She couldn't be more than seventeen.

Kati and Jon's eyes widened.

"Well . . . a little over a year." The young waitress smiled. "I'm glad I get to see you today. How are you doing?"

Will glanced at Kati and Jon, rolling his eyes. "I'm fine," he said through his teeth.

She smiled, turning her body toward him. "Are these your children? They've grown!"

Will set the menu on the table and stood up. "Ma'am, may I speak with you in private?"

The waitress pranced across the restaurant with Will. He turned to her, towering over her with his broad, tall frame. "Ma'am, I hope this doesn't appear rude, but the last time you waited on me, you flirted with me. And if you can't tell by me ignoring you each time, I'm not interested. Don't push your way into my life by referring to my children."

Her face reddened. "I'm sorry, I never meant to . . ."

A pang of guilt hit Will. "Listen, I don't mean to upset you . . . I just can't." He turned and walked away, leaving her with tears in her eyes. His family stared at him.

"William, don't you know that poor girl?" his mother scolded. "She's waited on us before."

"No, why?"

"Are you kidding me?" Kati interjected.

"No." Will's face reddened.

"It's Chief Erickson's daughter, Sammy. She's grown up." Jon laughed. "You're an idiot."

"I don't think she was flirting. She's a kid. She started working here just after her sixteenth birthday," Liz whispered, frowning.

Will put his face in his hands. He was an idiot. How did he not recognize the chief's daughter? It had been three years since he saw her last, at Shelly's funeral. She couldn't have been more than thirteen then, but now she was a grown woman. He struggled to recognize her, but then again, the funeral was a hazy memory for him.

Caden put his hand on Will's arm. "See, Daddy, now that's how I feel when people talk to me. Sometimes, I can't understand things like flirting, happy, or angry." He pointed to Liz. "Nana's angry." Then he pointed at Jon. "He's happy." Finally, he pointed at Kati. "Aunt Kati is hard to read."

Will glanced at his son. "Who taught you that?"

"Momma."

"I wonder what you'll say to the chief when he finds out you made his daughter cry. You seriously thought she was flirting with you. What an idiot," Jon laughed.

Will scowled. "Shut up, Jon." Will knew he needed to apologize to the chief's daughter, or he would hear about it.

Will had been having trouble sleeping for the last week, making him as friendly as one of the five-foot rattlesnakes that slithered along the pasture of his forty-acre ranch just outside Cardinal Creek. He and Shelly had bought the Rockin' D Ranch to open an equine therapy center for children with autism. Shelly had been working with Cindy Lopez, the Blue Bonnet Therapy Center director. Caden had been attending the center since he was two. Her dream was to help Caden and for the equine center to be a resource for other families. She'd been gone for three years; now, it was a lost dream. His thoughts drifted to another time before his life turned upside down.

The memory of the accident replayed on a loop in his mind, as it had every Memorial Day weekend for the past three years. He remembered staring at the shattered window of his SUV in disbelief; he'd focused on the giant shards of glass suspended in the window frame. In the blink of an eye, she was gone. The color vanished from his vision that day. It drained away, leaving him to see the world in black and white, flat and meaningless. His heart was broken into a million pieces, scattered on the ground, and left to die. He questioned how a perfect day could end so tragically.

His mind flooded with memories of that morning he'd spent with Shelly. She was still asleep in his arms; her golden hair cascaded across his chest and shimmered in the morning sunlight streaming through the window. Her eyes slowly opened, revealing that piercing blue gaze he'd fallen for when they were teenagers. She had smiled sweetly at him, her lips curving in a delicate bow. Will saw the love in her eyes as they gazed up at him, and he leaned down to press his lips against hers. Heat tingled throughout his body, and he'd held her close like he never wanted to let go. When they made love that morning, the world around them had stopped. He was reluctant to leave their bed, though he had to hurry to prepare for his shift at the firehouse.

An involuntary shiver ran down Will's spine when he fastened his shirt's last button. A sense of profound dread hit him as if something was off-kilter. He couldn't shake the foreboding that seemed to follow him into the morning air, and part of him wanted to turn back and hold her close just a bit longer.

Will hurried to his job at the Cardinal Creek Fire Department, running behind schedule as always. He had been working there for fifteen years, living out a dream he had since middle school, when he and his closest friend, Jon, discussed their aspirations of becoming firefighters/paramedics.

Will and Jon had been best friends since they were five years old. They went through high school together, participating in 4H and the roping team. They even joined the fire academy as a team. Their bond was strong, with a willingness to do anything for one another.

After graduating from the academy, Jon started dating Kati, but they never discussed marriage. When Kati's father passed away, their relationship became distant. When Shelly died in a tragic accident, Jon was never the same after he volunteered to be part of the team that recovered Shelly's body from her SUV trapped under a massive eighteen-wheeler.

When Will arrived, his coworkers were wiping down the fire trucks and doing daily chores. They worked, doing their daily tasks and waiting for lunch. The aroma of freshly baked lasagna wafted through the firehouse as lunchtime approached. Will took a bite, savoring the symphony of flavors that danced on his tongue. The chatter in the station grew louder as everyone enjoyed their meal together, bantering back and forth with each other.

A few hours later, Will was walking toward the fire station truck bay when he saw Shelly strolling toward him, smiling and waving. She'd stopped by on her way to get ingredients for cookies she was planning on baking with Eva. Shelly was glowing when she said, "I have news for you, but you'll have to wait until later to find out what it is." Then she'd kissed him goodbye, and a knot formed in his stomach as she drove away. No matter how hard he tried, he couldn't shake the uneasiness that swept over him.

Two hours later, a call came in for a car accident with a fatality. The sirens screamed through the streets as they raced to the accident site. Will never knew what to expect when he arrived on the scene of an accident. Only a few steps away lay a crumpled mess. The front end of an SUV stuck out from under the rear bumper of an eighteen-wheeler parked on the side of the road. As he moved closer, the fire chief, Luke Erickson, blocked him from moving closer to the scene. Jon sprinted to Will, tears streaming down his face. He pleaded with Will to hear what the chief was saying, but he didn't. He pushed past Jon and ran toward the wreckage. It took him several seconds to focus on who he was looking at: Shelly was pinned behind the steering wheel by what remained of her seatbelt. He remained focused on the wedding ring he'd placed on her finger the day they exchanged vows. The brilliant diamond glinted and flashed in the fading light of the late afternoon, casting shimmering rays in every direction. Will couldn't escape the churning in his gut. The red and blue emergency lights flashing around him only added to the chaotic scene. His eyes were fixed on the scene. It was like he had entered a dream-like state where everything was exaggerated and surreal.

A firm hand landed on his shoulder, but he shook it away and shuffled to the chief's truck. He looked back to see Jon working the scene using the jaws of life to recover his wife's lifeless body like any other accident, but this time, it was different and more personal. When Jon handed him Shelly's phone at the hospital, he opened it, and his text was staring him in the face. "Come on, tell me the news, please." Guilt filled his heart with sorrow for being responsible for this tragedy.

"Will? Earth to Will!" Kati said, waving her hand at him.

Slowly, he lifted his head, glancing around the room. He gave a wry smile. "Yeah, sorry. I'm tired this morning. What did I miss?"

"You seemed to drift off," Kati said.

"Aunt Kati, Daddy does that at home," Eva commented over the commotion at the table.

Liz scolded her daughter. "Kati, leave my sweet son alone. He just got off work."

Will scanned the table filled with his family, wondering how he would ask for their help with the equine therapy center, which he'd promised Cindy Lopez would open in September. When Cindy approached Will last week, she emphasized how important it was to the community to have the equine center open in the fall. Without a second thought, his overwhelming guilt led to him making a promise he wasn't sure he could keep.

He breathed deeply and cleared his throat, causing everyone to stare at him. "Listen, I'm not good at asking for help, but I need help opening the equine center by Shelly's birthday in September."

The silence was deafening. The group stared at Will. He shifted in his seat.

Liz's eyebrow raised. "I thought you were going to table that until you could figure out how to make it happen."

Will scrubbed his hand across his chin. "I was, but Cindy caught me when I left Caden's therapy last week." A lump formed in his throat, causing him to swallow.

"Do we have enough time to raise funds and complete the other paperwork? Have you found a grant?" Liz asked.

He shook his head. "I haven't found a grant, but I hope to get one." *I don't want to let Shelly down again. If I hadn't texted her, she'd be here to open the center. I should have waited to text her. If I had, she'd still be alive.*

Kati reached across, curling her fingers around his. "That gives us seven months to get this done. We can do it, big brother. Right, Jon?" Kati elbowed Jon.

"We'll all work together to get it done," Jon said.

"Thanks," Will said, squeezing Kati's hand once.

He shook his head, thinking about Shelly's notebook with all the plans she had written down, but she'd kept so much in her head. He had no idea how he could get it done. It was vital for him to open the equine therapy center. Shelly was passionate about working with children on the autism spectrum while integrating equine therapy. She eventually wanted to integrate equine therapy for veterans as well. They had so many hopes and dreams when they purchased the Rockin D. But now, those dreams have faded into nothingness with her gone.

Kati and Will had always been close. She had met Shelly in kindergarten, and they became fast friends. For as long as Will could remember, it was Jon and Kati and him and Shelly, the Four Musketeers. Shelly's sudden death left Jon and Kati in shambles. Their once vibrant love had dwindled to a distant flame, flickering in the aftermath of their friend's death.

It was not love at first sight for Will and Shelly. She was like another annoying sister until he noticed her during his senior year after Christmas. She was a good friend after his heart had been broken that summer. She'd kissed him on New Year's Eve at midnight; the rest was history. In the past five years, his family experienced significant loss with the deaths of their father and Shelly two years later.

It made his family closer, but recently, Kati had been encouraging Will to date, which irritated him because it was disrespectful to the memory of his wife. Will wasn't sure why she didn't understand that he couldn't open his heart to someone. It had only been three years.

Kati gazed toward the café door every time it swung open. Will raised an eyebrow, curious about her sudden interest. "Are you expecting someone?"

She glanced at Will, wide-eyed. "Um, no, not really." Her head shot up when the door opened, and a tall blonde woman walked in dressed in a shirt three sizes too small and fake from the top of her head to her waist. Will groaned, trying to suppress his anger because he knew what his sister was up to. Kati stood and walked over to greet the woman.

Jon raised his eyebrows and whistled. "Wow, she's hot."

"Don't you get into enough trouble with your carousing?" Will fired back, sounding harsher than expected.

Kati and the blonde woman made their way to the table, causing Will to squint and shake his head at his mother with disapproval.

"Hey y'all, this is Tammy," Kati said. "She just moved here from San Antonio. She's the new assistant manager of the emergency department. This is my momma, Liz, my brother Will, and his kids, Eva and Caden." She motioned over her shoulder. "This is Jon."

Will closed his eyes, took a deep breath, and painted on a smile. He knew precisely what Kati was up to with this new coworker thing. "Hello, Tammy."

She smiled, batting her long, obviously fake eyelashes. "Hey, y'all, it's nice to meet you. She turned to Will. "Kati has told me all about you."

"Oh, she has?" Will, speaking between his teeth, the heat rising in his neck. He glared at Kati, then stood. "Tammy, please excuse us." He took Kati by the elbow and pulled her toward the bathroom. "What the hell are you doing?"

"Nothing, she's new in town. I told her I would show her around town after we were done here."

"Yeah, sure. Why did you invite her to a family thing?" Will snapped, pointing at her.

Kati held up both hands. "Oh my God, we're almost finished, so I texted her to meet me here."

"I know you are trying to fix me up with someone again. I told you I'm not ready to date."

"It wasn't like that. You made it clear you don't want to date. I asked her to meet me here, and I would show her around, that's all." Tears welled up in Kati's eyes. "First Sammy, and now this. What's wrong with you?" She wiped her eyes. "You embarrassed me in front of a coworker."

He inched closer and hissed. "'Oh, Kati told me all about you, Will.' What does that mean?"

He heard someone clear their throat behind him. He turned slowly. Tammy stood looking at him, brow furrowed.

Shit. Shit.

"What it means is that your sister spoke with great respect for her brother and longtime friend Jon, the firefighters," Kati said, biting her quivering lip.

"Kati, I, uh . . ."

"No, Will," Kati scoffed. "I'm going to excuse myself, if that's okay with you before I say something I'll regret." She pointed her finger at his chest. "You need to get yourself together. You were rude and owe Tammy and the chief's daughter an apology."

Will closed his eyes and rubbed the back of his neck.

Kati pushed past him. "Forget it, Will." She walked toward Tammy. "Sorry, my brother is a jerk. A great firefighter, but a big jerk."

Tammy snickered and waved. "Bye, Will."

"Bye, Tammy. Sorry, I was a jerk."

"Is a jerk, Tammy. He is a jerk!" Kati yelled over her shoulder.

Liz's intense gaze was fixed on Will as he returned to the table. Her eyebrows were furrowed, and her lips were pursed tightly together. He slid into his chair with a heavy thud, letting out a deep sigh before staring at his hands, unable to meet her eyes. Her anger radiated across the table.

"That wasn't cool," Liz said, glaring.

"Hey, kids, why don't we go find some candy so Momma D can yell at your daddy," Jon said as he gathered Eva and Caden.

"I think watching Daddy get yelled at is better than candy, Uncle Jon," Caden said.

"Well, me too, but let's get candy anyway."

When the kids were out of sight, Liz reached for Will's hand. "Listen to me. I know you're not sleeping well. Now, you want to open the equine center. What happened here today isn't you." She took him by the chin. "You aren't the person you presented to both ladies."

"God, I just miss her," he croaked. "The thought of being with another woman makes me . . . I can't be with anyone."

"I know you miss her, but that's no excuse for being rude to other people who are just being nice."

"I know. I feel like I'm walking in a fog most of the time. I react before I realize I've misread the situation."

"You've always reacted, even before Shelly died, but now it's worse." She squeezed his hand. "Be an example for your kids. Treat people well."

"Can you bring Caden and Eva home?" Will asked. "I want to go riding."

"Of course. Take Jon with you." Liz raised an eyebrow as Jon and the kids reached the table with two candy bars. "Jon, why so much candy?"

"Well, see . . ." A sinister smile spread across his face. "They can be all sugared up for Will."

"Ha." Liz held out her hand to the kids. "Put the candy in Nana's hand. You're coming with me, and I don't need you all hopped up on sugar."

"Oh dang, Momma D, I'm sorry," Jon said.

"Guess what? You get to go riding fences with Will just for that."

"Yes, ma'am."

"Great, punish me, Momma." Will laughed. "Jon, it's okay. I would rather be alone." He grabbed his hat and threw money on the table. "Thanks for taking the kids, Momma." He gave Jon a friendly punch as he headed toward the door. Just before he got to the door, he ran into Sammy, who tried to walk around him. "Hey, Sammy."

"What?" She stood with her back to him.

"I'm sorry I was rude earlier. I didn't recognize you, but that's no excuse for being rude."

"I feel bad about your wife. I was trying to be nice." She paused, then added, "You're too old for me anyway . . . if you thought I liked you."

Will laughed. "I suppose you're right. I didn't take a good look at you."

When she turned to him, he looked at her and saw a child. He shook his head. "Sammy, I am so sorry. I was way out of line."

"It's okay. Don't worry, I won't tell my dad." Sammy paused, then said, "You know, I was only thirteen when your wife died. My dad was upset when he came home the morning after. I overheard him telling my mom about it. I can't imagine how your kids feel. I would be devastated if one of my parents died."

Will sighed. "You have a good heart. I appreciate your kindness. Again, I'm sorry."

"All is forgiven, sir."

He squeezed her shoulder as he walked out the door, left to deal with his shattered heart.

CHAPTER 2

Anna Samuels stepped onto the wrap-around porch of her grandparents' cozy white farmhouse. The late February wind blew across the snow-covered pasture, causing a shiver down her spine.

She sighed as warm tears slid down her cheeks. She'd just buried her grandfather. Anna looked at the sky, wondering how she would live without her papa. She had sat by his side for three months, watching him slowly disappear. He became a shadow of the man she knew.

When Anna was nine years old, she'd begged her parents to let her go to a horseback riding camp with the Girl Scouts. A week into the camp, she dismounted her horse when she saw her grandparents standing by the fence with the camp director. Even back then, she'd immediately known something was wrong. Her parents had been in an accident, and she lost them both that day. The next few days were a blur as she packed up her room, said goodbye to friends, and was driven to her new home in Marceline, Missouri, with her Nana and Papa.

After the accident, Anna's chest had been tight with grief and pain for months. It tightened again as she stared out over the cold pastures.

The front door creaked open, and she spun around, expecting to see Papa. Instead, she saw Maggie Calvert walking toward her with a warm smile. Maggie was no taller than Anna, with short hair dyed chestnut brown. She had a youthful appearance despite being fifty-nine years old. Anna had known Maggie since she'd moved in with her grandparents, and Maggie had been there for her during the rough times when Papa was sick. She was like a second mother to Anna, and she felt blessed to have such a fantastic friend.

"What are you doing out here, honey?" Maggie asked as she wrapped a jacket around Anna's shoulders.

Anna's heart pounded as she pulled the jacket tightly around her. This was the day she'd feared since the day her parents died. She was alone with no family. How could she explain to Maggie how empty she felt deep down in her core?

"I just needed some fresh air," Anna replied, her voice shaking as she tried to hold back the tears.

Maggie took Anna's chin so their eyes could meet. "I can see you've been crying. What can I do to help? Talk to me, Anna. Show me what's going on beneath that brave facade," she whispered.

A sob escaped from Anna's chest, and she closed her eyes to allow the tears to stream down her face. "I just realized I have no family—everyone is gone. Now it's just me, and I'm scared."

Maggie sighed. "I understand why it's hard for you. You don't have your real family anymore, but you have us."

Anna pulled back from Maggie. "That's not the same though, is it?"

"No," Maggie said firmly. "It's not the same as having blood relatives, but that doesn't mean we can't be family too."

Anna frowned and wiped her eyes again. "The problem is that I still don't belong anywhere," she mumbled, a lump forming in her throat again.

Maggie half-smiled and grabbed Anna's hands. "You belong here with us, even if things don't look quite the same anymore."

Anna sniffled and nodded before mustering up a small smile of her own. "Thanks, Maggie. We should get inside before Jenny creates mischief."

Jenny stood a full head taller than Anna and could have walked straight from the pages of an epic novel. She had chestnut hair, like her mother, that fell to her shoulders in soft waves. She possessed an intense energy that no one wanted to challenge. Growing up together in school, Anna had seen Jenny's power firsthand on more occasions than she'd care to recount.

Maggie rolled her eyes and laughed. "My daughter, the court jester."

They walked back into the house that was filled with people clad in black. Anna narrowed her eyes as she spotted Tony talking to her friend Emma.

For the past two years, Anna and Tony have been dating. While she dedicated herself to caring for her papa, their relationship had to endure the challenges of being long-distance for the last three months. Tony's on-call schedule for trauma orthopedic surgeons had made it impossible for him to make the two-hour trip from Columbia to Marceline. Anna's heart leaped as she walked toward him. She wanted desperately to ask him to stay the night; she just needed someone to hold her. But something inside held her back.

Tony met her halfway, wrapping his arms around her. "How are you doing?"

Anna laid her head on his chest, finding comfort in his arms. She looked up. "Stay with me tonight. I need you."

"I wish I could," he whispered in her ear, "but I'm doing a knee replacement in the morning."

Anna took a deep breath and tried to push her disappointment away. "I understand." Then she turned to Emma. "Thanks for coming, Emma. I didn't expect to see you."

Anna's eyes narrowed on Emma, feeling a mix of confusion and resentment toward her presence at her grandfather's funeral. They'd been close friends since Anna moved to Marceline, but things changed when they both enrolled in nursing school at the University of Missouri. Emma became fiercely competitive and often took credit for Anna's hard work and ideas. Their once strong friendship continued to deteriorate as they began working together at University Hospital, with Emma getting all the recognition and promotions thanks to Anna's grant proposal. And now, seeing Emma dressed in black at her grandparents' house, Anna couldn't help but feel conflicted. Part of her wanted to confront Emma, while another part just wanted to mourn her grandfather's passing in peace.

"Why wouldn't I come?" Emma's tone was crisp.

Tony wrapped his arms around Anna's waist. "Baby, I need to go. I told Emma I would follow her home. She needs to work in the morning as well."

"Yes, Tony said he'd follow me home since I don't like driving in the dark," Emma stammered.

Anna raised an eyebrow. She didn't recall Emma mentioning having issues driving at night, but she didn't want to argue. Instead, she turned to Tony. "What time is the surgery?"

"Uh . . ." He cleared his throat. "In the afternoon. I'll call you before I go."

"I thought you said it was in the morning."

"Maybe morning? Or afternoon. I left my schedule at home. Um, I'll text you later, okay?"

Anna's stomach churned. Tony wasn't usually so careless with his schedule. But she nodded and said to Emma, "Thanks for coming."

"We need to get going," Emma said as she reached for Tony's hand and pulled away.

Anna's heart raced as she watched Emma's hand intertwine with Tony's, her grip firm and possessive. Emma yanked her hand away from Tony's as if she was reading Anna's thoughts. She couldn't help but feel a pang of jealousy. Did Tony have feelings for Emma? Was that why he'd been pushing her away?

Anna's heart thundered in her chest as Tony kissed her. She experienced mixed emotions as Tony's body tensed in response to Emma's disapproving glare. Suddenly, Emma gasped sharply, interrupting their kiss. The tension in the air left Anna dizzy and overwhelmed.

Emma latched onto Tony's arm as she shot Anna a disapproving look. "Sorry about your grandfather, Anna. Hopefully, you'll be back in the office soon."

They left in a tense silence, leaving Anna to grapple with her conflicting emotions and unanswered questions.

Anna's eyes widened as she watched Tony and Emma through the window of her house. She saw them arguing, their arms flailing, and voices raised. Tony's car was parked in the driveway, but he was next to it, gesturing wildly. Emma was on the verge of tears as she stormed toward her car. Anna's heart raced as she struggled with conflicting emotions—should she confront them or stay put until they left? Her feet carried her toward the door as she tried to decide, unsure if she wanted to know the truth behind their argument.

Anna stood frozen near the door, and her mind was filled with memories of her grandfather. Three years ago, she woke from a nightmare and immediately drove two hours to see him, relieved when it turned out to be only a dream. But this time, there would be no waking up or rushing to his side. He was gone for real, and Anna's world would never be the same.

With a forced smile, Anna made small talk with the remaining guests in the living room. She glanced out the window and couldn't help but notice Tony's and Emma's cars were still parked in the driveway despite them saying they were leaving earlier.

She rushed onto the porch and walked around it, following the stairs into the yard. With every step, her heart sank. She froze as she got closer and saw Tony embracing Emma tightly while kissing her fervently. The sounds of his moans echoed in Anna's ears, making her throat tighten. She cleared her throat loudly enough to get their attention.

Tony pulled away from Emma, his eyes wide. "Baby, it's not what it looks like."

Anna broke into mirthless laughter. "What does it look like?" She took a step toward him. "It looks like you were kissing my supposed friend who stole my ideas, a promotion, and now my boyfriend." She turned to Emma. "Is there anything else you want to steal from me?"

Emma straightened her clothes. "It wasn't stealing. He decided he wanted a woman who could please a man."

Heat crawled up Anna's neck. "Oh, is that right?" She glared at Tony. "Well, are you with Emma because I don't please you?"

Tony shrugged Emma's hand off his shoulder. He moved toward Anna to take her into his arms. "No, baby, she was just a fling."

"A fling? A fling? Wow." Anna looked at Emma. "You are a fling."

Tony touched Anna's face. "Baby, you know I love you. Please let me explain."

Anna ripped his hand from her face. "What is there to explain? I just caught you making out with my supposed friend."

Tony tried to pull Anna into his arms again, but she stepped back and closed her eyes. All she could see was a countdown for a space shuttle take-off, and that was where her emotions were heading for launch. She took a deep breath, attempting to control herself.

"I don't understand why you two didn't just leave," she said. "Why here, why now?"

Emma stepped forward. "Oh my God. Why? Why? Because he can't keep his hands off me!"

The countdown in Anna's mind ended. She grabbed Emma's jacket and dragged her toward her car. "Get the hell off my property before I throttle you."

Emma grabbed Anna's wrist, but all Anna could see was red. Anna's grip tightened on Emma's jacket as she turned, getting inches from her face. Her pulse raced as the anger boiled inside her.

"You took my job, now my boyfriend," she spat. "You can have him, but not at my house." Anna's vision blurred with tears. "What the hell are you so jealous of, you bitch?" Her voice shook with emotion as she continued, "You have both parents and siblings, while I have nothing." A sob caught in Anna's throat, but she refused to let Emma see her cry.

Tony put his hand on her shoulder. "Baby, let her go."

"Baby?" Anna yelled as tears streamed down her cheeks. Rage glowed in her eyes. "Both of you leave. Now."

The front screen door slammed, and they all turned to see Jenny walking down the sidewalk. Emma jumped back and slunk up the driveway toward her car.

"Hey, stop!" Jenny yelled.

Emma froze where she stood.

"What the hell is going on, Anna?" Jenny rushed over. By this point, Anna was sobbing. "What happened?" Tony took another step, but Jenny stood firm. "Somebody better start talking."

"Jenny, let me talk to Anna alone," Tony pleaded.

"No, I'm not leaving Anna."

Emma grabbed Tony's arm. "Come on, Tony, let's go."

Anna covered her face with her hands, taking deep breaths to compose herself. Her mind was reeling. *What is going on? This is like a bad dream I can't wake up from.* She slowly took her hands from her face.

Tony took a step forward, but Jenny stepped in front of him. "Go before I punch your lights out." She jabbed a finger into his chest. "What is wrong with you? If you're going to be a cheating weasel, at least leave. How could you do this? Both of you." She shot daggers at Emma. "What has gotten into you the last few years? What's turned you into such a bitch?"

"Jennifer Calvert, watch your language!" Maggie yelled from the porch as she headed down the steps to the driveway.

Jenny rolled her eyes. "Oh, for Christ's sake, Mom. I'm thirty-six. I can cuss."

Maggie rushed over, draped a jacket around Anna's shoulders, and hugged her tight. "You all right, darling?"

Anna nodded. "Can you please tell them to leave before I hit one of them?" she whispered.

Jenny yelled, "Momma, take her inside. I'll smack them hard enough for the both of us."

"No one is smacking anyone. We're adults. Well, maybe not you two." Maggie scoffed at Emma and Tony. "Ya'll get out of here. This girl has been through enough."

"Oh yeah, Mrs. Calvert, poor Anna is always the victim," Emma sneered.

Jenny grabbed her arm and dragged her to the car. "Shut up and get the hell out of here."

Emma knocked Jenny's hand away. "Poor Anna always gets pity because her parents died. They probably died to…" She paused and huffed, "Get away from you."

"Emma! Leave!" Tony yelled, stalking toward her. He turned to Anna. "I'm so sorry, Anna. I have no excuses."

Anna's entire being shook with a mixture of grief and guilt. She couldn't help but wonder if she was cursed as those closest to her continued to leave this world one by one. Each loss felt like a blow to her worthiness, and she couldn't shake the feeling that she was somehow to blame. Anna was numb when Tony and Emma walked away. The realization of yet another loss was too much for her to comprehend. Was any of this even real, or just some cruel punishment?

Maggie leaned in and whispered, "Honey, don't you listen to that spiteful girl. I don't know what happened to her. She's changed."

Anna slowly nodded. Tony and Emma were arguing in the driveway, but she couldn't understand what was said. She did hear Jenny tell them that she'd break their windshield if they didn't get into their cars and leave. When Anna listened to the cars drive away, she fell into Maggie's arms and sobbed. She led Anna through the back door into the kitchen and settled her at the table.

"Honey, you stay here. Jenny and I will tell the guests you aren't feeling well."

Mascara streaked across Anna's face. "It's not a lie. Everyone heard and saw it all, didn't they?"

Maggie nodded.

Anna put her head on the counter. "How humiliating."

As the guests left and the food was cleared, Maggie and Jenny thanked them while Anna struggled to control her emotions. She couldn't understand how Tony could betray her like this; she never expected him to be capable of such betrayal. Emma, someone she once considered a close friend, had proven to be a backstabber. Anna couldn't help but wonder why they bothered to come to the funeral. Did they just come to rub salt in her wounds? A conflicting mix of anger and sadness consumed Anna as she tried to make sense of it all.

Though it had been a short time since Anna had caught Tony and Emma on the side of the house, she couldn't get the image out of her mind. All she wanted was to change into her pajamas, drink a glass of wine, and go to bed. Anna collapsed onto the wooden stool, her head heavy with exhaustion. She rested her head on the cool laminate countertop, took a deep breath in through her nose, and let it out slowly through her mouth.

A hand on Anna's shoulder made her jump. "Hey," Jenny said. "You want Momma and I to stay tonight? We could make it a girls' night."

When Jenny and Anna first met, they immediately forged an unbreakable bond. It was after the funeral of Anna's parents. They'd sat on her grandparents' porch, shared a love of horses, and endured the loss of a parent. They shared a piece of chocolate cake while Jenny told her that her father, a police officer, had died on duty when she was five. Since that day twenty-seven years ago, Jenny had been there for Anna through every joy and sorrow. This night was no different.

Maggie waltzed into the room, holding a bottle of wine in each hand. "I have wine." She motioned to the refrigerator. "And ice cream."

Anna squeezed Jenny's hand. "I would like that. I need a minute."

"Let me finish a few things. I'll be right back," said Jenny.

Anna stayed in the kitchen, her expression both vacant and frustrated. When Jenny brought the last dish in, Anna sighed heavily before looking up at her friend. "How am I supposed to feel?"

Jenny shook her head. "It's understandable that you feel so angry and betrayed by Emma, especially after she got the promotion that you deserved. But what do you think about Tony?"

Anna paused for a moment, considering before responding. "Sometimes it's best to keep quiet and drive on, right? My program made a difference to the people who needed it. It mattered to me—not some petty jealousy between me and Emma." Anna wasn't sure what to think about Tony.

Jenny threw her hands up in exasperation. "Who taught you to take this kind of abuse? I know it isn't something your papa or nana would condone!"

Before Jenny could continue, Maggie spoke sternly from across the room. "Jennifer Calvert, that's enough!"

"Oh, come on, Momma!" Jenny paced angrily around the kitchen before turning to Anna. "You can't let people like Tony and Emma walk all over you. How long do they think they can get away with this behavior?"

Anna held up both hands defensively. "I don't care anymore," she said flatly. "She's been playing these games since nursing school, pulling out her competitive streak every chance she could."

Maggie put her hands on her hips as she glared at Anna incredulously. "And what about Tony?"

Anna cast her eyes downward as she spoke. "I honestly don't know what I care about right now," she murmured. Her chest was heavy as she thought about how much had changed now that both grandparents had passed. She absentmindedly ran her fingers over the worn counter where they used to sit, barely noticing Jenny and Maggie exchanging a knowing look. At just thirty-six, she was the only one left in her family. Jenny and Maggie were family in a way, but it just wasn't quite the same. Sitting there, overwhelmed by grief and emptiness, she thought about Tony with a sense of longing that she couldn't explain.

"The only thing I had to look forward to after all this was being with Tony," Anna continued, her voice falling. She felt a tug in her chest as she thought of him, missing the comfort they'd shared when they were together. "I think," she added after a moment of hesitation, lifting her head from the counter. A somber hush fell over the room; their soft breaths and Anna's deep, mournful sigh were only heard.

The silence was broken when Jenny spoke in an overly cheerful voice. "Anna, it would help if Momma cooked us breakfast."

Maggie smiled as she walked across the kitchen, handing each of them a glass of wine. "Oh, why yes, I live to make my thirty-six-year-old daughter breakfast."

Jenny held her glass high, trying to bring some fun to the somber atmosphere around them. "Cheers to you, Momma, the best cook in the world!"

Anna laughed and grabbed her glass, taking a long drink of her wine before setting it back on the table. Anna glanced at Maggie and noticed sadness in her smile and her heart constricted.

Maggie grabbed an envelope from her purse and placed it gently in front of Anna. The familiar sight of her grandpa's handwriting brought tears to Anna's eyes.

"He gave this to me not long before he passed away," Maggie said.

Anna couldn't help but notice a faint hint of her grandpa's woodsy cologne as she ran her fingers over her name scribbled in his familiar handwriting. She closed her eyes and breathed in deeply. Her head whirled with memories of late-night movie marathons with chocolate chip ice cream, sunflowers at her parents' gravesite, banana splits at Dairy Queen, and hearing him cheer for her on graduation day. So many memories . . . And that's what was left: just memories and this letter from beyond the grave.

Anna stared at the letter, her fingers repeatedly running over the delicate cursive on the envelope. "Maggie, thank you for caring for Papa," she whispered.

Maggie placed her warm hand on Anna's and smiled. "It was a pleasure to care for him," she said, swallowing unshed tears. "Your momma and I were the best of friends ever since kindergarten. Somehow, our friendship kept your momma alive for both of us."

Anna's tears overflowed at the thought that her family was gone—not an aunt or uncle, nor even a cousin—she was alone in the world. She looked up at Maggie wild-eyed, clutching the letter to her chest. "I . . . I feel so alone." She slumped down, sobbing.

Maggie wrapped an arm around her shoulders and rocked until the sobs subsided.

Wiping away tears with a tissue, Anna stammered, "I'm sorry for implying that you have not been here for me."

Maggie brushed away her concerns with a wave of one hand. "Sweetie, you are grieving," her voice gentle. "This wound is fresh, and it feels like life has stolen all your happiness from you tonight. But I don't want you to think you are alone. We love you deeply."

Jenny echoed her sentiments with a nod and an understanding look. "Anna, we love you, and even though it's not the same as a blood sibling, I think of you as a sister."

The comforting words settled into Anna's chest, and she knew that while her family was gone, two wonderful people would always be there for her.

Anna stood up unsteadily and laughed as she wiped away her tears. "I think I need a group hug and a refill." They shared a warm embrace, laughter bubbling through their tears.

Two hours later, after two bottles of sweet Pink Catawba wine, Anna, Jenny, and Maggie sat at the dining room table looking through Nana's photo albums. The room was illuminated by the warm glow from the vintage chandelier overhead. The old pictures were tattered from being thumbed through many times before. They paged through the albums while sipping their wine and laughed at the memories from years ago. Anna paused when she came across a photo from one summer when she was sixteen. In the photo, her smiling grandparents were standing on each side of her with their arms draped around her shoulders. She had gone to a horse-riding camp in Cardinal Creek, a quaint town in Texas. She remembered her camp counselor taking this photo. Her grandparents had been so proud of her accomplishments at barrel racing camp.

Jenny grinned. "I remember you coming home from camp that summer, crazy about a boy with amazing blue eyes. 'Cowboy' was what you used to call him."

Anna playfully swatted her. "Shh! That's our secret!"

Maggie raised an eyebrow at her daughter and said, "Should I start telling secrets?"

"Nah, Anna knows all my secrets, even ones you don't," Jenny replied quickly, changing the subject. "Anna, didn't you have a picture of the cowboy and his sister?"

Anna shrugged. "I thought I did. It drives me crazy that I never asked his real name and can't remember his sister's name. His mom was so kind to me." Anna stifled a yawn. "I'm exhausted. Would you mind if I turned in?"

"We're all exhausted," Maggie added with a hug. "Go on and get some rest."

Anna walked into her room, exhausted from the day's events. She gazed at the envelope in her hand, kissed her grandfather's writing, and set it on her bedside table. She needed a good night's rest before reading what Papa had written; she collapsed onto her bed, knowing it would make more sense once sleep restored her mind. Her eyelids felt heavy as sleep overtook her. Her last thought before she drifted off to sleep was that despite being without family, she was blessed to have the Calverts.

CHAPTER 3

Anna's eyes flickered open, and her gaze immediately locked on the crinkled envelope on her nightstand. She reached for it, taking in her grandfather's scent. Slipping out of bed, she grabbed the threadbare pink quilt Nana had made for her and shuffled to the kitchen to make a cup of coffee before heading out to the weathered swing on the porch. She carefully opened the envelope and sipped her freshly brewed coffee. Inside, a glossy photo was tucked between the letter folds.

My Dearest Anna,

If you are reading this letter, it means I have left this earth. I am safely with your grandmother and parents. Please don't weep for me. I've had a good life. You probably feel very alone, but you are never alone. We live in your heart and memories. When you see a beautiful red cardinal, I'm flying by to see you. When I settle on the bird feeder, we're having breakfast together.

After your momma died, it left my heart broken. I didn't think I could be fixed until you came to live with us. I never forgot your momma, but you helped ease the pain in my heart. Life is a journey of trials and tribulations filled with many beautiful blessings. You were our blessing in so many ways. I love you more than you will ever know.

I know you have always wanted to return to that little town in Texas. Did you see something there that touched your heart, or was it the lovely family you met at camp? You seemed to like being with them because they were good to all of us. It doesn't matter why. I think you should go on a great adventure. I spoke with Maggie, and she's willing to watch the farm while you explore Texas. If it works out, keep it or sell it. It is now yours.

I am so proud of you, Anna. Remember, when you see the cardinals, your grandma and I are visiting. You are my little angel. You made my life complete.

Love you to the moon and back,

Grandpa

Anna stared at the letter in her hands, remembering her first summer love. At sixteen, Anna was immediately drawn to Cowboy, who was almost two years older. His tall frame emerged from the rustic barn, leading a majestic horse on a rope halter. The worn leather of his cowboy boots kicked up dust as he strode toward her, wearing tight Wrangler jeans and an indigo shirt with pearl buttons. A black Stetson shaded his piercing icy-blue eyes.

Her heart raced when she heard his deep voice call out. "Hey Ginger, are you just going to stand there watching or come riding?"

There was electric energy between them as he leaped over the fence and stood beside her, close enough for her to feel the heat radiating off his body. He playfully ran his fingers through her fiery red hair and asked, "So Ginger, are you here for the barrel racing camp?"

Without saying a word, Anna nodded eagerly.

And then, with a mischievous smile, he added, "Maybe we could hang out."

She tossed her hair over her shoulders and replied, "What makes you think I want to hang out with you?"

But when he leaned in close and whispered one word into her ear—*Fate!*—goosebumps erupted all over her skin, and she knew she wanted to know him better. They spent the whole summer getting to know each other, and their bond grew.

They'd swayed to George Strait's warm baritone voice, and all her senses were heightened. When his calloused hands cupped her face and he leaned in to kiss her, it was like an electric current ran through her veins. The intensity of their connection was like their souls had intertwined at that moment.

On the last day at camp, Anna was brushing her horse in the barn with another wrangler. They were sharing stories and laughter as they worked. Anna was taken aback when Cowboy became jealous, lashing out at her with baseless accusations. She'd tried to ignore him but soon lost her temper and walked away without saying goodbye, regretting it when they pulled away from camp.

Nana had assured her that she was young and would forget Cowboy eventually, but after all these years, the memory of swaying in his arms still evoked a chill down her spine. There was something about Cowboy that could never be explained. As things deteriorated with Tony, Anna realized she'd been seeking that with Tony. Still, it wasn't there for either of them, or he wouldn't have been making out with Emma after Papa's funeral.

Wrapped in a cozy quilt, Anna held onto a faded photograph. The corners were frayed and tattered from being handled so much. In the picture, Anna stood next to Cowboy, the young man who captured her heart first. His tall figure overshadowed hers, with his arm draped casually across her shoulder. Next to them stood his sister, who shared the same striking blue eyes as Cowboy and dark hair hung in waves around her face. The three were all smiles, frozen in a moment captured by Anna's grandmother that summer in Cardinal Creek, a time she often looked back on with nostalgia. A mournful exhale escaped her lips as the burden of loss over the past six months weighed heavily on her. Taking a deep breath, Anna dared to imagine a new future. What if she could return to Cardinal Creek and give herself the rest she deserved? She was giddy, considering seeing Cowboy again after all these years. How much had he changed? Was he married? Did he have children? Anna couldn't help but smile as the tension eased from her body. Maybe it was time for that adventure.

She wrapped her quilt tightly around herself as she walked across the porch and heard the familiar squeak of the board. She smiled and muttered, "That board always caught me when I tried to sneak up on Papa. Is that a sign?"

Anna stopped in the living room doorway, overwhelmed by nostalgia. She could see her nana chatting animatedly with the ladies from the quilting guild as they sat around the antique wooden quilting frame, needles and multicolored thread scattered across it. Jenny's laughter drifted in from under the edge, and Anna couldn't help but smile at the memory. As she entered the dining room, Anna smiled, reminiscing of Sunday dinners with her family came to mind—Nana's crispy fried chicken placed on the table next to mounds of mashed potatoes, fluffy biscuits, and lemon meringue pie.

The delicious smell of breakfast being prepared in the kitchen jolted Anna back to the present, and she followed her nose towards it. Not much had changed over the years. The vintage table, chairs, gingham curtains, and Pyrex dishes still existed. Stepping into the center of the room, Anna threw an arm around Maggie's shoulders and rested her head against her.

"He told me to go back to Cardinal Creek." She handed Maggie the picture. "This was the picture I was talking about last night."

Anna chewed her lip, hesitating. "Do you think I should go?"

"If Cardinal Creek is calling to you, what draws you there?" Maggie asked.

Anna paused for several minutes, reflecting on the question. Her gaze shifted out the window toward the horizon, where she imagined a different life with newfound freedom. "I don't know . . . to heal or have a fresh start, maybe figure out who I am without my grandparents. It's not to look for Cowboy. That dream died a long time ago."

Maggie squeezed her shoulder in affirmation. "I know you are wise enough not to leave here on a whim like that. The choice is yours, and we'll always be here waiting if you don't like it there." She pulled Anna close. "We love you very much."

"I love you too," Anna replied, her voice thick with emotion.

Maggie smiled. "Let's have some breakfast and discuss this as a family. Let's get my lazy daughter up."

Anna laughed. "Does she still swing when you try to wake her up? Maybe I should get a broom," she joked. Anna walked down the hall toward her bedroom. She had already decided she was going to Cardinal Creek, Texas.

∽

Anna curled her hands around the ceramic mug, its warmth seeping through her skin. The aroma of frying bacon and baking biscuits hung thickly in the air like a comforting blanket, reminding her of the time spent with her grandmother in the kitchen. She smiled as she blew on the steaming coffee, reminiscing about her nana's homemade biscuits spread with sweet strawberry preserves. Jenny charged into the room, disrupting the peaceful moment.

"Good morning! Yes, Grand Marceline coffee! Hazelnut is my favorite." Jenny inhaled deeply and closed her eyes before hopping onto the stool next to Anna. "How are you this morning?"

Anna paused before answering as she thought about the turmoil going on inside. The town of Marceline, Missouri, was the boyhood home of Walt Disney. With its small-town charm, it was easy to see what had drawn him here all those years ago. It held tight a sense of familiarity for Anna. She grew up here and knew every street and back road like the back of her hand. But while Anna felt the connection, it wasn't enough right now. She wanted a new adventure—in Texas.

Maggie laughed and handed Jenny a mug of coffee.

"Okay, Anna, spill it," Jenny said.

Anna looked up and noticed they were staring at her. "You two are so impatient." She laughed. "I read Grandpa's letter this morning." She handed Jenny the photo and grabbed the plates and silverware from the cupboard.

Jenny stared intently at the photo, her brows knitting together. "Where did you get this picture?"

"It was with the letter from Papa. He told me to go back to Cardinal Creek."

"To find this hottie?" Jenny said, pointing at the picture. "He could be fat and bald by now."

Maggie swatted her with a towel. "Jennifer, stop," she interjected sternly.

"Well, he could," Jenny insisted, earning a slap on the arm from Anna. "Look at Billy Morgan—remember how cute he was in school?—he went from stud to dud."

Anna smiled. "She has a point, Maggie. He could be a troll by now. As for Billy, he's a nice guy."

Jenny made a face and rolled her eyes. "He is, but not as beautiful as he used to be."

"But who is? We all get older," said Maggie.

"Well, Anna and I are just as pretty," Jenny teased. "And look at you. You're one hot old lady!"

"I'm not an old lady!" Maggie exclaimed.

A wave of tenderness washed over Anna as she watched Maggie laugh. She was so grateful for their presence easing the sting of the last week—first Papa, then Tony. Suddenly, her phone buzzed with an incoming message from Tony.

> Tony: Hey, Babe, can we talk?
>
> Anna: Did you mean to text Emma or me?
>
> Tony: Anna, please let me talk to you. I'll drive there.

Anna slammed her phone on the table. "What the hell is wrong with him? When Papa was sick, he couldn't find time to sit with me, but now he wants to talk."

"Oh, hell no." Jenny reached for Anna's phone. "I got this."

Anna slid her phone away. "That's okay. I want to let him sit while I choose my words."

"'Screw you' would sum it up."

Anna bumped Jenny's shoulder. "I appreciate that you want to tell him off, but this is a good way for me to start sticking up for myself."

"True."

They finished breakfast and cleaned up the kitchen. Maggie brewed another pot of coffee, and they gathered around the table for a second. Anna stared at the photo of Cowboy. "What if he's still hot?"

Jenny burst out laughing. "I knew you were thinking about him. He could be. What did his daddy look like?"

Maggie swatted her. "What does that have to do with anything?"

"Well, if his daddy is old and looks good, so will he."

Anna rolled her eyes. "Yes, of course. Thank you, Dr. Genetics. It's not just about him but about making a change for me. I have cared for others for so long, and now it's time to take care of me. Plus, I would like a change of scenery. What do you think? Is this crazy?"

Maggie took her hand. "What would it hurt to look into opportunities in Texas if that's where you want to go?"

"As much as I love my best friend, I think if you need to explore another place, do it. I'll always be here for you." Jenny pulled her in for a side hug. "Are you going to talk to Tony?"

Anna shrugged. "I don't know." She smiled, "Listen you all, it's okay to leave me. I'm gonna be fine."

∼

Jenny and Maggie left the kitchen, softly shutting the door behind them, leaving Anna alone in the quiet house. She thought of her beloved papa, who had passed away last week, and how fast life could change. Anna's mind drifted to a memory from last spring when she and Papa had spent hours planting colorful flowers in the garden: purple phlox, pink ranunculus bulbs, tulips in every rainbow hue, and golden daffodils. With trowels in hand, Anna and Papa knelt in the freshly turned earth. Papa carefully placed a rosebush with delicate pink buds and thorny stems in the ground. It was a tradition they upheld each spring to honor Anna's momma.

Afterward, they'd sit on the porch and drink homemade lemonade until sunset. There was a heavy ache in Anna's chest at the thought of spending the rest of her life without a family. She sat on the couch with Papa's letter clutched in her hand and closed her eyes. His words repeated in her mind: *Go to Texas.*

Anna loved her job at University Hospital, caring for those with chronic illnesses. She was a palliative care provider to improve the lives of patients and their families. Anna noticed caregivers who lacked breaks and overlooked themselves to care for their sick family members would experience burnout. With that knowledge, she made it her mission to educate these individuals on the importance of self-care and set up support groups where they could speak about their everyday struggles. She figured this attracted Emma to the palliative care department too.

As she reflected on the past, a knot tightened in her stomach. Emma had selfishly claimed credit for Anna's hard work, leading to a promotion and recognition that should have been hers. But Anna couldn't deny the satisfaction of knowing her project had helped countless caregivers. She struggled with bitterness toward Emma and guilt for not standing up for herself and her work. They had once been close friends, but living together in college had revealed a different side of Emma—a party girl who put her desires above everything else. And now, as Emma rose to the director position, Anna couldn't help but wonder if she should have fought harder for the recognition she deserved.

A fiery rage ignited inside her as she realized she'd have to go back to the hospital and encounter Tony and Emma together. She remembered how Emma had slyly manipulated everyone against her. Anna couldn't believe she had ignored it for so long. Now, she dreaded returning and dealing with unnecessary drama in her life again.

Anna's phone buzzed; picking it up, she saw another text from Tony. She read part of the message before putting it away.

> Tony: Anna, please talk to me.

Anna's anger barometer continued to rise as she read Tony's message. *"What does he want from me now? Haven't I been through enough already?"* She knew that Emma had a habit of gossiping about other nurses, and now she wondered if all her humiliation would be broadcast to everyone. Feeling powerless and naive, she threw her hands up and sighed. *"Did he tell her I wasn't even interested in dating in nursing school because I didn't want it to distract me?"*

Regrets flooded her mind—her inexperience with dating in school because she thought it would take away from her studies, her naivety when Tony had swept into her life with his sweet words and romantic gestures, and, of course, that night at the club where she'd allowed herself to get too drunk and gave up her virginity. Letting it happen was stupid and naïve, but wouldn't it be worse if people found out?

She picked up her phone to finish reading Tony's message, and she realized that this would be the perfect time to stand tall and remain strong, so she set the phone back down.

A wave of conflicting emotions flooded her mind. Tony used to be attentive and loving, showering her with kisses and taking her out on romantic dates. He had even wanted to introduce her to his parents. But when she returned home after Papa got sick, Tony gradually became distant and disappeared entirely from her life. Why wouldn't he break up with her? Was it possible that the man she'd spent two years with wasn't who she thought he was? She was being pulled in multiple directions and didn't know what to think anymore. Maybe she should see what he wanted.

> Tony: Will you please answer me? If you don't message me, I'll drive there to see you, and I won't leave until you speak to me.

Anna's face burned. *Who does this guy think he is?* Her fingers flew over the keyboard as she typed a message back.

> Anna: I don't know who the hell you think you are. You're the one who's done God-knows-what with my "friend," and now this? What do you need to talk to me about, the intimate details of our relationship you shared with Emma? Did you tell her I was a virgin and inexperienced?

> Tony: Yes.

A lump formed in Anna's throat. Her hands shook as she typed a reply.

> Anna: Why would you do that? Those were our intimate details. I loved you, Tony. I would never share such things about you with anyone. I hope you had a good time with Emma. Just a little heads up—she has slept with pretty much everyone in school, so it might be a good idea to get yourself tested. Now, I'm going to make a few things clear. I don't want to see you, speak to you, or text you. We are over. Done. Finished. I thought I meant more to you than that.

> Tony: Baby, I love you. She kept coming to see me. I saw her one evening when I was leaving the hospital. She told me she was worried about you because your grandpa was dying. We had a little too much to drink, and the following day, she was in my bed, and well . . . God, I'm so sorry. I tried to stay away, but she kept coming to the house. Let me see you, Emma.

Anna stared at her phone, reading the message over and over. *Did this ass call me Emma? Really?* She reread the text, shaking her head.

> Anna: You miserable piece of shit. You never came and saw me once in the three months my papa was sick. Read what you wrote at the end. My name isn't EMMA. Go ahead and come to my house. I dare you. I can't believe you called me Emma. I'm done.

She saw the three dots moving again. *Oh my God, what does he not understand? It's done.*

> Tony: Can I call you, please?

Anna sent a middle finger emoji. The three dots popped up. *Are you kidding me?*

> Tony: Does that mean no?

> Anna: How did you make it through medical school? It means to go to hell. We're done.

She placed her phone on the couch next to her, not intending to answer any more texts. She picked it up again and blocked Tony's and Emma's numbers.

Anna glanced at the table where her laptop sat, and her gaze fell on the paper with her papa's handwriting scrawled across it.

Go to Texas.

She walked over to the table, picked up her laptop, and settled onto the couch with her legs crossed. Her job search in Texas took her from Austin to San Antonio until she saw a listing for a "director of palliative care" in Cardinal Creek that caught her attention. Anna leaned closer to the screen as she read the qualifications. She fulfilled every one of them. A framed photo of Anna's grandparents beamed from the corner of the room, and an inexplicable wave of comfort washed over her. It felt like a sign telling her to apply. She said a silent prayer before hitting Submit. She recalled her past thirteen years working in palliative care and how taking this leave of absence to care for her grandfather had brought her here today. Moving to Texas was just what she needed—a new beginning.

She shut her laptop and took carrots from the refrigerator before heading to the barn. Her horse, Thunderbird, was always there for her, listening to her deepest thoughts and feelings. Aside from Papa and Jenny, he was the only one she told her secrets to. Anna enjoyed conversing with her horses; it gave her solace in times of distress.

After her parents passed away, Nana and Papa bought Belle as her first horse, but Belle eventually passed away, leaving her shattered. Then, they'd gifted her Thunderbird when she graduated from high school. Thunderbird was a painted horse with white on his back and legs, a solid chestnut head with a narrow white strip down the center of his face, and silver outlining the chestnut and white.

Anna opened the barn door. "Hey there, I'm here."

Thunderbird immediately answered her with a low whinny from his stall. She held out her hand with a few carrots as a peace offering. He happily accepted the snack and rested his head on her shoulder.

"I hope Jenny fed you well," she said. After caring for her trusty friend, Anna brushed him down while talking to him. "Thunder, Grandpa passed away. We might move to Texas if I can get a job there."

He lifted his head and nickered in response.

"Well, you think it would be good?" she asked. He lifted his head as she brushed his neck like he was saying yes. "Okay, we'll move to Texas if I can get a job." Thunderbird nickered again. Anna scratched behind his ears. "I love you, Thunder." She looked around at his stall. "Did Jenny come back and clean the stall?"

He lifted his head again. She held out her hand with another carrot. "I'll see you in the morning."

"I think he's talking to you."

Anna turned to see Maggie standing at the entrance of the barn.

"Why, yes, he is." Anna went to put the grooming tote in the tack room. "To what do I owe this pleasure?" she asked as she walked to greet Maggie with a hug.

"You may need to talk about everything without Jenny's two cents."

Anna sighed. "Papa knew I always wanted to return to Cardinal Creek, but I hope it wasn't to chase my thing with Cowboy. It can't be about that;

it has to be for a fresh start. I think it's best if I don't date for a while. I need time to grieve."

Maggie hugged her. "The man you are supposed to be with is out there, believe me, and when the time is right, he'll just show up."

All Anna could think about was how inadequate and lost she felt. "I think a change of scenery would be the best for me," she finally said.

Maggie's voice cracked. "You're gonna go?"

"Well, I applied for a job in Cardinal Creek in the palliative care department."

"Wow," Maggie said, clearing her throat. "That seems like divine intervention."

"I would say so."

"Well, you know I promised your grandpa I would take care of this place while you were gone."

"Oh, Maggie, I hate to leave you and Jenny, but I need a fresh start. Everything here reminds me of him and my grandma." Anna's throat tightened.

Maggie put her arm around Anna's shoulder. "Honey, we can visit Texas, and you can come back. We're not going anywhere. I promised your grandpa I'd always be there for you, and I will."

Anna looked at her, and tears welled up. "I'm not going to cry again," she said, wiping her eyes.

"You just buried your grandfather and your grandmother six months before that. Go easy on yourself."

Anna shook her head. Thinking about that would only help a little. "I applied for a director position," she said instead. "Do you think I'm ready?"

Maggie put her hands on her hips. "Anna Samuels, from one nurse to another, you are more than qualified for that job. You have been a nurse in the same department for thirteen years, wrote a grant for them, and started a successful caregiver program. Believe in yourself."

Anna smiled. "I'm trying. I never feel like I'm good enough for a leadership position. Despite everything I did for the department, Emma was promoted before I was."

"Listen to me. You are qualified to do a director's job. Look at what you did with the program at the hospital. You took over that project and led a team of people to get everything done ahead of schedule. You are great with patients, and you understand palliative care."

When they reached the porch, Jenny was waiting for them. "Hurry, I brought the food we need to eat while it's hot. Plus, I'm starved."

Maggie rolled her eyes. "Since birth, my child has always been hungry and never gained a pound."

"I'm still growing, Momma." Jenny laughed.

As they entered the house, Anna saw a vase of yellow roses on the table, along with mini Texas flags inserted in the vase.

Jenny looked at her. "Are you going to Texas to look for the blue-eyed cowboy?"

Anna shook her head. "No." She leaned in to inhale the sweet scent of the roses and smiled. "I'm going for a change of pace if I get the job I applied for."

"I'm not saying I'm happy to lose my best friend and sister, but I'm happy you're going." Jenny hugged her. "No matter where you live, remember we'll always be connected." She raised her sleeve, showing a bracelet made of red thread. They had worn them since college, though they'd through a few replacements since then.

Anna smiled and held up her wrist to show hers. "Yes, it's the red thread of fate."

In unison, they said, "There's an invisible red thread connecting us, because we were destined to meet."

"Remember, we're always linked no matter where you go," Jenny said as they hugged. "Now, let's eat before I die of hunger."

They huddled around the kitchen table, eating barbecue from Pop's BBQ, the tastiest rib spot in town. The trio dug into half-slabs of ribs, creamy potato salad, smoky baked beans with plenty of brown sugar, and tall glasses of sweet tea. Anna wiped some sauce from her chin. "Oh man, this is just what I needed."

"That's not all I brought," Jenny said, licking barbecue sauce from her fingers. "I brought molten lava cake."

Maggie grabbed the cake and a bottle of wine from the refrigerator and rejoined them at the table.

"I love you guys." Anna wiped her mouth with a napkin.

"Have you heard from Tony?" Jenny asked.

Anna frowned. "Don't ruin this piece of heaven for me."

Jenny raised an eyebrow. "Well?"

"Yes, I told him to go to hell. Emma was never my friend. She broke the sacred friend oath. I'm fine starting over alone. I can concentrate on healing and my career."

Maggie slapped her hands on the table. "That sounds like a great idea. Let's toast to that!"

They raised their drinks in a salute to Anna's new venture. Raising her glass with a smile, Anna said, "You know, ladies, that's exactly what I need. An adventure! Here's to my new journey in Texas." She smiled at them with joy, sad that her grandparents were gone but grateful for her grandfather's final permission to care for herself and embark on a grand journey to independence.

CHAPTER 4

Anna drove down the highway with the windows open, letting the warm Texas breeze blow away her worries. She had left the San Antonio airport two hours earlier after a short, bumpy flight for her interview at the hospital and was starting to feel her excitement grow as she approached Cardinal Creek.

The GPS on her phone directed her off the highway and onto Main Street, where Anna was surprised that not much had changed since she was sixteen. Main Street was lined with many of the same family-owned businesses and a few new ones. She recognized the Cattle Trail restaurant with its famous lemon meringue pie, almost as good as her grandmother's. A boutique, a yoga studio, and a coffee shop were new since she was last there.

After passing by court square, she arrived at Cardinal Creek Community Hospital. When she parked her car, she couldn't help but smile at how much smaller it was compared to the 247-bed hospital where she worked in Missouri. If she got the job, Anna would have the opportunity to help the people of Cardinal Creek understand the benefits of palliative care, just as she'd done in rural Missouri. Her chest warmed, and time seemed to stand still as she realized this small town could become home for her.

She looked at the email on her phone one last time before she entered the hospital. While Anna waited for her interview, a man stared at her with chocolate eyes, chestnut hair, and a goatee. He wore scrubs and a long lab coat. She couldn't read his badge as she made eye contact with him. A smile spread across his face, and she nodded. *Oh Lord, he's coming toward me. Please let them call my name.*

The director of nursing's assistant emerged from the administrative office. "Anna Samuels."

Anna stood, letting out a sigh of relief. *Thank God. I'm not interested in talking to a man, especially a doctor.* She plastered on a fake smile and followed the assistant to the office, trying to hide any negative emotions brewing. The man's eyes almost burned a hole through her clothes. Anna's stomach tangled into knots as she watched him out of the corner of her eye.

Anna walked to the director of nursing's office, listening to the sound of her footsteps and her slow, steady breathing in the sterile hallway. The door pulled open when they arrived, and a woman stepped out. She had sharp cheekbones and perfectly coifed hair wound tightly into an unyielding bun. Dressed in a pencil skirt and navy blazer, she welcomed Anna with a warm smile, introducing herself as Cathy Watts.

An intimidating mahogany desk dominated the room. Cathy sat in her leather desk chair, emanating a regal air as she perched on it like a queen on a throne. Behind her desk was a bookshelf filled with nursing textbooks. They talked about regulations and policies, patient care standards, and best practices for what felt like hours. When they finished, Anna stood up from her chair feeling confident and capable, ready to take on whatever challenges lay ahead.

After the interview, Anna was paired with another department director for a hospital tour and lunch. One of Anna's favorite things at University Hospital was showing potential new employees around and giving them a glimpse into their daily work lives.

The director with whom Anna had been paired entered the room and offered her hand. "Hello, I'm Kati Deluca," she said, "the emergency department director."

Anna reached to shake her hand. "I'm Anna Samuels."

"It's a pleasure to meet you."

"Same here."

They took a quick tour of the hospital. Cardinal Creek Community Hospital was smaller than the hospital in Missouri. The hallways were slightly narrower, but the lights were bright, and everything was spotless. Most of the medical staff spoke with a noticeable Texan drawl.

Anna stood in the small emergency department, taking in the sight of the ten beds compared to the University's seventy-seven-bed, level-one trauma center. Kati led Anna to her office, its shelf adorned with a photo Anna couldn't quite make out.

Kati grabbed her purse before they headed out the door and said, "Anna, I hope you don't mind, but I thought we would leave for lunch."

"Sure," Anna said. "That's fine with me."

"We can take my car. I know this great place on Main Street."

They headed to the Cowgirl Sweets and Treats. "This place makes the best panini sandwiches and potato salad," Kati said.

"That sounds great," Anna said.

They chatted about the hospital on their way to the restaurant. They discussed the many positive changes that had been happening at the hospital, like the new palliative care department, which was something Anna was particularly passionate about and enjoyed sharing with Kati.

Kati pulled into the parking lot, and they headed inside. The restaurant was quaint with cowgirl decor. The pictures on the wall were of female rodeo events, local and professional barrel racers, team ropers, calf roping, and tie-down calf roping. Anna's mind returned to the summer she came for barrel racing camp. Her body warmed up as Cowboy's face flashed through her mind. Butterflies danced through her stomach as she remembered his kiss.

A tap on her shoulder brought Anna back to reality. "You okay, Anna?"

She smiled. "Yeah . . . was just taken aback by the smell of cookies. I love the decor."

Kati raised an eyebrow. "Yeah, the owner was a barrel racer who decided to turn in her saddle for baking. If you're getting a cookie, go for the chocolate chip."

After ordering, Anna followed Kati to a table near the window. *Jenny and Maggie would love this place*, she thought. They were equestrians like Anna and loved all things Southern. *And this place is Southern*, she thought as she glanced at the gingham curtains.

"So, Anna." Kati smiled when Anna looked at her. "I've read your application. I see you're from Missouri and work at the university hospital. Can you tell me a little more about yourself?"

Before Anna could answer, the buzzer to pick up their food went off on the table. They went to retrieve their food.

Anna took in the scent of her turkey pesto panini. It was dripping with provolone cheese. "This smells fantastic."

Kati smiled. "Just wait until you eat it." They each took a bite of their sandwich and savored the flavors. Kati wiped her mouth. "Let's try this again. Can you tell me more about yourself?"

"Ever since I graduated from nursing school. I've been employed at University Hospital in Columbia. However, I had to take a family leave of absence." She paused and took a deep breath hoping to hold back the tears. "My grandfather was ill and recently passed away."

Tears welled up in Kati's eyes as she spoke. "My daddy died five years ago, and my best friend was killed in a car accident two years later." She reached for a paper napkin decorated with the restaurant's logo to wipe her tears. "She was my brother's wife," she continued, her voice breaking. "It's hard when your heart feels shattered into a million pieces. But somehow, we've managed to keep going without them."

Anna nodded in understanding while Kati recounted her experience. It resonated with Anna's loss and struggles. She tried to focus on the paper napkin with the restaurant's logo before her but couldn't help but think about the people she'd lost. They were like missing pieces of her heart that she couldn't find.

"Thank you for that." Feeling overwhelmed, she pushed around her food with her fork, trying to hold back the emotions threatening to spill out.

But Kati's hand on hers offered comfort, reminding her she wasn't alone in this struggle to keep moving forward without loved ones by their side.

"I know it hurts, Anna. It's okay to be sad."

"Thanks for that, Kati." Anna forced a smile. "I appreciate it." She wanted to thank Kati for being there, but she also resented her for making her confront these painful feelings when they just met.

Kati took a deep breath, then laughed. "I guess that's not why we're here though. Do you have any questions about the hospital or Cardinal Creek?"

"Yes." This was good; Anna could talk about work. It was better than talking about heartbreak, though Anna sensed that Kati understood what she was going through. "Do you know of anyone who boards horses or a place I could rent where I could keep my horse with me?"

"Oh my goodness! You ride?"

"Yes, since I was nine years old. I was a barrel racer in high school."

"I was a barrel racer too. Well, my brother owns a ranch outside of town. It's beautiful there, with all the bluebonnets starting to bloom. I can see if he has a cabin available, and you could board your horse there too."

Anna felt like the universe was lining up all the stars for her. "Oh, that would be wonderful."

"My momma and I share a cabin on the ranch. My brother has two kids, Eva and Caden. They're the best."

"Oh, that's exciting. We could ride together." She smiled, her heart speeding up.

"It would be great to have someone to ride with again."

"I'm glad they paired us up for lunch and the tour." Anna hesitated, then added, "I appreciate you sharing your story. It's good to know someone understands what I'm going through."

"Me too, Anna. Me too."

After lunch, they chatted about the hospital and their experiences as nurses. Anna listened intently to Kati's emergency room stories. Despite being a small town and hospital, Kati ran into various people in the ER. Out-of-towners, older adults who were forgotten by families, children too sick to make it to the larger children's hospitals, cranky folks from the outskirts of town, and a few troublesome teenagers. The hospitals may have been different, but the cases were the same.

When they returned to the hospital, Kati walked Anna to her car. "I'm so glad we met. It seems like we've been friends for years."

"I know, right?" Anna said, laughing.

Kati gave Anna her number. "Listen, I'll talk to my brother about the rental. Call me once you know you have the job or have any questions."

"Text me when you get home!" Katie shouted as Anna entered her rental car.

Anna nodded. "Thanks, Kati. Sometimes it feels like the universe lines up the stars so you meet just the right people."

"It sure does."

CHAPTER 5

Will's stomach churned as he heard the knock on his door. He hesitated before the door, a familiar knot of anxiety curling in his chest. Who could be here? He hadn't been expecting anyone. But when he opened it, Kati stood there, and anger immediately surged from within. He hadn't seen her since the incident at the restaurant two weeks ago because she was avoiding him, and now she was here. He wasn't sure if he was angry at Kati or feeling guilty. But anger seemed like an easier emotion to deal with.

"What do you want?" Will snapped, hoping his voice didn't betray his inner turmoil.

"Can I come in?" she asked without preamble, pushing past him before he could answer. She surveyed the foyer with cold eyes, and he was acutely aware of how much space there was between them.

With his arms crossed, Will leaned against the doorjamb, a wild storm of emotions raging inside him. "Be honest. Were you meeting what's-her-name, or were you trying to fix me up?"

Kati narrowed her eyes and sighed. "Do you have rocks in your head? I wouldn't fix Tammy up with you because you're a jerk." Her response surged a flare of anger within him.

"Why are you so concerned with me dating anyone, anyway? Work on your own dating life," Will spat.

"I don't care if you date anyone, Will. Is this all because I tried to fix you up a few times?" Kati said, folding her arms across her chest, frustration mixed with disappointment in her voice.

Will ran his fingers through his hair and let out a long breath, suddenly wanting to apologize, but he didn't know how. He felt guilty for overreacting but also angry at himself for not being able to apologize even as he searched for the right words. "I'm sure you didn't come to apologize," he muttered, breaking the heavy silence between them. "I've been waiting for you to do that for two weeks."

Kati shrugged, an edge of sarcasm in her voice. "Me, apologize? All the assuming you did that day made you a giant ass."

He let out a low groan and hung his head, ashamed of himself for not handling things better and for jumping to conclusions without giving Kati a chance to explain herself first. "That's what Momma said," he admitted, recalling their conversation after it had all happened. "I thought she was taking your side."

"Oh my God? Did you even apologize to the chief's daughter?" Kati asked. Much to Will's surprise, her icy demeanor softened slightly, though her brow was still furrowed in disapproval.

"Yes, I did, and I told the chief what happened for your information." A deep sigh escaped his lips, a sense of relief flooding him as he finally spoke the truth. It meant acknowledging his mistake in assuming Sammy's friendly behavior was flirtatious.

"Listen, the reason why I came by . . ." Kati paused for a moment. "I had lunch with the woman interviewing for the new director position. She was—"

"This is bullshit," Will spat, opening the door wider as he motioned for her to leave. He ground his teeth as he tried to stop himself from jumping to conclusions. He wished he could take it back, but it was too late now. His stomach churned as he imagined things he knew weren't true, yet he feared them anyway.

Kati shook her head, trying to make him understand what she was trying to say. "No, that's not it. Oh, for the love of God . . . Listen, I'm not trying to set you up."

But Will cut her off, raising his voice. "I said get out."

Tears pooled in her eyes as she stepped toward the door, her voice quivering with emotion. She pointed an accusing finger at him. "Why do you always jump to conclusions? And why are you pushing everyone away, including your kids? Even Caden can see what's going on. Because of your impatience and moods, he wants to stay with Momma and me." She paused. "Do you even care about them anymore? They're still alive, and they love you."

Will clenched his jaw and fists tight. He wanted to believe she was wrong, to tell her she didn't understand, but he couldn't find the words. All he could do was yell as he motioned toward the door. "Get out! Go!" He tried to contain himself, but it was too late. He'd already let himself go.

Kati stepped toward the door, her words ringing in his ears. "You don't listen to people. You cut them off and assume too much, making yourself an ass! For your information, I'm not trying to set you up. Did you hear that, or is your head too thick?" Her voice shook as she spoke. She pushed past him, nudging him with her shoulder on her way out. "You could use the money from having someone board their horse here and rent your place if they get the job. What the hell? Don't you ever think about anyone but yourself?"

Will's face heated, but Kati had already stalked off toward her cabin, muttering under her breath before he could reply.

Jon had just rounded the corner toward Will's house when he saw Kati storming away. He rushed to embrace her in a comforting hug. Kati buried her face into Jon's chest, sobbing.

"Kati!" Will called and started down the steps, guilt gnawing at him. Jon shot him a dirty look, then led her to her cabin and shut the door.

Will kicked at the dirt as he went back inside. The house felt empty, the air heavy. He wished he could control his emotions, but he felt so erratic. He was a changed man after Shelly's death. Grief could do that to a person.

At the sound of the front door opening, Will's heart sank. He glanced at his watch. Only an hour had passed since Kati stormed off. *Momma is going to let me have it.* He took a deep breath and braced himself as he shuffled toward the door, anticipating the worst. But instead of his mother standing there, it was Jon.

Will released an audible sigh of relief. "I'm glad it's you and not Momma. Is Kati okay?"

Jon pushed past Will and said gruffly, "Define *okay*. I need a beer. Do you have any?"

Will nodded, grateful for the distraction from his thoughts. "Yeah, bring me one too."

Jon returned to the living room, handed Will a beer, and slumped onto the couch. He took a long sip before speaking up again. "She's one of the most exasperating people I have met." He shook his head at Will with a look of disbelief. "And what the hell got into you again? You don't think we want you to get married again, do you?" He took another swig of his beer. "I want you to get laid already because you've been unbearable for so long. I don't know why I'm still your friend."

Will threw a pillow from the couch at him in response. "Don't be an asshole," he said, running his fingers through his hair. "I don't want to think about being with another woman. I love Shelly, and it feels wrong now." He shook his head, not wanting to think about being with anyone else. "I'm not like you, Jon. What do you know, having had a string of girlfriends but no real relationships?"

Jon sighed heavily before replying. "That's not fair. That was before I dated Kati. This isn't about me though." He finished his beer. "She understands you don't want to date," he added sympathetically. "You've made that clear. Plenty of times."

Will rubbed a hand over his face, the other clutching the cold beer. He'd been ruminating over Kati's words since their fight, and he couldn't make sense of any of it.

"I'm not sure why I get so angry when she brings up another woman," Will admitted. "But I'm always angry. The thought of bringing another woman around the kids just . . ." He shuddered. "I don't know. It just scares me."

"Oh, I understand, but she didn't bring Tammy to date you. She was meeting her there, so what difference does it make? What's all this anger about?"

Will put up his hand. "I can't talk about this stuff anymore. I need a few more beers for this conversation."

Jon placed his beer on the table. "Do you think I drink too much?"

Will shrugged. "No more than I do. Numbs the pain." He set his beer on the table next to Jon's and put his head in his hands. "I see the accident over and over again. When I'm awake and when I'm asleep. The damn phone is what gets me. If only I would have waited to text her."

"Hey, you aren't responsible if someone reads a text."

Will shot him a look. "So, I should blame Shelly?"

"Blame does no good in this situation. It was a terrible accident, Will."

"We'll have to agree to disagree on that subject."

"Are you going to talk to Kati? She didn't do anything wrong."

Will let out a low groan. "I know she didn't . . . but I'm embarrassed by how I acted toward her and that I accused her of trying to set me up with someone else again."

"Oh man, are you gonna wait until Momma D comes here to straighten you out?" Jon said, using a high-pitched voice. "Y'all always do this. Get mad and avoid each other. William, you need to talk. You aren't too big for me to kick your ass."

Will laughed. "Don't let Momma hear you say that. She'll kick your ass."

Jon put his hands to his heart. "Momma D loves me the best."

Will threw another pillow at him. "Shut up, Jon. I'm the favorite."

He knew Jon was right. If he didn't try to make things right with Kati, it would only be a matter of time before his mother would be pounding on his door to chew him out. Guilt seemed to be all Will felt. Guilt for Shelly. Guilt for being a jerk to a total stranger. Guilt for snapping at the chief's daughter. Shame for jumping to conclusions with his sister. Kati was right. He always jumped to conclusions and made judgments without the facts.

He headed for the kitchen for two more beers, knowing a few more would let him sleep without nightmares. There were better solutions than this, but for now, it worked. He handed Jon a beer and sat on the couch.

"So, what will you do about the equine center?" Jon inquired. Will tipped his beer back, drinking almost all of it with one gulp. Jon raised an eyebrow. "And your sister says I drink too much."

"Well, I guess we both do. I don't know how I'll ever pull this one off. When I spoke with Cindy at Caden's appointment last week, I should have told her I couldn't do it, but I've let so many people down lately that I couldn't say no." He polished off the rest of his beer and headed to the kitchen for another. "Want another one?"

Jon held up his beer. "Bring me a spare. Do you have the funds to open it? Do you know where to get the funds?"

Will shook his head. "No money and no idea where to get it."

"Did Shelly have any plans written? She was a planner; I'm sure she had something written."

Will entered the room with two beers. Shelly's notebook was still on her nightstand, but he hadn't looked at it since she died. "No, she didn't have anything planned. She and Cindy were in the preliminary stage of planning."

"We need an angel or some kind of divine intervention to fix this mess."

"Amen to that." Will needed a quick solution to his problem, but he had yet to learn what it could be. He also needed to apologize to Kati before Momma gave him a piece of her mind or a boot in the ass. After two more beers, Will took out his cell phone. He could at least talk to Kati the coward's way.

> Will: Hey Kati girl. I'm sorry for the way I acted earlier. I tend to jump the gun, and I'm sorry.

> Kati: I wasn't mad at you. It hurt my feelings. I tried to fix you up several times, but I wasn't trying to set you up this time. I wanted to ask about the potential new director at work renting a cabin and boarding her horse until she found something permanent. I like her; we clicked right away during lunch. It felt strange . . . almost like we knew each other already. But maybe it's just because I miss Shelly and could use another friend in my life.

Will's throat tightened. Sometimes, he forgot that everyone missed Shelly, not just him and the kids. How could he be so insensitive to others' needs? He looked at Jon, who was staring at the TV, cradling a beer. His friend hadn't been the same person since the accident. What Kati had said about Caden stung. His son would rather stay with his grandmother than be with his father. It said a lot about who Will had become and how much he'd changed. Now, he needed to figure out how to change despite wanting to. What would Shelly think about how he'd changed? He needed to try harder with Caden and Eva. He loved his children, and he would do anything for them.

> Will: I'm so sorry. I'm a selfish ass sometimes. The new director can board her horse and rent the cabin. I seem to overlook the fact you lost your best friend. I'll try to remember that in the future. Do you want to have a beer with me and Jon?

> Kati: You are an ass most of the time! Lol. I'm gonna hang with Momma, thanks for asking. Did you know the kids are here?

> Will: Oh, thank God, I had no idea. Lol. Yes, I knew they were there. They have been hanging there a lot since I've been a big grump lately.

> Kati: They told me you banished me from your house. I was out of line about what I said about the kids.

> Will: I could call them traitors, but I won't. I deserved what you said. I love you.

> Kati: I love you too, but you're still an ass. Is Jon okay? We fought.

Will closed his eyes, understanding what Kati and Jon had argued about. Ever since Shelly passed away, their entire world felt like it was slowly crumbling apart. He could hear the anger in Kati's voice in his head, her accusations that Jon drank too much and was sleeping with other women—something Will knew wasn't true.

He interjected, once again trying to explain the situation and assure Kati she had nothing to worry about. As he reached for his phone to check for new texts, a notification lit up the screen with Kati's rebuttal.

> Kati: He drinks too much.

> Will: So do I. He's been through a lot. Remember, he's the one who got Shelly out of the car.

> Kati: I know. I can't do the whole thing with him drinking too much. I know a relationship won't change that. He's got to change that for us to go any further.

> Will: You're not ready for a relationship; that will only push him further away.

> Kati: It's possible. We're a mess, aren't we?

> Will: The door's open if you want to drink with us.

> Kati: Sleep well. See you tomorrow.

> Will: Night Kati.

Will set his phone on the table. "I guess I'm out of hot water with Momma now. I made things right with Kati."

"Did she ask about me?" Jon slurred.

"She did."

"Is she mad at me?"

"That's the same question she asked me about you."

"She's so exhausting." Jon's head dropped back on the chair. "But I love her with all my heart."

"Give her some time. Love is crazy and painful when lost." Will began to feel the effects of the beer working on him. As his eyes grew heavy, he turned to Jon. "I don't know if I could ever love anyone again."

CHAPTER 6

Since she returned from Cardinal Creek, Anna had been a bundle of nerves. When her phone buzzed, she almost jumped out of her skin when she saw the number was from Texas. She took a deep breath and answered. "Hello." She sounded perfectly calm, but her stomach churned with anticipation.

"May I speak with Anna Samuels?"

"Speaking."

"Hi, Anna. This is Melanie from Human Resources at Cardinal Creek Hospital. I'm calling on behalf of Mrs. Watts to offer you the position of Palliative Care Director."

Anna's heartbeat drummed against her chest. Without hesitation, she said, "I accept the position." There was no doubt in Anna's mind that if she thought about it too much, she'd decline the offer.

"Great. Can you start on the second or fourth Monday in April?"

"The second week in April would work."

"Great, we'll get things started."

"Thank you so much." When she ended the call, she lay back against the couch.

I'm going to Texas.

She went straight to her phone to text Jenny the news. Her fingers couldn't move fast enough.

> Anna: I got the job. I'm moving to Texas.
>
> Jenny: *sad face emoji* I'm happy for you, sister, but I'll miss you.
>
> Anna: I'll miss you too, but we have three weeks before I leave.
>
> Jenny: I'm visiting Marceline this weekend to spend time with you.
>
> Anna: It's a girls' weekend. I'll see you then.

The next thing Anna needed to do was find a place to live. She found Kati Deluca in her contacts, took a deep breath, and called her.

Kati picked up on the second ring, "I knew you would get the job."

Anna laughed. "I sure did. Did you talk to your brother about renting a cabin and boarding my horse at his ranch?"

"I did talk to him, but an ambulance just rolled in, so I'll call you later."

"That sounds good."

Anna knew sitting and waiting for Kati to call would drive her crazy, so she went to the barn to ride Thunderbird. She saddled him up and led him out of the barn. Anna smiled as a cool breeze caressed her face, carrying the scents of spring with it. The yellow daffodils were starting to bloom, a bright contrast against the lush green grass. She passed dogwood trees in full blossom, and the sun's warmth blanketed her skin. This was the land her grandfather had worked since before Anna's mother was born. On weekends, he'd tend to the cattle or pull weeds out of Grandma's one-acre garden. It seemed like only yesterday that dinners relied heavily on whatever grew from Grandma's labor. Taking in the familiar sights, she continued riding across the rolling ten acres of farmland, a reminder of how much could change in just a few months.

She leaned over and stroked Thunderbird's neck. "Well, it seems like we're going to Texas, big guy."

He nodded.

"It's your job to make sure I don't let anyone talk me into dating. I'm done with men for a while." Thunderbird snorted, and Anna laughed. "Oh Thunder, that does not include you." He whinnied, and Anna scratched his neck. "Okay, let's get you back to the barn."

After Anna groomed Thunderbird, she went in and checked her phone. She saw a missed call from Kati and raced to call her back.

Kati answered on the third ring. "He said yes, Anna. I can't wait for you to get here. I can't wait to go riding with someone."

"I can't wait to go riding in Texas again."

"When will you be coming?"

"In three weeks. I plan to leave on a Friday and arrive on a Saturday. That will give me a week to get settled before I start work."

"Wait. Did you say you rode in Texas? When?" Kati asked.

"My grandparents took me riding one summer when I was younger."

"Is that why you want to move here?"

"I'm just looking for an adventure in a new place."

"Well, you're coming to the right place." Kati squealed. "I can't wait. See you soon."

"Thank you, Kati."

The next three weeks flew by as Anna prepared to move to Texas. She was excited and scared at the same time. She and Kati had exchanged several text messages, with Kati assuring her that the cabin and the horse stall would be ready when she arrived.

When moving day finally arrived, Jenny held out her wrist, displaying her red bracelet as Anna climbed into her SUV, "Always connected."

"Always," said Anna.

CHAPTER 7

When Anna arrived in Cardinal Creek, she stopped at the grocery store to pick up some items and stretch her legs for a few minutes before heading to the Rockin' D Ranch. Deep down, she knew she was procrastinating going to the ranch because she was nervous but excited to meet Kati's family.

She stretched as she got out of her SUV, then went to the horse trailer in the back to check on Thunderbird.

"Hey, buddy, how are you? It was a long trip, I know." She reached up and scratched behind his ears. He nuzzled her neck. She smiled. "You are the only man I need in my life." He nickered, and Anna laughed. "I'll get you some carrots."

The small family-owned grocery store was a more intimate environment than the Walmart and large grocery chains she was used to. Local growers and ranchers supplied a significant amount of fresh meat, eggs, and produce. They even had fresh cheese from a local dairy. Organic food without the inflated costs. She heard someone crying as she looked up and down the produce aisle, searching for carrots.

"Daddy, where are you?" a little boy yelled.

When she turned around, she saw a little boy with dark hair and icy-blue eyes filled with tears. His hands were balled into fists.

Anna knelt at his eye level. "Did you lose your daddy?"

He sniffled and swiped his hand across his eyes and nose. "No, he lost me."

Anna suppressed a smile. "You want to come with me? We can find a manager to help you."

The boy looked up. "Daddy," he said, then he rushed forward.

Anna turned to see a tall man wearing a black Stetson and a cobalt button-down shirt. His piercing sapphire-blue eyes were framed by furrowed eyebrows and softened only when the little boy ran to him. His five o'clock shadow contrasted the otherwise tidy ensemble, giving him a rugged appeal. She couldn't keep her eyes off him.

The man's eyes met Anna's as he pressed a palm to his heart. The boy ran to him. Something about his presence made the heat rise in her body. Their gaze remained locked as he swaggered toward her.

The cowboy scooped up his son. "Caden, how many times have I told you not to wander off?"

Caden looked down. "Lots, but Daddy, this lady was helping me."

When the man smiled, Anna's face warmed. "Thank you, ma'am. I'm sorry. Sometimes, he runs off so fast."

Anna slowly nodded. *Oh God, I'm staring.* She cleared her throat. "It was no problem. He's adorable."

"Daddy, you can put me down. Pinky promises I won't run off." The boy raised his pinky, and the man hooked his pinkie finger with the boy. He gently placed the little boy on the floor and approached Anna. "What's your name?"

Anna crouched to his level. "I'm Anna."

"I'm Caden."

Anna put her hand out. "Nice to meet you, Caden."

To Anna's surprise, Caden hugged her. Then he touched her wavy amber hair that lay across her shoulders. "You have pretty hair." Anna's face turned hot. She looked at the man, whose mouth dropped open.

He stepped forward and took Caden's hand. "Oh, ma'am, I'm so sorry."

She smiled. "It's okay. He's just so sweet." She looked at Caden. "You know, you made my day, Caden."

He smiled and hugged her again.

She stood, noticing the man seemed entranced by her. "He never does that to anyone except family."

Anna smiled. "I'm flattered he likes me. You have a real special boy there, sir."

He put his hand out to shake hers. "It was very nice to meet you, Anna." When they touched, his roughened hands showed warmth and gentleness, but her heart sank when she noticed the wedding band on his finger.

Anna took a ragged breath. "Uh, same here," was all she managed to say as she assessed an escape route. *I need to get out of here before I pass out.*

As she turned to leave, Caden yelled, "Bye, Anna."

She smiled and headed toward the door. She was almost at the exit when the man's baritone voice reached her ears. "Anna, you forgot your cart."

As she turned, her lips curved upward. "Oh, where is my head? Thank you." Grabbing the cart, she headed down the aisle. As she rounded the corner, she stopped and touched her racing heart. *Who was that man, and why did he ignite every cell in my body?*

She checked out and headed to her SUV to give Thunderbird his carrots.

As Thunderbird ate his carrots, Anna stroked his mane. "No men. That's what I said, right?" He moved his head up and down. "Well, I saw the most beautiful cowboy in the store, but what does it matter? He's married."

Thunderbird snorted. "I know, I know, and his little boy was sweet too." He rested his head on Anna's shoulder. "You're a good friend, Thunderbird."

WILL EXITED the store and noticed Anna standing beside a horse trailer attached to an SUV with Missouri plates, feeding a horse some carrots. When he got to his truck, he observed the crimson-haired beauty interacting with her horse. He smiled as he watched her. He felt a tap on his shoulder.

"Daddy, why are you staring at Anna?"

Will shook his head. "Oh, I wasn't. I was looking at the truck over there." Will pointed in the general direction of Anna's SUV.

"I don't see a truck, Daddy."

"I thought I saw Uncle Jon's truck."

Caden climbed into his booster seat and chuckled. "Okay, Daddy. I know you were looking at her."

Will shook his head. "Buckle up, Caden."

Will had mixed emotions as he watched Anna interact with the horse through the rearview mirror. He saw a familiar tenderness as she fed her horse another carrot, smiling and talking to him. Images of Shelly flooded his mind. Each one was like a sharp needle, overwhelming and physically painful. But at the same time, he was grateful for the memories that still brought him comfort. He thought of his kids, thankful they hadn't been with Shelly in the SUV. A shiver ran down Will's back, thinking he could have lost all of them. He mouthed a mantra to help himself cope with the painful memories:

"I am grateful for what I have; I am blessed."

CHAPTER 8

Anna slowly drove up the winding ranch road, a sense of uncertainty building in her chest. She never expected the Rockin' D Ranch to be so beautiful. Fields of bluebonnets swayed in the wind, providing a stunning contrast between the soft blues and their green backdrop. Further down, longhorns were grazing in a field. Her breath caught in her throat at seeing the horses in the next field. Something familiar stirred inside her as she pulled up to a set of cabins and what looked to be a meeting area and a separate main house. Taking a deep breath, she turned off the engine and tried to calm her nerves before she left the car.

The second Anna opened the door, and someone called her name from the corral where two horses stood. Shielding her eyes from the sun, she saw little Caden running toward her. He proudly told her he lived there with his daddy.

As the handsome cowboy approached Anna, butterflies danced in her stomach. He stopped in front of them with an intense look, and for a moment, Anna thought he would ask Caden about something else. But then he said, "Are you the new director at the hospital?"

Anna nodded, aware of Caden standing close by her side. The urge to flee surged inside her, but then she saw Kati's familiar face approaching them, and a small wave of relief washed over her.

"Anna, you made it." Kati looked at the man skeptically before turning to Anna. "Will, did you scare the hell out of her?" She turned to Anna. "This is my brother, Will."

"I wasn't trying to scare her. I'm sorry for staring. I've never seen Caden act like that with anyone but his grandmother and mother."

Kati slugged his arm. "And Aunt Kati."

Will chuckled and ran his hand through his hair, avoiding eye contact with Anna. "Yeah, and Aunt Kati. Let me go check and see if Garrett can help you get settled in."

As he walked away, Anna noticed that he had tensed up and kept his head low as he rubbed the back of his neck. She furrowed her brows, confused and slightly hurt by his attitude. Had she done something to offend him? All she could think about was their earlier encounter at the store. Had she said something wrong? *Great. I already pissed off my landlord.*

Kati put her arm around Anna's shoulder, interrupting her thoughts. "Oh my God, I'm so glad you're finally here!" she exclaimed. "How was the drive?"

Anna pushed her hair out of her face and smiled. "Long. Very long."

"Let me show you the cabin. Garrett is great; he just got out of the military. He's quiet but nice." She whispered in her ear, "He's very hot too. He's single, and so is my brother."

He's single? Anna glanced at the barn. *What about the wedding ring?* Then she rolled her eyes. "I'm not interested in dating right now, Kati. I need to get the new department running. A relationship takes too much time."

"Oh, wow. You sound just like Will."

Anna laughed. "Do you have more than one brother?"

Kati furrowed her brow. "Just Will. Why?"

"He's wearing a wedding ring."

Kati closed her eyes and took a deep breath. "He still wears it. If we bring it up, he gets angry."

Anna started walking, feeling slightly relieved. "So, he's single but not on the market. "Something like that, I guess." She shrugged and started walking toward the cabin.

When Anna stepped inside, the cozy atmosphere immediately made her feel at home. The pinewood beams lined the ceiling, and the walls were rough-hewn and exposed, lending a rustic charm to the space. In front of a tall stone fireplace was a vibrantly hued cowhide rug and an overstuffed brown leather sofa. Western-tinged trimmings, such as horseshoes, old wagon wheels, and traditional Indian blankets, gave it a warm, homey feel. Anna's gaze fell upon the large bedroom with its repurposed barn-door bed frame and dresser made from reclaimed wood. Adorning the bed was an earth-tone-and-turquoise quilt, which brought back fond memories of when she and Jenny learned quilting from her nana.

She turned to Kati, smiling. "Oh, Kati, it's perfect."

There was a knock on the door. Anna opened it to find a man in a white Stetson, jeans, and boots. His jaw was covered with a dark, scruffy beard with hints of gray, and his eyes a deep, solemn brown. He smiled at her, but the solemnness in his eyes seemed out of place for the occasion.

"Hi, ma'am," he said. "Will asked me to help you. I'm Garrett."

"I'm Anna."

"Hey, Garrett." Kati waved behind Anna as she spoke.

Garrett smiled and offered a small wave back. "Hey, Kati." He turned his attention back to Anna. "Let's get you settled. Do you want to get your horse first?"

Anna nodded eagerly. "He's my most important cargo."

The two went to work unloading the SUV and settling Thunderbird in his new home while chatting about their horses. Anna grabbed two water bottles from the cooler Garrett had just placed on the porch. She handed one to him and motioned to the porch swing for them to sit down.

As they sat chatting, Anna saw Will standing in the distance, leaning against the barn, watching them intently with an expression she couldn't quite read. She tilted her head in confusion before offering him a nod of recognition, but instead of joining them, he rubbed his fingers along his stubble-covered jaw and strode toward his house. Anna's eyes were locked on Will's back as he walked away, and her shoulders sagged, not understanding how she had offended him.

WILL'S mind raced as he watched Anna and Garrett unload her horse from the trailer. His heart thudded in his chest, and his hands trembled as he brushed away the cobwebs and swept the straw from her horse's new stall. He wanted to offer to help but instead kept his distance, pretending to be busy in the tack room. When she walked past him with boxes of supplies, his cheeks burned, and a lump formed in his throat. Even though he tried to keep out of sight, inevitably, whenever their eyes met, his heart raced, and his temperature rose. Uncomfortable with his intense attraction toward her, Will took refuge behind a wall in the tack room while Anna and Garrett finished settling her horse into his stall. He knew he had to maintain a good amount of space between them. Then, his thoughts shifted to confusion over his attitude.

What difference does it make if she looks attractive? That didn't justify rudeness. Being unkind would only make her feel unwelcome.

Will hovered near the barn, pretending to tinker with a wrench as he watched Anna and Garrett on the porch swing. His chest seized when he noticed Garrett's hand graze Anna's. The heat of jealousy smoldered in his stomach.

Why am I getting so jealous?

In a fit of self-loathing, he ran his hand over the back of his neck, and the sting of regret washed over him. *Why didn't I help her? I could have been sitting with her if I had helped her unload the car. They look so comfortable together. I could go over and see if she needs anything.* It was as if Anna sensed his eyes upon her, and she glanced at him, tilting her head inquisitively.

As if sensing his eyes upon her, Anna glanced at him, her head cocked inquisitively. He did not respond but shoved his hands in his pockets and walked away.

Eva was sitting at the table drawing when he walked into the house. Without looking up, she said, "She's pretty, isn't she?"

Will raised an eyebrow. "Who's pretty?"

"Come on, Daddy, you know who."

"How do you know what she looks like?"

"I saw her from the window when she first got here."

Will let out a loud groan. "Eva, she's renting the cabin."

"I saw the way you looked at her when she was talking to Caden. It's the way you looked at Momma."

Will folded his arms against his chest. "Eva, I'm not talking about this. I love your momma, and I need to concentrate on the equine center. You and Caden are my priority and all I need."

Eva got up and stood in front of Will with her arms crossed. "Daddy, listen to me. Caden and I are doing fine. I know you loved Momma, and you miss her. So do I, but you can't stop living"—she bit her lip, tears brimming in her eyes, and took a deep breath—"because she isn't." A hand went to her heart. "She lives here. The love never dies. Maybe that's why it hurts because we loved her."

She threw her hands up and walked around him. "What do I know? I'm just a kid. I'm going to the barn. I love you, Daddy."

Tears rolled down Will's cheeks. "I love you too. You're very smart for a ten-year-old. How did you get so smart?"

"I got it from my momma. She told me that after Grandpa died. I want you to be happy again like you used to be."

ANNA WAS in Thunderbird's stall feeding him carrots when a blonde girl with sapphire-blue eyes dressed in jeans and a T-shirt walked into the barn.

She waved at Anna. "Hi, I'm Eva. I'm Kati's niece."

Anna smiled and introduced herself.

"I know Caden has been talking about you since he and Daddy returned from town."

Anna laughed. "Oh, he has? What did he say?"

"Well, he said you helped when Daddy lost him. What's your horse's name?"

"This is Thunderbird."

Eva scratched his ear. "Hey, Thunderbird." He sighed and laid his nose on her shoulder.

"I think he likes you," said Anna.

Eva smiled. "He's a beauty." Thunderbird let out a snort. "And a talker."

Anna giggled. "He is indeed."

"You want to meet our horses?"

"Of course."

"I love horses. My momma and I used to ride a lot," Eva said, heading toward the first stall. "This is Cotton Candy, and she's mine. Look how her coat shines. I brush her every day."

Standing before Anna was a beautiful light-chestnut American Quarter horse with a blaze that covered her face from the forehead down to the nose.

"Cotton Candy has socks!" Eva said, referring to the white around all four hooves.

"She's beautiful, Eva." Anna pressed her face against Cotton Candy's soft fur and closed her eyes. A sense of comfort washed over her, like in a silent communication between horses and humans. She smiled and opened her eyes.

Eva was staring at her. "What are you doing?"

Anna scratched Cotton Candy's face. "I love placing my face on my horse's face. It always makes me feel better after a bad day. Have you ever done that?"

"Not really. I brush her and talk to her."

Anna stroked the horse's neck. "Cotton Candy is like a silent friend. Horses can tell how you feel, especially when you're sad or scared. As you groom her, she listens as you talk. Has she ever nuzzled your shoulder?"

"Yes, a few times. Especially after my momma died." Eva stepped up on the fence and scratched Cotton Candy's cheek as the horse nuzzled Eva's shoulder. She closed her eyes and placed her face against the horse's cheek. After a few minutes, she opened her eyes and smiled. "Oh, my goodness. When I was sad, Cotton Candy put her cheek on mine, and I felt better but didn't know she knew."

"They're smart."

"Who told you about this?"

"Well," Anna said, "I read about it after my grandfather bought me a horse because my momma and daddy died."

Eva jumped off the stall. "Your momma and daddy died?"

Anna tried to divert the subject because she didn't want to discuss this with a child she didn't know. "A long time ago." She ruffled Eva's hair. "Remember, you can tell Cotton Candy your troubles. She'll listen."

Eva jumped up and hugged Anna. "Thank you, Anna. I'm glad you're here."

Anna was surprised by Eva's hug. "Me too."

Eva continued the tour, introducing her to Buttercup, a dark chestnut

American Quarter horse with white around the hooves that extended up the legs. Eva stroked Buttercup's cheek.

"This one was Momma's horse." She quietly moved across to the third stall. "This one is Daddy's horse, Jake. He's a painted horse."

Jake was a large Tobiano with a vertical spotting pattern along the topline, a dark chestnut head part of the body, primarily white legs, and a multicolored tail. Eva stroked his cheek.

"Hey, boy, how are you?" she asked. Jake whinnied at her. "Daddy will be out to feed you later."

Jake neighed.

Both Anna and Eva laughed.

"Jake talks a lot," Eva said. She crossed to the last stall. "This is Caden's horse, Duke. Caden likes to ride a lot too. He comes to the stable with Garrett when Daddy is at work."

Duke was a black American Quarter horse with a white star on the forehead and a shine that made his color almost look blue. He stuck his head out of the stall.

Anna smiled. "Hey, Duke." He used his nose to nudge Anna's arm.

Eva laughed. "He wants you to pet him."

Anna smiled and stroked his cheek.

"I'm going to get the grooming tote in the tack room. You wanna come?" asked Eva.

Anna followed her. Eva brought the tote to groom Cotton Candy. They brushed the horse's shiny coat, starting at the top of the neck and moving along the body.

"You are a pretty girl, Cotton Candy," Anna said as she brushed her coat.

Cotton Candy neighed in response.

"You have a talkative group here, Eva. Thunderbird will fit right in."

Eva laughed. "Cotton Candy always answers when you talk to her. Momma always told her and Buttercup how pretty they were, and they would neigh and nod their heads to answer her."

"Well, Cotton Candy, you know you're pretty then." The mare nodded her head. Anna and Eva giggled.

"What else do you like to do besides ride horses?" Anna asked Eva as they continued grooming Cotton Candy.

"I love to draw and bake cookies. Nana likes to quilt, but I'm still too young."

"We have a lot in common. I love to draw and paint. I started quilting with my nana when I was in middle school, up until she got sick."

"Is she better now?"

Anna let out a deep breath. "She passed away last year."

Eva kept brushing Cotton Candy. "My momma died when I was seven. My daddy is still sad."

Anna fought back tears. She wasn't sure what to say. "And how are you?"

Eva put the brush in the grooming tote. "I miss her a lot."

Anna contemplated telling her about her parents because she wanted her to know she understood how she felt. She put the brush in the tote.

"When I was nine, my mom and dad were killed in a car accident. I went to live with Nana and Papa. So, I understand how you feel." The unspoken knowledge of losing a parent existed between them.

"Anna, I'm glad you decided to stay here. I think we're going to get along."

Anna smiled. "I think so. I live just over there." She pointed toward the cabin where she was staying.

They went to place the grooming tote in the tack room. Anna caught the smells of leather and saddle soap. The smell of hay and TLC permeated the small room. "I think I should get settled in my cabin."

Eva smiled. "Thanks for brushing Cotton Candy with me."

Anna squeezed Eva's shoulder. "Thanks for the awesome tour."

Well, that explains why he still wears his wedding ring. He's still mourning his wife.

She understood how Eva felt, that was for sure.

Anna was heading back to her cabin when a middle-aged woman with silver bobbed hair stormed across the yard, leaving dust in the path toward Will's house. Anna watched the interaction, wondering what was happening between the woman and Will. She was pointing a finger as she spoke to him.

CHAPTER 9

Will was sitting in his living room when he caught a glimpse of his mother storming across the yard toward his house. With a heavy sigh, he pushed himself out of the chair and headed toward the door. He knew his momma wasn't one to mince words when she was angry.

The loud knock on the door made Will flinch, a sound that was louder than a summons from the police. He took a deep breath. Kati must have told their mother that she and Will had reconciled, so he wasn't sure about this angry visit. Maybe his mom would finally tell him what a horrible father he was, something even Kati had brought up.

Will opened the door. "Momma, why are you knocking on the door?"

Liz stood with her hands on her hips. "I thought we discussed jumping to conclusions with your sister when we left the restaurant."

"Come on, we made up three weeks ago." *Why didn't Kati tell her we'd straightened things up?* "I even invited her over to hang out with Jon and me. Didn't she tell you?"

She slapped his arm. "Try again."

He lifted his eyebrow. "Ouch, why are you hitting me? We made up. Didn't you see the young lady move in? Anyway, why did it take you three weeks to come to yell at me?"

She pushed a finger at his chest. "Listen to me, William. I know losing

Shelly has been hard now that you've had the equine center on your mind, but that doesn't give you an excuse to treat people like crap." She poked his chest again. "Your kids have spent more time with me than you lately because you are so grumpy."

He lowered his eyes. "Yes, ma'am. I'm sorry. I guess the lack of sleep is taking a toll on me."

"Get your hat. We're going for a ride. Let's saddle up Jake and Queenie."

Will grabbed his Stetson on the way out the door. They silently headed to the stable, crossing the field and separating it from the cabins. A few birds sang spring songs, and a breeze rustled the grass.

His momma was right. He'd been a jerk to Kati. He shouldn't have yelled at her like he had twice. They'd always gotten along since they were kids. It was just that Will didn't understand why his sister, mom, and friends couldn't leave this alone. Shelly had only been gone for three years. He wasn't ready, was he? He couldn't dishonor her memory. Why didn't anyone understand that?

He saddled both horses in silence, then handed Liz the lead for Queenie. They both mounted and headed outside in silence. Will shifted in his saddle. The silence was killing him. He couldn't stand knowing he had upset his momma. He studied her face as they rode. Was she still mad? Sometimes Will couldn't read what others were feeling, especially when he was tired. Their family had always been close. He talked to Momma about everything until Shelly died. He never knew if he wanted to be alone or let others in. At times, he wanted everything to return to how it was before Shelly's passing.

"I'm sorry. I don't sleep well sometimes." Will swallowed the lump in his throat.

Liz fixed her gaze on him. "The silence is unbearable, right? You can't tell anyone what you're feeling. Instead, your emotions manifest as either silence or anger. That's why I was afraid to approach you after you argued with Kati. I was afraid of what I would say if I lost my temper. That's why I waited until now to come and talk to you about this. The passive-aggressiveness between you and Kati has been going on for years, breaking my heart. But now you treat Eva and Caden the same way. Either you're short-tempered, or you ignore them altogether. That must stop now. They've already lost their mother, and the last thing they need to think is that their father doesn't love them."

"What do you mean?"

"They think your silence is because they did something wrong or have lost your love somehow."

"Is that what they told you?" His voice quivered as he asked, "They feel like I don't love them?"

"No, they haven't said anything, but I was a schoolteacher for over twenty-five years. Remember, I know kids. They've been staying with me for a few weeks, and you don't even check on them. You have always been a good father. I'll tell you this once: Get it together for those kids."

"I knew where they were. Kati was texting me, telling me how they were." Will's voice was just above a whisper.

"They don't know that. You need to talk to them, got it?"

Will hung his head in guilt-ridden defeat. "Yes, ma'am. I'm sorry."

Will kept his eyes fixed on the road as he spoke. "I didn't realize the kids thought anything about how I acted. I assumed if they had you, it was all that mattered." A sob caught in his throat. How could he have been so oblivious to their feelings? He sighed deeply as if being suffocated by a wave of emotions. "Ever since Kati tried to fix me up, I feel like everyone is fixated on me dating again. And I miss her so much, and it feels like everything is . . . I don't know anymore."

"Oh, sweetheart," Liz said, her voice full of understanding and sympathy. "Caden and Eva love you so much. They're wondering if you're angry at them for some reason. They noticed the tension in your words and asked me why."

Will couldn't believe what he was hearing. How could he have been so oblivious to his own children's feelings? There was a whirlwind of turmoil inside him since Kati had tried setting him up on dates—it seemed like everyone was pressuring him to move on. His gaze cut sideways. "The pain is overwhelming. I want to..." He cleared his throat. "Be alone."

Liz drew a deep breath and said, "I truly understand what you mean. When your daddy died, the pain was more than I could bear alone. We'd been together since high school. He was my soulmate." Her voice shook with emotion before she continued. "I know the rest of my life will revolve around my family and crazy friends. I'm too old to find that kind of love again."

Will noticed the pain in her face, reminding him that her pain was still raw. Shelly died so soon after his dad that she never had time to grieve. She didn't run and hide from everyone like he did. "Momma, you're—"

"Let me finish. You aren't sixty. You still have a long life ahead. I know you love Caden and Eva." She threw her hands up. "I don't even know what I'm trying to say, so I'll just say it."

Will stopped his horse, and she followed. "You should think about dating. Shelly wouldn't want you to stop living your life. She would want you to . . ." A tear rolled down her cheek. "It sounds so insensitive when I say it."

He knew exactly what she was trying to say, and it made sense to move forward with his life, but it felt like a betrayal, and the thought sent guilt coursing through his body. "I don't know how to let go. I feel like I'm being disloyal if I start dating. I'm also scared of how Caden and Eva would take it if I started a new relationship. I'm terrified that the kids will think Shelly never meant anything to me if I move on. I'm also afraid they'll forget their momma."

"They won't forget their momma even though they were young when she died," said Liz. "You will keep her alive in their hearts by the legacy you will leave in her name. The plan for the equine center will show them how much Shelly meant to you. I'm not saying you need to join a dating service, but don't close the door."

Will and Liz nudged their horses. Liz smiled. "The bluebonnets look beautiful as always. I love spring."

"What makes you think you are too old to love again?" Will asked. "Is that why you haven't dated since Daddy died? I'm sorry I have been so wrapped up in myself. I never thought . . ."

Liz laughed, throwing back her head. "I wouldn't want to date someone because I'm too old and set in my ways. I love being here with you, Kati, and the kids."

"We don't think you're old."

"Well, thank you. We'll drop that subject right there."

"Oh, that's how it is? Hmm. I'll drop it after I say this: Don't close the door." Will snickered as he gave Jake a nudge. Jake picked up his pace.

"That wasn't nice." Liz gave Queenie a little nudge to catch up. "The other reason I wanted to ride was to ask you about the plans to open the center."

"I was going to tell Cindy there was no way I could get it done last week when I took Caden to therapy. When I saw Cindy, she pulled me aside to thank me again. Her excitement about its impact on the kids in the area made me lose my courage to tell her I couldn't do it."

Will finally looked through the notebook Shelly had kept for the equine center. It was brimming with all sorts of plans, including detailed notes on obtaining grant money and plans for a fundraiser. He could barely make sense of what she had written.

"Momma, I don't even know where to start. I have Shelly's notes, but I'm a firefighter, not a grant writer." He adjusted his hat. "When Cindy asked me if I could do it, I couldn't say no," he continued. "We need it in the community; there are only three equine centers from San Antonio to Dallas to meet the overwhelming need." He looked to the sky. "I owe it to Shelly and the kids. If I fail, it will hurt a lot of people."

"That's a big burden to put on your shoulders."

"I like to stay busy, Momma, then I don't have time to . . . feel."

They rode for a time in silence. Will wondered what she was thinking. Over the last three years, his momma had been a rock for him. She helped with the kids, never complaining or bringing up his father, who had just died before Shelly. He knew her heart was broken. He'd never forget his helplessness when his father dropped to the ground while mending fences. All of Will's efforts to do CPR had failed. He was gone before the ambulance arrived. The widow-maker was what they called his heart attack, and it took his daddy away from his momma, making her a widow at age fifty-five.

"Have you looked for someone to help you with the grant?" asked Liz, her voice bringing him back to the present. "Have you asked Cindy?"

He scrubbed his hand across his face. "Honestly, no."

She let out a long sigh. "Let me do some research and talk to the Quiltin' Bees."

He laughed. "The Hens of the South."

The Quiltin' Bees were a group of ladies from Cardinal Creek who, as their name suggested, loved to quilt. They were a force to be reckoned with when they set their sights on a new project.

"You're lucky you're sitting on Jake, or I would swat you."

He couldn't help but chuckle, knowing his mom would get annoyed if he teased her about her quilting circle. "What did you have in mind?" he asked.

"As you know, we've been creating quilts for different causes, like supporting veterans and cancer patients, since our 4-H days. Ever since Sissy opened her shop, her quilts have become a staple in almost every Airbnb and bed and breakfast around here. She has a knack for coordinating charity events with our group; let me talk to her."

Will unexpectedly released all tension, knowing the miracles he'd seen the Quiltin' Bees work since childhood. As much as he teased his mother about them, he knew the community had benefited from their charity work. After talking to his mom, at least he had a plan in mind.

They spent the rest of their ride in silence, enjoying the warm air. When they were almost to the barn, Will looked at Liz with a mischievous smile. "I'll race ya!" Will shouted before his mother responded. He had taken off, leaving her behind.

Will barely began to unbuckle Jake's saddle in the barn when he heard Queenie's panicking, whinnying, and Liz's screaming. Fear coursed through him as he sprinted out of the barn, and what he saw made his stomach sink. Liz's foot was stuck in the stirrup, and Queenie dragged her across the ground. Will leaped forward, wrapped his hands around the leather straps, and yanked them tight, bringing Queenie to an abrupt halt.

"Oh my God, Momma," Will breathed, noting with horror that Liz's right leg was splayed at an unnatural angle. Her jeans were torn, revealing a bone sticking out. Will's stomach churned as he realized she'd broken her leg.

Tears streamed down her face as she squeezed her eyes shut against the pain.

Will grabbed his cell phone and called 911. Relief flooded him as Garrett rounded the corner on his horse. He dismounted and ran to Liz's side. Will's mind raced. Even with the ambulance en route, they needed more help before it arrived.

"Hey, Garrett," he said. "Go get Kati and . . ." Will hesitated, conflicted between his guilt about being rude to Anna earlier and his need for her help as a nurse. His first instinct was to be selfish and find another solution, but he knew they needed all the help they could get.

Garrett interrupted Will's thoughts. "I'll get Anna too. She's a nurse."

"Yeah . . . good. Go."

Will tucked a horse blanket under Liz's head and retrieved trauma sheers from her saddle bag. A flood of relief overcame him when Kati, Garrett, and Anna approached the barn.

"Momma, what happened?" Kati asked.

"My boot got caught, and then I startled Queenie when I tried to keep from falling," said Liz.

Anna knelt beside Will. His stomach tightened as he carefully cut away the denim from around Liz's leg, but he dropped the sheers. Anna picked them up and wiped them off with her T-shirt before returning them to him.

Their gazes met and he flashed her a wry smile. "Thanks," Will muttered, as heat warmed his cheeks with a blush of embarrassment for his clumsiness.

"Do you have something to bandage her leg to keep the dirt out?" Anna asked.

Will nodded and pointed to his truck. "I have a bag in my truck. Can you grab it? It's a black duffle." Anna jogged to his vehicle and grabbed the bag, pulling out gauze as fast as possible for Will to wrap around Liz's leg.

Ten minutes later, the siren and flashing lights headed up the driveway. Eva and Caden came running out of the house. As soon as Caden got closer, he started crying and screaming as the paramedics worked with haste to help Liz.

Will watched as Anna moved toward Caden, his body taut with anxiety. Will was scared that the overstimulation from the noise would cause Caden to have a meltdown.

Without hesitation, Anna leaned closer and whispered something in his ear before gently tilting his chin to look into her eyes. With a smile, she spoke again, and Caden nodded in response.

Liz held out her hand to Caden.

Anna said, "It's okay to go hold her hand." She walked him over to Liz. He took her hand.

"Listen, baby, I'm okay," Liz said to Caden. "I just need to get my leg fixed. I'll be back soon."

He sniffed. "You aren't gonna die, are you, Nana?"

As those words left Caden's lips, Will's chest tightened. What if his mother died? He shook his head. *No, she won't. It's just a broken leg.* That didn't stop the heaviness in his chest. He knew the risks of a compound fracture, yet he also knew that early intervention gave his momma a good chance of not having complications in her recovery.

She shook her head. "No, sweetie. Let me kiss your forehead." He leaned in so she could kiss him. "I love you, Caden."

"I love you," said Caden.

Caden held Anna's hand the entire time. When they loaded Liz into the ambulance, Anna pulled Caden into her arms and whispered in his ear. Will's breath caught in his throat.

"Will, we need to get to the hospital," Kati said, touching his arm.

Will looked at Garrett and Anna.

"Get in the truck, Will. Anna and I have the kids," Garrett assured.

Anna nodded. "Yeah, we have this."

"Yeah, Dad, Garrett will have us out riding longhorns by the end of the day!" Eva yelled.

Will turned, one heavy eyebrow slanted in solid disapproval.

"Just the small ones." Garrett ruffled Eva's hair and poked her side. "Why are you trying to rile him up? Totally not appropriate."

Will climbed into the truck and drew in a long breath.

Kati wrapped her fingers around his and said, "It will be okay."

Fear prickled his scalp. He had no idea how to enter the same hospital where they brought his wife the day she died.

CHAPTER 10

Will's fingers tightened around the steering wheel as he drove to the hospital, anxiety curling like a snake in his belly. He was relieved when Anna handled Caden with such ease—familiarity even—but he was still uncertain if allowing him and Eva to stay with her and Garrett was the right choice.

Kati and Will arrived at the hospital just after the ambulance, and she dashed inside while he stopped short in front of the emergency entrance. His body trembled as memories of Shelly's accident filled his mind. Will took some time to compose himself, closing his eyes and taking a deep breath. He wiped away the sweat that had formed on the back of his neck with a shaky hand. *I can do this. I can walk in there. This isn't the same as when Shelly died.* Since Shelly's accident, Will stopped working the ambulance so he wouldn't have to make runs to the hospital. He was thankful for the opportunities to drive the firetruck or accompany the chief to fires. After a while, his primary task became chauffeuring the chief.

Kati placed a hand on his arm, causing him to jump. "Hey, Will. You, okay? You've been out here for a while. Momma's waiting for you," she said softly.

He fumbled for an excuse about why he was lingering outside, knowing she saw right through it. "Oh yeah, sorry. I just had to make a call." She raised her eyebrows skeptically but didn't press the issue further. "How is she?" he asked, shifting gears.

As they headed into the hospital, Kati explained, "She's in a lot of pain, but you know how stoic she is."

As they walked down the hallway toward Liz's room, Kati explained she'd already received x-rays, and the surgeon had been called in. They quickly entered the room to find Liz talking to the doctor. "Kids, this is Dr. Seth Watts. He'll be doing surgery to fix my leg."

Will and Kati reached out to shake his hand, and Dr. Watts firmly grasped it with a reassuring squeeze. The doctor had a kind face framed by chestnut hair with a hint of gray at the temples. His small stature was balanced by a goatee that gave him a distinguished air. His eyes were a deep shade of brown, the pupils wide and filled with an intensity that made Will uncomfortable. He could sense a hint of mystery and danger beneath the warm exterior, making him uneasy. He scolded himself for being overly suspicious without knowing more about the doctor.

Dr. Watts went over the procedure as if it were routine for him. He mentioned that the bone was fractured in multiple spots and would need to be repaired with hardware, cautioning that infection was the primary concern, but she would be given antibiotics. They were reminded she was in good health and active, so she'd likely spend one night in the hospital if everything went smoothly. He asked if they understood what he explained. Will and Kati nodded in unison.

Dr. Watts put an encouraging hand on Kati's shoulder and gave her a reassuring smile. "You don't have to worry," he said, "Your mother is in good hands."

Kati flashed a weak smile. "Thanks, Dr. Watts."

As Dr. Watts exited the room, a nurse quietly entered, her rubber-soled shoes squeaking on the tiled floor. She paused in surprise when she saw Kati. "Oh my God, Kati!" she exclaimed. "What are you doing here?"

Kati placed her arm around Liz's shoulders. "This is my mom. See, Momma, you haven't met everyone in town. This is Sylvia, one of our new nurses who moved from San Antonio."

Liz laughed, "Nice to meet you, Sylvia."

Will kept looking at the floor, not wanting to make small talk. "This is my brother, Will." She gave him a nudge to get his attention.

"Hey, Will."

He slowly lifted his head and nodded. "Hello." She smiled at him as she sashayed past him to leave the room.

Over the next few minutes, nurses came in and out of the room to prep Liz for surgery, hooking her up to IVs and monitors. Liz's eyes grew heavy from the pain medication. Will held her hand, his palm sweating, but he didn't want to let go. All he wanted was for everything to be all right. He looked into his mother's eyes and said, "I'm so sorry. This is all my fault. I should have helped you down."

Her eyebrows furrowed. "Don't you do that. I have been getting off horses since before you were born. It was a freak accident."

Will leaned over and kissed her forehead. "I love you." *Please let her be okay.* He knew she had a long road of recovery ahead. The biggest worry after surgery was infection, but they rushed to get her to the hospital and did their best to prevent infection when she fell.

She touched his face one last time before they wheeled her away. "I'll be fine. I love you too."

Kati kissed Liz's cheek. "I love you. We'll see you when you're done."

They watched the nurses wheel their mother down the fluorescent-lit hallway into the surgery holding area. All Will could hear were the squeaking wheels on the stretcher and his conflicting emotions—despair at the thought of losing his mother and hope that she'd make it through surgery unscathed. When the door shut, his chest tightened, and his breath became coarse. Kati put her arm around him and suggested they grab a drink and go outside—an escape from reality, if only for a moment. He managed a nod and followed her to the cafeteria in silence. He was in a daze as they grabbed two soft drinks and headed outside.

Sitting on a bench outside the hospital, Will and Kati let out simultaneous sighs. Will didn't expect the day to end like this. He should have helped his mother down off the horse. He removed his hat, placed it beside him, and said a silent prayer for his mother's successful surgery. All he wanted was for her to make it through without any complications.

Kati touched his shoulder and asked, "Are you okay?"

He gave a slight nod and forced a smile. "I suppose so, now that I'm out here."

Kati furrowed her brow. "It's hard for you to go into the hospital?"

"The ER mostly," he replied.

She nodded. "I understand." Then she nudged his shoulder and added jokingly, "You don't notice other women, do you?"

Will's eyes widened, and his breath hitched as he thought about Anna helping with his mother. "What are you talking about?" he stammered.

Kati gave him a knowing look. "You missed Sylvia eyeing you. If that were Jon, he would have noticed her . . . boobs."

Will managed a small laugh. "You broke up with him because he can be such a pig. I love him, Kati, but I hate how he talks about women." He looked away from her and stared at the sidewalk. He breathed deeply and admitted, "I didn't notice the nurse, but Lord help me . . . I noticed Anna." A knot tightened in his stomach as he thought about how beautiful she was.

Kati's eyes grew wide, and Will flashed her a look that told her to keep quiet, which she respected. As they sat silently, Will stared at his drink, his mind searching for something to say. He couldn't help but think of the times his jealousy caused problems between him and Shelly. With her gone, he couldn't shake off the guilt of possibly dating again. Memories of their life flooded his thoughts, causing his heart to ache. After a long pause, he cleared his throat and said, "I can't believe I said that out loud."

Kati looked at him with a side glance, a mischievous grin growing wider as she raised an eyebrow. "Brother, I'm not sure I heard you."

Scarlet heat warmed Will's cheeks, and he shifted uncomfortably in his seat. He didn't want to repeat what he said; it was embarrassing and revealing. But Kati wasn't going to let him off the hook that easily. "Please don't make me repeat it," he muttered.

She shrugged. The gleam in her eye made Will uneasy. "Whatever you say, man."

Will rubbed his chin. "I don't even know how to act around women anymore." He sighed. "I'm not sure I ever did."

Kati chuckled as she stirred her drink with a straw. "Just be yourself," she said.

Will let out a long groan, feeling frustrated and defeated by his self-doubt. He needed to be honest with himself. Part of the reason he didn't want to get into the dating scene was the fear of rejection that loomed over him like a dark cloud. "Tell me about her," he said finally. "What is she like?"

"All I know is she's from Missouri," Kati replied. "She loves horses and worked in a palliative care department there. She also said her grandparents raised her."

Will nodded, wondering if he'd have the courage to talk to her. Anytime Anna was near, he had an overwhelming urge to flee, just like when she arrived at the ranch. He was taken aback when she arrived and realized she was the same woman who had helped Caden at the grocery store.

"I'm sorry I've been so grumpy lately," he said suddenly, breaking the silence that had descended upon them again. "No excuses, but I'm not sleeping well."

Kati smiled. "It's all forgiven," she said.

After finishing their beverages in peaceful tranquility, they strolled back to the hospital to await their mom's emergence from surgery. As they walked alongside each other, Will bit his bottom lip, wondering if he had been using Shelly's death as an excuse not to date. Deep down, Will knew it was time to put himself out there, but the thought of rejection was almost too much to bear. He shook his head as he entered the hospital. *How could I be thinking about dating while Momma is in surgery?* He chuckled to himself. At least his anxiety came down a notch.

Two and a half hours later, Dr. Watts finally appeared in the surgery waiting room with good news. "Your mother did great," he said. "She should be up and around in no time. The biggest risk for this type of fracture is infection, but you got her here fast, and we started antibiotics immediately. She's in recovery now."

Kati shook the doctor's hand, thanking him profusely. He nodded before turning back to her with a curious gleam in his eye. "Aren't you the director of the Emergency Department?"

Kati nodded, red creeping into her cheeks. "I am."

The doctor smiled, his gaze scanning Kati. "Well, I guess I'll be seeing you around," he said, his voice dripping with charm.

Will and Kati raised their eyebrows at each other.

Will smiled, "I think he likes you."

She lowered her voice, imitating Will, "I am not interested in dating. Plus, he's married to the director of nursing."

Will playfully pushed her shoulder. "Touché. You didn't know him?"

"No, he's new to the hospital. Some of the nurses in the department have talked to him, but they work the floor more than I do."

A short time later, Will was relieved when he and Kati received word that Liz was going to her room. The tension in Will's body melted away when he entered the room and saw Liz lying in the hospital bed with her eyes open but glazed over from pain medication, slurring her words as she told Will to get home to the kids. She held out her hand—an invitation he could not refuse—so he grabbed it firmly before turning to Kati with concern, asking how she would get home when all was said and done. But Liz assured him Kati was fine; she'd sleep there or call Jon to get her. He kissed his mom on the forehead and promised to visit her in the morning.

Will's feet were heavy as he left the room. When he reached the nurses' station, he noticed something that made him pause. Dr. Watts stood extremely close to one of the nurses, resting his hand on her arm. Will watched in disbelief when the doctor tucked a strand of hair behind her ear. That wasn't an appropriate way for a married man to act with another woman. *What a jerk,* he thought. Will shook his head. He was exhausted and couldn't wait to go home to his kids.

CHAPTER 11

As the ambulance pulled away, Anna's gaze shifted to Garrett. His hands trembled as he jammed them into his pockets. She instructed Eva and Caden to wait on the porch of her cabin while she cautiously approached Garrett and touched his shoulder. His gaze was distant, and his body was frozen in place. Anna squeezed his arm, hoping to bring him back to the present. Garrett drew a long breath, clenching his jaw while sweat gathered on his forehead.

"Garrett," she whispered, "are you okay?"

He opened his eyes and rubbed them with the base of his palms before plastering a dazzling smile that lit up his brown eyes. He asked if the kids were alright. Anna scanned his face before responding quietly, "They're fine." Without thinking, she grabbed his hand and squeezed it reassuringly. She felt the tension leave Garrett's body as he started to relax. He offered a slight grin.

"Let's get them in my cabin and figure out what to feed them," Anna suggested.

Eva and Caden were ushered into the cozy cabin. As they settled at the wooden table, Anna and Eva browsed through the menu of various pizza options. Across the room, Garrett leaned casually against the wall, deep in conversation with Caden. Anna couldn't help but steal glances at him.

When he caught her gaze, he nodded in acknowledgment. A slight smile played at the corners of her lips. She sensed that something was bothering him, but the cause eluded her.

Anna propelled herself up. "So, after looking at the pizza menu with Eva, I think we need pizza."

Both kids jumped up, pumping their fists as they yelled, "Oh yeah, Pizza! We want pizza!"

Garrett laughed. "I can get it. One cheese and one pepperoni?"

"I like anchovies and mushrooms," Anna interjected, teasing.

Eva wrinkled her nose. "Mushrooms, yuck. I don't know what anchovies are, but they sound gross."

"They are," Anna laughed.

Garrett took his keys out of his pocket. "I'll go get the pizzas. Are you okay here, Anna?"

She put her arm around Eva and said, "We're fine."

Garrett glanced at Caden. "You wanna go?"

Caden quickly grabbed Anna's hand, pulling her toward the couch. "I'm going to stick with Anna," he insisted.

Garrett laughed, a hearty contrast to how he was before they entered the cabin. "I'm crushed, buddy."

Caden raised his hand in a wave. "Come on, dude, we're buds, right?"

Garrett chuckled. "Yes, we're buds. I'll be back, y'all."

Anna observed the exchange between Garrett and Caden and noticed how different it was when Will interacted with his son. Garrett was more relaxed and cheerful when talking to Caden, whereas Will was more controlling and tense. When Will interacted with Caden, he did his best to keep the conversation from spiraling. It was as if he didn't know how to talk to his son. Her heart softened toward Will for his uncertainty.

Anna jumped up from the couch when she remembered the horses needed to be fed. "So, y'all wanna go feed the horses? Caden, you haven't met my horse, Thunderbird."

Caden nodded, his eyes wide. "I saw him at the store after Daddy lost me. He was watching you while you fed your horse carrots. I think he likes you."

She forced a small smile, her cheeks burning with embarrassment. She couldn't understand what Caden had meant when he said Will had been watching her. Ever since she'd arrived at the ranch, Will had acted distant and cold. Was this his way of showing someone that he liked them? But then again, she noticed how gently he cared for his mom. She didn't know what to think of it.

Eva giggled. "I told him you were pretty."

Anna stood up abruptly, realizing she needed to change the subject before things got awkward. "Come on, you little matchmakers, we should feed the horses."

Smiling, Anna pulled a bag of bright orange carrots from her pocket and handed them to Caden and Eva. "Hey, let's pass these out."

Caden wrinkled his nose. "I am not eating carrots."

Anna ruffled his hair. "Not for you, silly; for the horses."

Caden and Eva followed Anna to Thunderbird's stall with handfuls of carrots in their fists. She stopped just outside the booth, offering Thunderbird an outstretched hand with a carrot before entering the stall. He snorted lightly as he took the carrot from between her fingers, then rested his head on her shoulders as she scratched behind his ears.

Caden held a carrot in his palm for Thunderbird. The horse nuzzled the boy's hand before taking the carrot from him, then gave him a gentle nudge with his muzzle. Caden grinned up at Anna before looking back at Thunderbird. "You're a good boy," he said, softly patting the horse's neck. Thunderbird nickered before trying to bite Caden's shirt with his teeth, forcing a laugh out of both Anna and Caden.

"He likes you," Anna said. "What do you say we head back to my cabin and wash up for pizza."

"Yes, ma'am," Caden said enthusiastically. "Come on, Eva, let's go wash our hands." The children sprinted toward the cabin. Anna had to jog to keep up with them.

After they finished washing up, Garrett returned with four large pizzas and some paper plates.

After everyone ate, Caden settled on the couch to watch a movie on Anna's phone. Garrett had walked Eva to her house so she could get her sketch pad and pencils, and now she was quietly coloring at the table.

Garrett stood with his shoulders hunched as if in deep thought. "Anna, can I talk to you outside?" Her stomach twisted at the worry in his voice, and she followed him out. "Will called while I was getting the pizza. Liz is out of surgery and doing well. She'll be able to come home sometime tomorrow."

Anna let out a sigh of relief. "Thank God."

He shifted his feet, cleared his throat, and looked at the sky. "I should go feed the horses," he said.

Anna shook her head. "It's okay. We did it while you were gone."

He shot her a grateful smile. "Really? What a first day you had here."

Anna ran her fingers through her hair before replying, trying not to think too hard about what troubled him. "Yeah, no kidding. Are you okay?"

Garrett opened his mouth to speak but paused before letting out a small chuckle. "Anna, it was nothing."

She kept quiet momentarily, allowing him to open up to her. "If you ever need to talk, I'm here."

He smiled again and nodded before taking a step back from her. "Thank you for that. Would you mind if I took off?"

Anna shook her head, still uneasy about what upset him in the first place. "No, I have it under control. Did Will say when he was coming home?"

Garrett looked relieved at the shift in the conversation. "He wanted to wait until Liz was in a room," he said before gently touching her shoulder and squeezing it lightly in farewell. "Caden and Eva are in good hands with you. I'll see ya on Monday."

What the hell was that? Does he like me? No, he's too old for me. This entire day has been surreal. Lord, I need to sleep.

"Good night, Garrett." Anna watched as Garrett drove away, wondering if she'd ever discover what had been troubling him. She pulled at her red bracelet, already missing Jenny and Maggie. It had been a crazy day. *Well, Anna, you wanted a family,* she thought as she walked into her cabin.

CHAPTER 12

As Will drove back to the ranch, the muscles in his body began to relax. He rolled his shoulders to ease the tension in the back of his neck. After parking his truck, he attempted to rub the knots from his shoulders while he tried to sort through all the day's emotions. He prayed he could keep his composure as he walked to Anna's cabin. As he climbed the stairs, his heartbeat quickened at the thought of being near Anna. By the time he reached the top, he was sure it would burst through his chest.

Will could see through the window as he approached the door. Eva was sitting next to Anna on the couch with her sketch pad, diligently adding color to her drawing with a pencil. Caden slept with his head in Anna's lap, and she carefully brushed her fingertips over his hair. He had such a peaceful look on his face. Will watched in awe. It had taken months for Caden to interact with Garrett when he arrived, but now they were the best of friends. A pang of jealousy hit Will as he realized Caden fist-bumped Garrett more than him. Caden instantly connected with her, and Anna had won the little boy's trust within hours. Will smiled fondly as he watched Eva talking to Anna with a twinkle in her eye, something he hadn't seen since Shelly died.

He knocked on the door. He saw Anna motion for Eva to answer the door. "Who is it?" Her voice was soft.

"It's my daddy," Eva whispered as she opened the door. She wrapped her slim arms around Will's waist and squeezed tight. "Is Nana okay? When will she come home?"

Will enveloped Eva in a warm embrace. "She is fine and is resting at the hospital. She'll come home sometime tomorrow."

Will looked at Anna. "How did you do that? With Caden sleeping in your lap like that?" He rubbed the back of his neck. "It took him months to get used to Garrett when he started working here."

Anna shrugged causally. "Oh, he was watching a movie on my phone and laid his head in my lap."

"He only does that with a select few," Will remarked with amazement. "Thank you for all you did today."

Anna smiled. "They're great kids. We fed the horses while Garrett got pizza. We had fun despite the circumstances."

Eva gushed. "Anna loves art, just like me. She paints."

Will glanced at Anna. "You don't seem like the type to paint. What got you into painting?"

Anna furrowed her eyebrows. "Painting has a type? I didn't know that." She sighed and stared off into the distance. "I started painting to calm my nerves when I was about Eva's age." They locked eyes for an uncomfortable few seconds, neither saying anything nor moving. Anna broke their gaze and looked down at Caden, who was still sleeping in her lap. She hummed the first few lyrics of "I Wish Grandpas Never Died" by Riley Green, and the words seemed to break her heart.

Will's chest rose and fell with rapid breaths as he glanced around the room, desperately searching for an escape. He had no explanation for how Anna knew Caden's favorite song or why watching her interact with him brought back memories of Shelly. His wife's soft voice and gentle touch could calm Caden's outbursts. She would cradle his head in her lap and sing "You Are My Sunshine," the words echoing in the air. Will cleared his throat, attempting to push away the memories.

"I should get the kids home," he murmured. As he bent down to scoop Caden into his arms, he accidentally brushed against Anna's arm, resulting in a jolt of electricity, throwing him further off balance. The tension between them grew more intense as he gazed into her emerald-green eyes. A thunderous humming filled his entire being, drawing them closer as they stood silently.

"Good night," she whispered before Will headed out the door and down the steps.

The screen door squeaked, and he turned to see Eva with her hands on her hips. "Daddy, you forgot me," she laughed.

He paused, chuckling at her words, and offered her his hand. "I'm sorry, pumpkin. It has been a long day. I'm not sure where my head is." Eva smiled, took his hand, and with a final goodnight to Anna, they headed home.

Will tucked Eva and Caden into bed before heading to the bedroom he used to share with Shelly. The room was frozen in time, just as it was on their last day together. The bed remained untouched, perfectly made, just as she had left it. He ran his fingers over her hairbrush, strands still caught in its bristles. As he laid his head on her pillow, memories flooded back from their time together. He could smell the faint scent of her jasmine shampoo. Somehow, he thought he could keep her alive if he changed nothing. There was a sinking feeling in his stomach for how his body and mind reacted when he was close to Anna. Everyone told him it was time to move on, but who could put a time stamp on loss? Of course, he missed the intimacy of a woman's companionship, not just the physical aspects. He hadn't been with a woman since Shelly's death. Women never caught his eye, much less affected him like Anna.

It was more than her physical appearance. Will didn't understand it, but how Anna was with his kids drew him in. She brought back the spark they lost when their momma died. A sigh escaped his lips, recalling the last morning he and Shelly spent in bed. His mind fast-forwarded to the accident. He wished he had kept her at the firehouse longer; maybe she wouldn't have gotten killed. He was lying to himself and everyone else. It was the text he sent that had caused her death. He and Shelly argued about distracted driving because she always answered a text. No matter how often he gave her the cold, harsh facts about the death rates from distracted driving, she never stopped being glued to the damn phone with complete disregard for anyone else. *Look at me blaming her. I knew she answered texts, and I sent the text anyway. It was my fault.* He jumped up and stormed into the bathroom for a shower. As the cold water hit his back, his mind filled with thoughts of Shelly. But then the thoughts quickly shifted to Anna, and he couldn't help but wonder what she was up to.

He turned, facing the cold water, making him jump a bit. "That will teach you to think of her," he mumbled. He shut the water off and wrapped a towel around his waist. He peered into the mirror, hating the reflection of the man he saw. He wasn't suitable for anyone, especially Anna. He was the reason his wife was dead. He needed to learn how to open the equine center or else he'd let the community down. He was broken beyond repair. He decided the best thing to do was avoid Anna altogether, but he needed to figure out how.

He dressed in shorts and a T-shirt, grabbed his bedding from the closet, and headed to the couch. As he lay there, his mind wandered to his mother and her recovery time. He couldn't imagine how he'd manage without her. She was the one who helped with Eva and Caden and always pitched in around the ranch. She picked up his slack when he worked. He let out a frustrated sigh and covered his eyes with his arm, overwhelmed at the thought of preparing to open the equine center by Shelly's birthday without her help.

CHAPTER 13

Anna's eyes slowly opened as her alarm blared beside her bed, and a wave of confusion washed over her. This wasn't the same twin bed from her childhood in Missouri, draped with a soft pink-and-white quilt made by her beloved nana. The dark wood and high wooden beams contrasted her old room's familiar pink daisy wallpaper. Nana and Papa wanted to change her room, but Anna didn't want to because it made her feel close to her momma. She took a deep breath to catch the scent of the pine from the queen-sized four-poster bed. She slowly ran her fingers across the stitches of the quilt featuring a Lonestar design in warm hues of brown and turquoise. The memory of Will's breath on her cheek when he picked up Caden came flooding back to her, as did the musky scent of his cologne. Scarlet warmth rose to Anna's cheeks at the thought, and she threw her arm across her eyes to block out the light.

She was simultaneously exhausted and exhilarated from the excitement of the day before. Suddenly, she threw the covers back, thinking about getting to the barn before Will to clean the horses' stalls before he arrived. Since Liz and Kati were at the hospital and it was Garrett's day off, Will would be alone to do the chores. Anna quickly pulled on a pair of Wranglers, a lavender T-shirt, and her boots. She fixed her crimson hair in a ponytail and put on a teal vintage ball cap with a patch that said, "Barn hair don't care." She stepped outside, surprised by the warm morning air.

The large red stable door greeted her, and she entered the barn. There were large rafters and a loft, and almost all twelve stalls had horses occupying them. Sweat trickled down her face as she grabbed a wheelbarrow and pitchfork, headed to the first stall, and mumbled, "Wow, it's much hotter here than spring in Missouri."

She opened the stall door and scratched Duke's cheek. "Good morning, big boy." She held out a carrot. "It's bribery." She laughed. She put in her AirPods and pressed play on her favorite playlist, then went to work, mucking the stalls and swaying her hips to the music.

She felt a hand on her shoulder when she reached the fourth stall and jumped. She turned to find Will staring at her. He wore a pair of Wranglers that accented his muscular thighs and a blue T-shirt that stretched across his broad, muscular chest.

She quickly took out her AirPods. "You scared the living daylights out of me." *Lord, I hope he didn't see me dancing.*

He stood with his arms across his chest. "What are you doing?" His tone was sharp, and it made Anna cringe.

"What does it look like?" She clenched her jaw and pointed to the wheelbarrow with remnants of the dirty stalls.

His eyes seemed cold and distant. "Why?"

She straightened her back. "Because I thought you might need the help since you had a long day yesterday, and no one is here to help," she snapped.

He closed his eyes and took a deep breath. "I'm sorry. I was just surprised to see you here."

Before Will left the stall, he turned to Anna. "Uh, those were some nice moves there. What are you listening to?"

Anna's face turned the color of her hair. "Um, I was listening to NSYNC," she mumbled. *Oh, he looks a little too amused for my liking.*

Will put his hand up to his ear. "Say that again."

Anna narrowed her eyes. "I accept your feeble apology. I'm almost done here. Do you want some help feeding the horses when I'm done?"

He chuckled. "I can't believe you're offering to shovel my horse crap."

Her lips twitch into a smile. "I am, sir."

Before he walked out of the stall, he said in a sing-song voice, "Bye, Bye, Bye," and waved his hand.

A burst of giggles stirred her belly and mingled with a thousand butterflies. *I would call that a truce. This man is a total mystery and has a good sense of humor.*

They worked together to finish feeding the horses and cleaning stalls. Will started at the other end of the barn and fed the horses with clean stalls. While they worked together in silence, Anna couldn't help but notice how Will filled out his T-shirt.

Get ahold of yourself, Anna! Despite being a widower for three years, he still wears his wedding ring, and you just got cheated on. She let out a low groan as she picked up a load and threw it toward the wheelbarrow with too much vigor, causing it to go over the side. She uttered a loud huff as she stomped around to pick it up. She tossed it into the wheelbarrow and saw Will leaning against the stall door, smiling.

She narrowed her eyes. "What?"

"Are you okay?"

She gave a half-shrug. "Yeah, I'm fine. Why?"

The corners of his mouth curved into a smile. "You seemed mad when you threw that load toward the wheelbarrow."

She dropped the shovel into the wheelbarrow. *Oh, I'm flustered every time you're in my vicinity.* "I'm not mad. Yesterday was crazy," she said abruptly, changing the subject as she rolled past Will with the stall contents. She caught the woodsy scent of his cologne, which teased her senses.

"Yes, it was. I appreciate your help." Will moved aside to miss being hit with the handle of the shovel.

She kept walking, trying to keep her composure. "Not a problem. Do you need help feeding?"

"Nah, it's okay. Just wanted to make sure you're okay."

She turned to him with a forced smile. "I'm fine. I was frustrated I missed, that's all."

"It happens." He chuckled. "I better get back to work."

Anna dumped the contents and put the shovel and wheelbarrow into the tack room. She grabbed the grooming tote and headed to Thunderbird's stall.

When she reached his stall, she scratched his cheek, reaching out her hand with a carrot. "Look what I brought, handsome." He rubbed his nuzzle against her neck. "Oh, you like it." He bobbed his head up and down.

Anna laughed as she brushed him. "I hope you like it here, buddy." He whinnied. "Good." She scratched his ear before using long strokes to brush his shiny coat.

Anna heard Will talking to her and turned, causing Thunderbird to snort in Will's direction. His eyes looked tired despite his smile. She scratched Thunderbird's cheek, "It's okay, buddy. It's just Will."

Will cleared his throat, then said, "Thank you again for helping with the horses. I'm sorry I was rude earlier. I didn't sleep well." He kicked at the ground. "I wanted to say something earlier, but you seemed mad."

"It's all good, Will." She scratched Thunderbird's ear. "I didn't hear you because I was talking to this guy, but you have some ninja moves." Thunderbird bobbed his head and nickered, "I know, baby."

Will laughed. "He talks to you."

"Yep, I share all my secrets with him."

He raised an eyebrow. "You do?"

"I do. Good ol' Thunder tells no one." Anna smiled as she worked, but inside, something tugged at her heart, making her want to escape this situation. An old fear of rejection bubbled to the surface and made her uncomfortable as he watched her intently. "What? Why are you watching me?"

He grinned as he scratched Thunderbird's cheek. "Would you like to have breakfast with us?"

Anna's heart raced, and the conflicting thoughts made it hard to answer. Should she say yes or no? She took a deep breath and mumbled, "Yeah, sure . . . I'm almost done."

After finishing, she put the brush in the grooming tote and affectionately scratched Thunderbird's cheek. "I love you, buddy," she said.

Will took the grooming tote to the tack room and closed the door. Anna was in disbelief when he'd asked her to come for breakfast with him and the kids. The signals Will sent were all over the board. *Does he like me or hate me?*

They exited the barn, and Will stopped abruptly in front of her. "I'm not good at asking for help. It makes me feel helpless, and then I act like a jerk. Again, I'm sorry."

She nodded. "It's okay, no problem."

He gave her a quick kiss on the cheek, and before she could respond, he walked quickly toward his house.

Anna stood rooted as if her feet were nailed to the ground. She pressed her hand to her cheek to steady her racing thoughts and breathing.

∼

IN A DAZE, Will walked back to the house, a maelstrom of emotions whirling within. *Why did I kiss her? What was I thinking?* He burst through the door, ready to shower and clear his mind, when he heard Eva's voice.

"Daddy, are you okay?" She was sitting on the couch, drawing.

"Yeah, I'm fine. I need to shower and straighten up . . ." His voice drifted off. He wished he could come up with some excuse to cancel breakfast, but how could he explain that? Guilt consumed him as his gaze settled on the wedding picture above the fireplace, a knot forming in his stomach.

Eva stood and walked over to him. "Daddy, what's wrong? Is everything okay?"

A lump formed in Will's throat, making it difficult for him to speak. He swallowed hard. "I invited Anna for breakfast."

Eva hugged him tight. "Thank you. I like her a lot. She understands what it's like to grow up without a momma."

Will's muscles tensed. He took a deep breath to steady himself. "She does? How do you know this?" He crossed his arms, expecting an explanation from her.

Eva rolled her eyes and tugged on his shirt sleeve. "You're getting mad before you know anything. I can tell."

Will relaxed his stance and nodded for her to continue. "Go on."

She told him they were grooming Cotton Candy when Anna had shared how she used animals to comfort her sadness after her parents died. But she didn't say how old she was when it happened, only that she understood what Eva was going through. A flood of emotions hit Will, but he was relieved that Eva had someone to relate to her experience.

Will pulled her close and rested his chin on her head. He could feel her body shaking as she fought back sobs. He murmured, "I know you miss your momma. I do, too." Their embrace lingered a bit longer before Eva wiggled out of his arms.

Eva wiped the tears from her face and, with a shaky voice, said, "Go shower. You stink. We don't need that when Anna gets here. I'll straighten up the house."

Will chuckled as he went to his bedroom, trying to ignore the sinking feeling in his stomach. He closed the door behind him and collapsed onto the bed with a groan before standing back up again. He paced around the room for several moments before catching sight of himself in the dresser mirror. "It's just breakfast, for crying out loud," he muttered as he pulled his shirt over his head. "What about this woman has me acting so . . . stupid." He caught a glimpse of himself in the bathroom mirror. "I'm not any good for her even if she wanted me. Besides, if Anna knew it was my fault Shelly died, she'd never want anything to do with me." He let out a loud groan. "It's just breakfast."

He undressed, stepped into the shower, and allowed the warm water to wash away his worries. He wondered what had happened to Anna's parents. Why did it bother him so much that Eva knew? He was sure she understood what it was like to grieve deeply for someone you loved, which made him feel an inexplicable connection to her.

Once showered and dressed in comfortable clothes, Will returned to the living room, where he found Eva had miraculously transformed the chaotic mess into a home like Shelly had kept when she was alive. It was beautiful how much Eva resembled her mother in looks and actions.

Eva was sitting at the breakfast bar in the kitchen, drawing. He kissed the top of her head. "Thanks for cleaning up. How about some blueberry pancakes?"

Eva raised her eyes and smiled. "If you make those, she'll marry you."

Will chuckled. "Think again, sister. My heart belongs to your momma."

Will went to work making the pancakes. Eva did not refute what he said about not starting a relationship with Anna, which was a relief because he wasn't in the mood to debate the point. While cooking the first batch of pancakes and bacon, Will made himself a cup of coffee. He watched Eva as it was brewing.

"Daddy, I feel your eyes burning the back of my head."

"Nothing to say?" he teased.

Will jumped, startled by the knock at the door.

"She's here."

Will's stomach did flip-flops. "Well, get it."

"I know you love Momma, but . . . oh, forget it." Eva started to head toward the door, but he reached out and grabbed her arm.

"Wait, Eva, what were you going to say?"

"She's not here," she whispered, then headed to answer the door, leaving Will even more conflicted.

He shook his head and muttered, "We've only known each other for two days. Isn't it a little too soon to talk about marriage? It's just breakfast."

CHAPTER 14

Anna knocked lightly on the door. Her legs felt weak as she stood there, and she wondered if she should turn around. She'd taken her time getting ready. She was dressed in Wrangler jeans and a cobalt-blue shirt, which made her eyes look deep blue-green. Her hair hung across her shoulders. She'd even put on some light pink lipstick. Will had sent so many conflicting signals in the past day that her mind was whirling with confusion as to why he'd invited her to breakfast in the first place. *Why am I doing this? Why did I say yes?*

She took a step back. "Okay, I want to experience family life again. I miss it," she whispered. A painful lump formed in her throat. She loved Nana and Papa, and they were beautiful to her, but they were sad after her parents had died. It was like a cloud that never entirely left.

She held her hand up to knock again but hesitated. She couldn't help but feel a mix of nerves and anticipation. Her stomach churned with anxiety and excitement. She considered turning back, but it was too late. The scent of bacon cooking mixed with pancakes danced through the air, making her stomach growl. She rapped on the door again, this time louder, preparing herself for whatever may come.

Eva opened the door, motioning for her to come in. "Anna, I'm so glad Daddy invited you to breakfast. Do you like blueberry pancakes?"

Anna tried to smile despite the knot in her stomach. "I do!" She passed through the doorway with Eva leading her toward the kitchen. As they went through the living room, Anna stopped in awe when she saw a wedding picture of a younger Will and a beautiful blonde woman hanging over the fireplace.

"That's my parents' wedding picture," Eva said. "Wasn't Momma beautiful?"

Anna gulped and managed to reply, "She was. You look just like her." Eva giggled, took Anna by the hand, and dragged her toward the large farmhouse kitchen. Eva announced their presence. Will greeted her warmly, unlike how he had acted since she arrived the day before. He offered Anna coffee, which she accepted gratefully while trying not to blush or fumble over her words.

She leaned against the counter, holding the cup with both hands, and smiled at Eva, drawing at the breakfast bar. Will stood near the stove holding a spatula. The silence was oddly comfortable. Caden entered the room shortly after, rubbing his eyes.

A smile spread across Eva's face as she exclaimed, "Caden, look who's here."

Caden beamed as he rushed to Anna, embracing her. "It's nice to see you," Anna said, rubbing his back with one hand as he clung to her.

"I woke up, and you were gone," Caden said, looking at Will, his gaze sharp and intense.

"I had to bring you home," Will said, his words punctuated as he held the spatula.

Caden shrugged, unconcerned. "Well, that's true, but I like staying with Anna; she rubs my head like Momma did."

Anna noticed Will's shoulders dropped slightly, and the stiffness in his posture was gone, replaced by a calmer demeanor. She wondered if he was expecting Caden to have a meltdown.

"Oh, she does?" he asked.

"We had pizza and fed the horses. Anna is the best," Caden said, clapping his hands, "We had so much fun."

Will and Anna's eyes met, and heat rose to her cheeks. "Mr. Deluca, your son is a flirt," Anna said, trying to hide her blush with a playful joke.

Caden put his hands on his hips, confused by their banter. "What is a flirt?"

Will winked at her. "He learned from the best."

Anna was shocked at how different Will was acting. *First, the kiss, now flirting. What is going on?* His demeanor allowed the tense muscles in her shoulders to relax.

Eva rolled her eyes and shook her head. "Gross, Daddy! Not before breakfast," she said, wagging her finger at him, "or after or ever!"

Will arranged the fluffy pancakes loaded with blueberries and strips of bacon on a platter. Anna's mouth watered. "I can set the table," she offered.

Will pointed to the plate cabinet and directed Eva to get the silverware and Caden to get the butter and syrup. Will's woodsy cologne hung in the air as he leaned over to place the platter on the table, and Anna breathed in the familiar scent. Will looked at her so intensely that she had to catch her breath as if the oxygen had escaped the room. She suppressed a nervous giggle and asked if he wanted coffee, breaking the trance. Eva stepped closer to Will, her eyes darting between them. Anna grabbed his cup to make him a fresh cup of coffee. Eva carefully moved Anna's cup toward Will's chair, a subtle gesture Anna noticed out of the corner of her eye, which made her uneasy. *I can't sit next to him. I'm a leftie!* Knowing they could bump elbows, she asked if he was right or left-handed. Will seemed thrown off by the question and replied he was right-handed.

Eva snatched Anna's cup and placed it at the end of the table. "Anna can sit here," she said as her lips curled into a smirk. She placed Will's cup on the right side of the table. "Daddy, you sit here so you won't bump elbows."

Anna slowly sank into her seat as she watched Will's reaction. He appeared to be as uncomfortable as she was, but after one bite of her pancakes, she closed her eyes and savored the buttery sweetness and the explosion of warm blueberries in her mouth. "Oh my . . . these are so good," she said.

Eva laughed in response. "I told you they were something special."

Will sipped his coffee and let out a low whistle. "Wow, what did you do to this? My coffee never tastes this good."

"It's a Missouri secret." Anna grinned enjoying their exchange.

"Keeping secrets, are we?" Will teased.

She winked at him. "Maybe." She liked this side of Will, but even as she flirted back, she couldn't help but wonder what had changed since yesterday that made him more openly playful with her.

As they ate, Eva shared stories about her love for English and art, Caden talked about his love of math, and Will bragged about his remarkable aptitude for numbers. Despite attending the elementary school in town, both kids preferred being at home on the ranch.

When they finished eating, Eva said, "Caden and I need to make a Welcome Home banner for Nana. May we be excused to do that?"

Will nodded. "Sure thing. Just take your plates to the sink first."

Eva and Caden hurried to their rooms, leaving Anna and Will in awkward silence. Anna cleared her throat and said, "They're terrific kids."

"They are, thank you." Will let out a long sigh. His expression changed, and she wondered if she'd said something to upset him. He opened his mouth to say something, then stopped.

Anna watched him with curiosity. "Are you okay?"

He nodded. "I was just thinking about how much Momma does around here. I'm not sure how to keep up with all the extra chores." He laid his napkin on the table. "I'm sorry. I'm not sure why I told you that."

"I can help," Anna offered without hesitation. "I'm used to doing chores and working."

"I can't ask you to do that."

"You didn't ask," Anna reminded him, "I offered." She glanced around the kitchen. She liked the cozy farmhouse décor with an apron-front sink, floating shelves, and exposed wood beams. She loved the butcher block counters and white cabinets with rustic handles. The exposed brick behind the stove and the soothing ivory walls provided a rustic appeal. The room was filled with comfort and the love of a family. One house wouldn't be too much to keep up with, but the ranch would be tough for Will.

Anna hesitated before asking, "Why do you have all the extra cabins, the lodge, and the arena?"

"My wife, Shelly, and I bought the ranch with dreams of creating an equine therapy center for autistic kids. We were in the planning stage with the autism therapy center Caden attends, but she was taken from us," Will choked out, his voice barely holding back a sob.

A sudden pang of empathy hit Anna as she placed her hand on his arm, wishing she could do something to comfort him in his moment of sorrow.

As their eyes met, an inexplicable wave of familiarity engulfed her. She noticed the tenderness of Will's soul, which stirred something in her. Before Anna could reflect on what was happening, she hastily pulled her hand away and averted her gaze, muttering a feeble apology. Shame descended on her as she remembered that he acknowledged his wife's death moments ago. Her mind swirled with confusion as she tried to make sense of the conflicting emotions.

"I'm trying to open the equine therapy center by Shelly's birthday in September, but now that Momma is hurt, I have no idea how to get it done."

She slowly looked up and mumbled, "Sorry . . ."

"It's okay," he said as he studied her eyes. It created an intense connection between them that Anna feared and didn't understand.

"I wanted to apologize about the kiss earlier." He leaned forward and wrapped his fingers around hers in a comforting and intense gesture.

Heat rose in her body, from the tips of her toes to her ears. "Uh . . . all right . . ." She leaned closer, taking in his scent, something she could get used to. She wondered what it was about him that was so familiar. Maybe she just felt comfortable with him. Through his grief, she knew he was a man who loved to help others.

Suddenly, Eva's voice barreled down the hallway toward them, causing them both to jump. "Dad! We need your help!"

Will smiled and gave her hand a quick squeeze. "I'll be right back."

Once alone, Anna rushed over to the sink and splashed cold water on her face to calm her nerves. *Come on, Anna, pull it together.* Just then, Will entered the kitchen as Anna dried her face. When she turned and saw him looking at her, embarrassment filled her cheeks as she realized how flush they must be.

He came closer, his gaze intense. Anna's heart revved up like a race car. He reached for the towel in her hands and softly whispered, "Let's finish our coffee." Anna found it hard to form coherent thoughts when she looked at Will.

"So, are you excited about starting your new job?" he asked as he grabbed his cup of coffee.

The question snapped Anna back to reality. "Yes, I'm looking forward to building the palliative care program. The program I worked for in

Missouri allowed caregivers to take breaks, which greatly benefits the patients and their families." Her cheeks burned, and she looked down. "Sorry, I guess I'm just passionate about my work."

"Don't be sorry. I understand wanting to make a difference in the community." He took a long sip of his coffee. "That's what I want to do with the equine center."

Anna held up her cup. "Here's to making a difference." She thought about the program she'd started at the hospital and wondered if she should offer to help Will with the equine center. *That's ridiculous; you can't just push your way into this family's life.*

Eva walked in just as there was a lull in the conversation. "Hey, Caden and I play that game too," she said, casually breaking the spell cast over the room.

Their heads snapped toward her. "Excuse me?" Will said, clearing his throat.

"The staring game," she said.

They burst out laughing. "We were just enjoying this great coffee. What did you need?" Will asked.

She shrugged. "Don't remember," she said as she skipped out of the room.

As Anna watched Eva leave the room, she wondered if this was a dream; it was so surreal. Anna slowly turned to Will, who was staring at her. She shifted in her seat, trying to figure out what to say. *What were we talking about? Me helping, that's it.* Without thinking, she touched Will's hand. "Please let me help you. I'll stay out of the way. Tell me when you need me, and I'll be there."

His eyebrows squished together. "You are not a bother to me, Anna."

She smiled. "I don't want to be one either. I want to lend a hand if I can."

Will furrowed his brow, deep in thought. Then he grinned, "You could make this coffee for me every day."

She couldn't help but return the smile. "Sure, come by my cabin every morning. Seriously, I can take the morning feedings if you like." She stood, already gathering the dishes. "Let's do these dishes so you can get on with your day."

Will quickly rose from his chair and stepped forward. "No, no," he said with a hint of authority. "I can do them."

Anna raised an eyebrow and motioned toward the sink with her chin as she walked past him with an armload of dirty dishes. "Four hands are faster than two. I'll wash, and you dry?"

They went about their task with an ease and comfort that surprised Anna. He smiled at her as they worked together.

"Tell me what else was on your playlist this morning?" he teased.

"No, sir, that's completely confidential."

"Oh, it is? Let me guess: NSYNC, Backstreet Boys, and . . . 98 Degrees. Am I right?"

A grin spread across her face. "Guilty as charged, but you forgot many good ones."

He narrowed his eyes. "Like who? Alanis Morissette."

"Oh, are you seriously from Texas?"

Will placed his hands on his hips. "Ma'am, I'm a born-and-bred Texan."

Anna threw her hands up. "I don't believe you." She turned back to the sink and continued washing dishes. Will snapped his towel in her direction. "Don't think about it, or I'll squirt you with this hose!"

Will fired back. "You wouldn't."

She pulled the hose from the faucet and playfully turned to him, smiling. "Oh, I would."

"Just tell me," he pleaded with a laugh.

Anna turned back to the sink. "Nope."

She watched him dry the dishes out of the corner of her eye, staring her down like someone getting ready for a dual. Anna smiled and started humming "Carrying Your Love with Me" by George Strait. He dropped a glass on the floor, and it shattered to pieces. Anna jumped.

"Will, I . . . um . . ." She bent down to pick up the shards of glass. Tears burned her eyes as the gravity of the situation settled in.

"Hey, it wasn't your fault. I haven't heard that song in years." Will reached for her hand. "Be careful; you'll cut yourself," he said as he picked up the pieces of broken glass. "I never much figured you for a George Strait fan. Now he's been my favorite since forever, I suppose."

As they cleaned the glass up, Anna kept silent. When they dropped the last piece in the trash, Anna whispered, "That's been my favorite song since I was sixteen. It reminds me of a good friend."

He looked up and smiled, but she could sense an inner struggle with him as if something were stopping him from getting too close. "Me too," he finally said before turning away quickly.

"Where's the broom?" she asked. He made her feel safe yet scared simultaneously with his touch, and she didn't know what stirred inside her more: comfort or fear.

"You don't have to clean up my mess," he said.

"I don't mind. I didn't mean to make you drop the glass."

"It wasn't your fault. It just slipped out of my hand." Will walked past her to get the broom. His arm brushed against hers, causing the hair on her arms to stand at attention. She took a long, ragged breath and headed to the table to wipe it down with a towel.

She felt his eyes on her, and she turned to find Will staring at her again. "What's wrong?"

He shook his head. "Thanks again for your help today and yesterday. I would love it if you would help in the stable when you can. As you know, it's hard for me to ask." He swallowed hard. "But I could use the help."

Anna nodded. "Sure, that's no problem."

"Can I ask you something?"

"Sure."

"Eva told me your parents passed away. When did that happen?"

It was like a movie of all the people she'd lost playing in her head at a warped speed. A tightness spread across her chest, and tears stung her eyes, begging to roll down her cheeks. Despite wanting to be strong, her lip quivered involuntarily. "They died when I was nine. Are you upset I shared that with Eva? I mentioned it in passing. I'm sorry." She tried to control her tone, but it came out shaky and unsteady.

Will placed his hand on her, attempting to provide comfort. But inside, a storm of emotions raged on. She had the urge to push him away and flee from his presence. Yet she kept a calm facade, struggling to rein in the turbulent emotions.

"I'm not angry," Will said abruptly. "Eva feels you understand how she feels about losing her mother."

Anna fought back the tears, but one nonetheless managed to find its way down her cheek. She opened her eyes when she felt him wipe it away, more confused than ever. "If there's one thing I understand, it's the loss of everyone you ever loved," she said, covering her mouth to stifle the words she hadn't meant to say aloud.

Anna started to turn away from Will, but he gently squeezed her arm, forcing their eyes to meet again. Her heart thundered so hard in her chest that she was sure Will could see it.

"I should go. Thanks for breakfast," she said before walking away quickly, willing the tears away with every step. She glanced over her shoulder only to find Will still watching her retreat, and she gave him a halfhearted smile before she went into her cabin and shut the door. *This isn't why I came here.* Anna thought as she realized how frequently their paths had crossed in twenty-four hours.

CHAPTER 15

The kitchen suddenly felt empty as Will stood there with a broom. He'd enjoyed breakfast with Anna and learning about her life, but her words of loss reopened old wounds. He yearned to return to the safety of solitude. He was flooded with guilt. Why did he crave a connection with someone other than his wife when his wedding ring still circled his finger? His gaze fell upon the photo of him and Shelly on their wedding day. The ache suffocated him as he remembered their last moment together. Did Anna notice his ring? What must she think about him wearing it and flirting with her? The phone vibrating in his pocket pulled him away from his thoughts. It was Kati.

"Momma is getting released soon. Can you come get us?" Kati said.

"I can. I need to get the kids rounded up."

"Jon could get us or come stay with the kids."

"Oh yeah, that's what we need: Jon flirting with Anna and no one to intercede."

Kati laughed. "True."

"I'll be there soon. How's Momma?"

"She's doing well. Ready to come home."

"I bet."

Will loaded his kids into the truck, glancing at the cabin where Anna was staying. He heard a gate creaking and walked toward it to investigate. That was when he saw Anna astride her horse, Thunderbird, gently leaning forward and whispering something in his ear. The horse neighed in response. Will had only ever known one other person who could communicate with animals like this: Ginger, a girl he'd known when he was younger and whom he hadn't thought of in years. Will shook his head and returned to the truck, feeling a strange combination of nostalgia for Ginger and something else he couldn't entirely put his finger on.

On the drive to the hospital, some of the morning's events came flooding back to him—the way Anna showed such passion for helping others, her sharp wit as she teased him with a hose, and, most of all, those emerald eyes that seemed to look right into his soul. The thought gave him palpitations—a mix of excitement and fear that he hadn't felt in a long time—and made him smile.

"Dad!" Eva and Caden yelled from the back seat.

He cleared his throat. "What!"

"You passed the hospital," Eva said, pointing behind her.

He looked in the rearview mirror. "I did. Uh . . . thanks."

Eva leaned forward as he turned the truck in the right direction, "What are you thinking about?"

He looked at her through the rearview mirror and avoided the question. "How are you sitting forward? Are you buckled?"

She laughed and sat back to buckle her seatbelt. "You like Anna, don't you?"

He looked at her in the rearview mirror. "For your information, I was thinking about your mother." He looked away and felt terrible for lying.

She sighed, "Oh."

"She's a very nice lady, Eva. I'm glad you connect with her."

"You are?"

"Of course I am. We talked about her momma and daddy."

"You did?" Eva leaned forward.

Will cleared his throat. "Yes." *She understands our family more than I do. She truly understands loss from a young age.*

Eva raised an eyebrow. "What else did you talk about?"

"Music."

"Oh, what kind of music does she like?"

"The same stuff Aunt Kati likes." Will smiled as he thought about Anna shaking her hips to NSYNC. "But I can forgive her because she likes George Strait."

Eva clapped her hands. "That's it, Daddy. You need to marry her."

"Yes, we like her. And want to live with her." Caden piped in, interrupting Will's thoughts.

Will gritted his teeth. He liked Anna, and he was grateful that his children felt a connection to her, but he didn't even know her. An ache settled in his chest. He knew where they were coming from. They missed their mom. They were just kids and didn't understand how complicated things were. He knew they didn't intend to replace Shelly, but it saddened him.

Will shook his head. "Caden, you can't live with a stranger."

A low growl came from the back. Caden was heading toward a meltdown. He saw things in black and white, getting angry when things came in shades of gray. So, Will dropped the subject.

Caden mumbled, "Doesn't matter. She lives on the ranch. I can live with her."

Will pulled into the hospital and parked the car. As they entered the floor where Liz was staying, he saw Dr. Watts standing behind one of the nurses, his hand grazing her shoulder as he bent down to whisper something in her ear. The nurse rushed to her feet and left the nurses' station after his words.

They walked into Liz's room. The same nurse Will had seen at the nurses' station with Dr. Watts was removing an IV from Liz's arm with gentle hands, speaking soothingly to her. But the nurse jumped when Caden shut the door, turning wide-eyed at them. Liz laid a comforting hand on her arm. "Are you all right, dear?"

The nurse took a tissue from her pocket and dabbed her eyes. "I'm so sorry, ma'am. I'm having a day."

"It's all right, dear. Are you new here? I know most people in this town. I roamed the streets with the Romans."

"Oh Lord, you aren't that old." Kati piped in when she came out of the bathroom. "That's Cassidy; she's new." She turned to Cassidy. "Are you alright?"

Cassidy nodded. "Yes, ma'am. I'm going to get Ms. Deluca's discharge papers." Then, she quickly left the room.

Will watched as she exited. "Has Dr. Watts been weird with you?"

Liz shrugged. "No, not at all."

He looked at Kati.

"He was standing too close to me the night Momma had surgery. But I have a large personal boundary space. Her eyebrows furrowed. "Why do you ask?"

Will waved his hand. "It was probably nothing." He noticed Caden and Eva standing close to the door. Eva was holding Caden's hand. "It's okay, guys. You can go see Nana."

Liz held out her arms. "Yes, come see Nana; she misses you."

They crept toward Liz's bedside, and Eva hugged her grandmother. "Are you going to be ok, Nana?"

Caden peeked around Eva. "We missed you, but it wasn't so bad. Anna came for breakfast."

Kati and Liz looked at Will with raised eyebrows. He rolled his eyes. "It was nothing. She helped in the barn this morning and needed to eat."

"What did you cook, big brother?" A smirk spread across Kati's face.

Caden and Eva spoke in unison, "Blueberry pancakes."

"I told Daddy that she's gonna marry him because of those pancakes."

Liz tried to hold back a laugh as their eyes met. Will knew exactly what she was thinking.

He growled and narrowed his eyes. "I'm gonna get you a wheelchair, Granny."

"William Deluca, don't call me that."

They all burst into laughter as he walked out of the room.

Will headed to the nurses' station to ask for a wheelchair. One of the younger nurses said that someone would come by shortly with the discharge instructions and to help get his mother out of bed. One hour turned into two, but they were finally discharged.

As Will wheeled his mother out of the hospital, he was relieved that she was looking like herself again. Liz was smiling as he helped her into the truck.

Concern marred his features. "You scared the heck out of me yesterday. I should have helped you off the horse."

Liz slapped his hand. "Stop, we already had this conversation." She placed her hand on his chin. "You're not responsible for all the bad things that happen to the people you love. Now take me home."

A smile crossed Kati's lips. "Hey, big brother, let's get Momma home."

Will spent the next week in agony as he tried to avoid Anna the best he could. He knew where she was, but he kept his distance. Despite his best efforts, he still couldn't get the memory of their breakfast out of his head. He felt shame for flirting with another woman in the house he'd shared with his wife. Every time he thought about it, the heat of embarrassment rose from his chest to his throat. But despite all this, he enjoyed Anna's presence and wished she were around more often—a feeling that filled him with guilt and confusion.

While working on the fence one evening, Will noticed Anna staring at him across the yard. Her expression was unreadable. He nodded and put two fingers to the brim of his hat as a gesture of respect, but instead of returning the gesture, she abruptly got up and went inside her cabin, slamming the door behind her. Maybe it was anger, but Will was never good at reading women—that was Jon's forte. Deep down, Will knew it would be better if she despised him.

CHAPTER 16

Anna arose with a combination of eagerness and apprehension the morning of her first day at Cardinal Creek Community Hospital. Despite the butterflies in her stomach, she was eager to embark on a new adventure and take on new challenges. She'd spent the last thirteen years at University Hospital, but today, she was ready to step out of her comfort zone in a new state with a new job.

Anna was grateful for the distraction of her new job as she tried to make sense of Will's sudden avoidance. She couldn't understand why he'd been so distant since they had breakfast. Their conversations replayed in her head, searching for clues about what she might have said to upset him. She thought they could be friends, but apparently not.

Thunderbird and Jake's familiar nickering greeted her when she entered the barn, and Garrett flashed her a warm smile as he approached. He stood tall and confident, with broad shoulders. When he removed his hat, his hair revealed a mix of red and blond shades. They had become fast friends over the last week since she hadn't seen much of the Deluca family. She and Garrett had gone horseback riding and eaten together a few times. Anna wondered if this was what it was like to have an older brother.

He gave her a side hug. "Are you excited for your first day?"

Anna shrugged. "Maybe."

Garrett's eyes narrowed. "You are such a liar, Anna Samuels."

"Okay, I'm excited and nervous—very much so." She placed a hand on her heart. "I think my heart is gonna beat out of my chest."

"You'll do fine. Did you talk to your friend back home last night?" he asked.

Anna twisted the red bracelet on her wrist. "I did." She headed to the tack room. "I should get the stalls cleaned up. I still need to get ready for work."

"Well, let's get to gettin'."

Anna headed down to the first stall and stopped before she went in. "Garrett?"

He stuck his head out of the stall. "Ma'am?"

"Thank you for being a friend. I know we haven't known each other long, but talking to you has kept me from feeling homesick."

"I enjoy the company. I also appreciate the help. The Delucas have been busy the last week."

"How's Liz doing?" Anna asked. "I haven't seen Kati."

"Well, you must come out of the cabin to see people."

Anna rolled her eyes and headed into the first stall. "Get to work." She put in her AirPods, turned on her music, and began humming to her favorite George Strait tune.

She felt a nudge on her shoulder as Jake nuzzled her neck. "At least you like me." Jake chewed on her hair, and she giggled. "Hey buddy, wish me luck today." He whinnied. She scratched his cheek and finished his stall. While she worked in the last stall, the song she'd hummed when she had breakfast with Will came on. She tapped her Apple Watch so hard to skip it she was sure she cracked the screen. She picked up the shovel, threw it into the wheelbarrow, and headed out of the stall.

As she latched the stall, Garrett grabbed the wheelbarrow. "Take off. I got this. Let me give you a good luck hug."

Anna wrapped her arm around his waist. "Thanks."

"Good luck. Text me how it goes today." He gave her a side hug.

As they released each other, Anna saw Will approaching the barn. He abruptly stopped in his tracks.

She turned to Garrett. "I'll text you later."

Will stood frozen as Anna walked past him. "Morning, Will."

He nodded as she eyed him on the way out of the barn. "Morning, Anna."

Anna quickened her pace as she returned to her cabin, muttering, "He's just so exasperating." As soon as she entered the cabin, she slammed the door.

⁓

WILL JUMPED at the sound of the cabin door slamming shut. His hands were buried deep in his pockets, and he stood frozen. He had heard Anna and Garrett talking over the last week whenever he passed the barn, and warmth washed over him, but he also had an ache he couldn't explain. Every morning, Anna was in the stable tending to the horses, and this morning was no different, except for Garrett wrapping his arms around her small frame. Will clenched his fists, seeing them together, knowing what it meant. He escaped into the tack room and threw himself onto a hay bale. He scrolled mindlessly through his phone, trying to avoid everyone. Lost in thought, he didn't notice when the door opened until Garrett's voice broke through his reverie. "Something wrong, Will?"

He raised his eyebrow in suspicion. "Are you and Anna dating?"

Garrett removed his hat and sighed. "Come again?"

Will narrowed his eyes as he stood up. "You heard the question. Are you two dating? You seem to be spending a lot of time together."

Garrett's expression shifted to anger as he put his hat back on. "Why does what I do with Anna matter? We're both old enough to make our own decisions." He stepped away, but Will pursued him out of the tack room.

"Come on, Garrett. I've seen you pick her up after work and ride horses. That's what people do when they're together."

Garrett stopped in his tracks and spun around, an intensity burning in his gaze. "Stop it, Will. This is ridiculous."

Heat burned his cheeks, and he realized he'd gone too far. He was about to apologize when he heard a familiar voice behind them.

"Will, knock it off now!"

He straightened and closed his eyes. As he turned, Anna stepped forward, looking at him with fury in her eyes. "You have ignored me for over a week. I'm sorry if I said something wrong but leave Garrett alone. He's been a good friend to me."

Will couldn't tear his gaze away from her. Anna stood wearing a sapphire-blue pencil skirt, blazer, and pale pink shirt, making her emerald eyes sparkle. Her auburn hair cascaded down her shoulders in curls, her Cupid's bow lips were painted in a medium red tone, and blue pumps accented her calves.

She marched up to him, eyes blazing and fists clenched at her sides. "If you want to know who I'm dating, come to my cabin and ask me. And don't you ever talk to Garrett like that again, do you understand?" She poked her light pink nail into his chest.

Anna turned to Garrett. "Hope you have a great day, sweetheart." It sounded like sugar coming from her lips. She blew him a kiss and walked away.

Garrett pretended to catch it and put it on his cheek. To add insult to injury, he yelled, "I'll text you later, my love."

"Okay, love ya." She shot Will one last glare before she got in her car and left a cloud of dust as she drove off.

Will stormed out of the barn with a growl so profound it felt like it came from his gut. He needed to talk to Liz about her physical therapy sessions but couldn't keep his emotions at bay. As soon as he burst into her house and slammed the door behind him, he knew he'd made a mistake. A shout came from the kitchen, where he knew Liz was having her morning coffee. "Don't slam the door."

He winced at her tone, recognizing the anger simmering beneath it. Despite his apology for slamming the door, she didn't look any less upset.

Will dropped his hat on the table and slumped into a chair, his mind consumed by guilt and anger. "Will I ever learn to keep my mouth shut?" There was no hiding the shame in his voice.

Liz peered at him with a piercing gaze. "What did you do?"

He was unsure if he wanted to look at her when he told her of his idiocy. "I accused Garrett of dating Anna." He looked up at Liz. "He's too old for her."

Liz grasped his arm. "What were you thinking? You're too old for that kind of nonsense."

Will rested his forehead on the table, the weight of defeat crushing him. "I can't explain it," he confessed.

Liz narrowed her eyes. He knew she was on to him. "Tell me the real reason. Don't you lie to me!"

He hesitated. Could he tell his mother how he felt? "I can't," he finally admitted.

Liz remained quiet, letting him suffer before she spoke again. "Ah, you like her."

Of course, but it was more complicated. Will was sure Anna hated him after their confrontation. "She was on fire, mad. You should have seen her coming across the yard," he explained and took a deep breath. "When I saw her coming, all I saw was Ginger. It was like the day she let me have it when I accused her of liking Jon. Anna even poked me in the chest the same way Ginger did." He ran his fingers through his hair. "Today was the third time I thought about Ginger around Anna. It's weird. She hummed the song I sang to Ginger, and I dropped a glass." He looked at Liz. "I feel like I'm losing my mind."

Liz wrapped her fingers around Will's hand and squeezed. "You never really got over her. I know you loved Shelly, but there was no closure with Ginger."

"We were just kids, but I loved her."

"Accusing Garrett of wanting Anna won't help you win her heart. You need to apologize to them."

Will let out a low groan. "I know. I feel like such a jerk."

Liz took him by the chin and looked him in the eye. "What makes you so insecure? You are a handsome man with a great heart. What makes you think you're not worthy of love? Jealousy is your weakness, and it almost cost you Shelly."

Will struggled to answer as a tightness gripped his chest. "I don't know," he choked out. He shoved his chair back, snatched his hat from the table, and stormed out of the room. His insides ached with guilt as he thought of how he'd treated Garrett and Anna. He shook his head as he mounted his truck and slammed the door. He stepped on the gas and sped away, desperately searching for a way to make things right.

CHAPTER 17

Anna's hands shook as she put the car in park. Will's harsh words toward Garrett had her simmering on the inside. Her hands quivered as she grabbed her lipstick and touched it up in the mirror of her visor before stepping out. She took a moment to collect herself, then confidently walked through the double doors of the hospital, ready to begin a new phase of her life.

Anna made it through the first part of her orientation, which included information on hospital policies, insurance, and patient relations. When it was time for lunch, Cathy Watts, the director of nursing, took her to the cafeteria. When they arrived, Cathy excused herself to use the restroom while Anna entered the line.

Someone behind her whispered, "What's good for lunch?"

When Anna turned around, she saw a doctor dressed in blue scrubs with a brown goatee flecked with gray. His closely cropped hair was like a military cut, and he extended his hand to shake hers.

"Welcome. I'm Seth Watts. I work in orthopedics," he said.

"I'm Anna Samuels. I'm the new director of Palliative Care." She shook his hand.

He smiled warmly and held her hand for a moment longer before leaning closer. "The burgers are pretty good unless you are one of those health nuts."

"No, sir, I like burgers just fine."

Anna watched as Dr. Watts transformed before her very eyes. His charming demeanor slipped away, replaced by a spark of fury that ignited when his gaze caught sight of Cathy. "Seth, it's lovely to see you. Anna, this is my husband," Cathy said as she kissed him. Anna watched in disbelief when he pushed her aside.

Dr. Watt's eyes raked up and down Anna's body as if he was undressing her, and when he turned to leave, he didn't acknowledge Cathy's presence, but his eyes scanned Anna again. "It was nice meeting you, Ms. Samuels."

Anna watched Cathy's face when he walked away. *Okay, that was weird. Anna, you are imagining things here.*

Cathy quickly pasted on a smile. "Should we get something to eat?" she choked out.

"Are you okay, Cathy?"

She nodded. "I'm fine, just starving."

They got their burgers and fries and then took a seat. The cafeteria appeared to be stuck in a time warp. Although it now fell under the category of vintage or retro, the orange and yellow chairs and booths gave off a 1970s vibe. Despite the outdated furniture, the place was immaculate and had a cozy atmosphere.

Anna tried to make small talk as they ate, but Cathy remained silent, barely acknowledging her words as she picked at her food. It wasn't until they finished that she spoke up, her voice barely audible. "I don't understand it.... He's never behaved like this before."

Anna didn't know what to say. She had only just met the couple and had no idea what could have caused such tension between them. But as she looked at Cathy's face, she knew something more profound was beneath the surface.

"I'm sure it's nothing," Anna offered weakly.

Cathy narrowed her eyes. "I'm not fond of cheaters or those they cheat with."

Anna raised an eyebrow at the rather abrupt comment. *Was that a warning for me? Okay, Anna, you had a rough morning after the confrontation with Will. You are imagining things.*

"May I excuse myself? I need to make a phone call before returning for orientation," Anna said.

Cathy's expression went blank. "Yes, that's fine. It was nice having lunch with you." Sadness stirred behind her eyes. "I look forward to working with you."

Anna hurried toward the exit; she needed some air. Since Papa died, she felt like she was in a fog, and today was no exception. She sat on the bench just outside the hospital entrance and closed her eyes, letting the sun warm her face. Her nerves were beginning to calm when she heard someone talking. "Did my wife bore you to death?"

Anna opened her eyes and saw Dr. Watts standing in front of her. "No, she didn't. She had some enlightening things to say."

Dr. Watts put his arms across his chest. "Oh, she did. About?"

Anna narrowed her eyes. "Let me just say we agree about certain aspects of relationships." *I can't believe I just said that. I'm going to get fired on my first day.*

"And that would be?"

Anna stood. "I'm sorry, sir. You'll have to ask her about that. If you'll excuse me, I need to get back." She walked to the orientation classroom like she was on fire.

∽

When Anna arrived home, she was surprised to find a note on the door from Kati. *Anna, join Momma and me for dinner tonight. We want to hear about your first day at work. I'm sorry I didn't get a chance to talk to you last week. We can catch up tonight. Kati.*

She took a quick shower, threw on some black yoga pants and a loose T-shirt, then put her hair in a messy bun. She grabbed a bottle of pink Catawba wine before heading to Kati and Liz's cabin. When Kati opened the door, she greeted Anna with excitement and curiosity. "Oh my God, please forgive me for not coming to see you for over a week."

Anna waved a hand at her. "No worries. I know you've been busy taking care of your mom. Garrett took good care of me."

Kati wiggled her eyebrows mischievously. "How good?"

Heat warmed Anna's face as she tried to dodge the question. "It's not like that—we're just friends."

"Well, that man is full of passion."

Anna laughed. "Why do you think that?"

"Quiet brooder."

"Not Garrett. He talks a lot."

"Our Garrett? How do you know?"

She didn't want to talk about Garrett. A storm brewed within when she thought about how Will stalked after him, demanding to know if they were dating. She hoped Kati would let this conversation go.

Liz sat at the kitchen table with her leg on a pillow.

"Hello, Mrs. Deluca. How are you doing?" Anna asked.

She raised an eyebrow. "It's Liz, darlin'. I'm not that old."

"Yes, ma'am. Liz, it is."

Kati smiled mischievously as if something had dawned on her. "Now, Anna, tell us about you and Garrett—"

Liz cut Kati off with a stern voice. "Just Leave it, she said before turning to Anna. "I hope you like spaghetti," she added, smiling warmly.

"I do." The conversation shifted away from the topic of Garrett, much to Anna's relief.

"So, how was your first day?"

"It wasn't entirely bad, but it was still a standard first-day orientation. I had lunch with Cathy Watts. I also met her husband. Their interaction was . . . strange."

Kati's eyebrows raised, hinting at an unspoken question.

"Dr. Watts gave me the feeling he has two sides," Anna said, "like Jekyll and Hyde. But it could have just been my imagination."

Liz took a sip of wine. "Dr. Watts was very professional with me, but that's his job." She pointed to her leg. "He put my leg back together, but you know how hospitals are, full of rumors."

Kati laughed. "This whole town is full of rumors. A couple of nurses in the OR said he makes them uncomfortable. The phrase they used was a little creepy.'"

Liz scoffed in disagreement. "My daughter thinks all doctors are creepy. She likes cowboys and firefighters instead."

Kati hit her mother with a towel. "It's not like that! We're not talking about this again."

Despite Kati's protests, Liz continued, "Kati and Jon—Will's best friend—have been playing this game for years, but for some reason, she won't date him. He's a nice boy."

Kati forced a smile as she placed spaghetti on the table. "No matter how nice someone is, being together is impossible if you don't trust them."

Liz placed her hand on Kati's, her blue eyes soft with sympathy. "I'm sorry. I know he hurt you after Shelly died."

Kati's voice trembled as she spoke, and she quickly wiped a tear away with her sleeve. "He betrayed my trust, and I can't be with someone I don't." She placed a basket of garlic bread on the table, head bowed in a silent plea for understanding. "I would rather be alone than be with someone who doesn't respect our relationship."

Anna understood how it felt to have someone cheat on her. She could still see Tony kissing Emma at her grandparents' house. A shiver ran up her spine. She raised her glass of wine in salute. "Here, here. I broke up with my boyfriend, a doctor. He was cheating on me with someone who I thought was a friend. I found them making out at my house the day I buried my grandfather."

Liz and Kati gasped in unison, their hands flying to their mouths, eyes wide in shock. "What did you do?" Kati asked as she handed Anna her plate of spaghetti and meatballs.

"Thank you," Anna replied as she took the plate from Kati. "I lost my temper and told them to leave with a few expletives. He tried to follow me, but I gave a clear warning that I would knock him senseless if he did."

Liz suppressed a giggle, trying unsuccessfully to hide the smile that tugged at the corners of her mouth. "Have a temper, do we?"

"Just a little, but Jenny's is worse," Anna said. "She wanted to hit him!"

Kati tore off an end piece of garlic bread. "You should have let your friend hit him."

Anna laughed and then took a sip of wine. The other women watched intently as she swallowed before answering. "Nah, good riddance. I gave him a double deuce when he left," Anna said, raising both middle fingers in victory.

Kati and Liz fought back another round of laughter sparked by Anna's unique farewell gesture to her unfaithful ex-boyfriend.

Anna smiled wickedly. "Let's just say I got the last word, so to speak." She took a long sip of her wine, trying to wash the memory away.

"So, how have you been since then?" Kati asked.

Anna placed her empty glass onto the table with a gentle thump, "Well, I'm here now with my full attention on making the palliative department a success."

"Where did you work in Missouri?" Liz asked between bites of food.

"I worked in palliative care at the University Hospital in Columbia. I was proud to witness the expansion of our services, but it was bittersweet, as I knew so many families were still without the resources they needed. Last year, I wrote a grant to extend our coverage to rural areas and create a caregiver's group for those caring for family members."

Liz's face was a mixture of shock and admiration. "That's incredible, Anna. I'm so impressed. Wait a minute—You wrote a grant?"

Anna nodded, brushing off the praise. Even though she'd worked in palliative care since graduating from college, she still couldn't believe her success and how the program had grown from small beginnings.

Kati interjected, "Is Will aware that you know how to write a grant?"

Anna shook her head. "No, we talked about my work a little, but I didn't go into detail."

Liz squeezed her hand tightly. "Honey, we need your help writing a grant for the equine center. We need your help a lot. Did Will tell you about it?"

Anna glanced at them and nodded. They depended on her expertise and needed her help to get the administrative part of the center started so they could get it open. This project meant more to them than anything, and it would help so many people.

"I can try," Anna said. She knew that she couldn't turn away from this project. It was more than just a business venture. Despite her doubts and fears, Anna agreed to help with the grant application process because it was a chance to bring hope to the community.

Anna took a deep breath. "I understand how important this is to you and the community, but I don't think Will likes me very much."

Liz burst into laughter. "I wouldn't worry about that. He likes you. He's just—"

"Mean to everyone. Let Momma handle him," Kati said.

"Yes, of course, I'll help," Anna replied hesitantly. "Will did tell me about wanting to open by September; that gives us about five months, so we have to start planning soon."

Kati leaped from her chair and embraced Anna, thanking her for the offer. "Will has a notebook with Shelly's plans for the equine center, but he keeps it hidden. You can ask him what Shelly found, though it's still touchy for him."

Anna swallowed hard and asked. "How will he take my helping him?"

"Helping who?" a deep voice sounded behind her.

Anna slowly turned to face Will, who had just entered the room. His eyes met hers as he growled, "Who said anything about needing her help?"

Kati quickly intervened. "Will! Anna told us she wrote a grant for her last job and increased palliative care in her rural community. She can help us with the administrative work on the equine center."

Will rolled his eyes. "Anna just started a new job. She doesn't have time for that."

Anna's heart sank. Did he not want her help? She got up and took a few steps toward him. "What are you saying? You don't want my help?" she snapped.

She clenched her jaw defiantly as she glared at him with blazing intensity. "Well, what *are* you saying?"

Liz stifled a smirk as Will backed away from Anna, scowling at her without blinking. "I'm sorry," he muttered. "I didn't mean to imply that you can't speak for yourself."

"Yes, Will, what are you saying?" Kati said in a mocking tone.

He shot a menacing glare at his sister. "When can we get started?" he grumbled through gritted teeth.

Liz bit her lip to avoid laughing while Anna crossed her arms and glared at him. He leaned down and whispered in her ear, "I'm sorry, Anna," causing chills to run up her spine as his warm breath danced on her neck. "I would love your help. When would you like to start?"

The hair rose on her neck as she glanced up at him with wide eyes. She cleared her throat before stammering, "Whenever you want."

His lips curved into a small smile as he whispered, "We can start at our weekend breakfast and continue at your place after." Her head bobbed slowly in agreement, and he walked away, leaving an awkward silence.

Liz and Kati tried to suppress their amused giggles before finally bursting into laughter. Kati exclaimed, "Whoa, girl, he has finally met his match. Even Shelly didn't stand toe-to-toe with him like that!"

Liz raised her glass in celebration as Anna finished her wine with a gulp. "Girl, you have gotten under his skin something fierce," Liz said admiringly. "Kati's right. Shelly never stood up to him like that." With a mischievous smirk, she added, "You two have a chemistry that heated this kitchen like Texas in July!"

Anna shook her head and sighed. "That was the second time today that he pushed my buttons. First, he accused Garrett and me of dating, and now this." With an exasperated groan, she concluded, "What is wrong with him?"

Kati poured another glass of wine. "Oh my God, I thought he was going to kiss you," Kati teased.

"No offense, but I'm not interested in dating anyone."

Liz bit her lip to suppress a mischievous grin. "Oh, we get it, honey. He said the same thing about not wanting to date, but you've piqued his interest."

Anna had been encouraged by the wine when she stood up to him. She was embarrassed, but he could have been more understanding. She picked up her plate and moved toward the sink, swaying. "I should head back to my cabin."

She hugged Liz and Kati. "Honey, you can come over anytime. We loved having you. Thank you for helping us."

"Good night, y'all." Anna stepped out into the night air and took a deep breath as she watched them close the door behind her with an audible click. Her stomach fluttered at the thought of Will's warm breath against her neck despite his absence. An unfamiliar fire smoldered low in her stomach until she stumbled, causing her to giggle. She steadied herself with outstretched arms and muttered, "I need to stay away from Will. He sets off something inside me. Mostly my temper."

∽

WILL SAT on the porch swing of Anna's cabin, his body swaying gently with each back-and-forth movement. He knew he needed to apologize for his behavior earlier that day. The scent of lavender shampoo still lingered in his nostrils, reminding him of her fiery spirit and how she had awakened something inside of him that he thought had died with Shelly.

When he saw Anna stagger toward the cabin, a mix of emotions swept through him: pleasure, excitement, and apprehension.

"Oh hey, Will," she said with slurred speech. As she climbed the stairs, her steps were unsteady. He could tell she had been drinking, and he couldn't help but smile.

When she stepped on the last step, her body swayed a little. Will stood and moved closer. He cautiously placed his hands on her shoulders to keep her steady. "I wasn't mad at you," he said softly, his gaze locked on hers.

"Why have you been avoiding me?" She hiccupped and blinked owlishly at him.

A slow smile spread across his face as he tucked a piece of hair behind her ear, noticing the sprinkle of freckles across the bridge of her tiny button nose for the first time. He let his fingertips linger on her skin as he tucked another loose hair behind her ear.

"I'm not avoiding you," he replied, his voice low and rough.

He looked into Anna's eyes, wanting to pull her close. She seemed smaller now, with parted lips, and he fought hard against the urge to press his lips against hers. His breath caught in his throat as he resisted temptation.

"I like your momma and sister," she said suddenly, her words followed by another hiccup. "They're sweet." She touched his nose. "So are you, but you are so . . . hot, and then you're cold . . ." she hummed in a sing-song tone.

He smiled at her. "You're drunk."

She half-shook her head in disagreement, her eyes twinkling with mischief in the fading light of the day. "I'm not drunk, just a bit tipsy. Your momma thinks you like me."

He raised an eyebrow. "She does, huh? Do you?"

"Do I what?"

"Like me," he replied softly, though there was still a hint of wariness beneath the surface.

She laughed, though it seemed laced with sadness. "Of course, I do . . . but you hate me. It was like you understood my grief when we talked at breakfast. I thought we connected. But then I made you mad. I'm sorry for that." Tears welled in her eyes. "Also, I'm sorry if I made you mad earlier," she whispered.

Will's chest tightened at her words. "Come on, darlin', let's get you to bed."

Anna pointed an accusing finger at him. "I'm not dating Garrett. I have no siblings, and he's been like a big brother," she murmured. "He just took me out to eat, and we went horseback riding . . ." her voice trailed off. "I'm here alone." Tears filled her eyes.

Will wiped away her tears with his thumb before he spoke again. "I'm sorry, Anna. I didn't mean to hurt you."

Her expression softened, and she smiled sadly while touching his face tenderly with her fingertips. "I forgive you," she whispered before muttering something else under her breath that Will couldn't quite catch. He tilted his head inquisitively and leaned closer to hear her better before freezing when it suddenly registered what she said: "Cowboy."

Why did she call him that? What did it mean? Will smiled despite himself and shook his head as if clearing away cobwebs from his mind. Then he remembered why he was here in the first place: to get Anna safely to bed before things went any further down this path of conflict and confusion between them.

She steadied herself on Will's arm. "Where's Eva and Caden?"

"They're at home."

She smiled, touching his face, "I love your kids."

He needed to get her to bed before this conversation went in another direction. "They love you too, darlin'. Let's get you to your room."

Anna pointed toward her room, and he directed her to bed. She lay down. He removed her shoes and gently covered her with a quilt. Grasping his hand, she said, "I hope we can be friends. What I feel for you is something I only felt once before."

He leaned over and kissed her forehead, letting out a groan. "What's that?"

She touched his face. "Safe," she said, her voice barely a whisper in the night.

"Me too, darlin'. I don't know what it is, but it scares me." He tucked the blankets around her.

"I don't mean to scare you," she croaked.

"I know, darlin'. It's me, not you. Get some rest." He squeezed her hands and smiled. "You better not be late to the stable in the morning."

She chuckled. "Good night, Will."

Good night, darlin'."

"I like it when you call me that," she said as she drifted to sleep.

He stood at the door, waiting for her breathing to slow down before he exited the cabin. He smiled. Alcohol was liquid courage, a truth serum. Anna only said what he'd thought about many times since they met. It was like they'd known each other forever. When he got back to his cabin, he was greeted by his wedding photo, bringing back the pain once more. He knew he'd have to put aside his feelings for Anna so he could open the equine center by Shelly's birthday. He had to fulfill Shelly's dream.

CHAPTER 18

It was a warm morning when Will entered the stable; he greeted the horses before heading to the tack room. When he opened the tack room door, he heard footsteps and held his breath. There was Anna, her hair tousled and clothes rumpled from the night before. He had hoped he'd catch her before she left for work. She seemed lost in her thoughts as she almost collided with Garrett.

"Good morning, sunshine," Garrett said with a sly smile. "Ya look a little green around the gills." He stood observing her with his arms crossed. "Did ya have too much to drink?"

She narrowed her eyes and stormed around him. "Maybe I'll start down at the other end." She rubbed her temples as she continued to the last stall.

"Okay, sunshine, just don't vomit in the stall."

"Shut up, Garrett."

He threw his head back, laughing.

Garrett approached the tack room as Will scrambled for the wheelbarrow and pitchfork. When Garrett pulled the door open, he jumped in surprise that Will was there. "Whoa, I didn't know you were in here," he exclaimed.

"Well, if you weren't busy flirting, you would have heard me," Will retorted with a smirk.

Garrett glanced around. "Flirting with who, you?"

Will walked around him with the wheelbarrow. "Let's just get to work." He pushed it down the stable aisle and halted when he saw Anna bent over as she mucked the stall. His face grew hot at the memory of their conversation last night. Had she been telling the truth, or had the alcohol clouded her judgment?

"Okay, boss. Anna is in the stall across from you," Garrett whispered loudly. "I think she's hungover."

Suddenly, Anna straightened up and turned around. "I can hear you, Garrett."

Will halted, amused, and turned to Garrett. He relaxed into a smile and threw his hands up. "How do they do that?"

Garrett slowly shook his head.

Anna narrowed her eyes. "Do what, boys? Appear out of nowhere and hear everything?"

Garrett laughed as he took the pitchfork from her. "Give me that before you stab us."

"I wouldn't do that." She winked at him as she took the pitchfork back. "Hey, I can finish everything at the other end."

Garrett looked at Will. "I guess that makes us safe."

She pointed it toward Garrett, mimicking him, saying, "I have my eye on you."

A smile tugged at his lips before he gestured for her to get to work. She saluted him before going back to finish cleaning the stall.

A mixture of envy and confusion coursed through Will as he watched them interact. He could tell she liked Garrett. She barely looked at him during their exchange, and his heart sank slightly.

Will forced himself toward the stalls across from Anna. They faced each other after finishing their tasks in the second stall. "Good morning," he said with a hint of hesitation.

She smiled back tentatively. "Good morning."

He inhaled sharply, trying to keep his composure. "How do you feel this morning?" He could barely meet her gaze, instead focusing on the ground between them.

She looked up to meet his gaze, her emerald eyes evaluating his question. Her delicate freckles stood out in contrast against the rosy hue of her cheeks.

After careful consideration she spoke, her voice trembling slightly. "I feel okay, considering. And you?"

Will shifted nervously, hands clasped behind his back. "I'm . . . okay too. Do you remember walking home from Momma and Kati's last night?"

Anna shook her head, looking away as her face turned crimson red like her hair. They stayed that way for what seemed like an eternity before Anna gestured to the barn behind them with her chin. "I—I should finish. I need to get to work."

She stepped toward the adjacent stall but stopped and looked over her shoulder at Will, her wide eyes plaintive. "Hey, would you want to start working on the grant tonight? At my cabin?"

Will nodded, though part of him wanted to ask if they could talk about what had happened last night instead. "We could do that. What time?" He needed to fight his feelings as he watched her work, including the desire to kiss her.

"I should be home around five o'clock. Let me know if anything changes," Anna replied, then quickly turned away before Will could make out the blush spreading across her cheeks again.

He cleared his throat. "Do you have your phone with you? I'll enter my number to stay in touch if any changes happen."

Anna handed him her phone, and he swiped past the wallpaper: a photo of an older man with a huge grin standing next to Anna. His mouth quirked up in surprise. "Who's this?"

She watched him intently as he added his information to her phone. "It's my grandpa."

Will raised his eyebrow. "He looks familiar to me. I'm not sure why."

"We came to Cardinal Creek, but I was young," Anna confirmed.

As those words tumbled from her lips, Will secretly wondered how they ended up in a tiny town like theirs, Cardinal Creek, where people rarely come or go. He handed her the phone, and she slid it into her pocket.

"How old were you when you came here?" Will leaned against the stall he was supposed to be cleaning.

She shrugged and replied, "Sixteen. I was almost a junior in high school." A nervous smile played along her lips. "Well, I should get finished. See you tonight." She headed back to the stall.

As she walked away, Will recalled a day when he was eighteen at the barrel racing clinics. He was a junior wrangler at the time. He had seen Jon talking to Ginger and noticed how her laughter lit up her face as he told her stories. Back then, Will was uneasy around girls due to his gangly frame and inability to find the right words. Jon always knew how to make people like him with his gregarious personality. After Jon left the barn, Will accused Ginger of liking him, prompting her to say her peace before she left in a huff. That was the last time he saw her.

Anna stuck her head in the stall. "Bye, Will. Have a good day."

He startled slightly, then smiled. "You too," he said warmly. "See you tonight."

As Anna left, Will returned to cleaning the stall. He wondered where he had seen Anna's grandfather before.

After mucking the stalls, he and Garrett sat on hay bales in the barn. Will took a deep breath. "I'm sorry for the way I acted the other day. Anna told me last night that you've been kind to her."

Garrett's head cocked slightly as he looked out at the field. "I appreciate the apology. Could I ask you a question?"

Will nodded, his mouth suddenly dry.

"Why do you care if Anna and I date? Do you like her?" Garrett asked, slowly turning to face him.

Will's face flushed as he frowned, his lips pressing together. A million thoughts raced through his mind, all telling him to tell the truth. But he couldn't bring himself to say the words out loud. In the end, he gave a slight shake of his head as he wasn't confident enough to say anything.

Garrett removed his hat and ran his fingers through his hair. "The look on your face tells me more than enough," he said. "First of all, I'm forty-five. It's not like Anna and I are going to date or anything. I'm here for other reasons; I rarely discuss my past." He adjusted his hat back onto his head. "Have you ever wondered why I'm here?"

Will raised his shoulders. "We all have our reasons. I just wanted to give you some room to think." His face softened. "Kati's right, I'm a jerk. I don't know what it is about Anna, but . . ." He rubbed the back of his neck nervously. "She has this effect on me that I haven't felt since Shelly. But I can't get involved with her. She's going to help me open the equine center."

Garrett gave him an understanding pat on the shoulder. "I get it, but seriously, aside from the age difference, I see her as nothing more than a friend. Now, let's get to work before we get gored by hungry longhorns." He gestured toward the truck.

While they loaded feed into the truck to feed the cattle, Will thought about Anna's age. If Anna was in her early thirties, and she was sixteen when she came to Cardinal Creek . . . He shook his head. There was no way Anna and Ginger were the same person. He would have recognized her.

"Did Anna tell you how old she is?" Will asked.

Garrett threw the last sack of feed into the back of the truck. "I think she said thirty-five or thirty-six. Why?"

Will shrugged. "Just wondering."

CHAPTER 19

Anna made it through the morning, but her pounding headache lingered, a reminder of her mistake from the night before. Last night had been a blur of too much wine and embarrassing moments that she now wished she could take back. When it was time for lunch, she headed to the cafeteria, famished. She glanced around for Kati or the two nurses from orientation but saw no sign of them.

Suddenly, she felt a presence behind her and heard an unexpected voice in her ear. Dr. Watts stood too close for comfort and spoke in a low hiss that sent shivers down her spine. She quickly moved forward, but he slithered even closer. Anna searched desperately for an escape. She finally found one at the sandwich counter and bolted for it while mumbling a hurried goodbye.

After she paid, her body relaxed when she finally spotted two nurses from her orientation class, Beth and Nancy. She headed to their table and sat down, hoping Dr. Watts wouldn't find her.

Beth and Nancy worked in the ICU on the night shift. They graduated from UT Austin four years earlier and had been best friends since elementary school. Anna listened to their stories of lifelong friendship. She shifted the red bracelet on her wrist, imagining Jenny's presence.

"How do you like Texas so far?" Bethany asked.

Anna smiled. "I like it a lot. I have my horse here, so I've been able to ride at the ranch where I'm staying. It brings me back to when I rode with my friend Jenny and all the fun we had."

"We both love to ride, too," Nancy chimed in. "Do you ride every day?"

"I don't get to ride every day, but I do spend time with my horse." She paused momentarily before answering, "Your friendship reminds me of my best friend Jenny and I. We grew up together and even went to the same college, but she's a physical therapist in Missouri."

Beth inquired inquisitively, "Does she plan on moving here?"

Just as Anna opened her mouth to answer, Dr. Watts appeared at the table. Anna's heart sank into her stomach as he slid into the chair beside her and whispered, "I am beginning to think you're avoiding me."

Anna stiffened up, her eyes widening in surprise. "No, I—"

He placed his hand on hers and gave it a light squeeze. Anna pulled her hand away. "Was there something you needed?" she muttered through gritted teeth.

He smiled warmly at her, almost amused by her reluctance. "Would you introduce me to your friends? I'm new to the hospital and trying to meet the nurses who serve me."

Anna scoffed. *The nurses who serve him?* She struggled to maintain a calm tone as she introduced him to Beth and Nancy even though she was fuming inside.

"It's nice to meet you, ladies. I'm Dr. Watts," he said with a polite smile. He stood and picked up his tray. "Well, I should be getting back as I have surgery this afternoon." His eyes met hers, and he added, "Ms. Samuels, I hope I didn't offend you. That was not my intention."

Anna nodded. *Maybe he didn't mean it the way I took it, but he still gave me the creeps.* "No offense taken," she replied through tight lips.

"Anna," Beth said, her voice filled with concern as she touched Anna's arm and drew her back to the conversation. "You, okay? Who was that doctor?"

"He's Cathy Watts's husband. She's the director of nursing. I met him when I had lunch with Cathy yesterday."

Nancy gave a deep sigh. "There's something off about him. He gives me the creeps."

Beth rolled her eyes and shook her head. "Nancy, you always look for the worst in people."

Anna tried to smooth things over by waving her hand in dismissal at Nancy. "He seems harmless enough."

Nancy appeared hesitant and uneasy, as if she had more to say, but decided against it. Eventually, she gave in and said, "Only time will tell, but he's setting off my alarm bells big time." She scoffed. "'The nurses who serve me' . . . What a misogynistic pig."

Anna laughed nervously, wanting to change the subject and lighten the mood. "That didn't sit well with me either."

With a groan, Beth glanced upward. "Oh, don't give her any fuel!"

Anna didn't want to be drawn into any further speculation. "We should get back to our afternoon sessions," she said. They quickly gathered their trays.

A chill ran down Anna's spine as they left the cafeteria. Dr. Watts had grabbed her hand without warning, but he'd apologized as if it was an automatic response and hadn't thought about his action.

Just then, Kati rounded the corner and approached her. "Hey, Anna, how's it going?"

Suddenly, tears blurred Anna's vision, and a flood of emotions assaulted her. *Why do I feel so overwhelmed and upset? Do I need some time alone? Is it because I miss Jenny?* With a forced smile, Anna mumbled a hasty goodbye and ran toward the bathroom, shutting herself inside a stall to cry out all the emotions that had been building up for some time.

ANNA ARRIVED home from work with her head spinning, a knot in her stomach, and a deep ache in her temples, thanks to Dr. Watts's unwelcomed closeness. His hot breath had lingered on her neck, distracting her the rest of the afternoon. She rubbed her temples as if that would somehow quiet the chaotic surge of emotions that ran through her body. With a deep sigh, she muttered, "What the hell is wrong with me?"

The only way she could concentrate on the grant proposal was to rid herself of lingering emotions, so she headed to the bathroom, desperate for a hot shower to help clear her head. The steamy water cascaded over her weary body like a healing balm, and the scent of lavender shampoo soothed her senses as it washed away the anxiety and confusion. After shutting off the water, she wrapped herself in a teal robe. She was drying her hair with a towel when there was an unexpected knock at the door. She quickly brushed her hair, secured her robe, and opened the door to see Will in jeans, a black shirt, Stetson, and roper boots, his glacier-blue eyes shining even brighter against his outfit.

His square jaw softened as he smiled and said, "Hey, I guess I caught you at a bad time."

The intensity of his gaze made Anna's heart flutter. *Those eyes...* "No, I spent a little extra time in the shower. I'm sorry."

Will tucked a strand of hair behind her ear, which sent tingles down her spine despite her efforts to remain aloof. He seemed to sense it too. Heat rose from her neck to the top of her head when he pulled his hand back quickly. "I'm sorry. I don't know why I did that."

She waved her hand at him, desperately trying to mask her inner turmoil. "It's okay. Let me get dressed. Make yourself at home." Her heart pounded as she went to her room to put on some clothes. She selected black yoga pants and an oversized T-shirt that hung off her shoulder, exposing a spattering of freckles. She hoped Will didn't notice the flush that rose from her neck like the mercury in a thermometer.

When she returned to the living room, Will stared at her wide-eyed. He cleared his throat nervously. "How was your day?"

Anna forced a smile. "It ... was good," she replied. "And you?"

"Same old, same old ranch work," he answered.

Anna grabbed a bottle of wine from the refrigerator and held it up. "Want some?"

He raised his eyebrow. "Do you drink every day?"

Forcing herself not to break eye contact, Anna replied with a chuckle, "No, I rarely drink. Why?"

Will's eyes filled with a hint of curiosity and amusement. He tilted slightly and asked, "Do you remember talking to me last night after you left my mother's cabin? What do you remember?"

Warmth rose in her cheeks and body, and she tried not to squirm under his gaze. She looked down at the floor before meeting his eyes. "I have a vague memory of talking to you. I regret being so forward, even if it was under the influence of alcohol."

He laughed, breaking the tension. "Don't be sorry. I like to call alcohol liquid truth."

Anna smiled, her nerves started to calm. She grabbed two glasses from the cabinet. "Do you mind if I have a glass of liquid truth, then? I promise not to say anything stupid tonight."

"Don't need my permission," Will said as he sat at the table. "Can I ask you a personal question?"

"How personal?" Anna asked.

He shrugged. "How old are you?"

That was what he wanted to know. Anna let out a relieved laugh as she sat down at the table. "Thirty-six, the same age as Kati. Why?"

He shrugged. "Just wondering." He glanced at the bottle she set on the table. "Does that wine bottle have a twist-off cap?"

"Why yes, it does. This is some good wine from Missouri wine country." She twisted off the cap, poured some into each glass with shaky hands, and then took a long sip. "Mmm, it's so sweet." She paused and asked, "Would you like to smell the bottle cap?"

Will chuckled, reaching for the second glass of wine, and she pushed it toward him with her slender fingers. He took a sip, and his eyes widened in surprise. "This is amazing. I never would've guessed you're into wine with twist-off caps and NSYNC."

"And the Backstreet Boys." A smile quirked as she studied his face and posed her next question. "Do cowboys drink wine? I thought they were whiskey and beer drinkers."

He smirked at her as he swallowed another long gulp of the pink beverage. "Now, this one does. I like this wine. What's it called?"

"Pink Catawba. It's my favorite from Missouri wine country. I love going there, especially in the fall." Nostalgia washed over her as she remembered when she and Jenny used to go to the winery and sit on a patchwork picnic quilt they had made from their old blue jeans, including pieces of her mother's and father's jeans mixed in. The trees in autumn were vibrant red, orange, and yellow hues, and the sun would warm their necks.

"Let me get my laptop," Anna said. "We need to start by figuring out what we need to do for the grant application."

A glimmer of admiration shone from Will's eyes as he watched her prepare for work, and he smiled fondly at her eagerness to get down to business. They settled down on the couch side by side and began creating spreadsheets and timelines of tasks that needed to be completed to get the equine center open by September. She pointed to the timetable while explaining her idea. "This is what we can use when you're having your breakfast meetings. That way, you can assign tasks to people."

He gave an appreciative nod before finishing his wine and leaning back against the cushions. "You know how much this means to me . . . and Caden and our community as a whole, right?"

She met his gaze, then turned back to her laptop, fingertips hovering over the keys as she spoke confidently, "I'll do whatever it takes to ensure we meet that deadline." With that resolution made, they got down to work, creating a Kanban board with a timeline of tasks that needed to happen to open the center by September.

Anna retrieved the second bottle of wine and poured them both another glass. As she drank, her mind became hazy, and her inhibitions were loosening. "Can we tour the ranch and share your program ideas?" Anna turned to face him, but he had a faraway look. "Will, did you hear me?"

He smiled. "I'm sorry. What did you say?"

Anna's mouth was dry. "Are you okay? I'm sorry if I overwhelmed you." The warmth of the wine was beginning to flood her veins.

He reached over and brushed his fingertips along her cheekbone, and the heat of his touch penetrated her skin. "I'm sorry for the way I treated you."

She focused on a spot on the wall across the room. She could feel him studying her, trying to gauge her reaction, and she tensed even more.

He leaned back, took a deep breath, and let his hand fall from her face. "You haven't done anything but be kind to me and my family, and I haven't been nice to you."

Anna swallowed hard past the lump forming in her throat. "I thought I made you angry somehow." She attempted to lighten the mood with a small joke. "The wine is getting to us."

But he wouldn't let it go and continued apologizing for how he treated her. He said that he appreciated her kindness, understood the pain of losing someone you loved and that he'd been wrong to ask Garrett if he was interested in her romantically.

Anna stared at him, blinking, unable to comprehend what he was saying until she finally understood. *He was jealous.*

She laughed. "Oh my God, who was drunk last night? Me or you? I told you this last night: Garrett and I are just friends. He's a very nice person. If I could pick a brother, it would be him."

He sat up abruptly. "You did, yes." After taking a long sip of his wine, he blurted, "I was jealous."

Anna froze. She didn't know what to do with his confession. The room felt heavy as she searched for something to say. Clearing her throat, she looked back at her laptop. "We should probably get back to work . . ."

"Yeah, sure." Will rubbed the back of his neck and sighed. "When would you like to take a tour of the ranch? I work tomorrow, but we can do it the next day or over the weekend."

Anna knew that he was trying to change the subject, so she obliged with a nod. "I think your next day off would be good."

"Would you want to go to one of Caden's appointments at the therapy center to meet Cindy, the director?"

Anna sensed the tension between them but forced herself to answer. She would do anything to break it. "I think meeting the director is a good idea." Cautiously, she said, "One thing I need you to do is figure out how much money you think will be needed to open the center and operate for a few months."

"I can answer that now because I have no idea," he said. "I don't know how to open an equine center, much less run one." There was a mixture of worry and desperation in his eyes. "I truly don't know how I'll do this."

Anna's voice was soft but unwavering. "I'll do everything I can to get the equine center open. You aren't alone in this."

Anna poured more wine into his glass and then filled hers. He drank the entire glass in one swallow. Will entwined his fingers with hers. His chest heaved as he took a deep breath as if he wanted to say something but didn't know how to express it.

After what felt like an eternity, he finally said, "I texted Shelly the night she died. She was always texting when she drove; we constantly fought about it. She visited me at the firehouse and then left to run errands. I texted her, knowing she'd look at it. She rear-ended an eighteen-wheeler, killing her instantly." He paused and looked down at his lap. "If I can't do this, I'll let her and my family down again."

Anna couldn't find any words of comfort, so she just sat with him until he broke the silence by asking for more wine as he wiped the tears from his eyes.

"I'm . . . I'm sorry," she whispered. Anna looked into his eyes, relieved to see a faint glimmer of strength returning to them.

"I'm sorry. I don't know why I told you all that. It feels like I can talk to you, and you don't expect me to always be strong," he said.

She gave him a reassuring smile. "No one can always be strong," she answered gently. It seemed that Will needed someone who wouldn't judge him for showing moments of weakness—someone who expected less from him than he did of himself—and it made Anna understand why he chose to confide in her. She placed her hand on his, attempting to offer solace through her words. "The accident wasn't your fault."

Again, the air seemed still as silence filled the room, leaving Anna wondering if Will had ever sought professional help for his grief. She knew it was more than grief that was tearing him apart.

Will gently touched the red bracelet on Anna's wrist. "What were you thinking about when you told me about Missouri wine? Your voice just trailed off. You had a peaceful smile." He ran his finger across the bracelet, causing Anna to shiver. "And you were tugging at this bracelet. This may seem random, but I was going to ask, and then we started talking about the equine center and . . ."

Anna smiled, glad for something to talk about that could lift the mood. Her voice was soft as she recalled trips with Jenny to wine country in the fall. She described the vibrant oranges, reds, and yellows of the foliage spread across rolling hills as far as the eye could see and how they'd crafted their picnic quilt from their parents' jeans. Her voice slowed as fresh tears welled up in her eyes. She wasn't sure why she missed Jenny so much today or if it was a combination of many things.

"I miss Jenny a lot today. We took that quilt everywhere, but when I left for Texas, she said I should take it." She turned to Will. "Would you like to see it?"

Will nodded, so she quickly got up and retrieved it from her bedroom.

Sitting next to him on the sofa, she carefully laid out each jean square, displaying the pockets that belonged to her parents and Jenny's father and the neatly embroidered pocket with a horseshoe from her barrel racing adventures during her sophomore year.

He looked at her and chuckled. "I knew someone with the same pair of jeans."

Anna raised an eyebrow. "Really? That's funny. My nana made those for me. She embroidered the pockets for luck."

Will's voice was husky. "Why did your family come to Cardinal Creek when you were sixteen?" His fingers traced the stitches on the horseshoe.

But Anna didn't want to recall her time in Cardinal Creek; it reminded her of a hurt that cut too deep. "Horses," she muttered. "We came for horses, then we left."

"What made you come back here?" he asked, seemingly unconvinced by her brief explanation.

She took a drink of her wine and handed him his glass. With a hint of hesitation, she replied, "Well, I suppose after I lost the last living member of my family, I needed a change." But if she were honest with herself, her cheating boyfriend and former friend had made her see that she needed a change of scenery . . . an adventure.

Will held up his glass. "Here's to new beginnings."

Anna smiled. "To new beginnings." They clinked glasses and took a long drink.

He gently squeezed Anna's hand. "I hope we can be friends." He chuckled. "I like talking to you, and I look forward to working with you on the equine center."

His touch sent electricity through Anna's veins, and she wanted to know more about him with every moment they spent together. She smiled bashfully. "We'll become friends as we work together. We'll get this done."

Anna shared her excitement for their upcoming tour of the ranch to gain a better understanding of their project. She held up her glass again, toasting to taking things slow so he wouldn't become overwhelmed.

Anna stood up, but her feet tangled beneath her, and she stumbled into his chest. He steadied her with solid hands, and his gaze penetrated her. Scarlet heat caressed her cheeks.

It's all right, darlin'," he said in a low voice. "Would it be okay if I hugged you? I could use a hug."

Anna nodded, barely able to whisper, "Me too."

He enveloped her in his arms, and she felt the world had stopped turning. His familiar scent surrounded her like a comforting cloak as she closed her eyes, wanting to stay here forever.

He softly kissed her head and spoke into her hair. "Anna, thank you for . . . well, for everything. I don't want to let go; this feels nice."

"Hugs are excellent," Anna murmured. It had been far too long since anyone had hugged her like this. When the hug finally ended, Anna was sad it was over.

"Thank you, darlin'," he said as he grabbed his hat. "I'll see you the day after tomorrow."

"Good night, Will," she said as she watched him leave.

CHAPTER 20

The following day, Will stepped into the barn, his boots crunching on the hay-strewn floor. Garrett had already moved through the stalls with practiced efficiency, mucking out the old straw and filling each booth with fresh fodder. As he walked in, Garrett stopped and leaned against the rough pine boards of the last stall. "I'm almost done. Let's talk."

"Is everything okay?" Will asked.

Garrett let out a long breath. "I've been working here for a while, and you don't know much about me. I wanted to say thank you for allowing me to have space since I've been here." He ran his fingers through his hair. "Did you ever wonder why I came to work here after the military?"

Will shrugged. "Honestly, it's none of my business. Plus, I thought you would tell me when you were ready if there was anything to tell."

"I appreciate that more than you know. I was injured on my last tour and sustained burns to my chest, arms, and legs. I was married at the time. My wife came to the hospital in Germany, and when she saw me, she told me I looked repulsive." Garrett began to pace as he continued his story. "She told me she wanted a divorce and left. When I got back to San Antonio, I was told my career with the military was over, but I would need therapy after I was released, so I opted to find something close to Fort Sam. After being released from the hospital, I decided to go for a drive and ended up in Cardinal Creek. The rest is history."

"You didn't want to go home to family?" Will asked.

Garrett shook his head. "No. This is where my feelings for Anna come in."

Will cleared his throat. "How?"

"I like Anna, but not the way you think." Garrett's voice caught. "She reminds me of my sister—the same fiery temper and passionate spirit. Every time I see her . . ." He trailed off and cleared his throat. "To me, she's like a sister. I want to protect her the same way you would protect Kati."

Will didn't know what to say. After losing his dad and Shelly, he knew it was best to be silent rather than offer the pearls of wisdom people often did when they didn't know what to say.

Garrett looked down at the ground and shifted some hay around with his boot. "My sister passed away before I joined the army. I was trying to find a new place without anyone knowing who I used to be and what I've been through."

Will scrubbed his hand across his face in disbelief. "I'm sorry. I don't know what to say."

Garrett wiped his eyes. "Listen, if anyone understands loss, it's your family. It changes people."

"Indeed," Will mumbled, "it does."

Garrett took a deep breath before continuing: "Sometimes it feels hard to believe that I've been led to a place where people can understand my loss without even knowing about it. It has been such a comfort for me." He continued with a slight smile, "I appreciate you respecting my time to heal." His eyes met Will's as he spoke, "And just so you know, you don't need to worry about me and Anna. Loss is something we both comprehend. As she mourns the loss of her last living relative, a deep emptiness has consumed her. She now navigates through life utterly alone without the comfort of a family by her side.

Will adjusted his hat, still speechless from this unexpected conversation. All he had come here to do was take care of the horses and head off to work, nothing more than a few polite words exchanged with Garrett.

"Did she say why she chose to come to Cardinal Creek? I asked her last night, but she gave me a non-answer," Will said.

"She said she wanted a new start after she caught her ex-boyfriend cheating on her at her grandfather's funeral."

Will was surprised to hear this. Of all the scenarios he thought up about why she'd come here, he wondered if it had to do with an ex-boyfriend. She had lost so much, yet here she was, providing comfort without mentioning her stories of loss and grief. He had known about her parents' death and her grandparents' passing, but he never realized the weight of the sadness surrounding her until Garrett put it all into perspective.

"How long ago did her grandpa pass away?" Will asked.

"I think it was the end of February." Garrett kicked at the ground. "Do you mind if I just put it all out there for you to think about?"

"Sure. I appreciate you sharing with me. I also appreciate you putting things into perspective for me."

Garrett slapped Will's back. "There could be a kinship between the two of you that could be a catalyst for healing from the grief you both have experienced. Just open your heart a little. You may be surprised."

"I never thought about it like that." Will took everything in, a sudden kinship forming between them. It never occurred to him, but there could be a connection between him and Anna—a bridge to understanding each other's grief. The thought warmed him.

"Just open your heart a little," Garrett repeated. "You may be surprised."

Will shook his head. "All this wisdom in my barn, and I didn't know it." He smiled feeling a renewed hope for what was possible between him and Anna. If he opened his heart, he could heal from the pain.

Will slapped Garrett on the back. "I better get to work."

"Remember what I told you," Garrett said as he left the stable.

Will stood watching, thinking about how you never really knew someone else's pain when you were too busy thinking of your own. "Hey, Garrett," he called. "Thanks. Talking to you helped a lot."

Garrett waved to him. "No problem. Just make sure I have help when you're at work."

Will chuckled. "Anna is going to help tonight with the evening feeding."

"Oh, she's a good one, Will. She gets most of the work done before I even get here."

They left the stable together but went their separate ways. As Will approached his house, he thought, *I still have Eva, Caden, Mom, Kati, and*

Jon. Anna had put in so much time since she arrived at the ranch. She worked tirelessly to help with the horses and was now helping with the equine center. How could she still be willing to give when she'd lost so much?

～

WILL and Jon settled into the plastic chairs on the wide concrete stoop of the engine house, squinting against the morning sun as they surveyed Main Street. People were already out in force, with joggers gliding down the sidewalk and locals milling in front of the small boutiques, eateries, the yoga studio, and the quilt shop.

Jon took a long swig from his water bottle and turned to Will with a wide grin, gesturing toward the women who passed on the street. "Isn't this the best part of working? Watching the people go by? Now and then, we even see some hot chicks. If one has a friend, we could double date."

Will groaned, rolling his eyes. "I'm not interested in picking up someone random off Main Street."

Jon playfully nudged Will with his shoulder and laughed. "We don't have to marry them, just have some fun," he joked, wiggling his eyebrows. He lowered his voice and clarified, "You know what I mean."

Will's features twisted into a scowl as he folded his arms over his chest and emitted an exasperated sigh, as if this joke had been told one too many times. "Have you ever wondered why my sister won't date you again?"

Jon glanced at him in surprise. "Come on, this isn't the first time we've looked at girls out here. Now you're mad?" His gaze narrowed suspiciously. "Is this about that hot little redhead at the ranch?"

Will furrowed his brows in response, the hint of a smirk playing around his lips. "Seriously? She's not some conquest, you know? Her name is Anna, and she's been helping since Momma got hurt." He shook his head slowly as a wry smile pulled at the corner of his mouth. "God, you will never win Kati back, and you do all the talking when we see women."

Jon raised his hands in surrender. "Whoa, I wasn't trying to hit on her or anything," he said quickly, looking between his feet as if searching for the right words. "I was just curious about her, what she's like . . ." His voice trailed off, and he was hit with a realization that suddenly dawned on him.

He widened his eyes, and his expression shifted to one of understanding. "You like her, don't you?"

Will clenched his jaw, desperately trying to keep his anger in check. "I want to have a relationship with her, but I feel like I'm being disloyal to Shelly's memory."

"Believe me, Will, I knew Shelly way before you did, and I'm sure she'd want you to be happy."

Will rose from the chair and started pacing. "What if the memories of her slowly fade as I begin to move on?"

"Excuses . . . all excuses. You are afraid to let someone else in." Jon stood, a fierce urgency flashing in his eyes. "Love doesn't die with the person," he said firmly, pressing his hand against his chest. "It lives on in the memories you leave behind and loving relationships like yours with Eva and Caden. I know she loved you, Will. I'm sure she would want you to be happy. She wouldn't want her children to go without a mother."

Will nodded solemnly, reluctantly shaking hands with Jon before gently embracing him with one arm. "Thanks, man," he said.

Jon sighed heavily as he looked away. "I miss her too." He cleared his throat after a few moments of silence. "Hey, Deluca, don't worry about me and Kati. I like her for real this time."

Will emitted a small laugh. "Are you ever going to give up?"

Jon smiled. "Never! She loves me. I need to prove I'm worthy of it."

Will chuckled softly under his breath. Despite everything he had said, Kati still thought Jon had cheated on her and had chosen to part ways with him. He knew Jon hadn't cheated, but even if he told Kati, it wouldn't melt her heart like it had so many times before. He knew it was unlikely that Kati would ever forgive Jon, no matter how hard they both tried.

Will knew Jon had been drinking more since Shelly had passed away, but he couldn't imagine Jon cheating on Kati. After all, Will had been with him on the night he was supposedly unfaithful, and Jon had been in no state even to consider such a thing.

It was clear that although Jon had grown distant from Kati since Shelly's death, his heart longed to win her back. But his words were rarely a good representation of what was going on inside his head.

Jon clapped his hand on Will's back. The gesture was both reassuring and firm. "Listen, I know you don't want to date, but what you are doing with the equine center will keep the memory of Shelly alive for you and the kids. Just see what happens. Caden likes her. He told me she's been nice to him and Eva."

Will furrowed his brow. "When did he tell you that?"

"He told me when I stopped by to see your momma. He said she rubs his head like Shelly used to and listens when he talks, unlike someone we know . . . you." Jon pushed his ball cap back and rested it on his head while a smile tugged at the corner of his mouth.

Will could feel a flush across his face as he realized the truth in Jon's words. "Shelly was much better at that than I am. I've been participating in Caden's therapy and improving communication with him. So far, it seems to be helping."

Caden went to therapy twice weekly, and Will always went unless he was working. His little boy had different communication needs, including occupational therapy and PECS, the picture exchange communication system. Before Shelly passed away, Will had been involved in all of this, but now it was up to him to meet Caden's needs. They weren't perfect yet, but they'd progressed since Shelly's death. At least, that was what Patty, Caden's therapist, had said.

Jon's blue eyes crinkled with compassion. "Look, you're a great dad, and I can't begin to imagine what it must be like to grieve someone while trying to take care of two kids."

"Thanks," Will muttered, his voice strained with the tightness in his throat. "And remember, you've been my brother for years."

Jon and Garrett's words echoed in Will's mind. The equine center could bring Anna closer to his children and serve as a way for Shelly's memory to live on, even if she were no longer with them physically. It wouldn't be a bad idea to try and get to know Anna better too. Having another adult to talk things through might do him good. After all, last night was the first time he'd told anyone the deep, dark secret he'd been carrying around, that he believed he was the reason Shelly had died. The tension around his neck and shoulders loosened slightly as the thought settled in.

CHAPTER 21

Anna sat in her office sipping on a cup of coffee. She was filled with excitement about touring the ranch after work. She and Will had worked on the plans for the equine center and made significant progress, and she was eager to see the property and continue building their vision together. Mixed emotions about Will flooded her mind, bringing back memories of his warm touch when he tucked a stray hair behind her ear. The thought of seeing him again caused butterflies to flutter wildly in her stomach. Her reverie was interrupted by the ringing of her phone. It was Kati inviting her to lunch.

Anna tapped a few buttons on her calendar app to check her afternoon schedule before heading to the cafeteria. She had been in several long meetings today, all devoted to planning the programming for palliative care. Her new ideas had been met with enthusiasm, particularly the concept of a caregiver support group. Anna's steps felt lighter as she walked toward the cafeteria. She breathed deeply, eager to enjoy the mouth-watering aroma of hamburgers and fries, causing her stomach to grumble.

When she saw Kati at the grill line, she rushed to meet her. "How did you know this was what I was craving? The smell made my stomach growl as I entered the cafeteria."

"Mine too." Kati draped an arm around Anna's shoulder. "How are you? I haven't seen you much. Work has been crazy."

Anna forced a smile. "I'm doing well. A little homesick at times."

Kati furrowed her eyebrows. "Well, we need to take care of that," she said firmly. "Is Will being nice?"

Anna chuckled as contentment washed over her like a warm tidal wave. "Yes, he's been a perfect gentleman."

Kati winked playfully at her. "Let me know if he gets sassy. I'll have Momma get after him."

They put in an order for cheeseburgers and fries. Anna's mouth watered as she walked to the table. It had been a while since she had a good greasy burger. They sat at a table facing the hospital gardens with bluebonnets and red poppies. Butterflies flittered around the flowers, creating a color spectacle of their own. "Wow," Anna said in awe. "This is a nice retreat while eating. That garden is very nice."

"The Ladies' Auxiliary did an excellent job." Kati smiled.

"It reminds me of my nana's flower bed around the porch of our house. She had tulips, hyacinths, and daffodils. I loved growing up there. It's a beautiful place, especially the old oak tree in the front yard that provided plenty of shade on the porch when Papa and I drank lemonade." Anna couldn't help but grin at the memory of her childhood home.

"That sounds beautiful. Did you sell it before you moved to Texas?"

"I haven't sold it yet," she explained. "My friend Jenny and her mom are looking after it until I figure out if I want to sell it."

An idea quickly formed in Anna's head, and she could no longer suppress her enthusiasm. "It would be amazing if we could plan a girls' trip after the equine center opens. We could take our horses and go riding with Jenny."

"That sounds like fun. I've never been to Missouri. We should plan to go in October."

Anna's eyes lit up. "That's my favorite time of year. I was telling Will about the wineries and how the trees make the hillsides look beautiful."

"Let's plan it," Kati said. "How are things going with the equine center?"

"I'm meeting with your brother tonight. We'll tour the ranch to get a full rundown of what needs to be done. I'm not sure how it'll turn out yet.

Money can be tricky. I'm going to apply for a couple grants, but we won't get those in time to open in September." Anna was eager for the equine center to open on schedule, as it was significant for Will and his family. However, she needed clarification on the required funds or potential financing options. She believed the center's opening would aid Will's recovery and hoped not to disappoint him.

"Anna?" Kati waved her hand in front of Anna's face, breaking her from her trance.

"Yeah, sorry," Anna mumbled, mustering a nervous smile. "Just got lost in thought for a moment."

"Has Will introduced you to Cindy at the therapy center?"

"Not yet, but soon. Actually—"

A heavy hand clamped down on Anna's shoulder, causing her to flinch in surprise as Dr. Watts joined the conversation.

"Good afternoon, ladies. Kati, I saw you sitting here and wanted to check on your mother." He gripped Anna's shoulder tighter with each word.

Her skin prickled under the warm weight of his hand. It was heavy and oppressive, as if to remind her of her place, but why? She shifted her position, desperate to shake his hand away, but his grip remained firm. *Why does he always have to say hi?*

Kati cleared her throat before responding. "She's fine, Dr. Watts. Getting stronger every day."

He then shifted his attention to Anna and squeezed her shoulder, causing her stomach to knot with apprehension. "And Ms. Samuels, how do you like your position here?"

"Fine, sir, thank you," she grunted while grabbing her tray. "Hey, Kati, I need to go. I have a Zoom meeting I forgot about."

"I'll catch up with you later," Kati replied, grabbing her tray and following suit behind Anna toward the cafeteria exit.

Anna rushed out of the cafeteria, relieved Dr. Watts had finally let go of her shoulder. His touch made her skin crawl, causing her to feel fear and disgust. This was the third time he'd touched her without her consent. The first time, she'd played it off, but now she was convinced his touches were intentional, not to mention inappropriate. She had never been in this situation before. Tears pricked her eyes. She didn't know what to do. She was overwhelmed with guilt for not standing up for herself.

∼

WHEN ANNA PULLED up to her cabin, she was taken aback to see Will lounging on the porch swing. His hat was pulled low over his eyes, and he appeared to be sound asleep with his long legs stretched out and crossed at the ankles. She hesitated before walking up the steps and touching his arm gently. "Will," she breathed.

He stirred, and a deep, rumbling voice replied, "Mmm . . . there better be a fire."

Anna laughed and asked if it had been a long day.

He muttered something under his hat before pushing it back and sitting up straight. He smiled when he saw her. "Oh wow, you look nice, darlin'."

Anna blushed. "Oh . . . uh . . . thanks. I'll go change." *Wow, it suddenly got hot out here.* She hurried into the cabin and quickly pulled on a pair of jeans and a T-shirt. After she pulled on her boots, she headed out the door. Will was leaning against the porch railing. A smile spread across his face when she stepped onto the porch.

"You got ready fast."

"I've been looking forward to hearing more about Shelly's vision for the equine center," Anna said sincerely.

Will turned toward her, appreciation shining in his eyes. "Thank you for caring about our dream."

Anna gently touched his arm. "If it helps you and the kids heal, it's a win."

Taking her by the hand, he led her off the porch and toward the lodge. "Shelly loved this place, but it needs a lot of work," he said. "Although the structure is solid."

As they approached the lodge, Will paused before grasping the door handle. "When we're done, do you want to grab dinner?"

"Sure, we could make some notes and do some planning."

He opened the door to reveal a lofty space with massive wooden beams crisscrossing the ceiling. A chandelier made from an old wagon wheel hung above them, casting a faint yellow light on the vast room. Several round tables were scattered across the floor, each with dust and cobwebs but intact. Anna couldn't help but smile in appreciation; it was a picturesque place.

While Will showed her the lodge, he explained that Shelly wanted a camp for the kids in the summer at no charge.

Anna glanced around, taking in every inch of the space. Several large round tables were arranged in the center of the room. Each piece of furniture was ready to be restored to its original condition with a good cleaning and minor cosmetic work. She smiled as she slowly rotated in a circle. "This is great. How's the electricity and plumbing?"

"I think the electricity needs some updating, but I'm not sure," Will said.

She nodded. "If the electric and plumbing are good, it needs some updates and decorating."

As they moved through each cabin, Anna admired the familiar rustic touch, which reminded her of her cabin. Finally, they reached the arena, where she could see the entire property from an elevated view. She paused to take it all in. "There's more to this place than the stable. It's beautiful and has so much potential," she said.

Will leaned against the weathered fence, his eyes twinkling as he proudly surveyed the arena. His battered hat was tipped back on his head, and his calloused hands rested easy at his side. Anna stood beside him, taking in the scene. A two-horse trailer sat off to the left, and a stack of hay bales lay nearby. He gestured toward the open grassy circle ahead of them. "I love this arena. Sometimes, Jon and I come out and rope like in high school." He turned to her, a hopeful gleam in his eye. "If you like, we could ride this weekend and tour the land by horseback."

A smile spread across her face. "I'd love to go riding to see the land." She tilted her head curiously. "Wait . . . you rope?"

"Yes, ma'am, for as long as I can remember," he responded with a chuckle. "My dad put us on horses when we were about two years old, according to my momma."

"Does Caden rope, too?"

Will shook his head. "He gets frustrated when I try to teach him, but Jon helps him without fail."

"You know how kids are. They think their parents know nothing."

Will smiled. "Yeah, but Shelly communicated better with Caden than I do." He cleared his throat. "I'm going to tell you something I haven't told anyone because somehow I feel you understand me." He took his hat off and ran his fingers through his hair. "I've never been sure how to communicate with Caden. I'm always afraid I'm going to trigger a meltdown. It could cause problems if I can't get past that." Will exhaled slowly as he placed his hat back on his head. "I feel ashamed," he confessed, "I should be able to communicate with him better. I'm his dad."

Anna shook her head reassuringly. "Will, give yourself a break. You seem to be very hard on yourself about everything."

"This, my dear Anna, is why I like talking to you. You're kind when I need it, chew my rear when I need it, and always help me even when I'm a jerk."

She placed a gentle hand on his arm. "Deep down, you aren't a jerk. Fear drives a lot of your aloofness."

His eyebrows rose in surprise, and Anna could almost see the wheels turning in his mind as he contemplated her words. "How do you know?"

Anna smiled knowingly. "My papa used to tell me that fear is often why people push others away. For there is no worse pain than emotional pain."

Will shook his head slowly, appreciation in his eyes. "Never thought of it that way. Your papa was a wise man."

She looked into Will's eyes. "He would have liked you."

He put his arm out, and she laced her arm through his. "Why is that?"

"Oh, the list is too long." She giggled. "Let's eat."

"Has anyone ever told you that you change the subject a lot?"

"Yep."

Anna gazed at Will as they walked toward his truck, realizing that he had many layers, and she was beginning to peel them back one by one. He was possibly doing the same with her. After the tour and listening to Will share his feelings with her, she was more determined than ever to make the opening of the equine center a grand event. She may need to call in her Missouri reinforcements for help.

CHAPTER 22

Will observed Anna sitting cross-legged on her yoga mat with her eyes closed. He spotted Caden walking toward her cabin and paused to watch their interaction from the side of the porch. From his spot, he could see her teal T-shirt, black yoga pants, and her hair in a ponytail. She was radiant. When Anna opened her eyes and saw Caden, joy shone in her smile "Good morning, Caden," she said.

"Whatcha doin'?"

"Meditation," she replied. "It's a lot of breathing and relaxing. It calms the mind and body."

Caden pondered this for a moment, scrunching up his forehead. "Why do you need to be calm?"

She gave him an understanding look before explaining further. "Well, it helps when I have a busy day at work or your nana gets hurt."

He nodded and looked down, jamming his hands deeper into his pockets.

Anna gestured for him to sit next to her on the yoga mat, which he did, mirroring her in a crossed-legged position. "Are there things that make you feel like you need a break to feel calm?"

After taking a moment to consider this, Caden replied, "When I'm at school, the cafeteria is so loud it drives me crazy."

She nodded and tapped her phone screen a few times. "We can meditate with or without soft music. Which would you like?"

After briefly considering it, he responded with caution, "I think soft music would be nice."

Anna tapped on the screen several times, then set the phone down with a satisfied smile as calm instrumental music began playing. Okay, place your hands in your lap, or you can hold your palms up and form an *O* with your first finger and thumb."

Anna demonstrated how to hold his hands. "Very good. Now close your eyes." She peeked out of one eye, watching him. "Okay, take a deep breath in now. Let it out slowly."

Anna's voice was calm and reassuring as she spoke to Caden. She used simple gestures and expressions to explain why it was essential to take a deep breath when he felt overwhelmed. Caden seemed to understand what to do when he experienced anxiety. Will's heart warmed at the scene. He was amazed at how she connected with the kids almost effortlessly. He hoped that he could learn to communicate with Caden that well.

She opened her eyes. "Did you feel your body relaxing?"

Caden nodded. "It's hard to explain. It's like I feel before I sleep, but I'm not tired." He jumped up and hugged her. "I want to do this again." He ran down the porch stairs and looked back. "Thanks. See you at breakfast." He barreled across the yard, yelling Eva's name.

Anna smiled to herself as she stood up and gathered her yoga mat. Will took a few steps back, and a stick snapped under his heavy boots. Anna jumped, and her hand flew to her chest. "Oh, hey, Will. You almost gave me a heart attack."

"I apologize," he said with a sheepish grin, gazing into her eyes. "Thank you for what you did with Caden. It's been tough for him since Shelly died. I wish I were better at handling difficult situations, like when Momma got hurt. It means a lot that you take the time to be with him."

She squeezed his arm gently. "You'll get there. Stop being so hard on yourself," she said reassuringly.

Will's pulse quickened as their eyes stayed locked in an intimate moment. He cleared his throat, breaking the spell. "I stopped by to see if you'd like to join us for breakfast, but Caden asked you first. The entire family and some friends gather at the Cattle Trail Café almost every week. We can chat about the equine center plans."

Her cheeks blushed. "You want me to go? Do I have time to shower?"

He placed his hand on her cheek. "Yes, I want you to go. And please shower and use that lavender shampoo. You have thirty minutes. Meet you at the truck." Will turned and walked toward his house, anticipating what the day would bring. First breakfast, then a tour of the ranch on horseback. It had been so long since he rode with a . . .

Will turned and said, "Hey, Anna. You've been a blessing to us." Then he bolted across the yard into his house and headed straight for the shower when Eva called for him.

"Daddy!" she yelled from the kitchen.

Will closed his eyes. "Yeah, baby?"

"I need to talk to you."

"I need to get into the shower. Can it wait?" He darted into the bedroom and shut the door.

Eva knocked on the door. "Wait, what is wrong with you? Why are you running into the house?"

He opened the door a crack. "Nothing is wrong."

She narrowed her eyes. "Did you make Anna mad, and she's chasing you?"

"No," he said. "Why would we be fighting?"

She chuckled. "Uh, you have a way of irritating girls," she said, matter-of-factly.

Will opened the door. "You're ten. What do you know?"

She threw her hands up. "I'm irritated now, and I'm a girl." She narrowed her eyes. "Did you at least ask Anna to come to breakfast? Caden said he invited her."

"Yes, I invited her. Would you get irritated if I said I need to shower?" He shut the door before she answered and leaned against it. His eyes drifted to the picture of him and Shelly on the dresser. Toying with his wedding ring, tightness spread across his chest. "What am I doing?" he muttered. Every cell fired in his body, thinking about being close to Anna, but thoughts of Shelly brought on a twinge of guilt. *There's nothing wrong with us being friends.* For now, he just needed to get to breakfast so he could get the center open for Shelly.

Will quickly showered and dressed, putting on his white Stetson as the final piece. When they headed outside, Anna was leaning against the truck, waiting. Eva and Caden sprinted toward her, grasping her around the waist. She laughed as she gathered them into a big hug. Will watched his kids with Anna, his stomach fluttering. Their laughter shined with a brightness that hadn't been seen since their mother died. Seeing them happy again brought him peace.

Caden jumped up and down, clapping, his cheeks flushed in excitement. "I knew you would come with us!" he exclaimed.

"You did?" Anna smiled, gently ruffling the boy's hair.

Eva squealed, "I'm so glad you're coming!" She turned to Will, her eyes wide with anticipation. "Are Nana and Aunt Kati coming with us?"

Will nodded as he opened the truck door for Anna, taking in her appearance. Her ginger waves cascaded down around her shoulders. She wore jean shorts and sandals that showed off her pink painted toenails. He offered her his hand.

She smiled, gazing into his eyes. "Your eyes are beautiful. The shirt you're wearing makes them look pale blue." She leaned in and whispered, "I swear I can see your soul."

Will's throat went dry as he placed his hands on her waist. She glanced at his white Stetson and asked with a sly grin, "How many of those do you have?"

He winked mischievously. "Just a couple. Do you buy that shampoo by the gallon?"

Anna threw back her head and laughed as Eva and Caden shouted in unison for food, begging their father to go before they rebelled against him. The sun sparkled off Anna's fiery red hair as she laughed at the commotion Caden and Eva were creating. With a smirk, Will settled into the driver's seat. He admired her long, slender legs dotted with freckles and the mischievous smile on her face. With one last sly glance toward Anna, he asked if everyone was ready and then drove toward the restaurant where Kati, Jon, Garrett, and Liz were expecting them.

∼

THE CATTLE TRAIL CAFÉ was bustling, the noise rising as more customers filled every table. Will and his family sat at their usual spot in the back. He studied Anna as she took in the hustle and bustle around them. Everyone was engrossed in their conversations, some louder than others. The overlapping voices created a chaotic atmosphere, making it difficult for Will to follow any conversation.

Will's hand brushed against hers. "What are you thinking about?"

She gave him a small smile and looked down. "I'm not used to this big family," she said. "It was always just Nana, Papa, and me. It hurts that they're gone."

As he reached for her hand, he intertwined his fingers with hers, hoping his touch could offer her the same comfort it gave him. Will enjoyed the peaceful and comfortable silence they shared while observing his family. Kati and Jon exchanged playful banter while Garrett and Caden discussed Mario Kart. Liz and Eva were whispering to each other about cookie recipes. Anna's shoulders loosened, and he hoped she felt the same contentment he did.

But when he looked at her, he noticed her eyes were filled with tears. He leaned in closer, hoping to provide some solace, whispering, "Are you sure you're okay?"

Her lower lip quivered, and a single tear slid down her cheek. "Yes," she said, dabbing her eyes with her napkin, "I'm thankful you brought me. You have such an amazing family. You have no idea how much this helps me."

Despite the whirlwind of emotions inside him, Will maintained a stoic facade, his face betraying nothing. A warm smile spread across his face as he affectionately squeezed her hand. It made him happy to know that being here provided her with a sense of comfort.

They ordered food and sipped on coffee—orange juice for the kids—as they waited for the food to arrive.

Liz quieted the group, "Okay, y'all. Let Will tell us what's going on with the opening of the equine center."

Will's head spun with all the information Anna had provided. Taking a deep breath, he tried to steady himself before speaking. He explained the spreadsheet she had painstakingly created and her tour of the property where she'd taken notes on each cabin and the lodge. They'd made an agenda, but panic engulfed him at what needed to be accomplished to open the center.

"Do you want help from the Quiltin' Bees?" Liz asked with an amused twinkle in her eye.

Anna raised an eyebrow and glanced sideways at Will, who couldn't help but smile. "Momma, why don't you tell her about the Quilting Hens . . . I mean, Bees?"

Liz narrowed her eyes. "William Deluca, I'll send Kati to slap you."

Kati threw her arms around Liz in glee. "Oh my God, Momma, it's a dream come true."

Jon jokingly raised his hand and declared he would volunteer for slapping duties.

Eva then jumped up, waving her arms wildly. "Ain't nobody gonna slap my daddy, got it?"

The entire table erupted into laughter as Will ruffled his daughter's hair affectionately and winked at Anna.

Liz cleared her throat to get their attention. "Moving on. Miss Eva, Nana will talk to you later. Anna, the Quiltin' Bees are a group of ladies I grew up with. We've been quilting since our 4H days. My friend, Sissy Hogan, owns Cardinal Creek Quilting on Main Street. We've made quilts for charities and hospitals for years. Sissy said she'd organize the Quiltin' Bees to raise funds." She flashed Will a grin. "So us hens are going to help, drink wine, and share some crazy stories."

Will chuckled and turned to Anna. "Despite their love for wine, they have contributed significantly to the community," he stated. He gave a playful wink to Liz. "Once we have finalized our plans, we can arrange to meet again," he added while shrugging. "That's all for now."

After eating, Anna got up and excused herself to use the bathroom. Garrett offered to show her the way. Will watched them talk, feeling excluded from something significant between them. Garrett possessed qualities that he lacked: confidence, protectiveness, and compassion. Though jealousy started to boil inside him, Will managed to compose himself. They had both assured him that they were not romantically involved.

As they walked toward the bathroom, Anna laughed loudly at something Garrett said before touching his arm. Instinctively, Will's teeth clenched until his jaw hurt. He stood abruptly, desperate for an escape from the table. "I'll pay the bill," he muttered before heading to the counter.

Just as he handed his debit card to the cashier, Jon's arm draped around his shoulders. "Man, I've seen that look on your face twice before," he remarked. Will rolled his eyes and gave a long-suffering sigh, knowing Jon would keep talking no matter what he said. "Yep, I saw it at roping camp with that little redheaded filly and again with Shelly."

A flare of anger shot through him. Why did Jon always mention roping camp when discussing his loves? But even as Will bristled at the reminder, a part of him knew Jon was right. That was why it infuriated him.

"Dude, only two women got under your skin." Jon leaned in close and whispered, "Now three. You better grab her up before Garrett or someone else does."

Jon paid his bill, and then he and Will returned to the table. Jon sauntered up to Anna and flashed a charming grin. "We haven't been formally introduced yet. I'm Jon, Will's good-looking best friend."

Kati rolled her eyes and stepped in front of Jon, but the corners of Anna's mouth twitched in amusement.

She extended her hand toward Jon and replied, "Nice to meet you, officially, Jon."

His face lit up with joy as he requested a hug instead of a handshake. His arms were already outstretched when Will stopped him from going further with a stern look and a firm "Think again."

A giggle escaped Anna's lips as she put her hand to her mouth.

Will tried not to smile, but it was complicated with Jon's antics. "My apologies for my friend here. He was dropped on his head as a child," he said.

As Jon and Will bantered back and forth, Garrett asked amusedly, "Do you all ever stop?" To which the rest of the group answered in unison with a resounding no.

"I'm going to head out. I'll see you Monday, Will," Garrett said. They shook hands, and then Garrett wrapped Anna in a one-armed hug. "Take care, Anna."

She looked up at him, her lips curling into a smile. "Bye, see ya Monday."

Jon whispered into Will's ear, "Dude, she likes Garrett. You're gonna miss out."

Will rolled his eyes and shot back with a quip about bothering his sister, then turned to the rest of the group. "Okay, y'all, we're gonna go." He embraced Liz with his long arms and kissed her on the cheek. "I love you, Momma," he said. She looked at him, concerned but reassured by his confident tone. "Kati, you get Momma home safe."

Kati gave him a quick peck on the cheek. "Always."

Eva and Caden hugged goodbye before Will finally shifted his gaze to Anna. "You ready, darlin'?" His voice was low and tender as he looked at her.

She nodded slightly and said, "Yes."

Will's hand rested on the small of her back, igniting a spark throughout his body when she shivered at his touch. He helped her into the truck and closed the door, releasing a deep sigh. Communication was never his strong suit, even with Shelly. And he wasn't exactly known for being outgoing. He always worried about losing the women he loved because of his communication issues and jealousy. With Anna, he knew he had to keep his jealousy in check or risk pushing her away.

While driving back to the ranch, Will remained silent as Anna stole glances at him. Upon arrival, the kids ran out of the truck while he assisted Anna.

"Thanks for brunch," she said.

He tucked her hair behind her ear and asked, "Will I see you later at the stable?" As he stared at her plump lips, he only wanted to kiss her.

She swallowed nervously and asked if anything was wrong. He leaned in and whispered in her ear, "I'm fine, darlin'." Then he left a gentle trail of kisses from her neck to her ear, causing her to inhale sharply. "Please don't be late," he breathed.

Will walked toward the house with thoughts running through his head —relief that this tiny act could give him so much pleasure and fear that she might reject him later—all swirling in his mind like an eddy in a stream. He looked back, smiling confidently, no trace of insecurity left behind.

CHAPTER 23

Anna returned to the cabin, her legs shaking like a newborn foal. She could still feel the trace of Will's lips on her neck. She had no idea what to make of him—one moment, he was silent and withdrawn, and the next, he seemed so intent on her affections. This sudden shift imposed an unfamiliar tension in the air that Anna could neither comprehend nor control.

An array of conflicting emotions flooded her mind—joy, confusion, excitement—all leading to a realization that she could no longer fight: she was falling for him. But before she yielded to her yearning and desires, she had to remind herself that it couldn't be. After all, he still wore his wedding ring. *He isn't ready to move on just yet. I can't risk being hurt.*

"Nope, not happening, remember?" Anna muttered as she stepped into her cabin. She grabbed her art journal and forced herself to focus on something else until it was time for the evening chores. But she couldn't stop daydreaming about Will, his strong arms wrapped around her waist and his lips pressed against hers. *No!* Her mind yelled. She stood abruptly and went to her room to change into jeans and a T-shirt before heading to the stable.

As she worked on mucking the stalls, she heard Will enter the barn, and her heart leaped into her throat.

Will smiled as he leaned over the box. "Garrett said you would beat me here and already have most of this done."

She continued working without saying anything, desperately trying to control her emotions. Will watched her for a minute before saying, "Well, thanks again for stepping in and helping."

Anna curtly replied, "Honestly, you don't have to keep thanking me." *Why am I so on edge?* He walked away but quickly made an about-face, prompting Anna's heart to jolt again. Their eyes met, and a wave of nerves coursed through her body.

He took a deep breath. "I . . . I noticed you and Garrett . . . You uh seem to..." He swallowed hard, causing his Adam's apple to bob up and down as his eyes filled with pain and anxiety.

Anna's face burned with anger as she processed what Will had just said. She couldn't believe it. Was it jealousy? She tossed the pitchfork on the floor and walked around him toward the entrance. "Are you kidding me? I thought Garrett and I were clear that we're just friends." She spun around to face him. "What made you think that this time?" Her voice quivered despite her attempt to convey strength.

He cleared his throat. "No, Anna, that's not what I'm asking." He took a deep breath.

"You laugh with him and seem relaxed when you talk to him."

The room fell into a heavy silence as Anna struggled to hold back the tears of anger that threatened to spill. She angrily threw her hands up and yelled, "That's enough! I don't want to hear anymore!" With a loud growl, she stormed out of the stable.

But Will was right behind her, reaching out to touch her shoulder and pleading with her in a hushed tone, "darlin', please let me explain."

Anna pushed him away and marched back into the barn to finish her chores. Then she headed to Thunderbird's stall and began saddling him for a ride.

Will leaned against the stall door, his chest rising and falling with each ragged breath. "Anna," he said, his voice low and strained. She continued to work, her hands moving quickly and expertly but not quick enough to avoid his gaze. He took a step closer, and Thunderbird snorted softly in response.

Will scratched the horse's neck, trying to break the tension. "I know sometimes I say stupid things," he muttered, his face mere inches from hers.

Anna looked away. Scarlet heat warmed her cheeks. His hot breath trailed down her neck, and for a moment, their labored breathing was the only sound.

Anna broke the silence. "Are you going to saddle up, or am I riding alone?"

They stood, toe-to-toe, in a pregnant silence until Will reached over and tucked a strand of hair behind Anna's ear. "I'm truly sorry, darlin'," he whispered.

Anna lightly jabbed him in the chest with her finger and said, "Don't do that." Anger stirred in her gut before she turned away abruptly. "Let's ride," she said.

"Come on, boy, I've made a mess of things," Will said, with defeat in his voice.

Jake let out a snort, pushing Will's arm with his nose. He led Jake out of the stable where Anna was waiting with the gate open and Thunderbird's lead rope in hand. Then, they hopped onto their horses and began their journey through the countryside.

The bluebonnets and other wildflowers spanned the landscape in a breathtaking array of blues, yellows, and pinks. The flowers swayed gracefully in the gentle breeze, almost as if they were dancing in the sunlight. Meanwhile, butterflies and bees buzzed around from flower to flower, gathering pollen as the sweet melodies of birds filled the air. Anna was utterly captivated by the stunning scenery around her. She soaked up the serenity of the world as she rode in silence. Every few seconds, she caught Will looking at her from under his Stetson hat; she could tell he wanted to apologize further but knew better than to try. So, instead, they rode in silence as they headed deeper into the wildflower meadows.

Anna's grin widened as she gave Thunderbird a gentle squeeze with her legs and set off at a trot, then a gallop. The wind whipped through her hair, boosting her spirits. Before long, she turned to give Will a devilish smirk before resuming her journey. He trailed behind for a while before passing her and gesturing toward a hilltop. When they arrived, Will dismounted, pulled out a blanket from his saddlebag, and headed off to find the perfect spot that offered them a bird's-eye view of the ranch. Will spread out the blanket and motioned for Anna to sit. Though part of her wished for conversation, she stayed silent, mulling over their heated exchange. *Did he think so little of her?*

Will finally broke the silence. "Are you going to say anything?"

Anna took a deep breath and looked straight ahead. "I do like Garrett, but not how you think. He's been through a lot. He helped me move in when I first got here. He's a good man." She looked at him, and anger began to rise within. "Besides, I don't need anyone's permission to talk to someone, so don't ever—"

Will held up his hand, stopping her. "Anna, I'm not jealous. It's that you seem more at ease when you talk to Garrett than when you talk to me . . ." He looked down and whispered, "Am I hard to talk to? You seem more relaxed with him."

She placed her hand on his, and electricity ran through her. A pang of guilt hit her for jumping to conclusions. "I should've let you talk. I interrupted you. I'm sorry. I was slightly irritated since breakfast, but that's no excuse for my reaction."

"Why did you feel irritated? Did I say something, or was it the kiss? I'm sorry if it was too forward."

She cleared her throat and hesitated before speaking. "Honestly, I don't know. To be truthful, I miss my grandfather, and the pain hits me at the weirdest times."

He gave her hand a gentle squeeze as he nodded in understanding. "darlin', I get that. It still happens to me with my dad and Shelly." His voice softened. "So, will you ever tell me why you came to Cardinal Creek, of all places? A fresh start is one thing, but as much as I love this town, there isn't much here. Seems like you would pick someplace bigger to start over."

She smiled, remembering the past that had brought her to this small town. "I came here right before my junior year in high school with my grandparents. Nana and Papa wanted me to go to barrel racing camp, but I wouldn't go unless they came with me because . . . well, the last time I went to camp without . . ." Tears were stinging her eyes as memories from that time threatened to overwhelm her. "A car accident killed my parents while I was away at camp the first time. So Nana and Papa had come with me a few years later."

She looked down, playing with a blade of grass. "That's when I met a girl around my age with long dark hair. And her brother, a wrangler with icy-blue eyes. We got along great until he got jealous of another wrangler helping me get on a horse. We had a big argument, and I left without saying goodbye. It's something I've regretted for years."

She toyed with his wedding ring without looking at him. "It was stupid, but I wanted to start over when I came here. My papa had written me a letter and thought it would be good for me." Anna's cheeks flushed when she finally looked at Will's gaze, searching for something familiar in his expression. His hand settled gently around hers, sending a warm rush through her body despite her nerves.

"Are you okay," he asked, and she nodded. "What was the sister's name?"

"I don't remember. Why?"

Will hesitated. "Did the wrangler have a friend? What was the wrangler's name?" His voice shook slightly, and Anna could see the anticipation in his blue eyes.

"I didn't know his real name," she confessed.

Will's eyes were wild as he searched for the words he wanted to say. "I was a wrangler at a camp for a couple of summers. One summer, Kati and I met a girl. I didn't know her real name because Jon and I gave her a nickname."

Suddenly, it felt like someone had sucked the air from Anna's lungs. Could it be him? The cowboy? The wrangler from camp all those years ago? She remembered that summer at the camp. The memory of him ran deep, and she hadn't been able to shake it since. Thoughts of Cowboy had been a constant companion, even after all these years.

Her stomach was in knots, butterflies fluttering around inside. She wanted to tell Will how much he meant to her, but the fear of rejection still lingered like an old wound, refusing to heal. "What was the nickname?" she asked.

Their gazes locked. "Ginger."

The words echoed in Anna's chest with a rhythm of their own. Her heart pounded against her rib cage. "Cowboy?" she said, instinctively reaching out toward his face. He released a slow breath before saying yes, confirming what she already knew.

She ran her finger down his jawline and looked away, embarrassment washing over her face in a heat wave. She looked at him again, unable to speak what was on her mind. "We had a crush, didn't we?" The question hung between them like a ghost from their past. She suddenly felt sixteen years old again, as if no time had passed since that summer.

"Why did you leave without saying goodbye? I couldn't get you off my mind for months."

She rolled her eyes. "We were young. Nana told me to talk to you, but I was stubborn."

He laughed. "You're right about us being young, but you drove me wild. I didn't know how to find you." He took her by the chin and turned her to him. "Is it too late to tell you I'm sorry?"

She smiled. "No, and you aren't hard to talk to. And the jealousy thing is still the same. I didn't like that wrangler. I don't even remember his name."

"The wrangler was Jon." He let out a long breath. "Jon has always had a way with women. I was so awkward, tall, and skinny. I guess I just thought you liked him."

"Jon at the restaurant?"

"The very same."

She ran her finger down his chiseled jawline. "Do you ever look in the mirror?" She looked down, her face flushed, and murmured, "I guess you see yourself differently."

Will traced his finger along her face, lifting her chin until their eyes met. His penetrating gaze probed her face. He leaned in, placing a gentle kiss on her lips. The fireworks tingled throughout her body like an electric current. The memory of their only kiss came flooding back. Will placed his hand on the back of her neck, pulling her closer as their grip became more intense and passionate, both wanting more from the moment that seemed to stand still. When they finally pulled away, their eyes locked intensely, both forgetting how to breathe.

"I came to look for you the morning after we argued, but you were gone. My feelings for you were strong; I had never felt anything like it. It was like our souls were connected," he said, trailing off, embarrassed by his confession.

She entwined her fingers with his. "I felt the same. At first, I tried to date some guys, but no one made me feel like you did." She shook her head ruefully. "Next thing I knew, I was a thirty-something-year-old virgin because life kept moving. And then I met Tony." She chuckled. "Let's just say it didn't end well."

Will moved closer, his lips inches away from hers. His hand snaked around her neck to pull her in, and he nuzzled her nose with his before pressing their mouths together. His tongue explored her mouth with wet, passionate strokes that set off sparks of desire throughout her body, just like the summer they met all those years ago. She opened herself entirely to him, and when the kiss ended, she kept her eyes closed, savoring the feeling she had longed for since the day she left.

"darlin', open your eyes." His breathing labored.

She kept her eyes closed. "Connected, very connected."

He laughed while he trailed kisses down her neck. "Yes, darlin'."

"Will?"

"Hmm."

"After I left, how did you end up with Shelly."

He let out a groan. "Not now, darlin'."

"Please tell me how you ended up together." Anna knew now might not be the best time to ask, but Shelly had been an essential part of Will's life. And he needed to talk about her. He needed to open up, and Anna wanted to know about her.

Will traced her lips with his fingers, then gently kissed her neck and whispered, "Shelly was Kati's best friend. They always hung out with me and Jon."

The breeze blew through their hair as he lay back on the blanket and continued his story, detailing how they started spending time together during Christmas break and eventually fell in love.

"I'm sorry, Anna. I didn't know your real name," he said.

She smiled. "We were kids, Will. It's okay."

Will ran his calloused fingers through Anna's hair, and she felt comforted by the gesture. He stood up and offered his hand to help her up. He pulled her close, engulfing her in the musky scent of his cologne. Her hands grasped the fabric of his shirt at the back as he tenderly cradled her head in one hand.

Breathless, he pulled away. "We should head back before things go too far."

Anna nodded in agreement but did not want the moment to end. She closed her eyes and savored the security within his embrace.

"Ginger, your kisses still affect me the same way," he said. She smiled contentedly and wrapped her arms around his waist.

They mounted their horses and held hands as they rode back to the ranch in silence, yet it was loud with the unspoken connection between them that Anna knew could never be broken.

CHAPTER 24

Under the clear sky, Will, Jon, and Garrett rode out to tend to the cattle and inspect fences. The sun's rays beamed through the clouds and danced across their backs. Will couldn't stop thinking about his kiss with Anna. Despite being drawn to her, fear held him back from fully opening up about his life with Shelly.

Will glanced at Jon as they rode and asked, "Do you remember that summer when Kati did the barrel racing clinic?"

"I do. Wasn't there a girl involved?"

Will rolled his eyes. "Jon, come on, you always bring it up."

Jon's lips curved into a smile. "Ah, yes, the redheaded filly we used to tease and call Ginger. That girl gave us a run for our money. I remembered how mad she was with you on the last day, and she left without saying goodbye." Jon shook his head and chuckled. "That Ginger was certainly fiery."

Will smiled, nodding. "Yes, her. You won't believe this, but Anna and I rode a few days ago. And . . . well . . . it turns out that Anna is Ginger!"

Garrett brought his horse to an abrupt stop. "Y'all want to let an outsider in? Do you know Anna?"

Jon chuckled at Garrett's bewilderment and piped up before Will could reply, "Well, this guy here met Ginger the summer before our senior year and fell in love at first sight. It was before Will and Shelly started dating."

Will narrowed his eyes at Jon but knew he was right; he had indeed liked Ginger fiercely when she came to visit for the horse clinic that summer.

"Come on, guys, back to the story," Garrett said.

Will's voice wavered. "We had a terrible fight because I accused her of flirting with another wrangler. It was stupid, I know, but my jealousy got the best of me. So, Anna left without a word, and I had no idea how to find her. I was hurt and angry when she left, but I blamed myself for pushing her away."

Jon shook his head, a knowing smile on his lips. "So, I take it this Anna is the one who's given you that faraway look, then?"

Will furrowed his brow in confusion. "What are you talking about?"

Jon reined his horse and turned toward him. "The stars in your eyes, buddy. Do you like her?"

Will paused for a moment as he thought about Jon's question. "I'm conflicted. She's been through so much with her grandparents dying and her boyfriend cheating on her. I don't want to lead her on and make things worse for her, but there's something between us—some connection to loss I don't have with anyone else. It just feels right."

Jon rolled his eyes and threw his hands up. "Dude, just take it slow, all right? Don't rush into anything before you're ready, or things could end badly for both of you."

Will shifted in his saddle, nudging Jake forward as they rode along the fence line, allowing himself time to ponder his conflicting emotions. He wanted Anna, but at the same time, he feared letting go of Shelly. Was he afraid to open his heart so he wouldn't get hurt or rejected? Even if he was willing to risk getting hurt again, he wasn't sure he was ready yet.

The memory of their kiss washed over him like a wave, filling him with warmth, and he smiled at the thought of it. Anna had been helping Will without complaint since she arrived, and the kids adored her. Will knew what he was going to do. There was no denying the feelings growing between them. *I need to take things slow.*

When they reached the stable, Garrett clapped Will on the back and said, "Hey, take a shower and go see her." Will gave him a questioning look, and Garrett continued, "Look, I know she's helping you open the equine center. Tell her if it isn't the right time to date anyone. I don't want her to get hurt."

Will nodded and rushed toward Liz's house to ensure the kids had somewhere to stay that night. He sat at the kitchen table and removed his hat, revealing unruly, sweat-drenched hair. Kati stared at him intently. He smirked and said, "What?"

Kati smiled. "There's something different about you."

Will rolled his eyes, knowing what she was thinking without her having to say it aloud. "I'm dirty and stink," he said.

She smiled and shook her head. "No, you look . . . I don't know . . . happier, and you stink."

"Anna and I went on a ride yesterday, and we started talking . . . She's Ginger."

Kati's eyes grew wide. "What? Ginger from camp? Ginger from long ago? The Ginger you whined about for months?"

Will nodded. "I figured it out a while ago, but it was too ridiculous and seemed so unlikely. But it's her."

"Don't mess it up this time, Cowboy," Kati said.

Will raised his eyebrow. "I'll try not to."

Kati playfully popped him with a towel before shooing him away. "Now get out of here. And take a shower. You stink!"

THE AIR WAS STILL warm as the sun slowly dipped below the horizon. Will hurried toward Anna's cabin. His heart thumped with anticipation, and he bounded up the stairs two at a time until he reached her door. Taking one more shaky breath, Will knocked softly.

Anna opened the door. Her crimson hair cascaded around her shoulders, bringing out the green in her eyes like glimmering emeralds. Her navy dress clung to her curves, its hemline teasingly resting just above her knees. She took his breath away.

"You look amazing."

A wide smile spread across her face as she replied, "So do you."

He couldn't help but stare at her beauty for a moment longer before giving her a subtle wink and asking her if he could come in.

She snapped back to reality. "Yes, where are my manners? Please come in."

As he crossed the room, Will nervously rubbed his sweaty palms on his jeans, then took off his Stetson and placed it on the table next to the couch before taking a seat. Heat flooded his body, and he hoped Anna couldn't tell how anxious he was.

"You want a beer or some wine?" she asked.

"You bought beer?"

"You mentioned you liked it." She headed for the kitchen.

He smiled. "I'll take a beer unless you have any of that Missouri wine left."

Turning to look at him with hands on her hips, she said, "You like that wine, don't you?"

"I do; it's sweet like you."

Anna laughed. "Flattery will get you everywhere, Cowboy," she said as she poured two glasses of wine.

Will forced himself to relax. "So, we'll start with some wine, then get to work?"

"Sounds like a plan."

He couldn't take his gaze away from her body as she swayed across the room with two glasses of sweet pink wine. Her every movement caused his body to tingle from head to toe. How her dress clung to her curves and exposed her cleavage only increased the intensity of his thoughts. She handed him a glass of wine and sat beside him on the couch.

As Anna reached for a spreadsheet on the coffee table, Will's neck flushed with desire as he inhaled the familiar fragrance of her shampoo. When their hands brushed against each other, he released a deep breath. He appreciated the distraction as she handed him some papers. *Pull yourself together.* He scolded himself. *She's trying to help you.*

"I wanted to show you what I've been working on," Anna said as she sat back with her laptop. Will tried to focus on the screen, but the desire to kiss her consumed his mind.

"This is what we need to do to form the nonprofit," Anna said. "I updated the timeline, so all we need to do is start checking off tasks as we do them."

He studied each line of her lips and had to restrain himself from leaning in right then and there. The scent of lavender shampoo filled his nose with something sweet that tickled his senses. He forgot about the business plan while she discussed the different grants and timelines she had researched.

Will tentatively tucked a strand of hair behind her ear, his fingers lingering slightly longer than necessary on her warm skin. "Anna," he said, his voice thick. "I've been thinking about you since our kiss." His gaze lowered to her lips as he leaned in and captured her in a passionate embrace. Giving in to his desire, he deepened their kiss eagerly, warmth flooding through his veins.

He pulled away, then murmured in her ear as he kissed her neck, "I need to kiss you again and again."

Will closed his eyes as he felt Anna's lips on his. Her hand slid down his back, sending sparks of pleasure throughout his body. His hands moved along her sides, feeling the warmth of her skin. Every inch of Will yearned for her. At this moment, all the pain from Shelly's death seemed to be gone.

Out of nowhere, Shelly's face appeared before him. It was the same expression she had the morning they made love before she died. The warmth of Anna's lips against his no longer comforted him because it felt like he was cheating on Shelly's memory. He quickly pulled away. His body shook as tears ran freely down his face, begging for release from the pain consuming him.

Will tried to push away the guilt, knowing he deserved a second chance at happiness, yet it lay just beyond his reach. He glanced in her direction as he felt Anna's fingers curled around his hand. Her eyes were filled with understanding and compassion, but what else?

Anna pulled him into an embrace and kissed away his tears. He relaxed into her arms as she whispered, "It's okay, Cowboy." Will's breathing slowed as he tried to calm himself; it was as if Anna were slowly breathing life back into him.

Trembling, Will choked out, "I'm sorry, Anna."

Anna pulled him close as she knew of his inner struggle. She whispered reassuring words and wrapped her arms around him like a warm blanket. It was like home. He could heal and open up again with Anna's gentle words. He knew that no matter what happened between them, it would be okay for him to move forward.

Anna kissed his lips gently. "You want a refill?" she asked.

Will forced a smile and nodded as he handed her his glass. She refilled the glasses, and he laid his head on the couch and closed his eyes. *It's time to open my heart.*

"Will?"

"Hmm?"

"Your glass of wine."

He sat up, looking at her. "Thanks, I . . . uh . . ."

She pressed her fingers to his lips. "Shh, there's nothing to say." She took a sip of her wine, then sat down on the couch next to him. The silence seemed to grow louder.

He nervously twisted his wedding band. "I have spent the better portion of the time since Shelly died running from my grief. There are times I don't know what I feel," he said. "To be honest, betraying Shelly is an excuse because I'm unsure how to move on. I've been stuck here for so long. Being miserable is my new normal."

Anna silently poured herself another glass of wine, avoiding Will's gaze. He wrapped his arms around her waist. She turned to him and smiled. "Dance with me, Cowboy."

His blue eyes met hers with compassion and understanding. "Lead the way."

She turned on a familiar song that played softly in the background. "If I remember correctly, we danced to this song the summer we met. I've only listened to it at least a million times since then."

They swayed to the music of George Strait's song "Carrying Your Love with Me."

Anna rested her head against his chest, "I thought about you often over the years. I started dating Tony, but he wasn't you. I guess he knew that. I guess that's why he started sleeping with Emma." She smiled. "It seems silly, but I guess I held onto some childish fantasy that we would meet again."

He stopped swaying abruptly and tipped her chin up so she was looking at him. "darlin', it wasn't childish. I didn't know how to find you. Shelly and I had been friends for so long. She listened to me talk about you endlessly for months. We started dating and fell in love . . . life kept moving until . . . But now you're here, and . . . I don't want to break your heart."

She touched his cheek. "I'm not going anywhere unless you tell me to go. I love kissing you and want all of you. We have time for that."

"We do have as much time as we need." He leaned down and whispered, "You have no idea how much I want you."

Her mouth curved into a smile. "I believe I do."

Will's face flushed.

"William Deluca, are you blushing?"

The song stopped. He pulled her into his arms. "Let's try that dance again."

Anna started the song again and snuggled closer to Will's chest. "I could stay here forever, in your arms, listening to this song.

As the song ended, Will kissed her with a growing passion. He lifted her from the ground and carried her toward the couch, where she clung to him with even more heat. Will moaned into her ear, "We need to stop, darlin'. I want to take you on a proper date."

Anna continued kissing his neck, driving him wild.

"Do you want to go on a date with me?" he asked in a husky voice.

"Of course," Anna replied, caressing his face.

Will's hands wandered up her back, toying with the spaghetti straps of her dress before he reluctantly pulled away. "We could double date with Jon and Kati," he said almost to himself.

Anna raised an eyebrow in surprise. "They're a couple?"

Will threw his head back and laughed. "He wishes. He's been trying since his major screwup. He's like a brother, but sometimes he only thinks with one brain."

Anna grabbed the front of his shirt, kissing and tracing his lips with her tongue. Undoubtedly, he wanted Anna, but he wanted to do things right. She deserved that. He let out a low groan and pulled away again. "Darlin', we need to stop. It's been a long time for me. I'm losing restraint."

She ran her finger along his face and then gently kissed his forehead. "That's my sweet Cowboy," she said.

Will pulled her close to his chest, desperate for more contact. "I want to know everything about you," he said with desire.

Anna looked into his eyes and smiled. "We have time for all of it, Cowboy."

He tenderly kissed her forehead and steeled himself to face the unknown waters ahead as he began his journey with Anna, praying not to drown.

∽

JON AND KATI were huddled around a glowing fire pit, leaving the night air filled with the scent of burning wood. The bottle of wine in Jon's hand glinted in the orange light, and soft laughter drifted from their conversation.

When they spotted Will, a mischievous smile spread across Jon's face. "Oh, Cowboy, how was your evening with Ginger?" he yelled. Kati shot him an exasperated look and jabbed her elbow into his ribs.

Will rolled his eyes. "Good God, you could wake the dead. Be quiet."

Kati looked at Jon curiously as he filled another glass of wine. "We were just discussing how much Anna fits in here—or should I say, Ginger," Jon said.

Without hesitating, Will said, "Jon, I think you should ask Kati out."

Kati choked on her drink as she sputtered, "What the fu . . . Will!"

He raised his hands in mock surrender. "You two are always trying to set me up with women from here to San Antonio, so I finally asked someone on a date and . . ." Will trailed off as Kati leaped from her chair, spilling some wine.

"Yes! I'll go out with Jon!" She ran over and gave Will an unexpected hug. "You asked Anna out?"

He grinned sheepishly. "I did, and I need my personal dating committee to come along," he said, chuckling.

Jon pushed his hat back and snorted with laughter. "Afraid you're gonna mess things up, bro? Need help with your game?"

Will spun around, pointing at Jon. "Since you've been drinking, your ass better be at my house."

Jon snickered. "Yes, Dad." As laughter faded behind him, Will shook his head before entering his house.

He grabbed a beer from the fridge and mindlessly flipped through channels as his thoughts drifted to Shelly. Was he using her as an excuse to avoid getting close? He'd done it before—first with Ginger, then later with Shelly after marriage. Why did he feel so unworthy of starting something with Anna? The door slammed, bringing Will back to reality.

Jon stormed into the living room, his jaw firmly set. He plopped down in a chair and crossed his arms. "Your sister drives me crazy," he muttered.

Will snorted. "You need to cut back on the drinking and stop boasting about your conquests from here to San Antonio."

Jon rolled his eyes. "I never cheated on her, Will. You know that, but am I supposed to be a monk since we broke up?"

Will held up a hand. "I know you didn't, but you led her to believe you did, and I don't need to hear about the other things. If she takes you back, consider getting tested for a few million things first."

"I always use protection," Jon grumbled. "No kids for me. I think I would be a horrible dad."

Will burst out laughing. "No kidding! But if you love Kati so much, why have you been with other people?"

Jon slumped further into the chair. "She dumped me, and I was angry and wanted to get back at her somehow," he admitted. A long pause followed before Jon finally spoke again. "It felt wrong, like I was cheating on her. If I could turn back time, I'd change many things."

Will nodded solemnly in agreement. "Me too."

"How did it go with Anna tonight?"

Jon's inquiry hung in the air between them. Will shivered as he thought of the intensity of their kiss and how it felt to hold her in his arms as they danced. He touched the gold band on his ring finger, feeling a sudden pang of guilt for enjoying himself when Shelly was no longer here.

"Every time we kiss, it's like the fireworks in town on the Fourth of July. It was so intense I couldn't take it."

Jon leaned forward. "You thought of Shelly, didn't you?"

"Yup, but not just that. It's more about me thinking I don't deserve to be happy. Am I good enough? Same old stuff." He toyed with his wedding ring, knowing it was time to start taking steps to heal from losing Shelly, as well as his dad.

"What are you going to do about that?" Jon asked.

Will squared his shoulders. "I'm going to start tearing down the walls I have built around me and have faith there's a greater plan here." He sighed heavily. "But Anna . . . God, I can't explain it. She has been working nonstop on the plans for the equine center. It touches my heart that she cares about getting the equine center open, about the kids, and that she's helped without any complaints since the first day she got here."

Jon raised an eyebrow in amusement. "I remember her yelling at you that summer. I don't recall why."

Will smiled wryly at the remembrance of Anna's fiery temper, appreciating how different she was from Shelly in some ways yet very much alike in others. "Do you want to know why?"

Jon nodded.

"I saw you and Anna in the stable talking while she was brushing her horse." Embarrassment pricked at his skin. "I approached her after you left and accused her of liking you instead of me. I did the same thing with her and Garrett too."

Jon furrowed his brows in disbelief. "You're joking, right?"

Will hung his head low. "No." Anxiety coursed through him as he waited for Jon's reaction.

An expression of disbelief and hurt washed over Jon's face. He rubbed his temples. "I don't know what to say. You honestly thought I would steal your girl?" he asked, pain written in his eyes.

He stood and headed for the kitchen, and a few moments later, he returned with two bottles of beer. He handed one to Will. "We need to discuss this . . . actually, no we don't. If I had known you had thought so little of me, we would have never been friends."

Will's mouth dropped open, shock washing over him. "No, Jon, it's not like that. Girls always flocked to you because you were so outgoing, and I was lanky and skinny compared to you. It had nothing to do with you. It was all about my insecurities."

Jon sat in the chair and took a long draw from his beer. "Listen, I didn't know you had so many insecurities. Not when your family seemed practically perfect compared to mine. Your dad was always the best role model around here, and Momma D is three times the woman my mother ever could be. You are like a brother to me. I would never move in like that . . . not then and not now." Jon chugged his beer and shook his head. "It all makes sense to me now." He set the bottle down on the coffee table. His face softened as he said, "A lot makes sense now . . . Shelly . . . I get it now."

Will looked at him in confusion. "What do you mean?"

Jon groaned. "Not now, man. I'm gonna sleep in Caden's bed so you can have the couch. This conversation needs sobering up first." He gave him a weak smile before heading for the bedroom.

Will watched him go with a heavy heart. He slumped on the couch, staring at the ceiling as realization dawned on him. He was hurting people with all his insecurities and self-doubt. This was a significant problem that had caused harm to those closest to him before Shelly died. He knew he needed to address this before he caused any more pain.

CHAPTER 25

A rush of excitement coursed through Anna when she received a text from Will inviting her to join him for lunch. The soul-cleansing cry from this morning had helped erase the dark cloud from her day, and she was looking forward to spending time with him. She hummed a tune as she carefully applied her pink lipstick and paused to admire her reflection. The extra time she took to get ready this morning wasn't just to boost her mood; she also wanted to look her best for Will. Now, all she had to do was wait.

Anna's fingers flew over her keyboard as she busied herself with morning meetings, setting up interviews, and working on a budget for the department. But all that was forgotten when she heard the knock on her office door just before noon. She opened it to see Will looking as handsome as ever. His eyes scanned her from head to toe with admiration. "You look beautiful, darlin'."

Warmth spread through her body like wildfire. "Thank you." She cleared her throat, nervous energy crackling between them like static electricity. "Come on in." So many emotions coursed through her at once that it felt like her mind was going to overload.

He leaned in and whispered, "Would it be inappropriate for me to kiss your cheek?"

She closed the door. "I think it should be fine. A hug could be included."

He slid his arm behind her back, pulling her close; strong emotion shimmered in his eyes. "I love this color on you. It makes your eyes look exotic." He placed a light kiss on her cheek.

Anna bit her lip. "Thank you."

He kissed her neck, causing her to giggle. "We should go eat."

"I agree. You went beyond a kiss on the cheek."

He grabbed her hand. "I know, totally out of my character. I'm sorry."

"I'm not complaining. We were in my office with the door closed," Anna said as they headed out.

As they strolled toward the cafeteria, Anna and Will chatted about their upcoming double date with Kati and Jon and reminisced about when they danced together as teenagers. Anna couldn't help but smile at the memory, and when Will asked her why she was smiling, she winked back at him. But as soon as they entered the cafeteria, she felt the color drain from her face when she spotted Dr. Watts sitting in one of the booths. The mere sight of him made Anna panic, and her morning efforts to keep her emotions in check came crashing down.

She grabbed Will's hand tightly and quickly pointed them toward the deli counter, away from Dr. Watts' line of vision. After they got their food, Anna slid into a booth, keeping her eyes downcast.

"Darlin', are you feeling okay? You're pale."

She nodded. "I'm fine."

From the corner of her eye, Anna saw Dr. Watts walking past their table, his eyes fixated on her. Then he spun around and strode toward them. "Good afternoon, Ms. Samuels and Mr. Deluca," he said, his voice deep and commanding.

Anna dropped her gaze to her sandwich, and Will politely greeted him, "Hey, Dr. Watts."

"How's your momma doin'?" he asked.

"Getting better every day," Will replied with a smile.

Dr. Watts touched Anna's shoulder and squeezed gently before saying goodbye. His touch sent icy shards through her veins.

. . .

Anna's whole face burned as she nibbled at her sandwich. She could practically feel Will's eyes boring a hole in her forehead.

"Darlin'?" he asked. "What's wrong?"

Today, she was just a jumble of emotions. Everything seemed out of control for some reason. Maybe she just needed to go riding. She remembered that grief seemed to come in waves. Today must be a wave.

"A headache suddenly came on when we came into the cafeteria. I'll take something when I get back to the office."

Will raised an eyebrow. "You want to go now?"

She nodded. Will put his hand on her shoulder after he dumped the trash, causing her to jump. He took her hand, helping her out of the booth.

"Are you sure you feel okay? You're trembling." He placed his hand on her forehead. "Are you feeling ill? You still look pale."

"I'm fine." She pasted on a smile.

When they arrived at her office, Will's eyes seemed to search Anna's face for something, and his brow creased further when he didn't find it. She placed her hand on his neck, kissing him on the cheek.

Will whispered in her ear, "I'll see you tonight."

Anna's muscles relaxed at the first touch of his breath on her neck. As soon as the elevator doors closed behind him, she turned to unlock her office door when she saw Dr. Watts walking down the hall, a smug smirk on his lips. Her breath caught in her throat at the sight of him, and she quickly entered her office, locking the door behind her and leaning against it for support.

Anna attempted to forget the encounter with Dr. Watts as she threw herself into her work, interviewing nurses passionate about caring for chronically ill patients and preparing her grant proposal for caregiver support groups. By four thirty, she had finished work for the day and gathered up her things, ready to go home and see Will. Her heart sank as she descended the stairs to the ground floor and Dr. Watts stepped onto a landing between floors. She froze, unable to move. Nobody was around, and there was nowhere else for her to go.

"Hello, Anna."

She nodded as she attempted to keep moving down the stairs. "Dr. Watts."

He stepped in front of her. "Seth, call me Seth."

She walked around him. "Okay, Seth, have a good evening. I'm sorry, I need to run."

He touched her arm as she tried to get past him. "How do you know Mr. Deluca?"

"He's my boyfriend," she snapped.

Dr. Watts's brows creased. "You have a boyfriend?"

"Yes." She wasn't sure what else to say. "Uh, we live together." *Why did I lie to him?* She attempted to step around him again, but he blocked her way.

He ran the pad of his thumb in a slow circle along her jawline. His finger lingered on her chin before he tucked a wayward strand of hair back into place behind her ear. His voice softened as he spoke. "If you ever decide you want a real . . ." His words hung in the air momentarily before he cleared his throat. "Good night," he said, his voice barely above a whisper as he slowly ascended the stairs.

As Anna watched him walk up the stairs, her feet were rooted to the spot, her body shaking. With a sudden surge of adrenaline, she bolted down the steps and dashed across the parking lot toward her car, barely avoiding colliding with other vehicles. She fumbled with the key fob as tears streamed down her face, and when she finally managed to unlock the doors, she scrambled into the driver's seat and locked the doors, breathing heavily.

Tears clouded her vision as she drove home. She sobbed, barely able to see. Her hands trembled, her heart raced, and her mind spun. When she got to the ranch, she parked, racing out of her SUV into the cabin, hoping no one saw her. Fear and anger coursed through Anna as tears streamed down her cheeks. She locked the front door behind her and slid to the floor, hugging her legs close to her body. What was Dr. Watts' game? And was he following her? Anna couldn't escape his presence. She hunched down even further, shrinking into herself. Dr. Watts's wife was *the* director of nursing, and she was Anna's boss. Who else could she turn to for help? Would anyone even believe her if she spoke up? Even Will had seemed to buy the doctor's act and brilliant smile in the cafeteria.

Anna got up and stalked across the cabin to the bathroom, stripping off her clothes on the way to the shower. She needed to wash the feelings of the day down the drain. The mere thought of Dr. Watts's hands on her made her stomach churn, and she desperately wanted to scrub it away.

After dressing, she lay on her bed, wondering how she would handle him. She couldn't tell Will or Kati. It would be her fault if she went to the director of nursing. After all, she was his wife. Last year, a nurse in the hospital where she worked reported a doctor. She ended up getting fired. She couldn't take that kind of humiliation after all she had been through this year.

There was a knock on the door, shaking Anna from her thoughts. She walked over and opened it.

Will stood in the doorway, his build imposing, and arms crossed. His voice was deep and gentle as he said, "Darlin', I can tell something's wrong. What is it? Let me help you."

Anna's chest tightened at his offer. If only she could accept that tenderness right now. She shook her head and raised her hands defensively in front of her. "Will, it's nothing. Just leave me alone." She slammed the door harder than she intended and leaned against it.

"Anna," Will called from the other side of the door, "I'm getting us some dinner. If you don't let me in when I return, I'll kick down the door."

She scoffed in disbelief. "You wouldn't dare!"

He chuckled without humor. "Try me." His boots clattered down the stairs as he left.

Anna stayed put against the door, contemplating how to escape this mess.

CHAPTER 26

Will drove to Brick Oven Pizza, a small mom-and-pop pizzeria, the same one he'd been going to since he was a kid. He ordered his usual pizza with provolone cheese instead of mozzarella, hoping it would put a smile on Anna's face and help break her out of whatever sad mood she was in today.

"Hey, Will." George, the owner, greeted him from behind the counter.

"How are you? Is the pizza ready?"

"I'm good. Give me ten minutes. Want a beer?"

"No, I'm driving. Thanks though."

"How's your momma's leg doin'?" George asked.

"It's getting better."

Will sat while he waited and tried to make sense of his conversations with Anna. She had obviously been crying, but he had no idea why, and she'd completely shut him out when he asked about it. It was the second time he'd seen her in tears today, yet she kept him at a distance. He had confided in her about his pain; did she not trust him to share hers?

After a time, George called Will and handed him the takeout box, asking him to give his regards to Liz. Will paid for it and thanked George before exiting the store. Driving home, he held on to the slim hope that Anna would open up to him when he arrived. He parked the truck and grabbed the takeout before heading inside. As he knocked softly on her door, he wondered if she would ever let him in, figuratively and literally.

When she opened it, her eyes were red and swollen, and she silently motioned for him to come in. All he wanted was to gather her in his arms and comfort her. As they ate in silence, Will's gaze was glued to Anna as she carefully plucked pieces of cheese from her slice of pizza, avoiding eye contact. He reached over and touched her hand. "Please talk to me. You're always here to listen to me. Let me help you."

She didn't answer. Instead, she got up and opened the refrigerator. "You want a beer or wine?"

Will stood up and walked over to her, his arms engulfing her in a hug from behind. "I know something is bothering you," he said. "You don't have to talk about it if you don't want to, but I'm here for you."

She shook her head again in response. He turned her to face him, laced his arm around her waist, and pulled her close, stroking her hair before tenderly kissing her lips.

Will's eyes widened when she returned his kiss with a fierce passion that he had never experienced. She wrapped her arms around his neck and pulled their bodies together. His heart beat fiercely as the warmth of her lips activated all his senses. He swept her off her feet and carried her to the bedroom, where they embraced. They were breathless when their kiss ended. He helped her onto the bed and stood back to take in the sight of her—hair spread across the pillow. Her porcelain skin with a spattering of freckles caused a wave of emotion that left no air in his lungs.

He kissed her neck and whispered, "Darlin, you are beautiful." He lay next to her and caressed her face with his fingertips, tracing the contours of her jawline. Anna curled one leg over his hip and pulled him closer; their kisses grew more passionate until Will pulled away.

Sitting up, he tried to catch his breath. "I can't do this. This isn't the right time." He put his head in his hands. "I think . . . this may be a distraction for you." He wasn't sure if that was the right thing to say.

A wave of emotion washed over Anna's face as her eyebrows furrowed and her lips pursed. "Distraction from what?" she asked, her eyes narrowing with suspicion. "Maybe it is. Forget it." She charged off the bed. "Sometimes it all feels so bad you just want something that feels good." She was trembling.

He grabbed her hand and met her gaze, suddenly vulnerable. "Anna, I'm not good at this stuff. Whatever I say, it's going to be wrong." He brushed his thumb across her cheek, tracing its contours. "Darlin', can we just lay together? I want to hold you and let you know I'm here for you."

She nodded in agreement and allowed him to guide her back to the bed. As they prepared to lay down, Will hesitated as he reached for her t-shirt, silently seeking permission. She reassured him with a nod. He gently removed her shirt and set it aside before she reached for his and slowly unbuttoned it, maintaining unwavering eye contact. They settled onto the bed beside each other, their bare skin touching. The warmth emanating from Anna's body radiated through him, something he hadn't experienced before.

"Darlin', I know I have said this before, but I'm here for you if you want to talk." He ran his fingers through Anna's hair. His heart raced with anticipation at the thought of being so intimate with someone other than Shelly. He wanted so badly to make love to her, but part of him needed to take things slow. Every time they touched and explored each other's bodies, he ached for more, and although Shelly was the only woman he'd ever made love to, he believed everything could be different with Anna.

Anna's lips traced a path along his jawline before she leaned back and met his gaze. "I miss home," she whispered before returning to his embrace. He frowned with a sadness that went deep—a despair he couldn't quite articulate. He feared that having pleasure might drown out the pain he carried inside. The pain served as a constant reminder of what he'd done—a punishment he believed he deserved—but Anna was more than pleasure from his pain.

"I know. I'm here, darlin'," he murmured, kissing her forehead. He wasn't sure what else to say, but it was a start. Was there a chance that Anna could ignite a fire within him and bring back the feeling of being truly alive? Despite his fear of being vulnerable and letting go of the pain, the idea also sparked excitement.

CHAPTER 27

*A*nna lay in Will's arms, quietly listening to his breathing become slow and steady. Anna toyed with his wedding ring, wondering if he liked or felt sorry for her. Maybe he was just being nice to her so she'd help with the equine center. After all, look what Emma did to her: she used Anna for a promotion and then slept with Tony. What if Emma was right, and people didn't like her but felt sorry for her?

She traced his full lips with her finger, then kissed his clean-shaven cheek. Anna quietly eased out of Will's arms, got up, and put on a pink silk robe. She decided to work on the grant while he slept, but her mind drifted to the ring on his finger as she sat staring at the computer screen. Will kissing her while wearing his wedding ring was difficult to comprehend. Was he just as confused as she was? Anna reached for her phone and sent Jenny a text. She hoped her friend could shed some light on the tornado of thoughts that whirled through her mind.

> Anna: I'm sorry. I was supposed to get back to you, but I got busy with work and helping with the equine center.

> Jenny: It's okay. How are you?

Anna sat for a moment, wondering if she should lay it all out for Jenny or keep it to herself.

> Jenny: Anna, are you okay?

> Anna: Can I talk to you about something?

> Jenny: Sure, do you want to FaceTime, or is texting okay?

> Anna: We can text. Will is asleep in my bed, and I don't want to wake him.

> Jenny: Talk!!!

> Anna: Will came to work on the grant. We were kissing, and things got heated. We ended up in my bedroom. When things got heated, he stopped because I had a bad day. He still wears his wedding ring. Do you think that was an excuse to stop?

> Jenny: Wait a minute. Why did you have a bad day?

> Anna: It doesn't matter. Do you think he's using me to get the equine center open?

> Jenny: Come on, Anna. Do you think he's pimping himself out for that?

Anna snickered at Jenny's reply. There was logic in what she said.

> Anna: Who knows? Maybe he feels sorry for me. You know what Emma said. It could be true of everyone.

Anna's phone started ringing, and Jenny's name appeared on the screen. She closed her eyes and answered. "Hey, Jenny."

"What the hell is that all about?" Jenny's tone was harsh. "We've been friends for a long time and been through thick and thin. Do you honestly think we're friends because I feel sorry for you?"

"No, I was speaking about the other girls in school who were my friends," Anna said.

"Emma's a raging bitch who used you to help her through school and to get a promotion. Tony is a jerk, and he didn't deserve you. I don't know if Will has a motive, but if you don't open your heart to him, he could drift away."

A knot formed in Anna's throat, and she swallowed hard. "The wedding ring . . ." She took a ragged breath, holding back the tears. "It isn't right to be with him while he wears it. I feel like the other woman."

Jenny's tone softened. "Aw, honey, I get that. Have you talked to him about it?"

"No." Anna wiped the tears from her cheek.

"Don't you think you should?"

"I guess, but what if he gets mad?"

"People grieve in their way, but he shouldn't take it out on you. He's got to deal with it."

"Yeah," Anna mumbled.

Silence buzzed in Anna's ears, but after a moment, Jenny asked, "Is there something else bothering you? You said he wanted to stop because you had a bad day? What happened?"

Where do I begin? I'm homesick. Will is wearing a wedding ring, but he stopped because I was having a bad day. I'm sure that's not the truth. Then there's Dr. Watts in the stairway. She wasn't ready to have this conversation with Jenny when Will was sleeping in the other room.

"No, everything's fine. I don't know what to do. You know I don't have much experience with men. You saw how things ended up with Tony."

"Don't make me fly out there just to slap you."

I would love for you to visit. "You wouldn't, but if you wanted to, I would be ecstatic to see you."

"Have you thought about coming here for a visit?"

Anna had thought of coming for more than just a visit. She longed to be home to feel close to her grandparents. A vision of the flowers blooming around the porch appeared to her. She remembered the year they planted the pink tulips. Papa watched from the porch swing with a glass of tea. "I can't. I'm forming my department and working on opening the equine center." Her eyes burned with tears. "I miss him, Jenny," she croaked.

"I know. I wish I could hug you."

"Shelly!" Will shouted suddenly, and Anna leaped with fright.

She dropped her phone on the floor and ran to him. Will was hunched over on the edge of the bed, his hands covering his face, almost as if to protect himself from something. Anna stepped closer, but he held out an arm to stop her. She sank to her knees and hesitantly gathered his face in her hands, looking into his eyes. He welcomed her embrace and laid his head on her chest, clinging desperately to her waist.

"I have nightmares," he stammered. "Only Jon and Kati know about them. I think Eva does too." He let out a ragged breath. "I saw my wife's car under the eighteen-wheeler. I tried to run to the scene, but Jon stood in front of me. I saw her arm out the window."

Anna stayed silent, her head resting on the top of his head. He pulled her into his lap.

Will glanced up at her and whispered, "Thank you." He lifted her chin to look into her eyes. "Have you been crying?"

Anna suddenly felt vulnerable and exposed. She stepped away from him and stood with a slight smile. "I'm fine, I promise. I was talking to . . . Oh God, Jenny." She darted out of the room to get her phone. "Jenny, I'm so sorry."

"Oh my God, Anna, are you okay?" Jenny asked.

"Yes, Will was calling for me."

"You know, you don't lie very well."

Anna looked over at Will. He was staring at her. *I can't tell her Will had a nightmare.*

"Can I call you tomorrow? We can continue our conversation about the spring flowers then," Anna said.

"Ah yes, the spring flowers. Liar." Jenny chuckled.

"Don't make me call you bad names."

"I'll tell my momma."

A smile spread across Anna's lips. Jenny always knew how to make her smile. "Oh, Maggie loves me more."

"I think you're right. Call me tomorrow. Love you."

"Love you too. Talk to you tomorrow." Anna hung up the phone and turned her attention back to Will. His shirt was open, showing his washboard abdomen and broad shoulders. *Okay, Anna, focus on his face.*

"Back to why you were crying," he said.

Anna shrugged and looked away. "It was nothing. I'm fine," she mumbled. The frown on Will's face told her he didn't believe her.

He let out a low growl of frustration. "You always do that, Anna."

"Do what?" she shot back with irritation and spun away. "I'm just having a bad day."

"I've seen you cry a couple of times today. I know something is bothering you." His deep blue eyes flashed with intensity, piercing her resolve into submission. "Do I need to make you angry?"

Anna pointed at the gold wedding band encircling his finger. "This, for one, is bothering me."

A storm rose in Will's eyes, and a low growl escaped his lips. Anna braced herself for an explosion of temper. "What about it?" he said through clenched teeth.

She nodded in resignation before turning away, but Will grabbed her arm gently yet firmly, halting her movement. "You aren't going to run because I get angry," he said.

Anna yanked her arm away and stared at him with defiance. "I can leave if I want to," she snapped.

Will met her gaze and leaned forward slightly, his voice barely above a whisper. "And so could I . . . but I want to discuss this."

Struck by the sincerity of his words, Anna softened and nervously tucked a loose strand of hair behind her ear. She squared her shoulders. "Will, I don't think you're ready. I think we should be friends."

As soon as the words left her mouth, Anna regretted them. She dropped onto the couch behind her, only for her robe to come untied, revealing creamy skin beneath. Will's gaze flickered downward briefly before shooting back up to meet hers, a small smile playing on his lips.

Crimson heat rose in Anna's face as she hurriedly fastened her robe closed again. "I didn't do that on purpose," she stuttered. "I'm sorry."

Will sat next to her at a respectable distance. "I could see that, darlin'," he chuckled. "Talk to me."

She ran her fingers through her hair, avoiding his steely gaze. "Why do you want to be with me? To scratch an itch?" The moment the words left her lips, she desperately wanted them back.

His left eyebrow rose in response, and his eyes softened with a hint of disappointment. "Darlin, why would you say that?"

Embarrassed and ashamed, she tried to find the words to explain herself. "I don't know why I said that. I'm confused. The ring—it makes me feel like I'm with a married man. Then you stop when we kiss because you're thinking of her."

Will took her hand in his. "Honestly, I never thought about taking it off. I wanted women to think I was married so they would leave me alone," he confessed. "But from the first moment I saw you in the store, it was like I woke up from a long nap." He smiled as he tucked a strand of her hair behind her ear. "Since you've been here, my world seems brighter. I know you've only been here for a short time, but my life seems better with you in it."

Anna sat stunned, trying to comprehend what he'd just said. "You mean that?" she croaked.

"Darlin', I rarely say things that I don't mean. Believe me, I want to be with you, but it's been a long time, and I have only been with Shelly. I waited to get married to be with anyone. So, this is big for me."

"That makes sense. Why haven't you talked to anyone about your nightmares? It must be tough to hold all of that inside."

Will let out a long sigh. "I didn't want the department to know I was having issues. So, I've only told Jon the details because he was there."

"Do you have to go through the department? Could you find someone outside the department?" *Oh God, Anna, don't push him.* "I'm sorry, that's not my business. It seems like the department would have a support system for something like that."

He wrapped his arm around her, and she rested her head on his shoulder. "They may have something, but it seems like there's a code of toughness on the job, but I guess we are human." He chuckled. "Honestly, I'm not ready to talk about any of it yet."

"I understand." *So, if we got together, he would keep all this inside.*

"I will eventually talk about it. Speaking of talking about things, will you tell me what you were so upset about when you got home from work?"

Anna stiffened. "As I told you earlier, I was missing home." She didn't want to think about the encounter with Dr. Watts. Just the thought of it caused bile to burn her throat. She hoped Will couldn't see right through her.

"I get it. What can I do?"

For some reason, his question made her angry. "Bring them back," she said, her voice laced with sarcasm. "Sorry . . . sometimes I just miss my grandparents and feel like . . ."

She stood and headed to the kitchen, grabbed a glass from the cabinet, filled it with wine, and drank it in one swallow. Her nerves settled quickly, and the heat from the wine warmed her. *I have two choices: argue with Will or open my robe and divert his attention. Both are bad ideas. It makes it seem like I don't trust him enough to talk to him and I didn't listen to what he said about being with another woman.* She poured another glass of wine and took two long swallows before the glass was taken out of her hand.

Will stood towering over her, holding the glass of wine. "Don't do this, Anna." She reached and started to untie her robe, but Will stopped her. "What are you doing?"

I'm making a wrong decision and acting stupid. "I'm not sure." She closed her eyes to avoid looking at him. "Trying to make the pain go away."

"Darlin, that's temporary, trust me."

"Or getting the courage to seduce you so I could feel something more than pain."

Will wrapped his arms around her and pulled her close. "First, darlin', it wouldn't take much to seduce me, but I want our first time special. I want everything about us to be special."

Anna could feel Will's bare chest against her cheek, causing her body to warm. The wine dulled her inhibitions. "I get that, but damn, you feel and smell good."

He leaned in to kiss her tenderly on the lips. "So do you." He toyed with her robe, exposing her shoulder, and kissed it, trailing up her neck. "But being together tonight may cause more pain than relieve it."

Anna's hand trembled as she reached for the wine glass and downed its contents. A surge of bravery coursed through her, and she trailed her fingers up from his waistband, planting soft kisses on his skin along the way until she reached his chest.

Will let out a long groan, then gently took Anna by the face and looked deeply into her eyes. "Baby, I want this too, but we need to stop."

"Why?" Her voice cracked as she looked away.

"Because you've been drinking. I want us to have the total experience. I know you want the pain to go away, and while this does feel good, that feeling won't last."

Anna pushed him away, again feeling exposed by her behavior. "How do you know?" she asked. Deep down, she knew he was right, but she desperately wanted to feel something other than the sadness she'd been carrying for months.

He embraced her and tenderly kissed the top of her head. "It seems like you might not trust me, but I want to be someone you can confide in and heal with."

Anna stepped back from him and gave his shoulder a friendly shove. "You don't need to listen to my stuff. Besides, I'm fine," she said gruffly, averting her gaze as a wave of embarrassment coursed through her for her attempts to seduce Will and for drinking. She could feel his eyes on her, analyzing her every move. Taking a deep breath, she tried to compose herself. *I need to get my head together.*

"Anna, please look at me," he pleaded, and she did. "That's where you're wrong. We can support each other by truly listening to one another. I know you understand my grief. You know the pain of grief just as I do. I hoped we could share our sorrow and find solace together. Your grief is not a burden to me."

Anna stared at him in speechless wonderment. Her emotions were about to bubble over. She wanted to talk to Will but was scared about exposing her vulnerable side. "Me too," she murmured.

Will kissed her forehead. "Darlin, I'm gonna go. You look exhausted." He turned toward the door, looked over his shoulder one last time, and said, "Night, my Ginger," before disappearing into the darkness outside.

Anna watched him leave, knowing without a doubt that despite her fear of vulnerability, she had strong feelings for Will, and if anything were ever going to work between them, she would have to make some changes within herself.

CHAPTER 28

Time seemed to stand still as Anna nervously watched the clock, counting the moments until her date with Will. She hadn't seen him in two days, and their last interaction wound up with her a drunken mess. She tried to focus on the application for nonprofit status for the equine therapy center, but her mind replayed her pathetic attempt to seduce him. She felt like such an idiot. Had she pushed things too far? Was he ready for this level of intimacy? A myriad of questions flooded her mind.

Anna lounged on the couch, her eyes fixed on the glowing computer screen in front of her. She absently fiddled with her phone, scrolling through the text conversation she and Jenny had started two days ago. Anna knew that Jenny's expertise in equine therapy could be a valuable resource for the new equine center. Even though Jenny had chosen to work at University Hospital after graduating, her passion for equine therapy still burned bright. Anna wanted to hold off on asking for her assistance now. *Why do I always wait until there's a crisis to ask for help?*

> Anna: So, on a scale of 1-10, I'm a zero as a friend. I just remembered I needed to call you.

> Jenny: I worked late last night, so it's okay. How are you? What happened?

> Anna: I don't know where to begin. Will had a nightmare, which is what you heard. He was yelling for his wife, who died.

There was a delay in Jenny's reply. Anna leaned back on the cushion, watching the three dots moving, waiting for her friend's incoming text.

> Jenny: What did he tell you? What do you think about that?

> Anna: He said he saw his wife's car under an eighteen-wheeler. He didn't see her inside the car but saw her arm. He's been having nightmares since the night of the accident. That doesn't bother me. I told him he needed to find someone to talk to. What bothers me is him wearing his wedding ring. I guess I don't want people to think I date married guys. Is that stupid?

> Jenny: I don't think it's stupid. People make a lot of assumptions without knowing the whole story.

> Anna: I hope he takes it off for our date tonight, but I can't make him. I guess I have the choice not to go if he doesn't take it off.

> Jenny: Could you do that?

> Anna: Probably not. I'm excited and nervous about tonight.

I may cancel the date until he takes the ring off. Come on, Anna, you know that's not what you want.

> Jenny: Both of you have been through a lot. It takes time to heal. If you hold in the pain, the healing process gets delayed, like a festering wound.

> Anna: Okay. I could visualize that. Gross. Lol.

She has a point. He said his world is brighter since I've been here.

> Jenny: I aim to please. Lol. Just go out and have fun tonight. You deserve it. Did you get a new outfit?

> Anna: Yes, I did. Do you want me to send you a picture after I get ready?

> Jenny: You better.

Anna toyed with her red thread bracelet. She missed Jenny and Maggie. She missed home. Most of all, she missed Nana and Papa.

> Anna: Tell Maggie I said hey and give her a hug for me.

> Jenny: Text me when you get ready and send a pic.

> Anna: I will!

Texting Jenny was just what Anna needed to change her frame of mind. Tonight, she would concentrate on having a good time with Will. She needed to show him patience and grace, not being judgmental and pressuring him to do things he wasn't ready to do. *Tonight, I will have fun.* A smile spread across her face. It was just what she needed to finish the nonprofit application.

Anna glanced at the clock when she closed her laptop. It was time to start getting ready. The outfit she'd bought from the Diamond Saddle Boutique was carefully laid on the bed. As the shower's warm water cascaded down her body, she took in the calming aroma of her new shampoo, which smelled of cloves, cinnamon, and vanilla.

Twenty minutes later, her crimson hair was straightened and lay across her shoulders. It was a subtle but noticeable change. She finished the look by applying coral lipstick.

Kati showed up with her overnight bag. "Can I get ready with you?" she asked.

"Of course," Anna grabbed her hand and pulled her inside.

Kati looked at her. "Oh wow. Wait until Will sees you, and you aren't dressed yet."

A flush of warmth spread across Anna's cheeks. "Let's go."

"Anna, are you blushing?" Kati teased.

Anna chuckled. "Let's get ready."

Anna slipped on the skinny jeans that hugged her curves in all the right places. She put on her button-up cow-print shirt with a turquoise tassel necklace. Her boots were brown with a fancy turquoise inlay. She stepped back to admire her reflection with a smile.

Anna and Kati touched up their lipstick before they headed toward the door. Anna touched Kati's arm. "Can I ask you a question?"

Kati shrugged. "Sure, anything."

"Are you looking forward to being out with Jon tonight?"

Kati furrowed her brow. "Why do you ask?"

"Y'all have chemistry. Is there anything there?" Anna cringed as soon as the words came out of her mouth. *Jeez, why did I ask her that?*

Kati huffed. "Jon needs to clean up his act first. He drinks too much, and he's a cheater."

Anna decided to leave it alone. "I'm sorry, it's none of my business. I appreciate you going out with us."

"Of course. Let's hope he can behave tonight." Kati shook her head. "He's so handsome. Trust me, it's hard not to give in, but I can't. He's a great friend to Will, making me love him even more."

Anna touched Kati's arm. "Please forgive me for bringing it up."

Kati smiled. "What do you say we get you out there to see my brother? That's what tonight is all about. I haven't seen him this happy in so long." She rolled her eyes. "And he's not as grumpy as he used to be. Momma and I thought Caden would stay with us if he didn't stop being so grumpy."

"That's good." Anna wasn't sure how else to respond. "Should we head out?"

"Yep."

They grabbed their purses and headed out the cabin door. As soon as they stepped onto the porch, Anna saw Will and Jon standing there. Will held out his left hand, which no longer bore a wedding ring. Her heart leaped at the sight of it missing, confirming what she'd suspected—he was ready to make changes.

"You look beautiful," he said.

Anna's heart raced like an overwound clock. "Hi, Cowboy. I missed you." She hoped she wasn't being too forward.

He wrapped his arms around her. "I missed you too, darlin'." He leaned in and whispered, "Can I kiss you?"

She answered without hesitation, "Anytime."

When their lips met, she felt the warmth of his breath on her skin. His hand snaked around her neck as he pulled her close. He sighed as he pulled away from her and said with a smile, "God, baby, you smell good."

Jon coughed loudly to get their attention. "I hate interrupting your love fest, but can we go? I'm starved," he said, gesturing toward Will's truck.

Anna quickly suppressed a giggle before Will touched her back, sending sparks up her spine. He leaned in and whispered, "Don't encourage him."

He opened the truck door and helped her get inside. Before he closed the door, he touched her hair. "Looks good," he murmured.

Anna's gaze moved from his finger, where a faint tan line still marked the spot where his wedding ring once sat, to his face with a glimmer of hope. *This is a sign he wants to make changes. That means I need to make changes too.*

"You look amazing yourself."

Will rounded the front of the truck, stepped up onto the running board, and swung himself into the cab. The engine coughed to life as he buckled his seatbelt. He turned on the radio, and country music flooded the cab. They drove down Main Street, the neon signs of closed shops casting eerie shadows on the pavement. The looming redbrick facade of Saddle Up Bar and Grill greeted them with warm light spilling out from its windows. Will tapped his thumbs against the steering wheel to the country tune on the radio. All the anxiety that weighed Anna down earlier in the day had disappeared.

The smell of sizzling beef filled the air as they drove into the parking lot. A bright neon sign shaped like a bull and flashing pink lights welcomed them to the "Saddle Up Bar and Grill: Home of the Most Delicious Burgers in Town." They stepped inside to find a group of Stetson-wearing cowboys playing pool next to a jukebox blasting George Strait tunes.

When they walked in, Will whispered, "I hope you like to dance."

She looked at him with wide eyes. "It's been a long time since I line danced or two-stepped."

"How long?" he asked.

"Twenty years." She hoped he'd forget all about dancing. She had two left feet.

He touched her back and whispered, "It's like riding a bike. Plus, I'm a good lead."

Once seated in a corner booth, a waiter came by to grab their order. All four ordered their famous artisan burgers, steak fries, and a bucket of beer to share, which Will and Jon insisted was the only way to get drinks. With the restaurant's festive atmosphere and the group's continuing jokes, Anna sipped on her beer and relaxed. Even Jon and Kati seemed to be getting along.

While they waited for their meal, they could hear the beat of the drums originating from the stage. The band was warming up. Steel guitar and bass notes rumbled across the floorboards beneath Anna's feet. She smiled at Will, who gave her hand a reassuring squeeze.

After Will and Jon drank their third beer, Kati held out her hand. "Okay, brother, give me your keys."

Will took out his keys and handed them to Kati.

The band came back on, and they started playing Garth Brooks's "Friends in Low Places." Will grabbed Anna's hand. "Let's dance, darlin'."

Dear Lord, please don't let me make a fool of myself.

As they danced, Will spun her around gracefully. She followed his lead effortlessly, impressed by his skill. His eyes shone with a bright smile as they moved to the music. When "I Cross My Heart" by George Strait began playing, he drew her closer. Anna rested her head on his chest while his hand rested gently on her back. She inhaled the comforting scent of his cologne, feeling happy and safe in his embrace. Being in Will's arms was like home.

He whispered in her ear, "I love George Strait."

She looked up at him and said, "That hasn't changed. You listened to his music repeatedly that summer."

Will said, "The morning you started humming 'Carrying Your Love with Me,' I almost had a heart attack."

"If I remember correctly, the glass lost the fight with you," she laughed.

"I can't believe it's you, Ginger," he said. "I won't let you down again."

Anna wasn't sure what was happening, but there seemed to be a change in Will. When the song ended, he kissed her so deeply she felt it in her toes.

"Damn it, Cowboy, you keep that up. We'll pretend we're teenagers and go to your truck."

"Good thing Kati has my keys." He led her off the dance floor back to the table while the band was on break. Will opened another beer and took a long drink. "This is good. You want one?"

She shrugged. "I would like some wine."

Will strode toward the bar, his Wrangler jeans and a navy button-down shirt with his white Stetson just spoke cowboy. Anna watched him like he was the only man in the room. He engaged in friendly banter with the bartender for a few minutes before his gaze moved around the room and paused when it landed on her. There was something different about him, and it made her heart swell when he gave her an unspoken gesture of familiarity, a smile, and a wink.

Jon and Kati returned to the table, interrupting Will and Anna's silent intimacy. "I haven't seen Will dance like that in a long time," Kati said.

Anna laughed. "He's good. I only stepped on his foot ten or twenty times."

Jon opened another beer and took a long drink before saying, "He hasn't been out for a while either. His usual routine is breakfast once weekly unless I can convince him to get coffee."

Will soon returned with a glass of wine in hand for Anna. He sat beside her, kissed her, and asked if she was ready to hit the dance floor when the band returned. Anna eagerly replied, "After this wine, I'll be more than ready to dance."

Will looked at Kati and Jon. "Y'all gonna join us?"

Jon finished his beer and held out his hand to Kati with a wide grin. "Yes sir, who knows when I'll get you out to do this again. Ya, comin', sweetness?"

Kati rolled her eyes. "I'm not your sweetness."

The band returned to the stage, and Will, Anna, Jon, and Kati headed to the dance floor. The band started playing "Head Over Boots" by Jon Pardi. They moved like they'd been dancing together for years. Jon looked at Will and smiled. Anna and Kati were both spun in synchronization. Will took Kati, while Jon took Anna.

As they twirled around the dance floor, Jon leaned in and said, "Thank you for what you're doing for Will. I haven't seen him this happy in a long time."

He spun her back to Will, and Kati returned to Jon. Will said, "Did ya miss me?"

"I did."

As the band switched songs to "Carrying Your Love with Me" by George Strait, Will pulled her closer and said, "I think they're playing our song." They swayed to the music. He looked into her eyes, singing to her. She was transported back to the summer they swayed to this song, and he first kissed her. It was like they were the only ones in the room. When the song finished, he kissed her tenderly, just like he did all those years ago.

Anna caught a glimpse of Dr. Watts with his wife, Cathy, from the corner of her eye. She took a deep breath. *Okay, he's with his wife.*

"Darlin, what is it?" Will asked. "You're trembling."

She shook her head. "Nothin', something startled me. I thought I saw someone I knew."

He took her hand, leading her back to the table. Before they sat, Anna asked Kati to accompany her to the bathroom.

Dr. Watts exited the men's restroom when Anna and Kati were outside the ladies' room. Panic seized her as his eyes scanned her body up and down with a hungry gaze.

"Hi, Kati," he said. "I saw you on the dance floor. I wanted to see how your mom is doing?"

"She's doing well, thank you."

Dr. Watts kept his gaze on Anna. It was like he was undressing her with his eyes. A thousand ants seemed to crawl over Anna's skin. "Kati, I'll meet you in the restroom," she said.

Kati looked at Anna. "Okay, see ya in there."

Anna shot into the bathroom as the panic swelled inside her, threatening to swallow her from the inside out. She entered the stall, closed the door, and leaned against it, taking deep breaths while her heart thumped against her chest.

When Kati entered the bathroom, she said, "Wasn't that nice of Dr. Watts to ask how Momma's doing?"

"Yes." A scream sliced through the fog in her brain. *Calm down, he's with his wife. What is wrong with you?* A cold sweat beaded on her forehead. It was like the blood was draining from her face. *All this panic, and for what?* Sure, he made her uncomfortable, but this kind of reaction? Anna mentally shook herself.

"Are you feeling sick, Anna?" Kati asked.

She cleared her throat, opened the stall, and said, "Just needed to use the restroom."

Kati looked at her. "Girl, you are pale."

"Too much dancing, I guess. Just needed a breather." She balled her hands into fists to control the trembling. *Pull yourself together.*

"Let's get back before Jon drinks all the beer."

"I hope not. I could use one," Anna said with a slight grin.

When they returned to the table, Anna noticed Will watching her, and his forehead creased with worry. He brushed the hair away from her face. "You okay, darlin'? You're pale." The warmth of his fingers felt good against her skin.

She forced a smile. "I'm fine, but I could use a beer."

Will handed her an ice-cold bottle and held her hand. "Are you having a good time?" His brows furrowed as he felt her tremble in his hands. "Baby, did something happen?"

Anna placed the cold bottle on her forehead. "No, I think I got overheated." She looked at Will. "Yes, I'm having fun."

"We saw Dr. Watts on the way to the bathroom. He was askin' about Momma," Kati said.

"Yeah, he stopped by the table to say hi and introduced us to his wife. She seemed nice," Will said.

"She's our boss," Anna added flatly.

Will took her hand in his large, warm one, offering her an escape from the moment's awkwardness. "Looks like you're starting to get your color back. Wanna dance?"

Anna gratefully grasped his offer and said, "Yes, please!"

Will gave Jon a friendly punch in the arm. "Come on, let's dance."

Jon raised an eyebrow with a smirk. "Asking little old *me* to dance? With Anna sitting right there? I'm flattered."

Will rolled his eyes in response and laughed along with everyone at the table as they headed to the dance floor. They moved around the dance floor doing the two-step when Will and Jon decided to change partners again. As they went to change, Dr. Watts intervened, and Will ended up with his wife. Anna gasped as Dr. Watts placed his arm around her waist, drawing her close as they gracefully moved across the dance floor. She attempted to push him away by pressing her hand against his chest, but he only pulled her closer.

"Anna, you look stunning tonight," he purred.

She was sure it looked innocent to others, but it was horrifying just having him near her, much less his arms around her waist. She tried to pull away, but he squeezed tighter. Her eyes darted around, looking for Will. Then Dr. Watts's hand brushed below her waist, causing her to jump.

She looked at him wide-eyed with shock and tried to release herself from his grip, but his fingers dug into her skin.

"I suggest you move your hand, or I'll make a scene you'll never forget," she said, her jaw clenched. There must have been venom in her tone because he moved his hand quickly. *God, is this ever going to end? Where the hell is Will?* Relief came over Anna when she spotted Will and Cathy walking toward them.

"Hey, ya'll disappeared on the dance floor," Will said as they approached them.

Cathy's eyes burned a hole in Anna. "Yes, Seth is very good at that." She glared at her husband. "Especially when there's a woman around."

Dr. Watts broke into a mirthless laugh. "My dear wife exaggerates a bit."

Anna saw the dumbfounded look on Will's face as he watched the interaction between the Wattses. Anna knew there had to be more to this whole interaction.

Dr. Watts took Cathy by the arm. Anna noticed he was squeezing her arm, causing her to wince. She wondered if Will saw it too. "If you will excuse us. Thank you for the dance, Anna." He quickly led his wife out the door by the arm.

Anna did her best to hide her shaking hands as she turned to Will. "What the hell was that?"

"Oh, she was pissed. She was shooting daggers at him the entire time you were in sight. When ya'll disappeared, her eyes were filled with rage. Let's say I'm glad I'm not him tonight."

"Or any other night for that fact," Anna mumbled. This was supposed to be a fun night, but all she wanted to do was leave. Anna's breaths came out ragged as she struggled to keep her composure. The short time she was with Dr. Watts was like an eternity of torture. Now, she had the urge to flee. She cleared her throat and took a deep breath before speaking. "I'm sorry, but could we go? I'm a bit overwhelmed."

Will nodded before his focus shifted to the door, causing him to curse under his breath. "Crap."

"What's wrong?"

"Jon just stormed out. Let's go back to the table."

They returned to the table, where Kati sat alone with a forlorn expression. "Where did Jon go?"

"He went outside."

Will's eyebrows knitted. "What happened?"

Kati's eyes brimmed with tears. "What do you think? He's drunk, starts saying shit. I laughed. He got pissed and walked out." She threw up her hands. "I thought he was kidding."

Anna curled her fingers around Kati's and squeezed.

"Come on," Will said. "Let's go." While Anna hated that Kati was upset, she was grateful to leave.

They headed outside, where Jon was pacing near the truck.

Jon threw his hands in the air. "When does this end, Kati? When will you forgive me?" He leaned toward her, his words slurred. "I don't care anymore. Maybe I should leave with someone else. Which is what I was blamed for anyway." His eyes were cold and distant.

Kati cut him a glare. "No one wants to get laid by a drunk."

Anna wrung her hands together. She hated confrontations even when she wasn't part of them. Kati and Jon were seething.

Will must have noticed her apprehension because he grabbed her hand. "I'd rather they scream at each other now and get it out of their system before we get in the truck. I think Jon will be sleeping at my house again."

"He may be walking to your house the way Kati looks," Anna said.

Will threw his head back, laughing. "She won't do that, but she'll make him sit in the back with me."

"Why punish you?" Anna inquired.

Will laughed. "Darlin', you catch on quickly."

Jon looked at him through red-rimmed eyes and slurred, "Hey, Will, can I sleep at your house? I'm too drunk to drive."

"Sure, you can sleep on the couch."

He whispered loud enough for Anna and Kati to hear. "Dude, you told me that's where you sleep."

Will covered his mouth. "Zip it, Jon."

"Are we still brothers? I love you, man."

Will patted him on the back. "Ya, we'll always be brothers. I love you too. Let's get you to the truck, and you better not barf in it."

"I haven't barfed in your truck since . . . oh, I don't remember. I love Kati, Will, but she doesn't love me back."

Will adjusted Jon's weight against him. "I know. Stop drinking and talking shit, man."

Jon stopped and whispered, "I miss Shelly."

Will deeply breathed, "I know, Jon, me too. Please don't go there, not tonight."

Jon's voice cracked as he said, "Sorry, Will. Sometimes I need to talk about it."

"I know, Jon."

Anna watched the interaction between Will and Jon. They had a bond she didn't understand. He was dedicated to Jon and defended him tirelessly to Kati. For whatever reason, Jon and Will had a bond that revolved around Shelly's death. She knew they'd known her for a long time, but it seemed like he was more affected than a friend. Maybe it was because he and Will were so close.

Anna felt terrible for Kati, and she could see she was angry. "Wanna talk about it?"

"He makes me so mad I could spit. He acts like he's the only one who lost Shelly. We all lost her."

Anna put her arm around Kati. "What happened?"

"Oh, the same shit. I love you, Kati, blah-blah, then he gets drunk and talks about getting a piece of ass again." Tears glistened in her eyes. "It's like a stab to the heart. I'm done, Anna."

Kati glared at Jon and shouted, "Will, you have to sit in the back with Jon, or I'll throw him out of the car." Then she got up in Jon's face and hissed, "I'm done."

Will helped Jon into the truck. "I guess she's pissed at me," Jon slurred.

"Yep," Will said.

Kati interjected. "You are a fu—"

Will held up his hand. "Get in the truck and don't say anything more to him," he warned. "Otherwise, I won't sit in back with him."

She nodded. "Sorry if I ruined your time."

"Kati girl, y'all need to fix this. I know he has a drinking problem, but that's my fault."

"Why is it your fault?'"

"Come on, you know he recovered Shelly's body. He removed her from the SUV himself. It's why he drinks."

"Come on, Will. We all lost her," Kati retorted.

Will cut her off. "Please stop."

Kati nodded with tears in her eyes. He kissed her temple. "Drive us home."

Anna stood dumbfounded as she listened to the exchange between Will and Kati. *Poor Jon recovered Shelly's body. I bet it plays over and over in his mind.* She couldn't imagine how Jon felt, and her heart ached for him. Now, she understood Will's protective nature toward him. He was an honorable man who would do anything for those he loved. Anna realized she wasn't so different from him.

Will walked around to help Anna in the truck and gave her hand a reassuring squeeze. He climbed into the back with Jon as Kati slid into the driver's seat. They rode to the ranch in silence. The tension between Kati and Jon was like a heavy fog; although they said nothing, the emotions were palpable. The truck was heavy with sadness. Anna had a newfound respect for Will as they rode in awe-filled silence.

CHAPTER 29

On the ride home, Will's mind was whirling like a tornado. He glanced at Anna in the passenger seat, her eyes shut and her head propped against the headrest. He had hoped for a peaceful evening with her, and he foolishly believed Kati and Jon would behave themselves. What he wanted was to spend the night with Anna. He finally felt ready to be with her.

Hopefully, the scene between Kati and Jon wasn't too much for Anna. There was a lot she didn't know or understand about why he protected Jon and took care of him. He owed Jon a lot because of what he did the night of Shelly's accident. *I'm not thinking about that tonight because this night is about Anna and me.*

Not that it stopped his mind from wandering. What was it about that interaction with Dr. Watts and his wife? It was strange that he disappeared with Anna into the crowd, and his wife's anger toward her was confusing. Anna had acted odd that day in the cafeteria when Dr. Watts came by their table. *Maybe they have . . . okay, stop overthinking everything. Thinking that Anna and Dr. Watts have a thing is the stuff that gets me into trouble. Jealousy . . .*

When they pulled up to Will's house, Kati parked the truck. Will stepped out and helped Anna from the truck, then assisted Kati.

Then he opened the back door and grabbed Jon's arm. "Come on, buddy."

Jon climbed out of the truck. "You sure I can have the couch?"

"Yep."

He looked at Will. "You aren't staying in the house tonight?"

"Nope."

Jon's expression turned sad as he said, "She'd be okay with it."

Will shook his head. "Come on, buddy."

He got Jon to the couch, laid him down, and covered him with a blanket. "Good night, Jon."

"Night, Will."

When he stepped outside, Will saw Anna and Kati leaning against the truck, talking. "Hey," he said as he joined them, "I got him on the couch sleeping. He should be fine tomorrow."

Kati half-smiled. "Night, Will. Love you."

"I love you too." Will then turned to Anna and took her hand. "You okay, darlin'?" His pulse raced at the thought of asking her to spend the night in her cabin. Would she say yes? What if she rejected him?

"I'm fine. Are you okay?"

He put his arm around her. "More than okay."

"What was Jon talking about?"

Will exhaled. "I can't tonight, Anna. I need it to be about us. Not Jon and not Shelly. Just us."

"I understand," she said.

"Momma is keeping the kids tonight."

"Oh?"

He took a deep breath. "Do you want to spend the night together?"

Anna's eyes got wide, and she nodded her head. "Are you sure you're ready?"

"Darlin', I have no idea, but I want to be with you even if I just hold you."

She smiled. "I like the thought of you holding me all night."

They headed toward her cabin, enveloped in a palpable silence. As soon as they stepped inside, Will tugged Anna toward him with a fierce embrace. He couldn't get enough of her—she was his everything—and seeing that same intensity reflected in Anna's eyes made his pulse race. He pulled her close with trembling hands and claimed her lips in a fiery kiss. Her arms wrapped around his neck, pushing their bodies together until there was no space between them. A low moan escaped from deep within Will as he broke away from the kiss, breathless and dizzy with desire.

"Do you want to go to bed?" he whispered, meeting her gaze.

"Will, are you sure? I don't want to push you." Anna ran her fingers through his hair, and her gentle touch sent a thrill down his spine.

Will cupped her face and said, "I'm sure. I know I need to deal with my grief, but tonight, it's about you and me, okay? It's just about us."

"Just us," she whispered.

Their eyes locked, and Anna led him by the hand into the bedroom without a word. She stood before him, slowly unbuttoning his shirt one button at a time until it fell from his shoulders. Soft kisses trailed up his chest and neck as she explored every inch of his skin, leaving him gasping for more.

"It's your turn, Cowboy," she breathed into his ear.

With a slow and deliberate movement, Will unbuttoned Anna's blouse. A faint blush rose to Anna's cheeks under his touch. His body tingled with anticipation as his hands grazed the pink lace of her bra. He gently removed her blouse, and his lips traced a path along her neck, igniting a wave of pleasure between them. She stepped back and stood before him; a coy smile played on her lips as she kicked off her boots, unbuttoned her skinny jeans, and gracefully stepped out of them.

"God, you're beautiful," he said huskily as his gaze roved over her body.

Anna traced her finger along the waistband of his jeans, unbuttoning them and sliding them down his legs. He kicked his boots off and removed his pants. As Anna's eyes took in his body, Will couldn't help but draw a sharp breath before meeting her gaze again.

"You okay, Cowboy?" she whispered.

"I'm more than okay, darlin'," he replied, kissing her with a fiery passion that left them both breathless.

With a gentle touch, he guided her to the bed and pulled her into a warm embrace. His lips danced across her skin, igniting a primal fire within them. He never stopped kissing her, each one more intense than the last. His fingers traced a path down her bare shoulders, sending shivers through her body before entwining with hers. With a soft sigh, he brought her hand to his lips, tasting the lingering passion on her fingertips. He could feel her heart racing against his chest as their souls merged into one.

As Anna lay in Will's arms, his touch roamed up and down her back, savoring every curve and dip of her silky skin. He couldn't get enough of her. Their connection was magnetic. A long-forgotten fire ignited within him, fueled by their intoxicating heat and desire, like that first kiss so many years ago.

Will kissed her forehead and whispered, "Darlin, that was out of this world."

She raised her head off his chest and looked into his eyes. "You have no idea." She curled up in his arms. "Cowboy, that was the best first date."

"It was, Ginger."

He held her until she drifted off to sleep, then pulled her close as he stared at the ceiling, listening to Anna's slow, steady breathing. The tip of his finger traced her jaw.

Although he'd been worried about being unable to make love to Anna, once he felt her body next to his, there was no one else. It was just the two of them. It was like his soul was at home with Anna. He'd loved Shelly. He knew he did. But things felt different with Anna. And maybe that was okay. He would always love Shelly, but perhaps he could love Anna too.

Will's eyes grew heavy, lulled by Anna's warmth and slow breaths. There had to be life and love after loss. Maybe he could have it.

THE SUN PEEKED through the window. Will opened his eyes. Anna was asleep beside him, her arm draped over his chest and her toned leg curled around him. He disentangled from her and headed to the shower. She looked beautiful with her crimson hair splayed across the pillow, her arm over her eyes, and one leg sticking out of the sheet.

It dawned on Will when he entered the bathroom to shower. It was the first time in three years that he'd slept through the night without a nightmare.

With a towel wrapped around his waist, Will emerged from the bathroom, sat on the bed, and said, "darlin', are you awake?"

She smiled. "Mmm."

He poked her side. "You coming with me to feed the horses? You can muck the stalls."

She peeked under her arm. "Cowboy, I'm insulted. You want me to shovel shit after last night?"

He poked her side. "Oh, darlin', I especially want you shoveling shit after last night so you can be close to me."

She wrapped herself in the sheet. "Let me take a quick shower."

Will grabbed the end of the sheet while she pulled from the front. "Why are you so shy now?"

She reached out to grab his towel while laughing. He let go of the bedsheet, and she hurried to the bathroom. Will chuckled as he dressed in the same jeans and shirt he'd worn the previous night. As he pulled on his boots, a sense of joy filled his heart, something he hadn't experienced in quite a while.

Will went to the kitchen, hoping to find some coffee and mugs. A wide smile spread across his face when he spotted the French vanilla coffee pods. He made a mental note to remember what coffee and creamer she preferred for future reference.

When he finished making coffee, he took it back to the bedroom. His heart skipped a beat when he thought of her emerging from the bathroom in a towel. The sound of the water shutting off added to his anticipation.

The door opened, and Anna pranced out, wrapped in a turquoise towel, her hair in a matching turban. The color made her emerald eyes look even greener. He cleared his throat, trying but failing not to lick his lips. "Darlin', you make a towel look good."

Scarlet colored her cheeks. "Will . . . I . . . uh."

Anna adjusted the towel wrapped around her. Will's eyes narrowed as he walked toward her with a Cheshire grin.

"Will, no, don't grab my towel," she giggled.

He swept her up in his arms, and she squealed. "I need a good morning kiss, darlin'."

He planted his lips on hers, his tongue exploring. "Damn, you smell and taste good," he murmured in her ear. He left kisses down her neck, causing her to giggle. "You should get dressed, or I'll be late for work. I'll wait outside since you're shy now."

She giggled and slapped his butt. "Not shy. You don't need distractions."

"True."

Will grabbed his hat and headed out to the porch while Anna dressed. He sat in the swing, lazily draped his arm across the back, and tilted his head to take in the sun's warmth on his face. The door opened, and Anna emerged dressed in jeans and a T-shirt, accentuating her thin frame. Her hair was piled on her head in a messy bun.

She put her hands on her hips. "Well, Cowboy, are you coming, or are you going to sit there with that smirk all day?"

He shrugged. "That wasn't a smirk, darlin'. That was admiration. How was your coffee?"

She held out her hand. "Perfect."

Will took her hand as he rose. "You ready to clean my stalls?"

"It would be my pleasure."

They walked to the stable together, hand in hand. Will was energized with hope, and he finally knew they could have a relationship.

CHAPTER 30

Anna walked towards the barn, basking in the warm embrace of the morning sun as it rose above the horizon. She was eager to complete her morning chores before heading to work. Secretly, she hoped to see Will before leaving.

"Good morning, Thunderbird. I have something for you." Anna said as she held out a bundle of carrots. Thunderbird eagerly stretched his neck forward to receive his treat. She took a brush from the tack room and groomed him, delighting in his soft coat and laughing as Thunderbird nibbled her earlobe. A snort from Jake caught Anna's attention, and she smiled wider. This was Anna's favorite part of the day: being surrounded by these gentle giants filled her with a deep contentment.

A smile crept onto Anna's lips as she reminisced about the night she had spent with Will. They had connected on a deep level, sharing their bodies and souls while discussing their dreams and laughing until the sun rose. It was a moment of true intimacy, where their hearts and souls were in sync. The more time she spent with Will, the deeper her feelings grew for him. He was a kind and compassionate man who valued those around him, showing them love without limits.

After putting Thunderbird's brush in the tack room, Anna approached the stall with a handful of carrots and held her hand out for him to take one.

As she stroked his cheek, she caught the scent of Will's cologne, and her heart fluttered in response. She barely had time to turn around before he wrapped his arms around her waist and kissed her neck. "Good morning, darlin'. Are you spoiling my horse?" he murmured against her skin.

"I am," she replied as she leaned back into him. "I missed you last night."

"Oh, you have no idea how much I missed you," he said as his lips brushed her ear. Anna shivered at the sensation and felt a heat bloom inside her chest when he whispered, "I love waking up with you."

Turning in his arms, she looked into his eyes and replied, "Me too, Cowboy." His black Stetson was pulled low on his forehead, tight jeans hugging his lean muscles, and scuffed boots completed the look of an all-American cowboy. She sighed wistfully. "We should get this done, or I won't be going to work today."

Will laughed. "I wouldn't complain if we headed to your cabin and spent the day in bed."

She shook her head and smiled. "As tempting as that sounds, I have several meetings today. I'm still getting this department up and running."

"How's that going?" he asked with interest. Unlike Tony, who never asked about her job, Will was genuinely interested in what she did.

"We've made a lot of progress already," she said with pride. "We've hired five nurses to see patients in the community and formed a caregiver's support group with regular meetings. I should get to it so I'm not late."

"Hey, before we get started, do you want to go with Caden and me to his appointment at the therapy center to meet the director? We can have dinner after."

"Sure, that sounds good."

She started toward the tack room when he grabbed her hand and pulled her into his arms. "Can I take you to work this morning? Then I can pick you up after you get off, and we can leave from the hospital."

"I'd like that. I better hurry so I can get ready."

"We should get to work," he murmured in her ear.

Anna and Will quickly cleaned the stalls and fed the horses. Anna promptly showered, dressed for work, and finished her makeup before stepping outside to find Will waiting on the porch. His dark hair was still wet. He smiled as his eyes scanned her navy pantsuit.

She narrowed her eyes. "Are you ogling me?"

He shrugged. "Maybe."

She headed down the porch steps. "Stop looking at my behind."

"Me? Never," he chuckled. "Let's get going."

They walked to his truck, and he helped her in. Anna was quiet on the way to the hospital. She was nervous about the possibility of seeing Dr. Watts after their last interaction. She thought about the fire in Cathy's eyes and how Dr. Watts had roughly grabbed her arm. She stared out the window, watching the fields of wildflowers before they entered town.

Will reached for her hand, squeezing it. "You look worried."

"I was thinking about what I need to get done today. I always do this on the way to work," she lied. She didn't want him to know what Dr. Watts had done when he danced with her. Her stomach churned at the thought of his sleazy hand touching her backside.

Anna's stomach sank as Will parked in the hospital lot. She rubbed her neck, trying to release the tension building in her muscles. Will helped her out of the truck, then pulled her close and kissed her, causing every cell in her body to fire from her head to her toes, and she was left weak in the knees. "That was a little thing to remember me by," he said.

She ran a finger down his cheek. "I could never forget you . . . I never did, Cowboy."

He smiled. "I know, Ginger. I'll meet you here after work."

Anna's stomach was in knots from anticipation and dread as she walked through the doors of the hospital. She paused outside her office door and quietly uttered a prayer.

Her morning consisted of meetings to discuss palliative care and paperwork, but when her office phone rang, the sound pierced her ears.

She took a deep breath and picked up the phone. "This is Anna. How may I help you?"

"This is Cathy Watts. Report to my office immediately," she said with an icy tone.

Anna's pulse quickened as she nervously approached the administration offices. The entire hall seemed to be watching her as she walked by, their eyes heavy with judgment. Cathy stood outside her door when she arrived, shooting her a fiery glare. Nausea threatened to overwhelm her as she stepped into the office.

Cathy walked to her desk and pointed to a chair. "Sit." She sat at her desk with her fists clenched in front of her.

Anna obliged. Beads of sweat were forming on the back of her neck. She thought about running out the door and back to Missouri, but something kept her rooted in place.

"I don't know what you have going on with my husband, but it stops now. Do you understand?" Cathy barked.

Anna opened her mouth to speak, but no words came out. She just sat wide-eyed. She wanted to yell and scream, but she just stared.

Cathy slammed her hands on the desk, stood, and pushed the chair back, leaning across the desk as if poised for an attack. "Did you hear me? Leave my husband alone."

Anna quivered at the memory of his touch and was filled with disgust. Her tongue darted out of her mouth to lick her dry lips as fear flooded her body like an electric shockwave. She rose and steadied herself on the arms of the chair. "Mrs. Watts, I can assure you I don't want him," she said, barely able to keep the tremor from her voice. "Please believe me when I say nothing is happening between us."

Cathy paused momentarily before delivering her ultimatum. *"And I assure you,* if you don't stay away from my husband, I will destroy you. Now get out of my office."

As Anna slowly backed away, unsure if she should stay or go, conflicting feelings warred within her. Part of her wished to escape, while another wanted to stand up for herself and refuse to be intimidated by Cathy's threats. Shaking with fear and anger, Anna quickly walked to her office, hoping she wouldn't run into anyone. She trembled as she fumbled with the lock before finally gaining entry into safety.

Anna stumbled into her office, closed the door, and burst into tears. She'd done everything she could to keep her composure in Cathy Watts' office and was grateful that she'd held it together until now.

After falling apart, Anna quickly straightened up and took two deep breaths before wiping away her tears. She forced herself to focus on her work, but the possibility of running into Cathy or Dr. Watts around every corner loomed over her like a dark cloud. Anna had to find a way to stay hidden to avoid their wrath. It was clear from her meeting with Cathy that she had no allies. Even if Cathy believed in her innocence, she would never openly support Anna and turn against her husband. The stress was taking a toll on her. *If only I could become invisible, maybe I'd be safe.*

Anna stared at the clock, willing it to move faster toward four-thirty. She prayed she wouldn't run into Dr. Watts on her way out and took the elevator as a precaution. He was smiling at her as she opened the door leading to the exit.

"Hello, Anna," he said. She glared at him.

"I-I need to go. My ride is waiting for me," she stammered.

"Oh, your fireman boyfriend?"

Anna couldn't comprehend what was happening, that this slimy man dared to ask her such personal questions. Finally, after what felt like an eternity, Dr. Watts moved aside so that Anna could leave and escape his gaze. She quickly walked to the hospital entrance and saw Will standing outside his truck, a smile spread across his face, but when he saw her, the smile faded and turned to concern.

"Hey, are you okay?"

She blankly nodded. "I'm fine. Can we leave?" Her heart hammered in her chest. *Where will the confrontation with Cathy Watts lead? What is Dr. Watts going to tell her about today? She said she would destroy me.*

CHAPTER 31

Will watched as Anna settled into the truck. He knew something was wrong but struggled to summon the courage to ask her what it was. Would he have to tear down a wall to get her to reveal whatever troubled her? As they drove toward the therapy center, an oppressive silence hung like a dark curtain between them, and he couldn't stay quiet.

"Okay, Anna, what did I do to make you mad? Whatever I did, I'm sorry," he said.

A weak smile spread across her lips. It was like it was raining with the sun out. "Oh, Will, I'm not mad at you."

He curled his fingers around hers. "Then what's wrong?"

"Truthfully, I'm scared to tell you." She let go of his hand and reached for her purse. Her hands trembled as she opened it.

"Don't be afraid to talk to me. I would never hurt you."

"I know. I'm not afraid of you. Let's get through this tour of the therapy center, and on the way home, can we stop at a park and talk? I'll tell you." She dabbed her cheeks with a tissue. "Right now, I need to pull it together to meet Cindy." She turned to look in the backseat. "Where's Caden?"

"His therapist was sick today, but Cindy said you and I should come anyway."

She took a long sigh. "Thank God. He doesn't need to see me crying."

"It's okay to cry."

Anna chuckled. "Oh, sure. Says the guy who bottles up as much as I do."

"Touché."

The truck was quiet as they made their way to the therapy center. Will pulled a parking spot, quickly getting out to assist Anna out of the truck. He wrapped his arms around her, holding her close to comfort her.

"I thought you needed this more than an interrogation," he said.

She let out a long sigh. "This is so much better."

Her grip around his waist tightened. He placed a kiss on top of her head. "Are you good to meet Cindy? We can always cancel. You don't have to pretend to be okay right now."

Anna nodded. "Let's do this. I'll be fine." She straightened her shoulders, flashed a smile, and grabbed his hand. "It's important to you, so it's important to me too."

"darlin', you never cease to amaze me." Will knew something was bothering her, but she could turn off her pain in minutes. He wondered if that was how she was when it came to love. Could she act one way toward him and, deep down inside, not want to build on their relationship? His chest tightened.

She squeezed his hand like she knew what he was thinking. "Let's go, Cowboy."

Will opened the door for Anna and stepped inside the therapy center. A sense of dread overcame him as he strolled toward the front desk, where Cindy conversed with the receptionist. She was a petite woman with chestnut hair flecked with gold, her age betrayed only by the soft laugh lines around her eyes. Jeans and a polo shirt embroidered with the center's name on its chest conveyed an air of authority. His mind flashed back to Caden's first meeting here; he had been only two years old then. He remembered how foreign it all seemed as he'd tried to understand why Caden was so angry and frustrated, but thanks to Cindy and her staff, he saw glimpses of progress in his son, which seemed impossible after Shelly died. Before Shelly's death, Caden would throw a temper tantrum, and Will would just let Shelly handle it. He was starting to understand Caden but still had a long way to go.

Cindy's face brightened as she greeted Will, opening her arms wide to embrace him. "Will," she said, "Thank you so much for coming." Her voice softened as she added, "I'm sorry we had to cancel Caden's appointment. His therapist's son is sick."

"It's okay. He's hanging with my mom." He put his hand on Anna's back. "This is Anna Samuels. She has graciously offered to help get the equine center open."

Cindy and Anna shook hands. "It's nice to meet you, Anna. I can't thank you enough for helping with this project. Y'all can follow me to my office."

As they walked to Cindy's office, Will remembered the last time he and Shelly had made this journey down the same hallway. He imagined his wife, notebook in hand, as she scribbled notes, full of plans for the ranch they'd moved to just before his father died.

He hadn't realized he had stopped moving until Anna touched his arm, concern knitting her forehead. "Will, what's wrong?"

He forced a smile. "I'm sorry, I was just thinking about something."

Cindy glanced over her shoulder. "Hopefully, you've found Shelly's notes."

When they reached Cindy's office, she invited them to sit at the round table in the corner. Anna sat in the same spot Shelly used to occupy. Will placed his hat on the table before sitting next to her. He knew now wasn't the time to remember everything he and Shelly had shared at the center. Anna's hand encircled his thigh, gently squeezing it as if she could sense his thoughts. He held tightly onto it for support as images played out like a movie in his mind, the waves of emotion crashing down like a tsunami.

Cindy asked again if he had found Shelly's notes, but all Will could focus on was how tightly he gripped Anna's hand. He had to pull himself together and concentrate on what Cindy was saying. Anna gave his hand a reassuring squeeze, and he closed his eyes briefly before looking back at Cindy and Anna, their concerned gazes meeting his.

"Do you need some air?" Anna asked him.

"No, darlin', I'm fine. Why?"

Anna leaned toward Will and whispered, "Cindy asked you a question, and you were somewhere else."

He rubbed the back of his neck, struggling to decide whether to tell the truth. He knew where Shelly's notebook was and wanted to wait to part with it. It was the last thing he had shared with Shelly, and although it brought him pain, it kept her memory alive. He could still remember her excitement when she showed him the plans; it felt like a lifetime ago. "Oh, sorry, my mind was on the notebook. I don't know where it is," he lied.

Cindy let out a long sigh. "Dang, that would be very helpful to Anna. Shelly had all the plans in it. Do you know if she saved them to a flash drive or a computer?"

Will bounced his leg up and down rapidly. "I don't think so. I haven't seen anything."

Every time Anna squeezed his leg, she told him it was okay.

"So far, Will and I have been working on a grant and a budget," Anna said. "I have some contacts in Missouri that can help us organize the equine center."

Will jerked his head in her direction. "You do? How? Why?" He couldn't get out a complete sentence. This woman never ceased to amaze him. He'd given her nothing to work with, yet she worked endlessly to help him.

Anna and Cindy giggled. "Well, Anna, it seems you made Mr. Deluca speechless. That's a first."

Will narrowed his eyes. "Oh, ha-ha. This is the first I heard she was looking for help."

Anna chuckled again. "I have been researching and asked my friend Jenny, who works in PT, to find out if anyone in Missouri has an equine center. I thought if she made contact, we could model it after their center. I need information on the center's financing besides any money we might get from a grant. Why are you so surprised? How long have I been riding horses?"

Will wondered when his torture was going to end. He had no idea what he was getting into when he told Cindy he would open the center, and then he decided to give himself a short window to get it done. The muscles in his neck tightened. He should have listened to his mother. He rubbed his temple. His mind was at war with itself. He cleared his throat and stood up. "Could you take Anna on a tour of the center? I'll catch up with you when I'm done in the restroom."

He looked at Anna out of the corner of his eye. She furrowed her eyebrows. Will inched toward the door. He could swear the room was getting smaller and smaller. Beads of sweat formed above his lip. He got to the door in two strides. "I'll meet you in the OT room."

He quickly left the room and dashed to the restroom. Sweat ran down his back, and his chest heaved. He hadn't had this reaction since the chief had taken him off the ambulance. Before Shelly's accident, he and Jon worked the ambulance together. It was a tough job and not for the faint of heart. Paramedics dealt with every type of emergency imaginable from car accidents to domestic violence calls, overdoses, and heart attacks. Some things broke his heart, like the death of a child or anyone. Suddenly, the image of Shelly's arm hanging out of the SUV flashed through his head. He'd tried to reach his wife, but Jon and the chief stopped him. He leaned against the wall with his head back, waiting for his body to realize everything was okay. He pushed off the wall, went over to the sink, and splashed water on his face. A lump formed in his throat. *God, where is this coming from?* He wiped his face with a paper towel, took two deep breaths, then opened the door.

Anna was standing there, waiting for him. "It's okay, Cowboy. I'm here." She pulled him into an embrace. "Did you have a panic attack?"

He held her tightly, desperate for the solace she offered. "Can we go now?" He inhaled deeply, his heart racing as he inhaled her familiar scent. Closing his eyes, he tried to ground himself in the moment, pushing away the memories clawing at him from the depths of his soul. He remained rooted to the spot until he could pull himself together and focus on the present. He stood there for a few minutes, trying to compose himself while embracing Anna.

"I told Cindy I would take a raincheck on the tour. I wanted to be here when you came out so you'd know you weren't alone." She smiled. "You ready?"

The compassion in Anna's eyes comforted his soul. "Yes, darlin', thank you." He took her hand. "You're amazing. You have a crappy day, and now you're taking care of me."

Anna shrugged. "Sometimes it's easier to take care of others than yourself. I've seen you do the same thing."

They headed outside, and Will was grateful for the fresh air. He helped

Anna into the truck. "You want to grab some takeout and go back to your cabin? We can drink some wine or something harder."

"Do you think that's a good idea? If we share what happened, we should do it sober.," she said.

"True, so wine it is. That's totally grape juice."

She laughed. "You are insufferable."

Will walked to the other side and climbed into the truck. "Thank you. I don't know why that happened in there. I haven't had a panic attack like that since the chief took me off the ambulance."

"How long ago was that?"

"When I went back to work after Shelly died. Now I go on fire calls and drive the chief."

"I've asked this before, but have you ever considered seeing a therapist?"

"I don't need therapy. I need time."

"Look, I don't want to make you angry, but it might be good to talk to someone. In some ways, you'll never get over the loss of your wife, but what happened in Cindy's office was extreme. A therapist could help you process your grief, and there are medications to help with anxiety."

Will drove for a while without saying anything, tuning her out. He wasn't sure how to respond. He knew she was right. When he first started having panic attacks, he would drink to ease it; he liked the numbness alcohol gave him. Just like Jon. "Can I take you somewhere before we get some food and go home?"

"You aren't going to kill me, are you?"

Will raised an eyebrow. "Are you trying to lighten the mood?"

"I am," she said, smiling.

He glanced at her. "You aren't wrong, Anna. I need to be able to do my job, but I'm not sure I can. And to be honest, I don't want therapy right now."

Deep down, it wasn't just Shelly's death eating away at him. His dad's death haunted him too. He would never forget the day his dad died. They were putting up fences at his dad's ranch when he dropped over and died instantly. That didn't stop Will from doing CPR until the paramedics pulled him off. A widow-maker killed his dad. And he would never forget the look on his mother's face. He felt like he'd let her down. He seemed to disappoint so many people: his dad, his mom, Shelly, and Caden.

Anna wrapped her fingers around his. "Fair enough."

They rode in silence until he pulled into the parking lot of a scenic overlook. Anna gasped, and her face lit up at the sight. "Oh, Will, this is amazing."

It was a bird's-eye view of the state park near Cardinal Creek. The alluring sight of bluebonnets, Indian blankets, and other wildflowers blowing in the gentle wind created an almost ethereal atmosphere. It looked like a million butterflies moving below them. A gentle breeze moved the beauty of the red, blue, and yellow flowers below. They got out of the car, and Will led her by the hand to a nearby deck where they could watch the sun drop from the sky and sleep for the night. He tenderly put his arm around Anna, pulling her close. She sighed and rested her head on his shoulder as they watched the giant orange ball fade into purple, magenta, yellow, and orange streaks before disappearing below the horizon.

Will broke the silence and asked, "darlin', what happened at work today?"

Anna tensed up for a moment before taking a deep breath. Will prayed that she trusted him enough to reveal some of her inner struggles.

Anna started slowly, her voice soft and hesitant. "Remember when we saw the Wattes when we were out on Saturday? You said Cathy looked mad. Well, you were right." Her voice shook as she continued. "She threatened me and accused me of things I haven't done . . . She said she would destroy me, and I believe she will."

There was fear in her eyes. Will remembered how Dr. Watts had been overly familiar with one of the nurses at the station when he was at the hospital for his mother's surgery.

Not wanting to appear jealous, he cautiously wondered if anything like that had ever happened between Dr. Watts and Anna. "Can I ask you something? Please don't get upset."

Her eyebrow raised. "Don't you dare ask me what I think you will ask?"

"It's not like that, Anna. When Momma was having surgery, I saw how Dr. Watts was interacting with one of the nurses at the nurse's station, and she was visibly upset when she came in to take out Momma's IV. Has he ever tried anything like that with you?"

Anna looked down and shook her head. "No, no . . . nothing happened."

He watched her hands tremble. A mixture of jealousy and concern rose within him. He tried to push the conflicting emotions away, but they were difficult to suppress at that moment.

He should only be concerned for her well-being, nothing more. Something about the situation didn't sit right with him. He wanted to ask her what had happened but didn't want to push too far. Instead, he wrapped his arms around her and offered comfort.

"If he ever does anything to hurt you, please tell me," he said. "I want to protect you." He couldn't quite grasp it, but something about that guy made him uneasy.

"I appreciate that. His wife scares me. What if she ruins my nursing career? Maybe it was a mistake leaving my job in Missouri. Maybe I should go back."

Will gasped. "Don't say that, darlin'. Please don't be afraid to talk to me."

"Okay." And just like that, she quickly changed the subject. "Are you hungry?"

He laughed. "We're making progress. Thank you for sharing what happened at work today. If you need help with anything, we can talk to Kati too."

A flash of panic came across her face. "No, Will, please don't tell anyone. It will be okay. I promise."

They walked hand in hand back to his truck. Will felt a little lighter after talking to Anna about his panic attacks. That was the first time he got through one without drinking. He liked that she was honest with him and respected that he wasn't ready for therapy. They made progress: Anna shared with him, and he didn't have to make her mad. He wondered if she felt relieved too.

CHAPTER 32

Anna's gaze was glued to the computer screen as she furiously worked to find answers to the million questions she had about opening an equine center. She clicked through page after page of information.

The grant application was easy; she was truthful about that. However, she hadn't told Will she was lost when it came to setting up an equine center or that she hadn't talked to her contact in Missouri, nor did she know of a center they could use as a model, as she had told Cindy and Will.

She nervously twirled a pen between her fingers and typed "equine centers Missouri" into the search bar. Her eyes quickly scanned the list, searching for one near Columbia. She jotted down a phone number and then read the list of staff members. A slow smile spread across her face when she saw that one of the physical therapists was from Mizzou. She wondered if Jenny knew her. Taking a deep breath, Anna reluctantly picked up her phone to text Jenny. She hated having to ask for help, but this wasn't about her—it was about Will and Caden. Her thumb hovered over the message button, and Anna sent a text with determination filling every ounce of her being.

> Anna: Hey, I need some help. As you are aware, I'm helping Will with the equine center. We went to the center where Caden goes for therapy to meet the director. I'm so stupid. I lied and told him I was acquainted with someone I would call. I just looked up the Tranquility Ranch near Columbia. There's a physical therapist who went to Mizzou. It's a long shot that you may recognize her. Her name is Kitty Love (what were her parents thinking? lol). If you know her, could you help me contact her? Jenny, can you help me, please? Save this text. It will be a golden classic someday.

Anna sank into the couch, glancing at her phone every few seconds. She had already finished filing for their nonprofit 501(c)(3) designation, and now she was stuck on the grant paperwork, which seemed almost impossible. The next step would be to raise funds, but every time Anna asked Will about the financial status of the center, he remained evasive. She wanted to understand, but his lack of transparency made it hard to move forward confidently. Anna wasn't trying to be nosy; she needed to grasp what was going on to make progress and get the center open.

She slid down the couch, her body melting into the worn leather cushions, and closed her eyes. Images of Will's face when he hurried out of Cindy's office flooded her mind. His ordinarily stoic expression had been replaced with one of shock and fear. She could only imagine how difficult it had been for him to be at the center with so many reminders of Shelly. She paused, reached out, and grabbed her phone off the coffee table. Her fingers paused over the keys as she thought of what to say, then quickly tapped out a message to Will.

> Anna: Just checking in to see how you are. I miss you.

Anna waited as she watched the three dots moving. Butterflies danced in the pit of her stomach.

> Will: I miss you too. I'm 100 percent better since I got this text.

She struggled to find the right words. Should she talk about the budget now and risk upsetting him at work? She worried about that, so she kept quiet. It was more about how awkward she was around men, except for Garrett. She wasn't sure why. Her thoughts were interrupted by the three dots that appeared on her screen again.

> Will: Did Cathy Watts leave you alone today?

Anna hid from Cathy and her husband all day. She only left her office if she had a meeting. She ate lunch at her desk and then prayed as she took the stairs out of the hospital that she wouldn't encounter Dr. Watts.

> Anna: I stayed in my office most of the day.

> Will: Did Dr. Watts bother you?

Anna's eyes widened as the words on the screen slowly sunk in. Her stomach twisted into a tight knot as she read his message, wondering if he was being protective or possessive. She had to choose her words carefully, understanding that any misstep may trigger an argument. Anna hesitated before finally typing out a response.

> Anna: Do you think something is going on between us?

Her phone began ringing. *Oh God, I don't want to fight.* She answered. "I don't know how to respond to what you asked. I don't want to fight," she said firmly.

"Darlin, I just wanted to know if he bothered you today. I wasn't accusing you of anything." His tone was calm.

Anna exhaled. "Oh, no, I didn't see him."

"You'll tell me if he bothers you, right?" he asked.

Anna ran her fingers through her hair and closed her eyes. She had no idea what to say; she didn't want to lie and tell him yes because that wasn't true. So she changed the subject. "How are you? Is work okay?"

"Okay, darlin', I'll play along with you, changing the subject." He cleared his throat. "It's the status quo here. How was work for you today?"

"You asked me that question already," she gave a nervous laugh. She was glad he dropped the subject. Dr. Watts needed to be an off-limits subject. She still needed to figure out what she was going to do. *I don't want to say something. What if I'm overreacting?*

"I did. Sorry. I didn't ask what you were wearing."

"You have a key. Come in and see me in the morning."

"Oh really?"

"You'd better bring breakfast."

He cleared his throat. "I'm afraid Garrett is on his own tomorrow. How's the grant going?"

"I'm over halfway done with it. I should be soon, and then we can mail it," she said.

"Did you get ahold of your Missouri contact?"

Anna cleared her throat. "I called and left a voicemail, but nothing else yet." That wasn't exactly a lie, just deceptive.

"We've established the nonprofit, and the grant will be done soon. Our next step is to establish the structure of the center. This includes figuring out the personnel and the logistics of the cabins." Will took a deep breath. "We've made good progress so far."

"You forgot the budget. Do you have any money for things that need to be done, or do we need to organize a fundraiser?" There was a long silence. This was typical of Will when she asked that question. "Will? Can you look for the notebook? Maybe Shelly had something planned." She hoped she wasn't pushing him too much but needed the financial information.

"Anna, I have no idea where it is. I've looked." His voice was strained.

Anna's stomach tightened. She shouldn't have asked about the notebook. That was what had triggered his anxiety attack yesterday.

"I'm sorry, I shouldn't have pushed you about the notebook." Anna sat in silence as an uneasiness built up inside her. She heard him inhaling and exhaling on the other end of the line, but still, he said nothing. Even though it seemed like an eternity had passed, she hoped that just knowing she was there would comfort Will. Tears started to blur her vision as frustration rushed through her veins. How could she be so foolish? She needed to be more sensitive.

"Will . . . are you okay?"

"Can I call you back?" His voice cracked.

Anna whispered, "I'm sorry."

"Darlin', this is not your fault. I'll call you back."

She hung up the phone. Then, her phone started buzzing with a text message.

> Jenny: Haha Kitty Love. Yes, that's her real name. I do know her and the equine center. It's a fantastic place.

> Anna: How did I not know you've been there?

> Jenny: Well, you've been busy caring for your grandparents, working, and dealing with your scumbag ex-boyfriend.

> Anna: No sense in talking about all that, especially the scumbag ex. Can you help me with something? We won't go into how stupid I am and how I got in over my head planning an opening for an equine center.

> Jenny: How can I help?

> Anna: Can you set up a Zoom meeting with Kitty Love? I'll be forever in your debt.

> Jenny: I'll reach out to her. Would next week work for a Zoom meeting?

> Anna: Next week is fine. Just let me tell you what day, and I'll take PTO. I also need to ask her about fundraising. Will is very elusive about the money part.

> Jenny: When does he want to open?

> Anna: September.

> Jenny: After we talk to Kitty, we'll understand what they need to open. Then, he needs to tell you if they need to plan a fundraiser immediately.

> Anna: He had a panic attack yesterday when he was asked. Today, he had another panic attack, I could tell.

> Jenny: What do you think is going on?

Anna's mind was in a fog. He had lost his father and Shelly two years apart. His anxiety attack happened shortly after inquiring about the notebook.

> Anna: It's just an emotional time for him.

Anna hesitated, knowing it was time to ask for Jenny's assistance. Jenny had the certification and the drive necessary for this task. Anna didn't like asking for help but knew it was necessary.

> Anna: I might also need your input with the equine center. Between you and Kitty Love, we could design a unique program.

> Jenny: Just let me know when. I'm always here for you.

She pushed herself off the couch with a sense of urgency. She slipped on her Crocs and headed to the bathroom to peek in the mirror. Her hair was messy, and she had thrown on black shorts, a T-shirt, and a jacket without much thought. She didn't care what she looked like as she left and went to Kati and Liz's cabin. Her heart pounded in her chest as she approached their door. Should she be doing this? What if they said it was none of her business? Or worse, what if they told her it was a family matter? She lifted her arm to knock but paused, holding her breath, as doubt crept in. Ultimately, she took the plunge and knocked firmly on the door.

Kati opened the door. "Hey, Anna, how are you?"

"I'm good. Can you take a walk with me? I need to talk to you."

"Sure, let me put on some shoes."

Anna's feet were like lead weights as she descended the stairs. She steadied herself against the railing, gathering the courage to ask Kati when Shelly had died. Images of Will's breakdown kept playing through her mind, and she experienced a crushing sense of guilt. Why had she pressured him on the phone? Anna searched for answers and hoped she hadn't sent Will into an emotional tailspin.

When Kati stepped outside, Anna jumped at the sudden sound.

"Are you okay?" Kati asked, placing a hand on her shoulder.

"Yeah, I'm okay. I need to ask you a question, and I'm only asking because I'm worried about Will."

Kati stopped in her tracks. "Is Will okay? Did something happen?"

"He's not hurt." Anna hesitated. She chose her words thoughtfully, not wanting to pry into their personal lives. Despite the uncomfortable realization of being an outsider, she tried to support Will. "Yesterday, when we went to the therapy center, Will had a panic attack. He just froze up and it was like he wasn't there. He raced to the bathroom, and when he came out, it looked like he'd been battling some demons. When I talked to him today, I asked him about Shelly's notebook, which triggered a panic attack yesterday, and he quickly got off the phone." She hesitated, then said, "I'm aware I'm not family, but Will is very closed off. He's opened up a bit, but I still have questions. It's okay if you don't want to answer, but can you tell me when Shelly died?"

Kati looked at the ground and kicked at the dirt. "It's the end of May," she said. "Usually, the panic attacks start, the nightmares get worse, and he starts drinking a lot with Jon."

"I understand I'm not family, but I still want to help him," Anna said.

"Why would you say that? We care about you!" She pulled Anna into a hug.

"Thank you for letting me know. I know how difficult grief can be. You might want to ask Jon how Will's doing at work," her voice trembled.

Kati gave her a side hug. "Thank you for really caring about my brother. You have made such a difference in our family."

She nodded with her head down. "Thanks for saying that." She wanted to believe they would want her in their family.

"Good night, Anna," Kati said with another hug.

Anna returned to her cabin and stepped into the warmth of her living room. She dabbed her eyes with her jacket sleeve. Her phone buzzed. She fumbled with it. It was a text from Jenny asking if she was okay. Anna played with the red thread bracelet on her wrist. *How did she know?*

> Anna: I'm fine. Can you let me know when you have the meeting with Ms. Love?

> Jenny: Is the thing with the Deluca family becoming too much? Are you afraid they're going to leave you out in the cold?

> Anna: Shut up and stop reading my mind.

> Jenny: You want to fix Will and hide all your baggage in the box you have packed since your parents died.

Tears burned Anna's eyes as she considered Jenny's words. She realized Will's family was too good to be true, and she couldn't help but think the same of Will. Despite her doubts, she still wanted to help him overcome his grief. She had tried to support his children, and she understood that by doing so, she avoided confronting her pain.

> Anna: Shut up.

> Jenny: Lol, I had a feeling I was right. Don't make me come there and kick your butt.

> Anna: I dare you. Double-dog dare you.

Anna knew that a double-dog dare would get Jenny to visit. She just needed something familiar right now.

> Jenny: You have a family. Momma and I are your family. We're sisters from another mister. Lol

Anna decided the best way to end an emotional time was to watch a beautiful sunset like last night, but it was too late. The next choice was to go to bed. She heard a knock at the door when she was in the bedroom, pulling down the sheets. She prayed it wasn't Kati. She strode toward the door and took a deep breath before she opened it.

"Can I come in?" Will whispered. His face was red and blotchy, his eyes bloodshot, and his eyelids were puffy.

Anna nodded. "Will, aren't you supposed to be working? What's wrong?"

He shrugged. "Well, since I'm just a driver and the chief can do that himself, he told me I could go home. I'm a useless fireman."

Anna wasn't sure how to respond to him. He was distraught, and she didn't want to worsen it. She took him by the hand and led him to the couch. "First, you aren't useless. You're just in pain." She bit her bottom lip to summon the courage to ask, "Did I upset you? Is it me?"

"No, darlin', it's not you." He pulled her into his arms and kissed the top of her head.

They sat in the dimly lit living room, not saying a word. He drew her closer and sighed. "The anniversary of Shelly's death is in a few weeks. I relive that day every year, wondering if I could have done something to save her life. It started yesterday when we took that stroll down the hallway at the clinic. Everything seemed so familiar, but the images of the accident and our time at the clinic suddenly began returning, like an old VHS tape repeatedly replaying itself."

"I triggered it again when I asked about the notebook. Didn't I?"

"No, darlin', it's not your fault. I was already thinking about it. Jon and I can empty a liquor store this time of year," he chuckled.

"We'll get through this. Just tell me how I can help," she murmured. "I talked to Kati and asked her to call Jon to ensure you were okay."

"Thank you for checking on me," he whispered into her ear. "Now, you could kiss me. Then let me spend the night with you, and we'll see what that leads to."

Anna smiled. "I can do that." She kissed him with a passion that took her breath away. "How was that?"

A wicked smile spread across his face. "Hmm, maybe try again."

"Now, I'll change the subject before we get busy. We should have a meeting this Saturday and invite everyone." She put her hands on his face.

"We need to talk about the budget. You don't have to hide anything from me. We will get through it."

"I believe you'll make it work. I'm working through my thing about the budget, to be honest."

"Cowboy, now is the time to let us help you."

"I promise I'll tell you."

"You feel a little better?"

Will hugged her tighter. "How can you make me feel . . . I guess . . . safe at home?"

"I'm gonna change the subject again," she giggled. "I can make you feel great."

He raised an eyebrow. "Oh, you can?" He picked her up in one quick swoop that caused her to squeal. He took her to the bedroom and kicked the door closed.

CHAPTER 33

The truck's engine hummed as they drove closer to the Cattle Trail Café. Anna sat beside Will, her hands in her lap and her eyes fixed on the passing scenery. Eva and Caden were in the backseat. He had noticed this distant look on Anna's face before. It almost always indicated she was upset about something. The uneasy silence between them filled the truck's cab until it felt like an intruder in their relationship. A few days earlier, he'd been overwhelmed with anxiety, and Anna had done everything she could to calm him down. Somehow, she had managed to soothe him.

Will grabbed her hand. "Hey, you okay?"

She glanced at him and smiled. "I'm fine."

"Was work okay yesterday?"

She chuckled. "You asked me that last night."

"I'm just making sure."

"Cowboy, I haven't seen Cathy all week."

Will shook off his nerves. Things were moving forward with the equine center. They needed to keep diligently working on the grant. Now, they needed to ask his friends and family for financial help.

"Can we go for a ride after we eat?" Anna asked.

"Sure, if you want. You aren't going to take me on a ride so you can take advantage of me, are you?"

"Oh my God, Dad, that's so gross," Eva yelled from the back seat.

"What did I say?"

Anna looked at Eva. "Please don't repeat it." She gave a friendly punch to Will's arm. "Stop, kids today know way more than we did when we were ten."

"I know about Mario brothers," Caden yelled.

Will laughed. "Me too, buddy. We should play that tomorrow."

"Oh yeah!" Caden exclaimed as he fist-punched the air.

Will pulled into the parking lot, leaned in to kiss Anna, gave Eva a side-eye, and smiled.

Eva leaned forward and declared, "Disgusting Daddy, this is the part where you let us out."

As Will and the kids stepped out of the car, he chuckled. He offered Anna his assistance, gazed into her eyes, and said, "I appreciate everything you've done. But above all, thank you for being my friend."

He held her hand as they entered the restaurant to greet the tribe he was building to bring Shelly's dream to life. He prayed they could pull it off, but he knew there was a chance it wouldn't happen unless Anna was an angel sent from heaven to perform a miracle.

Liz was already seated at the head of the table. Her smile was warm, as always. Caden and Eva ran into her arms for a hug. Will kissed her on the forehead. "Hey, Momma, how are you?"

"Getting better every day. How are you? I know this begins a rough time for you." She touched his face.

He glanced at Anna. "I'm doing okay, thanks to Anna," he said. "She's been great. She listens to me when I talk. I've made it through with no alcohol."

"Have you talked to Kati?"

"Not yet," he said. "But I will."

Liz touched his arm. "We need to talk, okay?"

He nodded. "Okay, I promise."

Will led Anna to a seat next to Garrett, taking in the meeting of family and friends around the table. Kati and Jon were across from her, Eva and Caden settled next to Liz, and the Hens, Sissy, and Peggy Sue—his mother's quilting friends—were next to Caden. He briefly introduced them to Anna, promising a more formal introduction after breakfast.

He looked around the table, feeling blessed by all the love in the room. His gaze eventually met Anna's, and he felt a wave of tenderness swell within him. He was so grateful that she'd found her way back into his life.

Anna and Garrett engaged in conversation, laughing and smiling. Then concern washed over Garrett's face as Anna leaned in and whispered something to him. A surge of jealousy stirred within him, and he realized his jealousy had morphed into something new. He no longer questioned whether Anna and Garrett had a romantic relationship. Instead, he didn't understand why Anna could be so open with Garrett but wouldn't talk to him. He had a strong desire to support her.

Rising abruptly, he leaned close to her ear and said, "I'm gonna use the restroom. If they come for drink orders, I want coffee."

She smiled. "Okay, I'll get it for you."

He kissed her forehead. "I'll be back in a few, darlin'."

Anna motioned for him to come closer. "I'm very nervous about all of this."

He looked at Garrett. "Tell her it's going to be okay. She doesn't always believe me."

Garrett shrugged a shoulder. "That's what I've been telling her."

Will pointed to Garrett and himself. "We believe in you." He pointed to everyone at the table. "We all have faith in you." He squeezed her shoulders and murmured, "Baby, believe in yourself." Will headed to the bathroom, masking his uncertainty. Taking off the mask didn't accomplish anything.

Will slipped into the bathroom, his chest heaving. He leaned against the wall and closed his eyes, hoping to gain a moment's peace. But as soon as he heard the door open, he moved quickly to the sink and turned on the faucet, letting out a deep sigh as he glanced nervously in the mirror and saw Jon standing behind him. His brow furrowed with worry.

"How are you doing, Will? Usually, we hit the bars to drown our sorrows."

Will glanced at him in the mirror. "Do you think that helps?"

Jon shrugged. "Probably not, but it numbs it. What's up with Ginger?"

Will shook his head. "No wonder Kati won't date you. You want to know if I'm tapping it."

Jon creased his forehead. "Christ, Will, respect the lady. She's very nice. Caden likes her."

Will rubbed the back of his neck. "Why do you care?"

"What's your problem?" Jon took a step toward him. "I meant that Ginger seems nervous. Do you think I want her or something, that I'll steal her away from you?" He laughed.

Will grunted but said nothing.

"Come on." Jon rolled his eyes. "Where does this come from?"

Will stepped closer, his gaze radiating an intensity, but Jon's gaze had an equal power. "I saw you two laughing that day. I confronted her and . . . and she left!" His voice rose with accusation, nearly making Jon push his chest out. "Girls have always liked you better because you were more outgoing," he continued bitterly. "And now, she's out there holding Garrett's damn hand!"

Jon's hands tightened around the front of Will's shirt, pushing him back toward the wall with fire in his eyes. "What are you talking about? That camp again? Didn't we discuss this? I guess your apologies don't mean a thing." He yanked on the front of his shirt again. "This isn't about Anna, and you know it. This is about the night Shelly died. Are you pissed because I didn't save her?" He yanked Will's collar again. "Don't ever mention anything about my interest in Anna, now or in the future."

Will shoved Jon away and straightened his sleeves, ashamed of himself for losing control. "God, I'm sorry . . . I'm not myself these days." He'd just told his mother that Anna was helping him through, and that was true. But drinking himself into a stupor with Jon—as they always did—sounded pretty good too. Guilt hit Will like a ton of bricks. He scrubbed his face, trying to release some of the tension that built up between them this time of year. He knew Jon was battling his own emotions.

"If anyone should hate Anna, it should be me," Jon said. "This year, I'm all alone. You know I'm in love with Kati! Why are we even friends if you think so little of me?"

A heavy weight of guilt pressed on Will as tears stung at his eyes. He cleared his throat before speaking again. "Shit, Jon, I'm sorry. I told you I'm not feeling like myself. Why are we so angry with each other lately?"

Jon gave a slight shrug and opened the bathroom door slowly. "I have no idea," he said. "But sometimes, I want to punch your face."

Will chuckled. "You do?"

A faint smile tugged at the corner of Jon's mouth as he glanced at Will one last time before stepping out into the hallway. "Yeah, I do. You need to figure your shit out. But right now, I want some pancakes drenched in syrup. And a bottle of Crown later."

"I'd like that combo myself," Will said. "I've got a full bottle of Crown Apple at home if you want to join me later."

Jon raised an eyebrow. "What about Anna?"

"Didn't you hear there's a bonfire and music tonight?" Will asked.

"I'm invited?"

"Yeah, of course, you plus one."

Jon pushed his shoulder. "My plus-one is a bottle of whiskey to drown my sorrows."

Will clapped him on the shoulder. "Exactly."

Anna's lips turned up as she spotted him returning to the table. He wanted to bask in her warm smile and dismiss his earlier doubts about her feelings. Still, he couldn't shake the sinking sense of doubt as he watched Anna and Garrett engrossed in conversation. Did his unpredictable emotions make it impossible for her to trust him enough to share her grief?

The café was buzzing with the low hum of conversation. The thick scent of buttery pancakes wafted through the air, and almost everyone at Will's table had ordered them. Plates were being passed around as people nibbled on their breakfast and discussed the equine center as they ate. The knot in Will's stomach grew tighter as they faced reality about finances once everyone finished eating.

Anna squeezed his hand. "Hey, I was asking you a question."

He shook his head. "Sorry, darlin'. What was the question?"

"Do you have any donors so far? Garrett was asking."

He looked at Garrett. "Uh, no."

"Garrett has some experience fundraising. He said he's willing to help."

Will looked up. "That's what you two have had your heads together about all this time?"

Anna bumped his shoulder. "What else would we be talking about besides the horses?"

"William, we hens need to know what you need so we can begin to plan!" Liz yelled from the other end of the table.

Sweat trickled down Will's back as he pushed his chair back. He knew he had to stand, but his body was heavy, weighted down by the pressure of not having enough money to fund opening the center. The thought of everyone finding out caused panic to set in. He couldn't let Anna down. They had planned to announce their fundraising efforts together. *Is there even a plan? I need to pay more attention.* But fear prickled his scalp, making him doubt if they were ready for this step.

The warmth of Anna's hand touched his sleeve, and her soft voice broke through his fear. She stood beside him and smiled. "Hey, y'all excuse us. I forgot to tell Will something."

She turned to him and said, "Get up and follow me to the bathroom." She took his hand and led him away to the privacy of a hallway. "Garrett and I are here. We'll tell them what we know. Maybe the Hens can make some quilts for an auction?" Even with her comfort, some of him wanted to hide from the truth.

"Auctioned where, Anna?" His voice cracked.

"Will look at me. We can do this. You have a good support system. They want to help—Garrett, Jon, Kati, Liz, her friends, and my friend Jenny.

"How is Jenny involved?"

"She's my contact in Missouri." She smiled. "I've got it all under control. We'll discuss finances later. Now repeat after me: 'Fake it until you make it.'"

He wrinkled his brow. "Really, darlin'?"

"Cowboy, say it."

"Fake it until you make it," he mumbled.

Anna smiled. "Good boy." Then she moved her hands over the back of his neck and kissed him lightly on his lips, sending fireworks from his brain to his toes. "Now, let's go tell them what we know." She smacked his backside and winked. "You got this."

A smile spread across his face. "Yes, ma'am." This rollercoaster of emotions this morning was giving him a headache. He needed to drink tonight.

Will listened as Anna explained what they'd done so far. His lungs expanded to their fullest through deep, satisfying breaths as she assigned what must be done to the Hens, Garrett, Kati, and Jon. She let them know that the next time they met, she would give them more information about what they needed financially, and they'd most likely need to set up a fundraiser. To his surprise, all the ladies at the table clapped their hands at the thought of dressing up to raise money.

"Anna has done a great job handling this," Liz yelled from the other end of the table at Will. "Can you bring her down to this end and formally introduce her to Peggy Sue and Sissy?"

Will grabbed Anna's hand. "Come on, let me introduce you to the two best quilters I know besides my momma."

His heart swelled with pride, thinking about what Anna had done that day. "Thank you, darlin'," he said.

She smiled. "Don't you know I care about you and your family?"

"I can't wrap my head around someone like you."

Her eyes narrowed. "Why?" She pointed to his mom, sister, and the other people around the table. "All of these people are just like me. It's called unconditional love."

Will's heart skipped a beat. *Did she say she loved me? No, we haven't known each other that long. I guess we have. I need to get ahold of myself.*

Will watched as Sissy and Peggy Sue, two grandmotherly ladies he had known his entire life, warmly welcomed Anna. His mother had been friends with the quilting pair since they were in elementary school. Over the years, Will and Kati used to go to Cardinal Creek Quilting on Main Street while their mother sewed. Sissy owned the quilt shop, and Will fondly remembered visiting her shop with Kati while his mom sewed with the other women. The older ladies would pinch their cheeks, but mostly Jon's, because he was a charmer even in kindergarten.

Sissy grabbed Will's hand and said, "Don't screw this up. She's what you need."

Will shot her a look. "What?"

Peggy Sue interjected, "You heard what she said. Don't screw this up. She loves you."

Will raised an eyebrow. "How do you know that?"

Sissy smacked his thigh. "You love her too. You both don't know it yet. Sissy and I have started a pool on your wedding date."

Will shook his head. "The older you hens get, the crazier you are."

Sissy yelled to Liz. "I'm gonna smack him."

Liz shrugged. "I give you permission."

Will held up his hands in surrender and turned to Anna. "Darlin', did you hear that?"

Anna smiled. "I'm sorry, love. They invited me to the sip and sew."

Sissy yelled, "Jonny, come hug us. Will is insufferable."

Jon walked up behind Will. "Anna called you 'love.' Not me, not Garrett, so don't screw it up."

Will elbowed him in the ribs. "Are we good?"

Jon clapped him on the back. "Always. Meet you at the firepit later. Now I need to see Miss Sissy. She needs to pinch my cheeks." He wiggled his eyebrows. "She's kind of a cougar."

Will laughed. Jon's humor could always bring him out of whatever funk he got into. He turned to Liz. "Momma, can Caden and Eva go home with you? Anna and I are going riding to talk finances."

Jon shook his head and laughed. "Is that what they call it now?"

Sissy smacked his arm. "Behave, Jon."

Will wrinkled his nose. "Why are you so nasty?"

"Do you want apple or regular Crown? Honey Jack?" Jon kept talking like nothing was said.

"Surprise me."

Will was ready to leave so he could be alone with Anna. He kissed his mom on her cheek. "Campfire later, okay?"

"I'm proud of you. Let's get through this next week without so much drinking." She squeezed his hand. "Anna is good for you. This is the first year Kati and I are not picking you and Jon up off the floor drunk off your butt."

Will stayed silent for a few minutes. "I'm drinking tonight."

She grabbed his hand. "Don't screw this up, Will."

He kissed her forehead. "I won't. Now let me go so I can go riding. See you at the campfire. Don't be late."

Everyone had warned him not to mess things up with Anna: his closest friend, the Hens, and even his mother. He could hear their voices in his head, like a chorus of warnings. He could feel their silent alert radiating an unspoken message to not screw this up because of his tendency toward jealousy. His head swirled with a chaotic mix of emotion as he tried to figure out his feelings. He didn't want to screw things up.

Will grabbed Anna's hand and headed toward the door. He was eager to kiss Anna when they got to the truck. He took long strides to the parking lot, and she practically ran behind him.

"Will, are you angry with me?" she asked.

He stopped, pulled her into his arms, and kissed her until they were both breathless. "No, darlin', I'm not mad. I wanted to get to the truck so I could kiss you." He hugged her tight. "Thank you for all you are doing. I was nervous today, but you stepped up and didn't let me fall on my face."

"You are worth helping and worth more to me than you know," she said.

He couldn't believe what he was hearing. Tears burned his eyes. "What did you say?"

She looked him in the eyes. "You are worth helping and are worth more to me than you know."

"Thank you, darlin'." Those words rang in his ears all the way home. He could hear her sweet voice saying he was worth it. She thought he was worth it. He hadn't felt he was worth anything in the last three years, and because of Anna, maybe he could learn to believe in himself. She meant the world to him. He could love her, but it was too soon to say that.

CHAPTER 34

Anna and Will trotted their horses across the pasture, the sun warming their faces. Anna took in the kaleidoscope of wildflowers surrounding them, every color from deep blues to fiery reds and bright yellows. She watched the vibrant flowers swaying in the breeze. As they slowly rode forward in silence, Anna noticed Will seemed far away—his gaze distant, his posture rigid. Whenever she tried to talk to Will about finances, he seemed agitated and unwilling to discuss it. When she explained this to Garrett, they'd devised a plan to ensure the center would open on time. If they wanted it to open in September, they needed to get his numbers soon and implement their plan.

Will stopped his horse and turned to look for her. "You comin', Ginger?"

Anna shrugged. "Just enjoying the flowers . . . the view. What was wrong with you at the restaurant?"

"What do you mean?" Will nudged Jake and headed toward the hill.

Thunderbird followed him. Anna didn't answer because she knew it was his way of avoiding the question. When they reached the top of the summit, they headed toward a tree across from where they'd shared their first kiss. The panoramic view had many beautiful spots. She noticed the tree the day they kissed, but they hadn't been there since. They dismounted their horses and strolled toward a stone bench nestled under the expansive branches of an oak tree. Will carried a blanket over his arm, ready to enjoy the peaceful surroundings.

"You like to come here, don't you?"

He nodded and motioned for her to sit beside him on the blanket. Her gaze was drawn to the stone bench she hadn't noticed before on their previous ride. She gasped when she read the inscription: "Michelle Lynn Deluca: Wife, Mother, Sister, and Daughter." A beautiful angel with a horse adorned the top of the bench, and intense emotions filled her chest. Anxiety struck like a lightning bolt. Why had he brought her here? She desperately wanted to run away but forced herself to stay in control.

Will reached out and grasped Anna's hand. "To answer your question, I was jealous when you talked to Garrett." She tried to pull away, but he kept a firm grip. His voice was intense when he spoke, his gaze never leaving hers. "Hear me out, please." He seemed to struggle for words as if his thoughts were tangled threads that wouldn't untwist. "It's not that I think you're gonna leave me. It's just . . . there's a connection between us, but there's still a wall that we've both built up around us. And when I see you with Garrett, you seem so at ease. I want us to feel comfortable with each other." His voice faltered, and he swallowed hard. "Anyway, it's stupid, never mind." He let out a long sigh.

"I knew you were upset about something."

He shrugged. "It just seems like you find it easy to talk to him. You always seem guarded when you talk to me." He rubbed his neck. "Why don't you talk about your grandparents or parents with me? Or talk about your ex-boyfriend, Jenny, or anything else? It's always about me." He touched her arm. "It's not always about me."

Anna wasn't surprised. She hadn't shared many things with Will, and he hadn't shared them with her. Why was it so hard for her to tell him how she felt? Maybe it was because she was still figuring things out. "I'm sorry. I was telling Garrett how concerned I was about the finances for the equine center. I don't want to let you down." Her voice cracked.

Will nodded, urging her to continue.

"I don't talk about my grandfather or my life back at home because it's hard. I want to move forward and not talk about the past. I know you understand. I moved here to start over, and that's where I am emotionally."

Then, an image of Dr. Watts's slimy smile flashed before her. She realized that part of the reason she was so closed off about her life back in Missouri was that it meant she would need to confront what was going on in her life in Texas. Anna wasn't sure what to say to him about her grief. She didn't want to burden him with her stuff, especially since he was so distraught about the anniversary of Shelly's death.

So she turned the discussion back to Will like she always did. "I understand how important the equine center is for you, and if I can't figure out how to get money or how much we need, I'll fail you and your family."

Will gathered her in his arms. "I'm sorry I'm causing you so much stress. I know we need to talk about finances, but if I say the truth out loud, it could all end."

"Garrett said there's enough time to raise funds, but you have to tell us how much we need."

He kissed the top of her head. "I will, darlin'. I need more time."

Anna bit her lip, suppressing the urge to shout her frustration. Deep down, she knew there was no money. Why wouldn't he tell her? She should team up with Garrett to raise funds without telling Will.

Now wouldn't be the time to start pressing him about Shelly because that could be a possible powder keg. She walked on eggshells when it came to talking about Shelly. At times, it was like Will was still married to her. Even though he hadn't been wearing his ring, they never went to his place for dinner or stayed the night there. Anna's mind raced with possibilities as she watched Will gaze out over the ranch below, seemingly lost in thought. *Just a little more time* echoed in Anna's mind repeatedly.

"Shelly loved the view, so I brought her ashes here and buried them by that tree." Will pointed to the memorial bench.

"It-it's beautiful." Her breath caught in her throat, and tears blurred her vision as she stared at her hands. *He needed time . . . time away from me . . . time for what?* Her eyes were downcast as she twisted her hands together. A million things were going through her mind. It took all she had to remain seated because she wanted to get on Thunderbird and run away from everything as far as she could.

"I loved what we shared a couple weeks ago. I love waking up with you in my arms. I don't sleep well when you aren't there, but . . ."

Anna's shoulders were slumped, and her gaze was glued to her lap. Her breath hitched in her throat. Will licked his lips and looked away, unable to meet her gaze as he spoke. He slowly inhaled and exhaled before he said. "I thought I felt guilty for being with you, like I was cheating on Shelly, but I feared getting hurt and feeling vulnerable. I told myself it wasn't right, but it was."

"Just say it so I can leave." She was tired of these games. Neither of them was ready for this relationship.

She tried hoisting herself up, but Will gently caught her wrist. "Please, let me finish. You're always trying to run away."

She looked at him, eyes filled with pain. "You want me to leave, right?"

His eyes widened. "Darlin', didn't you hear what I said?"

She wiped her eyes. "The last thing I heard was that you needed time."

"First, when I said I needed time, I meant time to discuss finances. Second, I wanted to bring you up here to share some things with you. Please sit. Long story short, I'm ready to open my heart to you. I won't hide behind the death of my wife."

Anna settled back down. She could see the sincerity in his eyes.

"Something you said to me earlier keeps ringing in my ears. It means so much that you believe in me and think I'm worth helping. The more time we spend together, the more I care about you. I've never met someone like you. No matter the cost, you put others before yourself. I want to be there for you, too."

Anna nodded, urging him to continue.

"Darlin', I'm working hard to change my line of thinking. It's never about you but more about me. I'm sorry about the way I acted at the restaurant. I know you and Garrett would never try to hurt me. That's why I went to the bathroom to regroup. I admit it's been hard with the anniversary of Shelly's death coming up. I relive the time she was alive to the accident." He paused, then said, "My feelings for you grow every day. I'm still in awe that you stepped in at the restaurant when I was going to panic about the finances. Then there's the therapy center. I couldn't believe you were so in tune with my feelings. It means a lot to me, Anna."

He lifted her chin to kiss her. The kiss released butterflies in her stomach that fluttered to her heart. He looked her in the eyes. "Darlin', I promise I'll share the finances with you soon."

Anna sat for a while before she said anything. She wasn't sure how to respond to his beautiful words. He opened his heart to her. It was something they both guarded. She understood that the anniversary of a loved one's death would always bring up feelings that could turn a person upside down, especially when a trauma was involved. She knew that all too well because she had experienced loss through trauma.

He pulled her close. "Anna, you have been a blessing to our family, and I truly appreciate all you've done."

Anna took a deep breath. If he was ready to open his heart to her, then she should share part of her heart with him. "Thank you for sharing," she said.

The warmth of Will's body comforted her. She looked around the countryside and spotted a hawk hovering in the sky, looking for its next meal.

When she turned back to him, his eyes were filled with compassion. She took a deep breath, steeling herself to open up. "Tony betrayed me when I shared my heart with him," she said softly, her voice catching in her throat. "It's not that I don't trust you . . . you're nothing like Tony. But he wasn't the only one who hurt me; Emma did, too, in a different way. It's not that I trust Garrett, and I don't trust you. Garrett is more like a brother, which is different. You know, like you and Kati." Finally, she said, "I miss my grandparents and feel alone."

There, I said I'm sad.

The warmth of Will's embrace was like a shield around them against the sadness they both felt. His musky scent filled her senses and eased the ache in her heart. After silence, he whispered into her hair, "Thank you for trusting me." Anna closed her eyes and leaned into him, thankful for opening the door just a little.

CHAPTER 35

Will's leg incessantly bounced as he watched Anna work diligently on the grant paperwork. He was grateful she'd opened up to him, though he could feel her loneliness. He wanted to know more about what happened with her ex-boyfriend but didn't want to pry. As the anniversary of Shelly's death grew closer, Will's anxiety rose. He just wanted to drink until it was all over. His leg moved faster as his thoughts kept jumping to the day Shelly died and other memories he wished he could forget. It had been hard before Anna came into his life; he had nowhere to turn and no one to talk to. Because she was here, he had some solace from the pain.

Anna placed her hand on his knee. "What's up with your leg going like a motorboat."

He shrugged. "Just restless." He bolted off the couch. "You want a beer?"

Will needed something to take the edge off his nerves. It was nearing the middle of May, and he still needed to figure out how he would get funds to open in September. His palms began to sweat as he opened the refrigerator door. He reached in, pulled out a beer bottle, cracked open the cap with one hand, and brought it to his lips. From the corner of his eye, he caught sight of Anna peering up at him from behind her laptop screen. "Um . . . thirsty?" he said between sips of beer, a hint of forced cheeriness.

He leaned against the countertop as he nursed his beer, contemplating his situation. How would they raise enough money to open if they couldn't afford to finish the cabins and refurbish the lodge? He guzzled what was left in his bottle before he pulled another one from the fridge and twisted the cap off. His shoulders slumped. He should set up another meeting with Cindy or tell Anna what was happening. He knew not telling her was irrational, but fear kept him from doing many things.

"How long does it take to get the grant money? Will we have it in time?" Will asked.

Anna looked up. "Talk to me, Will."

"Could you explain this to me? I need to understand so I know what I need."

Anna set her computer on the table and walked over to him. "Well, it's likely we won't have the grant in time to do the work that needs to be done. Do you have bids for the repairs and materials?"

Will's mind was clouded with irrational thoughts. He knew they needed a fundraiser but was unsure how to tell Anna without exposing his attachment to Shelly's notebook, which contained the plans she'd made. The notebook was filled with Shelly's notes, her writing still vivid, but he couldn't read it thoroughly. Maybe if he could find something valuable inside it . . .

He tried to hide his turmoil as Anna explained what they needed: repairs, equipment, insurance, plus enough to run for six months or more. "If you think we'll need a fundraiser, please tell me now so we can organize it."

"I don't know if we need one," he replied hesitantly. Anna returned to the couch and sat down without a word, leaving Will in internal torment. Should he tell her they needed a fundraiser? How much of himself should he reveal why this project was so important? His mind raced as he wrestled with what to say.

There was a loud knock on the door that caused them to jump.

When Anna opened the door, Kati stood smiling at her. "Wow, you sounded like the police. Come in."

She bounced inside. "Remember, we're having a bonfire and smores tonight. To celebrate the end of the school year or that it's Saturday."

Will finished his beer. "Kati, you just like parties."

She shrugged. "True. Guess who showed up?"

Will scratched his head. "I don't know, Jon?"

Kati put her hands on her hips. "How did you know?"

He held up his phone. "He texted me, and I invited him this morning."

She shook her head. "Well, never mind, just come. We built a fire. Momma hobbled out, and we even invited Garrett."

Caden yelled from the porch, "Come on, Daddy. I want Anna to come. It's going to be fun."

Will pasted on a smile. "I guess we're having a party. Give us a few minutes to wrap things up." The last thing he wanted was to be around people. His chest tightened every time he thought about letting everyone down. A couple of beers had taken off the edge. Maybe he could relax and enjoy time with Anna and his family.

As they wrapped things up, Anna said, "Things are coming together, but I need a bit longer to finish the grant. I'm trying to plug some holes. I don't have answers to some questions, but I'm working with Jenny. Do you remember *any* of the plans Shelly talked about?"

He rubbed the back of his neck. "Not really, I'm sorry."

Anna frowned. "You looked worried."

He wrapped his arms around her, kissing the top of her head. "It's all good. Let's go to the bonfire."

Will's mind returned to the notebook and how much it could help. He would finally muster up the courage and look at it . . . tomorrow. A deep breath and a sense of resolution settled over him, and he reached for Anna's hand. "Let's go have some fun."

Together, they stepped out into the night, joining the revelers around the bonfire. Garrett and Jon were deep in conversation while Eva and Caden sat with Kati and Liz, all in fits of laughter at something Kati had said. Liz kissed each child on the head before wrapping her arms around them.

Will smiled, grateful for this family he was so lucky to be a part of. But as his gaze drifted to Anna, doubt crept in like a fog. Could he ever be the man she deserved? He cared for her deeply but felt unworthy. How could he lie to her about still wearing his wedding ring? He had taken it off on their first date, but he still wore it on his finger when he worked at the fire station. It disappeared into his pocket whenever he was with Anna. He wished he could explain why. Was it emotional baggage? Why couldn't he let go? The guilt and regret were palpable as Will realized the full extent of his lies—about money, the fundraiser, and his ring. He was a fraud. He needed another drink.

When Caden saw them, he sprinted toward them and caught Will around the waist, returning him to reality. "I love you, Daddy."

Smiling, Will ruffled his hair. "I love you too, buddy."

Eva strolled over. "Daddy, what took you so long?"

Wrapping his arm around Eva, Will said, "We had to finish something up."

She wriggled free from his grasp, then grabbed his hand. "Let's go make s'mores!"

Even as Eva dragged Will, he never let go of Anna's hand. She followed behind him laughing.

When they reached the fire pit, he gave Garrett and Jon a friendly pat on the shoulder. "Hey, ya'll." He grabbed a beer from the cooler and drank half of it in one swallow. He noticed Anna watching with a furrowed brow. Too much was going on, and he needed to relax. The mask of happiness wouldn't work tonight without something to numb his mind.

"How was the ride?" Jon asked Will.

Will took a long sip of his beer. "Good, we rode up and sat on the hill."

"Talking finances," Jon said, using air quotes.

Will bumped his shoulder as he finished his beer. "You're an idiot. Where's the whiskey?"

"I'm making s'mores. Ya'll want some?" Garrett said as he stood. He gave Anna's shoulder a friendly squeeze as he walked by.

Anna kissed Will's cheek. "I'm going to make s'mores. Want some?"

"No, I'm good."

She went by the fire, and Eva handed Anna a stick with marshmallows pierced through it.

After his fourth beer, Will's head was clouded as he watched everyone laughing and enjoying a good time. The kids' faces were sticky with chocolate and marshmallows. The bonfire threw shadows across their faces. Anna and Garrett were happily chatting. He clenched his jaw so tight his teeth hurt as he watched his family enjoy themselves while he tortured himself with irrational thoughts. He decided to put his worries away for the night, determined to join the others and put on a facade. *Anna said fake it until you make it.*

Liz yelled, "Y'all, I have the graham crackers and chocolate."

Will walked behind Liz's chair and kissed the top of her head. "Hey, Momma. How are you?"

"Well, it's almost time to get this cast off. Then I can come back to the stable."

"We miss havin' you. Don't we, Garrett?" Will said.

"Of course we do, plus her coffee is better than yours," Garrett said.

Will placed his hand over his heart. "Garrett, you wound me." A feeling of guilt washed over him. Garrett had always been a friend to the family and him.

Will grabbed another beer and settled in front of the fire, where Jon joined him with a bottle of Crown Royal and a six-pack of Coke. He handed Will an aluminum cup, filled it with a shot of whiskey, topped it off with soda, and then poured himself one. Raising his cup in a salute, he said, "Here's to Shelly."

Their cups touched with a soft clink as Will murmured, "To Shelly."

At the bonfire, his gaze landed on Anna with Eva, Caden, and Liz. Warmth surged through his body when he watched Anna wipe marshmallow from Caden's cheek and hug him tightly. When they finished making s'mores, Kati cranked up her favorite tunes—the boy bands she loved—and dragged Caden and Eva onto the grassy dance floor. Anna followed despite her face turning redder than her hair. Will grinned at Jon as they watched Anna and Kati jump and spin to music more suited for teenage girls than grown women.

After several songs, Kati announced, "Hey, Eva, check this out." She held up two wireless karaoke microphones.

Eva screamed, "Oh, Aunt Kati, I love it. Anna, are you going to sing with us?"

Anna declined with a shake of her head and raised her hands. "No . . . I've already made a fool of myself."

Her eyes landed on Will, and a grin stretched across her face. Using one finger, he beckoned her over. She went to where he was seated with a drink; the liquor was undoubtedly working its magic. She leaned in and kissed him. "What are you doing over here?" she asked.

Will was on a plastic Adirondack chair with his long legs crossed in front of him. Jon sat beside him, his eyes fixated on something only he could see. "He doesn't know how to behave when he drinks," Will said, nodding toward Jon.

Jon flipped Will off. "I wish I had more middle fingers."

Will laughed. "Great song."

Jon nodded. "It is."

Will grabbed Anna by the waist and pulled her onto his lap. He wrapped his arms around her and whispered, "I love how you are with Caden." Then he started kissing her neck, causing her to giggle. "Can I stay with you tonight? I promise I'll be good."

Jon slugged Will's arm playfully. "Oh my God, get a room. Not enough whiskey for that."

Kati yelled, "He's jealous!"

Will expected Jon to say something, but he didn't. He refilled his cup with more whiskey than soda. Will handed his cup to Jon and asked for another round. Will knew Jon's silence wasn't good. Should he say something to Kati or let it go?

Eva appeared by Anna's side and grabbed her hand. "You have to sing with us!" she exclaimed, pulling Anna away.

Before Anna was tugged onto the dance floor, she kissed Will and whispered, "You can stay if you don't behave."

NSYNC's "Tearin' Up My Heart" began to play, and Anna, Kati, and Eva danced and squealed. Will's mind drifted away, and his heart felt so conflicted. Were his feelings for Anna enough? He wanted to share this moment with her, but his mind was stuck in the past. *Maybe drinking wasn't a good idea,* he thought. Then his thoughts shifted to the equine center, and the notebook tucked away in Shelly's nightstand. He just couldn't let it go because that would mean letting go of Shelly entirely. He finished his drink, but he knew no amount of alcohol could ease this pain. He yearned for Anna's kiss, yet he knew that if he made even one move, he'd be forced to confront his unresolved memories of Shelly.

Jon tapped on his shoulder, holding out the bottle to fill Will's cup with whiskey.

"Look at Anna with Eva. Dude, she's so cool," Jon slurred.

Eva and Anna talked animatedly, sharing stories with laughter in between. He smiled at the sight of them. Anna's inner beauty was even more captivating than her physical appearance—it emanated from deep within her soul. Since her arrival, she'd brought warmth and compassion to the family that had been missing them for far too long.

Kati played George Strait's "Give it All We Got Tonight" and gave Will a thumbs-up. Will got up on shaky feet and walked over to Anna.

"Would you like to dance with me?" he asked as he held out his hand.

She took his hand, sending electricity up his arm. "I'd love to."

Will wrapped Anna in his arms while she laid her head on his chest. He pulled her closer. They swayed to the music, and he lost his footing a bit, but Anna steadied him.

She looked at him, smiling. "Are you okay? It's not like you to stumble."

"I'm fine." His mind was beginning to be clouded by the liquor. The conflict in his heart left a sinking feeling in his stomach. *Just take it slow.*

Jon asked Kati, "Do you want to dance with me?"

Will raised an eyebrow when Kati accepted. "Shit."

Anna looked at him. "What's wrong?"

"Jon and Kati are dancing."

She placed a hand on his cheek. "It'll be okay."

Will was suddenly distracted as his gaze kept drifting to Jon and Kati. When the dance ended, Jon kissed Kati, pulling her close. When the kiss ended, Will braced for the fireworks. When Kati didn't slap his face but touched it tenderly. Will sighed long and yelled, "It's about time."

They looked at him and smiled.

He whispered to Anna, "Darlin', I'm going to talk to Jon." She smiled and nodded.

He grabbed two beers and took a seat next to Jon. "How are you doing?"

Jon took the beer. "Better than you for once. Are you okay?"

Will shot him a glance from the corner of his eye. "Yeah, kind of . . . I don't know."

He took a long drink. "I know this time of year is tough for all of us. How are the kids?"

"They seem fine, but I'm so self-absorbed as usual, I don't know. I'm surprised Kati let you kiss her."

He finished his beer. "A pity kiss, I'm sure." He kicked the dirt with his boot. "I'm gonna go."

Will touched his arm. "You've been drinking, no driving." He felt Jon relax. "Come on, talk to me. What was up with the kiss?"

"Oh, she feels it as much as I do but won't give me a chance."

Will chuckled. "Here we are drinking beer."

"I think you may be a little drunk."

Will laughed. "Just a little." He pushed himself to stand and stumbled. "You're sleeping at my place tonight."

Jon flashed a face-splitting grin. "Yep, another beer, please."

Will came back and handed him another beer. "Jon, you know you need to get help before Kati will let you back in."

He hissed out a breath. "What about you?"

"What about me?" Jon struck a chord with Will because he knew it was true. His PTSD was so out of control that he couldn't be anything at the firehouse except the chief's driver. At least Jon had returned to working the ambulance and going into the hospital.

"You know what I mean. When are you coming back to the ambulance?" Jon asked.

Will leaned forward, resting his elbows on his knees. "I don't know if I can ever come back." He couldn't look at Jon when he said it. "Truth is . . . I know I need help. But I don't want it."

"You should because Anna wants you drunk, sober, messed up . . . she wants you and has for a long time." He poured whiskey into his cup and drank it. "Kati doesn't want me because I'm not good enough." He let out a bitter chuckle. "Just like my parents."

"You want me to talk to her?"

Jon shook his head. "No. Look, Will, you need to fix this. Anna is good for you. I know you love her. It's obvious. I need help, too, but I don't want it either. What's the use?"

Will held out his cup. "One more."

Jon poured whiskey into both their cups, and they drank it in one swallow.

Anna was now sitting with Caden in her lap, rubbing his head. For a moment, he didn't see Anna. He saw Shelly. He shook his head. He walked toward where she was sitting. "We should get him to Momma's."

Anna looked at him with concern. "You okay to carry him?"

Will laughed. "Probably not."

"Is it okay if I ask Garrett to carry Caden? He hasn't been drinking?"

He chuckled. "Yeah, that's probably a good idea; I'm a bit wobbly."

Will fetched Garrett, who carried Caden to his mother's house while Kati assisted Liz into their cabin. When Will and Anna headed for her cabin, Kati sat beside Jon by the fire, holding his hand. Anna smiled at him as they walked by. Will was riddled with anxiety about being with Anna tonight. When they arrived, Will tugged Anna inside and pulled her close, his hands finding the small of her back. His kiss was hungry and fierce, pushing at her lips with such passion that he eventually had to pull away, his chest heaving. He searched her eyes, concern lacing his voice as he asked her, "Was I hurting you?"

She looked confused. "No. Why?"

"It seemed like I was being aggressive."

Anna took him by the hand and led him to the couch. "How much did you drink?"

He sunk into the couch. "A lot."

"Do you feel better?"

Will laid his head back on the couch. "Not really." He turned his head toward Anna. "I don't deserve you. I think I was a bad husband to Shelly. I got jealous. She threw me out once." He wrapped his fingers around Anna's. "I had to stay with Jon for two weeks. She wanted a divorce, but Jon talked to her, and she let me come home." He lifted his head and looked at Anna. "Do you want to have babies someday?"

Anna chuckled. "That was random."

"I'm drunk, darlin'. It may take you a week to assemble my drunk ramblings."

He put his arm around her. "Can I hold you?" She nodded, and he pulled her to his chest and stroked her hair. "You aren't alone," he whispered. He contemplated expressing his true feelings but feared it would push her away. In the end, his drunk mind opened up. "I'm falling for you, Anna, but I am so insecure that I'm afraid I may run you away."

Silence hung in the air until he heard her murmur into his chest. "I fell for you long ago, Cowboy."

CHAPTER 36

A few days after the bonfire, Will was mucking out stalls. He still felt emotionally hungover. He overindulged in so much alcohol that night that he vaguely remembers returning to the cabin, and then everything went black. The next thing he knew, he woke up on the couch with a splitting headache. Anna was asleep in an armchair nearby, her feet propped up on the table.

She didn't seem angry when she woke up, but he couldn't remember what he might have said or done while under the influence. Drinking only magnified all his doubts and fears, and he knew it was the wrong way to cope with his grief after almost four years. It only strengthened his resolve never to mix thoughts with emotions and drinking again.

Just then, a noise in one of the stalls startled him. Eva stood at the entrance with tears streaming down her face. She was holding a picture in her hands. Her eyes were red-rimmed, and her nose was swollen. Without hesitating, Will took off his gloves and stepped closer to her. "Hey, what is it?" he said.

Eva sniffled before she spoke. "Could you take me to see Momma? I need to go . . . please," she murmured, not meeting his gaze. He put his hands on her shoulders for comfort and asked her why she was upset.

Understanding that this was something serious for Eva to ask, he promised to do anything he could to help.

"Well, let's saddle Cotton Candy and Jake," he said.

Will grabbed the saddle blanket and draped it over Cotton Candy's back. A knot formed in his stomach as he tried deciphering all the emotions that crossed Eva's face. He watched her lovingly prepare Cotton Candy, fastening each strap with precision. When she finished, she led her horse into the morning sun and mounted without saying a word. Will followed close behind as they rode toward Shelly's resting place.

They rode in silence, the clomp of horses' hooves pounding the ground beneath them. Eva's shoulders were hunched as she wiped away tears with the sleeve of her shirt.

"Eva, why have you been crying?"

She shifted in the saddle. "I miss Momma." Sniffling, she added, "I feel closer to her when we visit the bench."

"I can understand that. I miss her too. Some days are better than others."

"I was looking at a picture I made today," she continued. "It's a picture of my heart shattered, and I painted the broken pieces with gold, trying to put it back together, but it's still cracked and will never stop hurting. Then I thought about some things that Anna told me, and I wanted to talk to you about Momma."

Will's brow furrowed in confusion. "Did you make the picture with Anna?"

She nodded swiftly. "Yeah, Caden and I went to her cabin one day while you were working, and she spent the entire afternoon helping us. Caden made one too. Anna was so patient with him. He finished the whole thing."

Will was surprised he hadn't seen any of the pictures yet. "I'll look forward to seeing it when we get where Momma is." Anna had never mentioned spending the day with the kids.

Will studied Eva as they rode; his little girl grew up faster than he wanted and was wise beyond her years. Eva's suffering caused his heart to ache. They dismounted and secured the horses when they reached the hilltop. Will laid a blanket next to the bench dedicated to Shelly, who loved watching sunsets from that spot. He leaned against the bench; it was like Shelly had him in a warm embrace, like when they watched the sunset together.

He wrapped an arm around Eva, pulling her onto his lap. She looked up at him with tears in her eyes. "Daddy, was it my fault Momma died?"

Will felt a sudden blow to the gut. Why would she think such a thing? His eyes widened. "Baby, why would you think that?"

She trembled against him and whispered, "She went to the store because we were going to make cookies and . . . well . . . uh . . ." She sobbed into his chest.

Will's chest was so tight he couldn't breathe. *It was my fault, not Eva's. I should have done something to keep her safe. I shouldn't have texted her, knowing she could never wait until she stopped the car to open a message.*

He cleared his throat, cradling her in his arms like he had not long ago. "No, Eva. Look at me, baby. It was an accident." *My poor girl has felt guilt all this time. She shouldn't be dealing with this at such a young age.* "God, baby, no, it wasn't your fault." He pulled her in tight. Tears trailed down his cheeks. He let her cry until she was exhausted and stroked her hair while she calmed down.

A yellow butterfly caught their attention as it fluttered over a small star-shaped purple wildflower in the middle of the dirt path. Eva sat up, wiping away some of her tears with her sleeve. "Look, Momma came to visit us."

Will shoved upright and creased his forehead. "How did you learn about that?"

Eva leaned against his chest and sighed. "Anna told me that love never dies; it lives forever in our hearts. We see our loved ones in the butterflies, cardinals, the dragonflies. Those are our personal favorites. Anna says her grandparents are together when she sees a boy and girl cardinal. Sometimes, they come together or separate. I like Momma as a butterfly. Somedays she's yellow, other days blue, or some days a monarch." She stood up using her whole body, waving her arms. "Anna says when we see the wildflowers moving in the wind, that's Momma dancing in the wildflowers. She's everywhere." She knelt, putting her hand on Will's heart. "Especially in our hearts. Love never dies. It must be true because Momma told me that, too."

She pulled out the picture from her satchel and handed it to Will. He stared at the picture, tears brimming in his eyes. He noticed the torn pieces of paper carefully placed in a heart shape and surrounded with golden paint. Little photos of Shelly, also decorated with gold, were scattered around it.

"The gold is the love of our family and friends, helping to heal our broken hearts. Mommy lives in your heart too, Daddy, and there's enough room for Anna too."

Will was speechless as he tried to comprehend what Anna had said to Eva.

He nodded slowly. Anna was helping his daughter, and he had been lying to her about the finances, needing a fundraiser, wearing his ring, and maybe something he did the night of the bonfire. The realization hit him. *My actions affect everyone: my kids, Momma, Kati, Jon, and Anna. I am missing their pain and concentrating on my own. I'm selfish.*

"Daddy, I need to know you forgive me."

He wrapped her in his arms. "Nothing to forgive ever. It wasn't your fault, Eva." He squeezed a little tighter. "Oh my God, baby, I'm sorry. I should have been more attentive to you and your brother. I promise I'll do better. Thank you for what you told me. I love you. Thank you for teaching me."

"Caden and I love Anna. We think you do too."

The words tumbled on Will's tongue, and he was desperate to release his love for Anna. He wanted to scream it out, but fear paralyzed him. Loving Anna meant he'd finally be ready to put the past behind him. He closed his eyes while the sun's warmth washed over him like a soft caress. He needed something to hold on to... hope he would change.

"Eva," he croaked, swallowing hard. "Can I hold on to your picture?"

"Sure."

A weight lifted from his chest as Will rode back to the ranch. The wind blew through the grass, and he took a deep breath, feeling an indescribable warmth spread throughout his body. As the horses clopped along the trail, he embraced the path forward.

∽

WITHOUT BOTHERING TO KNOCK, Will gently opened the door to Anna's cabin and saw her sleeping peacefully on the couch, her long, shiny hair framing her cheeks. Taking a moment to appreciate her beauty, he walked over to the table facing the sofa, placing his hat beside him. He leaned in close, gently running his fingers through Anna's hair.

His loved ones' advice filled his ears: *Open your heart. Take it slow. Love never dies. . . .* And the big one, *Don't screw it up.* He slowly exhaled, mustering all his courage for what would come. With one swift motion, Will leaned in and kissed her lips. Her eyes fluttered open.

"Hello, Sleeping Beauty."

Anna brushed his face with her fingertips. "Hey, Cowboy."

"You looked beautiful lying there," he said, captivated by her beauty.

"Where have you been?" She playfully messed up his hair. "Your hair is all over the place."

"I went riding with Eva." His fingers slid down her arm, leaving a trail of energy infusing his soul. He took a ragged breath and tried to find the words to express his feelings. "Anna, I'm so thankful for all you have done for the kids. I know I've been distant lately, and it's not fair to you. The other night when I got drunk . . . I don't even want to think about it. But since you've been here, I've leaned on you more than I should have. You just lost someone, too, and I always ask for your help. That's why I wanted to thank you . . . and apologize for being so needy."

He rubbed his sweaty palms against his jeans. He cleared his throat again, realizing he'd forgotten to remove his wedding band. When their eyes met, Will remained quiet, praying she hadn't noticed it. But when he saw her expression, he knew she had seen it. The tension between them was palpable. She sat up, turned on the light, and stared at him as if expecting an explanation.

Anna glanced away as she spoke. "I'm so lucky to have Eva and Caden in my life."

Will's gaze softened, and he moved closer to her. His hands were gentle on the back of her neck, and when their lips met, a wave of electricity surged through him, making it hard to concentrate on anything else. Time stood still as their lips touched, as if nothing else existed but them and this moment.

I love you, Will thought. *Maybe I should try to slip the ring off or not be a coward and come clean, at least about the ring.*

Anna looked into his eyes. "What is it, Will? Are you okay? It's like you want to tell me something." She glanced down at his hand again.

Emotions of love stirred within him, yet he remained silent. He breathed out in resignation. "Eva and I had a long conversation about Shelly's accident. She blames herself for Shelly's death because she went to the store to get groceries to make cookies with Eva." Will paused, wondering if he'd said the words out loud. "I told her it was an accident, and no one was at fault. It was just an accident."

Anna closed her fingers around his, and their combined hands comforted Will. "Do you believe it wasn't your fault? Because no one else thinks so."

Will shrugged and let out a sigh. "No, it couldn't be my fault if it wasn't Eva's," he reasoned." But deep down, he knew the truth: it was all his fault. He reached for Anna's cheek and caressed it with his thumb. "One thing's for sure . . . I missed you," he admitted. As he took his hand away, Anna's gaze shifted to the band on his finger. There was no point trying to conceal it.

Anna's expression hardened, and her eyes remained fixed on the ring. "This may make you angry, but I'll say it anyway. I care about you more than I want to admit, and I want to support you, but this situation is bigger than both of us. You need professional help. You admit that the chief covers for you when you shouldn't be on the job," she said.

Will's chest tightened, and anger coursed through him because he knew he needed to hear these truths. He wanted to yell at her and tell her it was none of her business, but he held his tongue and instead stormed toward the door.

Anna strode across the room, her eyes blazing with a fierce anger that made Will take an involuntary step back. She stopped in front of the refrigerator, pulled out a bottle of wine, uncapped it, and raised it to her lips. She narrowed her eyes and continued to stare at the ring on his finger, daring him to move. He was paralyzed as a heavy silence filled the air. He knew what she was trying to communicate without opening her mouth: he couldn't expect her to trust him if he lied about wearing his wedding ring. The guilt was like a physical weight in his chest.

Anna broke the silence. "I can't compete with Shelly."

Will stepped closer to her so he could look directly into her eyes. "What does that mean?" His voice was a low rumble.

She grabbed his hand, lifting it slightly so she could see the wedding band. Then she dropped it with disgust and let out an accusing laugh. "You lied. . . . And you want me to trust you?" Her gaze seemed to pierce his soul.

Anna looked away for a moment before turning back to face him. Tears glistened in the corners of her eyes as she picked up the wine bottle and took another swig. "I can't compete with a dead woman, Will," she said, defeated. "I'm not a fool. You will always love her." She pointed to the ring and shook her head sadly. "My God, you wear your wedding ring like a shield to keep your heart from opening."

Tension hung thickly in the air around them like smog. Anna brought the bottle of wine back to her lips, but before she could take another drink, Will snatched it out of her hand and slammed it down on the counter with a loud thud. Startled by his sudden movement, Anna flinched and glared at him defiantly. His face was just inches from hers, and he spoke through gritted teeth. "Do you feel that wine yet? Do you think that's going to help?"

Her body was rigid, eyes blazing; she seethed. "I don't know, Will. Did it help the night of the bonfire? All I know is that you had a big headache and had to sleep on the couch while I got a string of broken promises. God, I'm so angry, I could scream!" She stormed over to the chair and buried her face in her hands, her shoulders shaking with silent sobs.

He knelt next to her, his mind racing for the right words. An apology wouldn't be enough. "I've been lying about wearing my wedding ring," he said, his voice barely above a whisper. "I put it on when I go to work, then I take it off when I see you. How could you trust me after that?"

Her eyes were red-rimmed and glistening with tears. "The trust is broken. You broke my heart." She stared ahead blankly, her breathing ragged and uneven.

Tears welled in Will's eyes as he realized what she was implying. He whispered, "What can I do to fix this?"

She met his gaze, her expression unreadable. "I want to go home," she said. "Everything just hurts too much here."

Will's heart sank as he understood the gravity of her words. He couldn't bring himself to look at her as he muttered, "Anna, you are home."

Her gaze sharpened, and she shook her head adamantly. "No," she said firmly. "This isn't home. I'm just a guest."

He could only nod silently in response.

Anna's chest heaved with each breath. Will couldn't help but feel the overwhelming urge to comfort her. He stepped closer and took her hand. "I'm sorry," he mumbled.

"Why can't people just say what they feel?" Anna asked, placing a hand on her heart. "Honesty, that's all I wanted from you."

"I can't speak for everyone, but for me, it's fear, I suppose." His words felt inadequate. He was speechless.

"I've learned that life is short, and fear holds us back from many things. Me included. Then, your whole world can change in the blink of an eye. I've seen that a few times, and so have you." She looked up at him, her eyes searching for something. "And yet here we are, still letting fear get in the way."

Will could feel time slipping away like sand through his fingers, knowing he had to act before it was too late. Taking a deep breath, he closed his eyes and searched for the courage to open his heart to her.

"With the anniversary of Shelly's death coming soon . . ." His voice cracked as memories flooded his mind. "My mind is all over the place. I keep seeing the accident, the days before the accident . . . everywhere I look reminds me of that day." He cleared his throat and tried to steady himself. "Apparently, this affects Jon and the kids, but I'm too selfish to see anyone's pain but my own."

Anna softened a bit. He gathered her in his arms as grief and pain collided inside of him like a tidal wave. Finally finding his voice again, he whispered, "I-I'm sorry; I never meant to break your heart. I don't want to lose you, but I'm struggling."

They held each other as the world around them faded, each lost in their thoughts and feelings.

Will's steps faltered as Anna took his hand and led him to the couch, where he stopped short. His icy-blue eyes met hers, their faces mere inches apart. Her love was so evident, yet her pain was just as intense.

"I'm going to set some boundaries here. You need to get me the information for the finances in two weeks, and I also need to know if you need a fundraiser. Taking off the ring has to be your decision; I won't put an ultimatum on that, but I may need to step back." Her hand brushed his cheek. "Cowboy, you are still all that I want. I know you're hurting, but I don't know how to help you. No matter how much love we have, it doesn't fix PTSD. Time may be able to fix this, but no more lies."

He wrapped his arms around her and pulled her close. He desperately wanted to tell her everything he felt, but fear held him back. He could only pray that one day he'd be able to work through his trauma and be the man she deserved.

CHAPTER 37

Over the next few weeks, Anna worked diligently on the grant application, texting and emailing Jenny and Kitty Love for information to build a program she was completely unfamiliar with, desperately gathering whatever information they could provide. The more time Anna spent digging, the more delayed she was in finishing the grant, causing increasing pressure. The anxiety weighed heavily on her shoulders; it seemed like there was something to worry about everywhere she looked. Her head throbbed from concentrating so hard at work, and the stress of learning everything she needed to know about the ranch had caused knots in her neck. She thought so much about the equine center that it interfered with her concentration at work.

She leaned back in her desk chair, wondering if she would ever feel comfortable at her job or the cabin. She longed for the comfort of home. Her mind drifted to memories of her grandparents' house: sitting with Papa on the porch swing, watching Nana as she planted flowers, sharing meals, and talking with them about everything. She smiled at memories of them going out for dinner—Papa always ready to devour twice his weight in food—and she missed his laugh the most.

A knock at the door made her jump. When she opened it, she was surprised to see Kati with an excited smile. "Let's go out and have some fun.

It's Friday, the start of the weekend. You deserve it after all the hard work you've been doing to help Will with the equine center. So, what do you say? Let's go to happy hour and dinner."

She wanted to go out and have fun, but guilt gnawed at her for not working on the grant; it needed to be finished. Could she enjoy herself when there was still so much work to do?

"I'm sorry, I can't. I have to finish the grant application, and I'm struggling."

Kati entered Anna's office and said, "Will is working today, so there's no need to rush home. One night won't make a difference."

"Kati, I'm exhausted. I want to go home."

Kati gave her puppy dog eyes and batted her eyelashes. "I'll beg, Anna . . . pleeease."

A laugh broke from Anna's chest. As Kati begged and made facial contortions, her gentle chortle became a hearty, genuine laugh. "Okay, okay, I'll go," she said breathlessly.

Kati put a hand on Anna's shoulder. "I will see you after work. I'll meet you at the front door."

Kati bounced out of her office, leaving an air of relieved energy behind. Despite the recent laughter, Anna couldn't stop thinking about Will's struggle with the upcoming anniversary of Shelly's death. Then there was his dishonesty about wearing his wedding ring—though they had talked it through. The grant process took longer than expected due to a lack of financial information, and the two weeks had come and gone, making Anna even more stressed. Although she'd established boundaries, she neglected to uphold them. "Come on, Anna," she whispered, "Let it go, and enjoy the rest of your day. Go out with your friends tonight."

She glanced at the clock as she opened her laptop. She quickly organized the nurses' schedules for their upcoming home visits. Then, she drafted a grant proposal to provide a caregiver program for Cardinal Creek, just like she'd done at her old job. She knew the tight-knit community would be behind it, just as they'd been when they proposed starting an equine therapy center. As Anna clicked through spreadsheets and pulled up documents, her mind wandered to the equine center. May was almost over, and she had yet to finish the grant application or determine its financial status. A fear of failure weighed heavy on her shoulders. Taking a deep breath, Anna played soft music and forced herself to focus on her work. Then, her phone lit up with a text from Kati.

> Kati: Hey, where are you?

Anna looked at her watch. It was 4:45 p.m. She signed off her computer and grabbed her purse and backpack.

> Anna: Sorry, I lost track of time. I'm on my way now.

> Kati: Hurry up, woman!!! LOL

Anna took the stairs two at a time, eager to reach the exit. She was almost there when she saw Dr. Watts and Cathy near the front desk. His eyes lingered on her a moment too long. She quickly raced outside, breathless. She was angry that she'd let her guard down again. The last few weeks, Anna had taken almost every precaution to avoid running into either of them, eating lunch at her desk and changing her route to the exit daily. But sometimes, it was hard to escape Cathy because she was her boss.

"Oh, I didn't mean for you to run down here. Are you okay?" Kati laughed.

Anna, still breathless, nodded. "Let's go," she managed to say in between panting.

Kati slapped her on the back. "You need a drink?"

"You have no idea," she said.

Kati threw an arm around Anna. "I'll drive. We can leave your car here. I can drive home if you have too much to drink."

Kati and Anna stepped into Saddle Up Bar & Grill and were met with the boisterous sounds of a happy hour crowd unwinding from their day. Kati spotted four nurses from different hospital departments: two from surgery and two from post-op recovery. They were gathered at one end of the bar, waving their arms for them to join them.

"Listen, these are great ladies. We all went to school together, and they're about our age." She leaned in and whispered, "They're unattached, like us."

Anna's head whipped around. "I'm unattached?"

"Oh yeah," she said as a sly smile crossed her lips. As they approached the bar, Kati yelled, "My friends, what are we drinking first, and who's the designated driver?" She held up her hands. "No, wait, first introductions. Everyone, this is Anna. She lives in one of the cabins at the ranch. Anna, this is Sylvia Martinez, who moved here from San Antonio; Becky Larson, whose family has been here since the town was founded and is named after her great-great-grandmother, Rebecca Larson, who came to Texas from the East Coast by wagon; Jessie Ramsey, another family that has been here for at least a century, and Vanessa Hodges, who's named for her great-grandmother who was on a board or something here in Cardinal Creek."

Anna giggled, watching them make faces at Kati as she talked about their families.

"Don't let Kati scare you. We're just plain down-to-earth rural folk here," Vanessa said as she shook Anna's hand.

Becky chimed in, "Hi, Anna, come sit. I say no one is the designated driver. We have options. Kati's brother, Will, or her love interest, Jon."

"Uh, no way," Kati exclaimed. "They're working tonight. How about Sylvia's hunky, dark, and handsome brother? What's his name, Hottie?"

Sylvia held up her hand. "Don't even think about it. Ricardo would lecture us all the way home."

Becky batted her eyelashes. "Will he pick us up on his horse? I love to watch him ride, rope, breathe." She looked at Anna. "The man can fill out a pair of Wranglers."

Anna felt the heat rise in her face. It wasn't about how Ricardo filled out a pair of Wranglers but how Will filled out *his* Wranglers. *These ladies are all like Jenny.* Kati ordered tequila shots with salt and lime and handed one to Anna. *Well, if I'm going to let my hair down, now's the time.*

Becky bumped Anna's shoulder. "Don't be embarrassed. You have plenty to see in Wranglers. Kati's brother, Will, is hot in a brooding way, and her hottie love interest, Jon." She waved her hand in front of her face. "He's on fire."

Jessie picked up her shot of tequila. "Here's to a night to remember . . . or not." They all drank their shots, and Anna's lips pursed at the tequila shutter.

Kati put her arm around Anna's as they smiled and waved at the bartender. He stood over six feet tall with auburn hair and a neatly trimmed goatee. His T-shirt fit snuggly over his broad shoulders, emphasizing his muscular frame. As he walked closer to them, Anna noticed a slight hitch in his step, and when his hazel eyes met Anna's, they sparkled with warmth, and he smiled. "What can I do for you lovely ladies?"

Kati leaned across the bar. "Hey, JW, how's the ankle?"

He shrugged. "Who's the new lady?" His voice was smooth like silk, causing Anna to raise an eyebrow.

Kati tugged on his bearded face. "Pipe down, buddy. Anna is taken. She just moved here from Missouri a little over a month ago."

He winked at Anna. "Not many of us around here, darling."

Anna wrinkled her brow. "What do you mean?"

He tugged her hair. "Us gingers."

She slapped his hand away. "Don't touch my hair, buddy."

He laughed. "Yep, that's not bottle red. She's a feisty one, Kati."

"Yeah, she is, and she's my brother's feisty one."

JW looked at Anna. "I shouldn't have teased you like I do to these ladies. Please accept my apology. I may be a beat-up bull rider, but I should have minded my manners."

Anna faked a smile, her face strained. "It's okay. I knew you didn't mean any harm." She suspected JW had no malicious intent, but she was still so shaken up after seeing Dr. Watts and Cathy. She promised she wouldn't let it ruin her night.

"Anna." Kati's voice snapped her back. She handed Anna another shot of tequila.

Becky yelled, "Here's to tequila making our clothes fall off."

JW said, "Becky, my floor is waiting for them."

Becky narrowed her eyes. "You are a pig."

He laughed as he limped to the other end of the bar.

Kati leaned in and whispered, "He's a good guy. He loves to give us trouble. I feel bad for him. He's been brooding a lot since he had to leave the rodeo circuit. There are a lot of videos on YouTube of him riding. There's one of when the bull trampled his ankle." She shivered. "It was awful."

"Why are you telling me this? Do you want me to like him? I don't need another project. Your brother is enough." Anna was frustrated. What was Kati trying to say? She drank the shot and took off toward the bathroom.

Kati yelled, "Anna, wait."

Anna paused and turned to Kati. "I'm just going to the ladies' room."

She dug her debit card from her purse. "Order two shots and a margarita. Buy a round for everyone on me." She stumbled toward the ladies' room, hoping the wave of nausea would pass. Once inside, Anna soaked a paper towel and draped it over her neck to cool down the fiery heat radiating through her body. She caught her reflection in the mirror—wild eyes staring back at her and lips that moved with unspoken words. *I don't even know who I am anymore . . . Nothing seems real. That's just the tequila. Speaking of tequila . . .* She flashed herself a weary grin.

Gathering herself together, Anna left the restroom and returned to the bar. She downed both shots without hesitation and then drank half a margarita with one swallow. Suddenly, she felt fingers encircle her hand, and when she looked up, she saw JW, his eyebrows drawn together in concern. "Ma'am, you should slow down, or I'll have to carry you out of here."

Anna's head was spinning, and she couldn't focus. It was as though the ground beneath her feet could give way at any second. She pointed at JW. "My clothes are not falling on your floor." She gestured for him to come closer, and when he moved in, she slurred, "I've loved Will Deluca since I was sixteen, but please don't tell anyone, my fellow ginger." She hiccupped. "I have no idea why I told you that. I guess I just wanted to say it out loud."

He ran his hand through his hair and sighed. "Darlin', I would never take advantage of a lady, no matter what. I know Will's a good guy—we graduated together after all. But I've always been angry at him for convincing Jon to join the fire department instead of going pro on the bull-riding circuit like he wanted to." He looked over at Kati and the group of nurses. "Looks like it may be up to me to Uber for this whole lot of you tonight."

"Thank God. I don't want them to call Ricardo, Jon, or . . ." Anna hiccupped, "or Will."

JW leaned against the bar. "Why not Ricardo?"

Anna leaned in and whispered, "I don't speak Spanish. I think Sylvia said he'd yell at us in Spanish." She picked up the shot glass. "Hit me again." She turned to the girls, laughing and talking at once. "Hey, you gals want more on me?"

"Hell yeah," they all yelled.

Someone yelled, "Great song."

Anna leaned on her hands. "JW, my new friend, a round on me, plus one for you."

JW laughed. "You are a hoot, girl." He poured two tequilas for each of them.

Kati threw her arm around Anna. "Girl, we should slow down. I can barely stand. I've had three beers and three shots. It's Friday."

Anna shrugged. "Yep."

Becky, who worked in the OR, walked over to Anna. "Hey, we girls were discussing something we noticed at the hospital. Can we get your opinion?"

Anna's head was spinning. She hoped she could answer them because she barely knew her name, much less something medical. "Sure."

"Do you know Dr. Watts?" Becky asked.

Anna's mind swirled, and terror rushed through her body as she was sure he was following her. She couldn't shake the sense of dread that consumed her. "Why is he here?"

The ladies surrounded her to show support. "She knows him," Becky said.

Kati touched Anna's arm. "Hey, are you okay? You just turned a pasty white."

Anna looked around frantically. "Is he here, Kati?" she said again, her voice trembling.

There was a deep-set frown on Kati's face. "What has he done to you?"

Anna shook her head, saying, "Nothing at all. I just saw him around," she lied.

But Becky chimed in with her own story. "Get this, his wife pulled me into her office and threatened me!"

Anna wrung her trembling hands as she fought to control her rising anxiety. The combination of intense emotions and alcohol left her nauseous, and the acid in her stomach burned her throat, causing her to swallow hard, trying not to throw up. Summoning all her courage, she eased herself off the stool and steadied herself on shaky legs. "I need to go to the bathroom. My stomach feels sick." *I'm not the only one, but he told Cathy I'm pursuing him.*

"You should eat. I'll order us something," Kati said. "I'm sorry, Anna. I shouldn't have encouraged you to drink."

Anna's shoulder bumped Kati. "It's okay; I'm a big girl. I'm going to go use the restroom."

"I'm quite tipsy myself," Kati laughed.

Anna steadied herself again. "Is Will doing okay? I haven't seen much of him. Just been busy with work and stuff."

"With the anniversary coming up real soon, he's better this year than the last three. He's drinking much less this year." Kati threw her arm around Anna. "I know he's stubborn, but I'm sure he loves you." She put her finger to her lips. "Shh. Don't tell him I told you. He'd kill me."

Anna placed an invisible lock on her lips and headed toward the bathroom, yet her thoughts were in turmoil as she walked. The words *he loves you* played repeatedly in her mind, leaving her confused and unsteady. She struggled to remain upright, clinging onto chairs for support as she walked. As Anna attempted to steady herself, she lost her balance and fell into someone's arms. Her eyes widened when she looked up and saw Dr. Watts. Had he followed her here? His arm was around her waist, and he pulled her close as she begged him to let go. He whispered that he'd take her home. Anna squeezed her eyes shut, praying it was all a nightmare.

"Let me go," she pleaded. Her feet were unsteady, and she tried to push him away, but she was fumbling and drunk. "Your wife will destroy my career. She told me that. Let me go," Anna pleaded.

Dr. Watts grabbed her arm and hissed, "She's all talk. Besides, she won't be doing that again." His grip tightened as he tried to help her walk.

It was all surreal, and Anna tried to understand what was happening. She continued struggling against Dr. Watts's grip. He tried to support her with his hand, but when it landed on her chest, Anna let out a bloodcurdling scream.

In the next moment, Kati had Anna in her arms while Dr. Watts was being dragged by the collar toward the door. Anna trembled in Kati's embrace, afraid to look around and see if they'd made a scene.

Then she saw a pair of black boots near her feet, and she slowly looked up to see a smiling fellow ginger. "Okay, Red, old JW took out the trash," he said. "Now I'm gonna take you ladies home. Can you promise not to puke in my truck?"

Nausea threatened Anna with the spinning of her head. "I promise nothing except to be eternally grateful for saving me from him."

Anna hung onto Kati and JW as they went to his large F-350. Anna looked at Kati. "How am I going to get up there? It might as well be a mountain." They roared with laughter.

JW opened the passenger door and offered Kati a hand when she stepped up to the running board as she climbed in. He looked at Anna. "I saw some of what happened with whoever that was, but I need to get you in my truck, and I have a feeling I'll need to pick you up. Are you okay with that? I promise I won't hurt you."

Anna stared at him for a few moments. "Can I try to get in like Kati? If I fall, the ground won't hurt too much."

"Anna . . ." Kati started.

JW put up his hand to Kati. "Hold onto my hand and to the door as you step up. You got this."

Anna did just as he directed and collapsed into the seat. When JW got into the truck, he looked at Anna and said, "You okay?"

She leaned against the headrest, praying the world would stop spinning, and nodded. "It was like climbing on a horse."

"Oh, little ginger, here is a rider," JW teased.

"Please don't call me that. Will has called me that since we were kids."

"Noted." That was all he said before Kati told him about how Will and Anna met when they were younger.

Anna opened her eyes and rolled her head toward JW. He glanced at her, and she mouthed, "She never stops."

"I heard you, Anna."

Anna laughed. "How?"

Kati leaned forward. "I hear everything. How are you?"

"I'm fine. You guys are my heroes. You can't . . . Will . . . promise me." She pointed at them. "Both of you."

"No, not a word."

"Don't tell anyone," Anna said.

"At least talk to Garrett about it, please," Kati pleaded.

"I just want to forget it."

When they pulled up to the ranch, JW helped Kati out of the truck. Then he helped Anna get down. She noticed how careful he was when he helped her. "Thank you, JW."

He squeezed her shoulder. "If you don't want to tell Will, let me program my number in your phone in case you need the trash taken out again."

"I agree with JW, Anna. Please, I would feel better if you told Will or Garrett to have someone to call if you ever need help."

Anna pulled her phone out of her pocket and handed it to JW. "Thank you again."

He touched his fingers to his hat. "Good night, ladies. I'll watch you get inside."

"Anna, can I crash at your place tonight?"

Relief flooded Anna's body when Kati asked to stay. "Yes, that would be great."

As they walked up the porch steps arm in arm, Anna and Kati turned around together to wave to JW, leaning against his truck. After she got ready for bed, Anna couldn't help but worry about what Will would think if he found out what Dr. Watts had done. As she dropped into bed, Kati's words *I know he loves you* echoed through her mind and brought both fear and solace. She desperately wished for Will's embrace, dreading his possible reaction to what happened. Anna's mind spun in circles of guilt, regret, and shame for letting herself become vulnerable to such a predator; it was all her fault.

CHAPTER 38

With a loud thud, Anna rolled out of bed and quickly shielded her eyes from the blinding sun streaming through the window. The room spun around her like she was on a roller coaster. Images of last night's party floated through her mind, and she could almost taste the tequila in her mouth as she thought of Dr. Watts. *Was he there?* She remembered him grabbing her, and she'd tried to fight back. It was all a blur.

Anna's stomach churned, causing her to sprint to the bathroom. She managed to reach the toilet before she retched. A knock at the bathroom door interrupted her moment of relief.

"Anna, are you okay? It's a stupid question, sorry. Do you want coffee?" Kati asked.

Anna smiled as she rinsed her mouth. "Yes, on the coffee. What did we drink last night? Tequila or diesel fuel?"

"If it's any consolation, my head is pounding."

"The coffee is in the cabinet. I'll bring the ibuprofen." Anna washed her face, brushed her teeth, and put a messy bun on her head. As she exited the bathroom, she saw Kati rubbing her temples with a cup of coffee on the table.

"Here's something for your pounding headache." Anna placed the pills on the table, grabbed a cup, and poured coffee. She leaned against the counter, wondering if she should ask Kati what had happened last night. Her brain was telling her one thing, but she wasn't sure. *It was probably my imagination.* She headed to the table to get her phone. When she opened it, there was a text from JW. Anna was confused. *Why would the bartender ask how I was doing?*

"Kati, why would the bartender have my phone number and be texting me?"

She looked at Anna over her coffee cup. "What do you remember about last night?"

Anna shrugged. "Not much. It's very fuzzy."

Kati let out a long sigh. "After you had I-don't-know-how-many tequila shots, you said you were going to the bathroom. I'm not sure how long it was, but we heard you screaming, and Dr. Watts seemed to be helping you up, but JW saw him touching you, and you were telling him to leave you alone. So, JW threw him out and gave us a ride home." She took a sip of her coffee. "You begged us not to tell Will. I didn't think it was a good idea for a few reasons, but I know Will."

Anna swallowed hard. "What does that mean?"

Kati rolled her eyes. "He builds things in his mind." If he hears the story from someone else, he'll think you were hanging on Dr. Watts while you were drunk."

Anna put her cup on the table. "Surely not. I can't stand Dr. Watts." *There, I said it.* A chill ran down her spine. "Was he trying to get me to leave with him?"

"I have no idea. It looked like he was trying to hold you up. JW was the one who noticed him touch your chest." She lowered her voice, imitating JW. "Oh, hell no. He doesn't need to do that to steady a lady."

Anna couldn't believe she put herself in that situation. She knew that anything could happen when drinking around strangers. Well, anyone for that fact. She was angry at herself for becoming someone that she scarcely knew anymore. It wasn't like her to drink to drown her problems, but lately, that was all she had done.

Kati's voice snapped Anna back to the present. "Are you going to tell Will? Do you want me to talk to him?"

"No," Anna snapped. She took a deep breath and closed her eyes. "I'm sorry, Kati. If anyone should tell him, it should be me." A million things whirled through her mind.

All of this was too much for her. Dr. Watts, the equine center, Will's incessant leaning on her, and the loss of her grandpa. She knew he cared for her, but his reluctance to face Shelly's death and the accident drove a wedge between them. He'd been indecisive about wearing his wedding ring.

Kati stood up and walked over to Anna. "I understand that losing your grandpa was tough for you. I'm sorry we asked for your help with the equine center, especially considering how Will has been since Shelly passed away. How are things going with the planning?"

Tears burned Anna's eyes. She couldn't pinpoint the reason for the sudden emotional rush. Was it frustration or fear that Will was keeping something from her?

"Budget has been the problem. I think Will is planning on the grant money to open, but we won't get the grant in time to do what needs to be done. He avoids questions about what needs to be done and how much money we need for the opening."

She took a deep breath. "It's hard for me to plan or know what to do. I'm talking to Jenny today to get the last things we need for the grant. Thanks to an equine center in Missouri, we have the stuff we needed for the grant."

"Momma and I had no idea this was happening. Why didn't you say something?"

"I don't want to let your family down."

She put her arm around Anna. "That's impossible. We appreciate what you've done so far. Do you have plans to talk about the budget with Will?"

"He told me we'll discuss it in a few days."

"If he doesn't, let me know. We'll talk to Momma. He doesn't want that."

Anna chuckled. "We all know he doesn't want that."

"Thank you for all you have done. I'm sorry I didn't go with you to the bathroom last night. It's not your fault Dr. Watts is a pig." Anna wanted to say more about what Becky had discussed the night before but hesitated.

Kati patted Anna's shoulder. "I better get out of here before Momma thinks someone kidnapped me. I didn't text her last night."

Kati pulled Anna into a quick hug, which Anna leaned into. With one more goodbye, Kati left for her cabin.

~

After taking the ibuprofen, the train calmed to drums pounding in Anna's head. She stared out the window and saw Will working with Garrett on a fence. She contemplated talking to him about what had happened last night, but he was busy. Will could be unpredictable sometimes, so she thought it was best just to let it go.

Grateful it was Saturday, Anna grabbed her computer and sank into the couch. With a sigh, she opened the laptop, staring at the screen, trying to figure out what was needed to open the equine center. She also needed to know the repairs required to get the first clients. She would devise a phase two plan when the grant funds came in. Anna had asked Will for numbers at almost every meeting, but he was vague with answers, especially when she asked about research Shelly had done. She opened her bottle of water and took a long drink. Her phone buzzed, turning her attention to a text.

> Jenny: Hey, Anna, do you have time to talk now? Momma is here. We could FaceTime.

> Anna: You bet. I miss y'all so much.

A heaviness settled in her chest with everything that was going on. She hoped talking to Jenny and Maggie could ease that.

Her phone showed a FaceTime call coming across the screen. Jenny's and Maggie's faces filled her screen, their smiles ear-to-ear. Anna's chest tightened as she saw the two women she considered family. Home. God, she missed them, home, but most of all, she missed her grandparents.

Some of the heaviness lifted as the warmth of home began to fill her.

"Oh my God, it's so good to see y'all," Anna squealed.

Jenny clapped. "It's good to see your face."

Maggie blew her a kiss. "It's like one of my daughters is a million miles away."

"Right now, Maggie, my heart hurts for home." Anna swallowed hard to keep from crying. She changed the subject. "So, thanks to you and Kitty, things are coming together with the grant. I know you have more information for me today, but that can wait. Tell me, what's going on with y'all?"

Jenny shook her head. "Uh, no, tell us what's going on with Will."

"Well, he and I have been spending time together." She closed her eyes. "There's fire between us, but he needs help. He's still grieving the loss of his wife. It affects all parts of his life, but that's my opinion. It's magical when we're together, and he opens his heart, but I feel like an outsider when he's closed off."

Anna could see the concern on Maggie's face.

"Maggie, don't worry. I don't think he realizes how much he's leaning on me. I think he forgets my grandpa just died, or maybe he thinks I understand him more because of my parents and grandparents." She threw her hands up. "I care about him, and I think he feels something for me, but he becomes so closed off, leaving me confused."

Anna let out a long sigh. "Y'all, I'm so homesick. I want to come home. I miss y'all."

"How's the job? Don't you like it?" Maggie asked.

"Yes, I love it." *That's not the total truth. I love the job, but then there's Dr. Watts.* "But I want to come home now. I promised Will and his family I would help set up the equine center."

Jenny cleared her throat. "Anna, I spoke to Kitty yesterday and will email you the information she sent me. I could have texted you that I emailed it, but I miss your face."

"That's awesome." Anna closed her eyes and exhaled slowly. She admired Jenny's dedication to her work and how she took an individualized approach with each client and created a partnership that led to positive outcomes. Anna knew it was time to ask for help; she gestured toward Jenny, hesitantly saying, "I know we talked about this when I talked to you about Kitty Love. I need your help designing the program and determining what equipment is needed. Kitty has greatly helped, but your input would make the program unique."

"I wondered when you were going to ask me," Jenny said. "This project is exciting. Equine therapy is my passion, but I haven't found my place doing it in Missouri."

"I just didn't want to drown you with your job and this," Anna said, sighing. "It's been stressful and exhausting."

"Have you asked Will if his wife had any written plans, even if it was scribbled on a napkin?" Maggie asked.

Anna rolled her eyes. "About a hundred times, but he evades the question or says he'll look."

"Anna, what's going on?" Maggie blurted out, then she bit her bottom lip.

"What do you mean?" Anna's eyebrows were drawn.

"I've known you a long time. You're fiery and take no crap from anyone, but you're taking all this from Will and saying nothing to him," Maggie said matter of fact. "And you just confirmed what I thought when I saw you. If this is too much, tell him. What have you done to take care of yourself?"

Anna paused, considering her words carefully. After a moment, she remained silent, letting her thoughts consume her.

"Maggie, I don't know why I keep taking it. I care about him, but I'm tired and homesick. Right now, I want to come home." *I wish I could tell them what was happening with Dr. Watts.*

"What if I come to stay with you in a few weeks and help you get this all figured out," Jenny said.

Anna's head shot up. "Really, Jenny? You would do that for me?"

Jenny smiled. "Of course, I would. We could work on the program there. I have some time off."

"I wish I were there to hug you. Please don't decide to move back here until the dust settles with the equine center," Maggie said.

Anna shook her head, a tear trailing down her cheek.

Jenny interjected, "Y'all are gonna make me cry. I'll be there in a few weeks. I'll make the arrangements and let you know about my flights."

"Really?" Anna said enthusiastically, drying her eyes with a tissue.

"Yes, really. Can we shoot for the end of July?" Jenny said.

"Anna, I will interject one more thing to see what you think. I hope you don't mind," Maggie said.

"No, anything you have to add would be so helpful."

"Do you think you should start planning a fundraiser, just in case?" Maggie asked.

"We've discussed it but haven't planned anything because I wasn't sure how much we needed. We discussed it at one of the breakfasts, but Will keeps stalling," Anna said. "Short answer: yes, we need a fundraiser."

"Well, you can never have too much money to get a place up and running, right?" Maggie chuckled. "If you want, I can come help with that part. Maybe it's just the medicine you need for your homesick heart."

Anna put her hands to her mouth, tears in her eyes. "I would love it if you came to see me. Anytime is perfect. Thank you. Both of you."

Anna's heart was whole. The call to Jenny and Maggie gave her hope for the equine center. Jenny coming for a visit may be what she needed to ease her homesickness. They had so many good ideas to fix this mess. She realized spring turned to summer. Time was passing quickly to get the equine center open. Anna closed her laptop and decided she would take Thunderbird for a ride. It may be just what she needed to work through her mixed emotions.

Anna walked into the stable, seeking solace to clear her head. She didn't want to see Will because she didn't want to tell him about the bar incident. She planned to avoid him, except when working on the grant, and keep the conversation on the equine center. As much as she cared for Will, she needed to care for herself. Since she came to Cardinal Creek, grief had been put on the back burner. If he couldn't get help with his grief and PTSD from Shelly's accident, it was time to pull away.

Heading to Thunderbird's stall, Anna sighed with relief that the stable was empty. She noticed he wasn't there as she walked past Jake's stall. *Will must be out with the cattle.*

Anna groomed and saddled Thunderbird. When she mounted her horse, she nudged him, getting him to trot. She was glad she wore a hat. The sun was hot on her skin. Thunderbird slowed from trotting to walking, allowing Anna to take in the wildflowers mixed within the swaying buffalo grass. It amazed her how a small flower would grow in the middle of dry, rocky soil. The butterflies danced among the wildflowers like nature's symphony. Anna smiled at the beauty. She noticed the days were becoming scorching hot, and it was just mid-May.

Thunderbird started to climb up the hill where Anna and Will had ridden together. She enjoyed the quiet and the bird's-eye view of the ranch. When she came over the ridge, she saw Will sitting under the tree, leaning against Shelly's memorial bench where she was buried. She pulled on Thunderbird's reins, stopping him. Will looked up, their gazes locked. Anna's throat constricted. She turned Thunderbird around, nudging him into a trot. She trotted down the hill back to the stable without looking back.

~

ANNA HEARD WILL ENTER the stable with Jake. She closed her eyes tight. *Please don't let him talk to me. Not now.* As she continued to groom Thunderbird, she prayed he would take care of Jake and leave. Then she heard his baritone voice behind her. She closed her eyes. *Feel nothing. Please feel nothing.* She turned slowly, gazing at the ground. Thunderbird nudged her with his muzzle.

Will said, "Are we working on the grant tonight?"

Thunderbird nudged her again, pushing her toward Will, and he grabbed her shoulders when she almost lost her footing. Part of Anna wanted to say no and walk away; another part wanted to help Will, but she wouldn't make it easy. "I guess. Are you ready to discuss the budget?"

Will's lips curled to a smile when Thunderbird nudged her for a third time.

She narrowed her eyes and shot a look at Thunderbird. "Really, Thunderbird." She turned back to Will and said, "The budget?"

"Darlin', I want to spend time with you."

His hand was on her neck, leaving a burning sensation where he touched. Anna took his hand off her neck and pulled away. "Come when you want, but we will discuss the budget. Bring wine." She grabbed her grooming tote and marched out. She stood at the door. "Well, are you coming out or what?"

There was a flicker of irritation in his eyes. He moved across the stable and stopped in front of her. "Darlin', we can play this game for a long time. I'll see you at six. I'll bring beer." He kissed her forehead and walked out of the stable.

Anna shouted for Will to stop, but he continued his swagger without glancing back. Her frustration rose to boiling, and she yelled, "STOP! Will!" He paused and turned to look at her.

"I can't stand beer," she stated with her arms across her chest.

A smile tugged at the corners of his mouth. "I know, darlin'. I know." He swiveled around, striding away toward his house.

"He infuriates me sometimes," she snarled through gritted teeth, her eyes flashing angrily. "Why does he always avoid the important things?"

Thunderbird snorted.

"I don't need your help, traitor."

She slammed down the grooming tote in the tack room, and trucked out of the stable to her cabin in a huff. *How can you love someone so much and want to punch them at the same time?* She knew it was time to show more restraint when she got inside her cabin. He couldn't have his cake and eat it too.

CHAPTER 39

Will had been dreading talking to Anna ever since she'd left him sitting alone in the meadow near Shelly's memorial. After all, he knew why she'd been so distant from him lately. The longer he stalled on the budget, the more distant she became. He'd sought refuge under the tree to find some peace. Will wanted nothing more than to make things right with her by explaining his reasons for being there. He also knew she was right in suggesting that he seek help for his PTSD, even though he'd rather pretend it didn't exist. So, with a deep breath, he raised his hand to knock on the door of Anna's cabin. Half of him was prepared to apologize and tell her how much he missed her, while the other half wanted to turn and walk away, never looking back.

Anna opened the door. She was wearing black yoga pants and a pink tank top. He could see the spattering of freckles on her chest.

"May I come in?" he asked.

She nodded and moved aside. "Come on in."

He noticed the laptop sitting on the couch. Had she been working on this thing all day while he was sitting on a hill trying to think of how to continue this lie to Anna? He didn't understand why he didn't come clean with her about not having any money. He was embarrassed that this whole thing had gotten out of control.

"Let's sit." Anna pointed to the couch.

He set his hat on the table and sat beside her, wringing his hands. Anna laid her hand over his and squeezed it. A tightness spread across his chest. "Anna, I'm sorry about our argument the other day. I realize I've been selfish to your needs. I'm trying, but I feel like I take two steps forward and three back." He could only imagine what she thought when she saw him sitting where Shelly was buried. He swallowed the lump in his throat and continued. "I went up there to clear my head. Planning for the equine center is getting to me. I'm afraid I'll let everyone down if I can't get it open." Will ran his fingers through his hair and looked down. Anna was still holding his hand, comforting him.

He pulled away his hand and stood. "I don't deserve you. I give you nothing except grief. And you comfort me repeatedly. I don't know why I sabotage everything good in my life. I've been doing it since we first met." Will stopped what he would say next because he was afraid to say it out loud. God, he loved Shelly. He loved Caden and Eva, but he'd always loved Anna, then and now.

Anna stared at him, not saying a word. Will wasn't sure if she wanted to yell at him, kick him out, or hug him. The silence was deafening. He came here to tell her all of that but couldn't.

"The budget, Will. Can you tell me about the budget?" Anna said flatly.

Will creased his forehead. "That's what you have to say? Even after what I just said?"

"What do you want me to say?" She stood and moved toward him. "I think you don't want the truth." A fire burned in her eyes. "You want me to open this equine center, but you lie or avoid my questions about the budget. I cannot figure out which." She took another step toward him. "I understand the magnitude of what your family has been through, and I have empathy for that, but you want something but avoid making it work. Why?"

Will hung his head and whispered, "I don't know."

She took his hand. "You need to decide how bad you want this, or we can't do much more on the grant. There are too many moving pieces for you to be so aloof."

"I don't have any money," he said. "None."

Anna's eyes widened. "What?"

"There's nothing."

Her breath hitched. "When we meet again, please come prepared with a date to set up the budget for the opening, or we can discuss it further. If not, I cannot continue with this project." She threw her hands up. "I can't do this anymore."

Will's heart jumped into his throat. He swallowed hard. "The equine center or us?"

Tears brimmed in Anna's eyes. "Both. My heart can't take it anymore. I have my stuff too."

"Are you leaving Cardinal Creek?" The air suddenly became thick when Will asked that question. He stopped breathing as he waited for her answer.

She placed a hand on his face. "Yes, I will leave."

He nodded and whispered, "I guess I should go."

"It might be best. You have a lot to think about."

CHAPTER 40

Anna clicked through the pages of the grant application, her fingers flying over the keyboard as she filled in each section with the information Jenny and the director of the Serenity Equine Center in Missouri had provided. Anna needed help to complete the application. Despite working every night after work, time wasn't on her side. Will texted her a few times about wanting to see her, but she always made an excuse about needing to finish the grant. Deep down, Anna knew she was avoiding him. She didn't want to stop helping with the opening of the equine center, but she needed some boundaries for her sanity. Being close to Will was like kryptonite; it weakened her.

A week without seeing Will had taken a toll on Anna—she hadn't slept or eaten and found it hard to talk to anyone. On Friday, Will showed up dressed in a black Stetson and a blue shirt that brought out his deep blue eyes. Her heart raced in her chest.

He smiled. "Hey, darlin', I saw your car. What are your plans tonight?"

She looked down, avoiding eye contact. "Nothin', just hanging out here." She couldn't believe he stopped by like nothing happened.

"Do you have time to work on the grant in a bit? Did you eat? I could go pick something up." He lifted her chin to look at him. "Please, Anna."

Kryptonite, I can't say no. "Well, I am hungry." She relaxed into a smile. *Maybe he's here to tell me more about the budget.*

"I'll go get us something. The kids are with Momma and Kati, so we have the evening."

Anna drew in a deep breath, taking in his familiar scent. *I've missed him so much.* She melted into his embrace, gently touching his cheek as he gathered her in his arms, holding her tight. "Oh, Will," she whispered, "you have no idea how much I've missed you."

"I've missed you too." He looked at her when they reluctantly let go. "I won't be long."

He descended the stairs, looking back and giving her a wink. When he was out of sight, Anna closed the door, leaning against it with her eyes closed. She knew she was weak when it came to Will, but why did she have to fold so quickly after holding her ground all week?

Anna quickly showered, then put on a turquoise V-necked sundress with spaghetti straps embroidered with small pink flowers on the bodice, making her eyes a Caribbean green. She took a last look at her hair lying across her shoulders. She dabbed on some vanilla perfume she'd found at the Diamond Saddle Boutique. Light pink lipstick was carefully painted on her lips. Anna placed her hands over her heart, which beat like a drum in her chest. She closed her eyes, slowly filled her lungs with air, then let it go. *Please let him give me what I need for this grant. God knows I don't want to leave, but I will.* She shook her head. *Maybe if I keep saying that I'll believe it.*

As Anna was heading to the kitchen, the door opened. Her heart stumbled before finding its rhythm once again. "Hey, Cowboy."

Will's gaze swept over her body, clearly approving how the dress hugged her curves. He held the takeout and a bottle of wine, mesmerized by her beauty. He cleared his throat. "darlin', you look beautiful."

She wrapped her arms around his neck. "I owe you an apology. I'm so sorry."

He pulled her close, resting his hand on the small of her back. "Why are you apologizing?"

"I've been avoiding you because I don't want to fight."

He pulled her in tighter. "I know, and I don't blame you. I need to get my shit together."

As they separated, his soft and graceful touch on her face caused a fluttering in her stomach. He spoke, his voice trembling. "I apologize for everything. I promise I'm going to be the man you need."

"Oh, Cowboy, it's not for me. It's for you. The change needs to be for you first."

He nodded and captured her hands in his. "It will be, Ginger. I promise."

When Will called her Ginger, it softened her heart. Her lips curled into a smile.

The look on his face pulled at her heartstrings. "Are you hungry?"

"Famished." A small, breathless whisper escaped her lips.

Will pulled out a chair and motioned for her to sit. "I hope you don't mind burgers from Saddle Up."

"I love their burgers."

He smiled. "Me too. You want some wine?"

"I'll take water. We need to talk about the grant, and I need a clear mind." She headed to the refrigerator. "You want one?"

"Please. We still have a long way to go. Are we going to meet the deadline?"

A smile crossed her lips as she handed him water and two plates and then sat down. Will took the burgers from the bag and put them on the plates.

As they savored their juicy burgers, Anna couldn't contain her excitement. "I've been collaborating with my friend Jenny and an equine center in Missouri this week." She got up from her seat and handed him a business envelope. "It's finished."

He paused, wiping his mouth. "I don't know what to say." His eyes scanned the envelope. "You said you wouldn't finish it without me telling you about the budget."

Anna stood frozen, biting her lip. "If I tell you it still stands, would you be upset with me, Will?"

His eyes were as soft as a whisper. "darlin', I'm speechless. No, you need to stand by the boundaries you set. I'm far from upset. I'm so thankful for you."

She kissed him on the cheek. "Now we can start planning the opening. I have been working on some things we need and how to structure it. So when can we talk about the finances?"

A bulge spasmed in Will's jaw. "I need to look at my schedule. I want to make you dinner at my place."

Anna stared at him, blinking. "You want me to come to your house?"

He nodded.

Anna contemplated asking him again if Shelly had anything written. She took a deep breath and quickly fired the question with her eyes squeezed shut. She gulped air. "Have you come across any research Shelly had done on opening the center? Like where to find funds or how to do the fundraising? I want to make sure what we do honors her wishes."

Will murmured, "I'll look around and see if there is anything. I'm sure she did, but I have no idea where it would be." He closed his eyes as he took a long drink of water.

Anna watched him as he picked at his food. It seemed like he was hiding something. The tension in his face was evident. She wasn't sure if he was upset with her for finishing the grant or asking questions.

Anna curled her fingers around his hand, "Hey, are you ok?"

"Yeah, I'm fine. Let's go out to dinner tomorrow. Eva and Caden want to stay with Momma. They texted me earlier about cooking and spending the night with Nana."

She cracked a smile. "Is dancing involved?"

He raised an eyebrow and slowly relaxed into a smile. "Do you want it to be?"

"Since I love dancing with you, yes."

Putting his hands to his chest, he asked, "Me?"

She pointed at him. "Yeah, you. I love being in your arms; your voice is smooth when you sing."

Will pulled her into his lap. "God, Anna, I love being with you." He moved his hand over the back of her neck, then kissed her lightly on the lips.

There was a tug on Anna's heart as she sank into the warmth of Will's arms. She wanted nothing more than to get lost in his embrace and experience the gentle brush of his lips on hers, but she knew that if she did, it would undermine all the boundaries and rules she had set to ensure he'd take her seriously.

"Should we get to work?" Anna said.

"Mmmm, can we stay like this for a few more minutes?"

"We should work, Cowboy," she said as she pushed herself off his lap.

After they finished eating and cleaning up, Anna gathered her laptop and trifold project board she had put together on the couch. The project board was covered in colored sticky notes. His eyebrows went skyward.

She giggled at his reaction. "Don't worry, it's not as complicated as it looks. Each goal is put into columns, and all tasks are separated. I like it organized."

He smiled. "I see that."

Anna reviewed all the tasks that needed to be completed by a specific date. She pointed out things that needed to be completed before patients could be seen on the ranch. She mapped out a list of therapies Kitty and Jenny had told her about. Will leaned forward, nodding slightly as he grinned. She had not seen that look before. She wondered what he was thinking about. Did he like the plans? Was now the time to talk about doing things in phases to alleviate financial worries?

Anna looked at him, smiling. "What?"

"Thank you for all your hard work while I've done nothing."

Her face flushed. "Stop," she said, giving him a friendly bump to his shoulder. "Your work comes after we get the money to get the ranch ready."

She opened the envelope and handed him some documents. "You need to sign where the tabs are." When he finished signing, she placed the papers in the envelope, sealed it, and placed it close to her heart.

"What are you doing?"

"Blessing them."

Leaning in, Will placed a tender kiss on her lips. "There's something I've wanted to say for a long time," he whispered.

Anna swallowed hard. "What is it?"

He ran his finger down her cheek, his gaze soft and warm. "I'm in love with you, Anna. I've wanted to tell you for a while, but I just kept finding reasons to push you away, and I'm sorry for that. I'm so, so sorry."

Anna sucked in a breath as she stared at Will, taking in his kind, beautiful eyes and his nervous smile. She didn't know what to think, especially given their push and pull lately, but she knew one truth profound in her heart.

She wrapped her fingers around his and said, "I love you too."

He gathered her in his arms, holding her against his chest. Anna closed her eyes, listening to the beat of his heart, knowing he'd conquered one of his fears. They both finally said what they'd been feeling all along.

"Will?"

"Hmm?"

"My friend Jenny is coming to visit in a few weeks. She's going to help us."

Will lifted her chin. "Look at me," he said with a tenderness.

Sadness filled her eyes. It was easy to think about leaving before Will said he loved her, but now . . .

"What is it, darlin'?"

"I'm homesick. I miss my house there, my friend Jenny, and my surrogate mom. I told them I wanted to move back home the day I took Thunderbird riding."

Will took a deep breath. "Are you leaving, Anna?"

"That's why Jenny is coming to visit." She looked at him and paused, then said, "I love your family, but I just need something familiar." Tears trailed down her cheeks. "I miss Jenny and Maggie, something fierce." She took a ragged breath. "They're a connection to my grandparents. I miss them so much," she mumbled.

He took the bandanna from his pocket and wiped her tears. "Ever since you got here, so much has been about me. I've been so wrapped up in my pain that I miss others'. That's not how relationships work. I'm sorry I've been that way to you and everyone, for that matter." He took a ragged breath. "I could take some time off to take you home for a visit. I would love to see where you grew up."

She opened her mouth to speak, but nothing came out. Will was changing. He loved her and wanted to take her home. "You can put this one in the books. I'm speechless. Thank you for offering to take me home. I'd love to do that after we open the equine center."

He stroked her hair. "You sure, darlin'?"

She nodded. "Jenny is coming to visit. Then we'll see." She sat up facing him. "Last summer, we sat on my grandparents' wraparound porch, swinging and listening to the bobwhites. My grandfather would whistle, and they would answer. I miss the yellow daffodils and purple hyacinths planted around the porch. I miss the green."

He laughed. "We all miss green. I'm sorry, but I forget that it hasn't been long since your grandfather passed."

"Jenny and I have been texting and talking on the phone since I got here, but with everything going on, when I saw their faces, I saw Papa."

He pulled her in, kissing her forehead. "I'm sorry, darlin'. Are you considering quitting your job, or would a visit help?"

"I'm not thinking about anything until we open the equine center. I gave you my word I would help."

She lay in Will's lap. With a feather's touch, he ran his finger from her shoulder to her hand. "Anna, please don't go."

"Cowboy, I'm hoping Jenny coming to visit will help."

Was Will saying "I love you" enough to keep her in Cardinal Creek? Anna didn't know. She wasn't sure how Will would handle his PTSD; he hadn't mentioned going to therapy.

Concentrate on the things he's accomplished since I got here, she reminded herself. *His jealousy has been much better. I haven't seen the ring since we last talked. He said he loved me. Now, we need to tackle the budget.* It wasn't about the budget for Anna; it was about trust. She needed to have faith in Will for their relationship to work. Without trust, there was no foundation for their connection. If she couldn't trust him, then she would go home.

Will's voice tore her from her thoughts. "Did you hear me? You looked a thousand miles away."

A heated blush rushed to her cheeks. "I'm sorry, I was thinking."

Will brought her hand to his mouth and kissed her knuckles. "The kids are staying with Momma tonight. Could I stay with you?"

Her pulse quickened, and she responded in a low, sultry voice. "What did you have in mind, Cowboy?"

He trailed his finger down her cheek. "We could cuddle and see where it goes. Just holding you all night is good enough for me."

She slid him a curious glance. "So, we could cuddle all night. Are you okay with that?"

"Yes, darlin', if you're okay with it, I'll get a change of clothes."

She sat up and hugged him. "I'm fine with it. Hurry back."

He kissed her on the forehead. "I'll be right back."

When the door closed, Anna jumped up to change her clothes and brush her teeth. She quickly changed into pink pajama shorts and a pink tank top and let her hair down. As she applied pink lip gloss, she smiled. She wondered if that was too much when she dabbed some vanilla citrus perfume behind her ear. When she looked down, she realized her toes matched the overall look.

Anna walked into the bedroom and got the bed ready. Sure, she and Will had been together before, but the thought of him making love to her set her on fire.

At least now she understood how Will felt and what he wanted. He wouldn't say he loved her to get her to stay, right? No, she didn't think so. He was doing better. They both were.

There was just that budget... and Dr. Watts. *If I want honesty, I need to be honest*, she thought. *Tonight is ours. I'll tell him tomorrow.*

Those were her last thoughts as she drifted off to sleep, waiting for Will to return.

CHAPTER 41

Will watched Anna's delicate fingers work the keyboard. The glow of the computer screen illuminated her face. Just last night, he had mustered up the courage to confess his feelings for her, and now there she was, sitting beside him. The memories of their morning together flooded back to him - waking up with her in his arms, their passionate embrace, the alluring scent of her skin, and the undeniable connection between them.

They'd been organizing spreadsheets and project boards since they finished with the horses. A budget sheet with Will's name on it caught his attention. Why couldn't he give her the book? Fear held him back. He'd promised her he would change, but he harbored this lie. Deep down, he knew this would work out, but not if it cost him Anna's love.

Anna was saying something, but Will was so lost in thought that he didn't hear her.

"I'm sorry," he said, rubbing his chin. "What were you saying?"

Anna pointed to the task labeled *Budget*. "This is the big thing you need to take care of so we can plan the opening. While I know you don't have money to open the center, I need you to come up with what you need to get done and prices." She took a deep breath. "And if you can find the notebook, it would be helpful."

Will rubbed the back of his neck and bounced his leg.

Anna placed her hand on his knee. "There goes that leg again. That seems to happen whenever the budget is brought up. Is there anything else you need to tell me?"

Will intertwined his fingers with hers. "No, this is just a lot." He rubbed his sweaty palms on his jeans and caught sight of his left hand. He couldn't believe he'd forgotten to take off his ring again. He'd promised changes. It was time he started making them. Anna was intensely focused, so hopefully, she didn't notice. The hope he had this morning was dissipating, but Anna needed the truth, and it was time she got it.

Anna touched his arm. "Will, now is the time to tell me if there's a problem so we can fix it."

His eyebrows drew together in anguish, and his stomach was in knots. Things were getting out of control. They only had the summer to open the equine center. *Where am I going to get the money needed? No, I need to concentrate on assessing what needs to be done.*

Will cleared his throat. "You know, I'm hungry." That was the truth, but the wrong one.

Anna side-eyed him and opened her planner. "We can discuss the budget when we meet again. When is your next day off? What do I need from you?"

"Tomorrow and Wednesday." Will chuckled, "And I need to get any information so we know how much money is needed."

She smiled and nodded as she took out a pen. "We could meet on Wednesday after I get off work."

Will suppressed his turmoil and gave her a side hug, kissing her softly on the lips. "I promised you I was going to change. We'll discuss everything on Wednesday."

Anna looked at him. "You sure?"

He gave a reassuring smile. "Yes, I'll give you the truth." He kissed her head. "I'm gonna go shower and change. Can you be ready in thirty minutes?"

"Yes, I can meet you at your truck."

He grabbed her, lifting her off the floor. "No way. I'm coming to get you. My momma taught me manners."

She stole a kiss before he put her down and walked out the door. *Hopefully, I won't lose her when she knows the truth.*

~

As he prepared for their date, Will's heart swelled with anticipation, but fear weighed it down. As he carefully applied shaving cream to his face, the flash of gold on his finger again scolded him for not taking off the ring. *I hope Anna didn't notice I was wearing my ring again.* After leaving Anna's cabin that morning, Will showered, dressed, and put on his ring out of habit. That had been his routine ever since he married Shelly. *A habit I need to break.*

After he showered, he placed the ring into Shelly's jewelry box on the dresser, and a sense of resolution washed over him. He dressed in Wranglers, a black button-down shirt, boots, and a black Stetson. He'd decided it was time to return to work the ambulance with Jon. Maybe he would do that on his next shift. Will didn't take telling Anna he loved her lightly. A person shouldn't ever play with someone's emotions like that. It also meant it was time to change the man he'd become since Shelly died. He needed to be a person Anna could count on when she needed someone, just as she'd been for him.

When he reached the cabin, he rapped his knuckles against the door. When there was no answer, he opened it, stepped inside, and called out. "Anna?"

"I'll be right there," she called from the bedroom. Will's pulse quickened when she emerged dressed in black skinny jeans that hugged her curves like a second skin and an emerald-green T-shirt and boots. Her makeup was subtle but drew attention to her full lips, which were painted coral. A slow smile spread across her face as she met his gaze. "Hey," she said.

Will's heart swelled at the sight of her, reminding him of what it was like to be alive again after three years of being numb. He kissed her deeply, savoring her sweet taste. "You look amazing," he murmured as they parted.

Anna let out a low laugh and pushed him away playfully. "If you keep doing that, we'll never eat."

With a grin, Will took her hand and led her toward the doorway. "I'm starving. Let's go."

Anna giggled, linking arms with him. "All right then, Mr. Hungry! Let's get some food in your belly."

As they drove into town for dinner at Saddle Up Bar & Grill, Will glanced at Anna. "You ready to dance?"

She looked at him with longing in her eyes. "With you, always."

"But first food."

They both laughed as he parked. He walked around the vehicle and helped Anna out of the passenger seat, curling his fingers around hers as they walked to the entrance.

He leaned in and whispered, "I like your new shampoo. I'm not sure if I told you, but I like it better than the lavender." He placed his hand on the small of her back as they entered.

Anna smiled. "The smell of the burgers makes my mouth water."

"I know what you mean," he mumbled. Her thoughts were of food, but his thoughts were on her vanilla scent.

She raised an eyebrow. "What?"

Will groaned. "You smell so good it's driving me mad. I want to get you alone and . . ." He wiggled his eyebrows.

"Will?" Anna tapped his arm.

"Hmmm?" he responded, realizing she was trying to talk to him.

"Are you okay? It was like you were a million miles away."

A grin spread across his face. "I'm great. When I'm with you, my hormones forget we aren't teenagers anymore."

A wicked grin spread across her face. "Wait until we're dancing."

He placed his hands on her hips and guided her to their table. Before she sat, he put his mouth close to her ear. "You better behave," he whispered as he nibbled her ear, causing her to giggle.

She patted the seat next to her in the booth. "Sit next to me."

He pointed his finger at her. "Are you going to behave?"

She placed a hand over her heart. "Me? Not behave? Never."

As Will slid into the booth, Anna had a mischievous look in her eye as she laid her hand on his knee, moving it slowly up his thigh.

Will bit his bottom lip, giving her a side glance. "Ginger." Her hand continued creeping up his thigh. He closed his eyes, placed his hand on hers, and moved it back to his knee. They sat quietly for a while before he took his hand off hers. He loved it when she was playful.

Anna looked at him with a sly grin as he continued to look straight ahead and slid her hand up his leg again. He grabbed her hand as the waitress breezed in to get their order.

Will cleared his throat. "I'll take a sweet tea." Anna was staring at him with seduction in her eyes. "What would you like to drink, darlin'?"

Her voice was low and sultry. "Same as you."

When the waitress walked away, Will glanced at her with narrowed eyes. "What are you doing?"

She gave his shoulder a friendly push. "Messing with you."

He leaned in, nibbling on her neck. "It's working."

She giggled. "We need to stop."

He kissed her cheek and whispered, "Never."

The waitress arrived with the drinks and placed them on the table. When she moved away, Anna squeezed his hand. He looked at her. The blood had drained from her face, and she was biting her bottom lip.

"darlin', what is it?"

She sat staring blankly ahead, not answering.

"Anna?" Will had no idea what the sudden change was all about. A million things ran through his mind. His thoughts were interrupted by a greeting from Dr. Watts.

"Good evening, Ms. Samuels and Mr. Deluca."

Will wiped his hands. "Good evening, Dr. Watts."

He put his hand out, gripping it. " How's your mom doing?"

"Ready to get that cast off and return to riding horses."

"It will be soon enough." Dr. Watts looked at Anna. "Ms. Samuels, how are you?"

Anna answered like the air had been squeezed out of her lungs. "Fine, thank you," she said with a hitched breath.

Dr. Watts put his hand out toward the empty seat. "Can I sit for a minute? I'm waiting for my wife, Cathy. She should be here any minute."

"Sure," Will said with hesitation. Anna shot him a furious look. Will wasn't sure what was going on between them.

Dr. Watts slid into the empty seat and turned his attention to Anna. "Ms. Samuels, how do you like the new job?"

"It's fine, thank you for asking," she said, strained. She dug her fingers into Will's thigh. Will side-eyed her with an eyebrow raised. A heaviness spread inside his chest as the green-eyed monster took over his body. Something wasn't right. Dr. Watts touched Anna's free hand. She pulled her hand back like it was on fire. "If you need anything, you know where to find me." His voice was primal. "I know Cathy can be difficult to work for at times."

Will looked at them. *What did he say?* Anna's breathing was so hitched her chest was nearly heaving. Will wanted to say something, but he just kept quiet. Anna grabbed his hand and squeezed like she was sending him a message he didn't understand.

His mind went back to the day his mother had surgery. Dr. Watts had been at the nurse's station, rubbing the shoulders of one of the nurses. She'd had the same look Anna had on her face now. Anna had told him nothing was happening, but now Will questioned it. *Is he bothering her at work?*

Dr. Watts shot Anna a smile. *Maybe she finds him appealing—he's a doctor and has more to offer. No, Will, come on. He's married, and Anna isn't like that.* He heard Dr. Watts's voice but didn't hear what he said because the green-eyed monster's voice was louder. *She wants him. He's a doctor, and you have nothing to offer. You need help to pull together a budget for the equine center.*

A familiar voice interrupted his thoughts.

"Well, well, Ms. Samuels, why is it that when I need to find my husband, he's always near you?" Cathy Watts said, anger laced in her voice.

What's going on? Will turned to Anna, whose nails dug into the palm of his hand.

Dr. Watts stood up, took his wife's hand, and kissed her. Then he said, "Dear, don't let that green-eyed monster blur your vision; you know I only have eyes for you."

Cathy winced at his words . . . or was he squeezing her hand? Will's chest tightened.

Anna drew in a sharp breath, remaining mute. Her eyes were wide as saucers. Will leaned in and whispered, "darlin', you, okay? Dumb question, I know."

She nodded blankly but didn't speak. Will cleared his throat and broke the awkward silence. "Hey, y'all have a nice evening."

Dr. Watts nodded. "Yes, of course. You too, good night."

Cathy's eyes cast down as she whispered, "I'm sorry. Have a good evening. I'll talk to you on Monday, Anna."

"Oh . . . okay," Anna managed to say. She rested her trembling hand on Will's thigh.

Dr. Watts nodded. "Good night, and I apologize for my wife's behavior." He stuck his hand out. Will shook it, squeezing it harder than he should, causing Dr. Watts to wince. As they walked away, he noticed Dr. Watts grab his wife by the arm and practically pull her toward the exit.

Will touched Anna's leg, and she jumped. "What was that?"

Dissatisfaction plowed her brow, and she speared him with another glare. "Did you just witness the same thing I did?" Something bitter dripped from her tone.

He gritted his teeth so hard his jaw hurt. "Is there something you need to tell me?" he growled.

"Like what, Will?" she snapped. "Are we back to the jealousy thing?"

Will took a deep breath. He needed to trust Anna if he loved her. The whole interaction was like something out of *The Twilight Zone*. He intertwined his fingers with hers.

"I'm sorry." He trailed kisses to her ear. "That was weird."

Anna jerked her head back. "Ya think? But of course, it's my fault—"

Before Anna could say anything else, the waitress brought their food. The burgers and fries sitting in front of them had lost their appeal. His hungry stomach was replaced with a strange hint of bile in his throat.

Will watched as she stared at her food without touching it. "You got quiet." *Of course, she did. I accused her of wanting Dr. Watts.* "I'm sorry, Anna."

She looked at him out of the corner of her eye. "Do you think I would cheat on you after all I went through with Tony?"

He shook his head. "darlin', I'm sorry. I know I've been saying that a lot lately. I'm changing, I promise."

She slowly looked at him, tears threatening to spill down her cheeks. "I don't like either one of them." The storm formed in her eyes, and her anger flashed. "As for you, it would be best if you *listened to me*," she said, emphasizing the last three words. "The jealousy thing better not come up again. This is not a threat. It's a promise. I will disappear without a word," she hissed. "You know I will. I've done it before."

Will knew he deserved what she told him. Something was wrong with the interaction between Dr. Watts and his wife. His gut told him that Anna was in a war between the two.

He took a minute to choose his words carefully. "Baby, I'm sorry. No excuses, except sometimes my insecurities outweigh my good sense." He prayed that his apology would help. He could do nothing more to make it right except never do it again.

Anna let out a ragged breath. "If you love me, Will, you would believe I would never break your heart by cheating. Dr. Watts is awful."

Will knew it was true. Even when they were sixteen, she had a heart like no other person he'd met.

He just wanted to take the food and head out. He wrapped his arm around her shoulders and said, "Hey, want to take this food to go? We can build a fire and dance under the stars."

She nodded, and a pained look marred her face.

"I'll pay, and we can go." He took her hand. "I'm sorry. Can you forgive me?"

Anna nodded, tears in her eyes.

A lump caught in his throat that promised to cut off his air. He hoped this wouldn't seal the deal on her decision to leave Cardinal Creek. He was such an idiot. Dr. Watts was slimy, and he couldn't imagine someone like Anna—with such a pure heart—would be interested in someone like him. But the situation was bizarre.

When they left the restaurant, they walked in silence to his truck, hand in hand. Still, the tension between them hung in the air.

Will loosened the ever-growing tightness of his collar before opening the door for Anna. He started to lend a hand but stopped and closed the space between them. The comforting aroma of vanilla engulfed him, stimulating his senses. He played with the tendrils of her hair, contemplating what to say that didn't start with *I'm sorry*.

He let out a long sigh and moved his blue gaze to blink up at the sky filled with stars. "Anna, I'm not sure what to say about what happened with Dr. Watts and his wife, but I know one thing." He lifted her chin to meet her gaze. "I trust you. I'm not sure I trust Dr. Watts, but I trust that when you say you love me, you mean it." His hands moved over the back of her neck before he lightly kissed her on the lips. "I mean it when I tell you that I love you."

Anna wrapped her arms around his neck. Her emerald eyes tugged at his heart, knowing it was his fault that he'd upset her.

Will gently stroked her hair, unsure of what to say. Her silence was deafening. Was she going to leave?

Relief washed over his body when she whispered into his chest, "I forgive you. Can we go home?"

She called the ranch home. Everything will be okay.

CHAPTER 42

As Anna worked at her desk, her mind returned to Saturday night. She wished she could tell Will about what had happened with Dr. Watts. Kati was the only one who had some idea of what was going on, and JW had had an inkling that something wasn't right, but she still felt so alone. She couldn't let this go on any longer. She needed to tell someone. It was tearing her apart. When Will became jealous, Anna was ready to return to Missouri. She didn't want to deal with the constant mistrust.

Accusations of cheating arose when someone didn't fully trust you. She couldn't understand why Will would think so little of her. But his reassurance after they'd left the restaurant warmed her heart. It was the perfect end to the evening, and waking up in his arms gave her the hope of continuing her life with Will in Cardinal Creek. Anna wasn't at fault for what happened at the bar, but would Will's jealousy let him see it that way? Suddenly, Anna's office door opened and slammed shut, causing her to jump and snap back to reality. She gasped when she saw Dr. Watts lock the door. She shot up from her chair, heart drumming so hard she felt it in her ears. Dr. Watts leaned against the door, arms crossed and a sinister grin. Her throat constricted, making it hard to swallow.

"What can I do for you?" Her voice cracked.

He crept toward her, his gaze undressing her. "I think you know what I want." His voice was husky with lust.

Anna's body trembled. "This needs to stop. I've asked you on many occasions. Your behavior is inappropriate. Your wife thinks I'm leading you on. I should report you." She took deep breaths, looking for a way to escape.

His eyes lit, and his lips curved in malicious pleasure as he moved closer. "Why do you think that's happening?" He closed the space between them, and his hand moved toward her. She lurched back to prevent him from touching her. "I've been telling her you follow me and meet me in the stairway. So, you can either let this happen, or you could lose your job and license. Nobody will believe you over me."

Anna's stomach tightened as he ran his finger down her cheek.

"This will happen."

Anna took a deep breath; it was time she fought back. She grabbed his hand and pulled his fingers with all her might, hoping to break them. "I—I told you no, and I mean it." She pushed him, causing him to stumble, grabbed her purse, and ran out the door. Then she shot on unsteady legs down the hall to the steps, too scared to look back and praying he wasn't behind her. The door slammed as she raced down the stairs and jumped the last three steps to the landing.

He charged forward and grabbed her, thrusting her up against the wall. His face was red, and he gasped for air, his eyes dancing with flames.

"Okay, this is how it's going to be. If you say anything to anyone, I will end you. I'll make sure you lose everything, including the cowboy." His face was inches from hers. "I told Cathy the whole Anna-wants-me story after we saw you in the restaurant."

Anna was trapped against the wall, trembling.

"Believe me when I say Cathy believes me, and your man will too. If you go to administration, this will blow up in your pretty face," he whispered in her ear, sending shivers throughout Anna's body.

A fire burned in the pit of her stomach. *Act now!* she thought. She narrowed her eyes and placed her hands on his chest. He smiled, leaning in to kiss her, then she pushed him so hard he stumbled to the ground. Anna ran down the stairs and out of the hospital until she got into her SUV, locked the doors with a trembling hand, and burned rubber out of the parking lot. Her body shook as she drove, tears streaming like a river down her face. When she was sure no one was following her, she pulled over, placed her head on the steering wheel, and sobbed.

Men like Seth Watts always won. She shuddered at the memory of a nurse in Missouri who had reported a doctor for harassment and ended up losing her job. Anna worked too hard for everything to go down the toilet because of Dr. Watts.

As much as she loved Will and his family, she knew she must leave Cardinal Creek. At least at University Hospital, she had her reputation as a nurse, but no one knew her there. She leaned her head on the seat. The thought of leaving Will made her heart ache, but there was nothing else she could do.

~

BACK AT THE RANCH, Anna changed out of her work clothes and headed for the stables. Her nerves were shot. She had even pulled out a suitcase to pack her stuff and had planned to leave without saying goodbye. *Going for a ride will clear my head.*

She grabbed Thunderbird's saddle and grooming tote. While tending to him, the powerful horse gently nudged her—twice. As he nuzzled against her neck, Anna stroked his mane and asked if something was wrong. He snorted in response and affectionately rested his muzzle on her shoulder.

"I need help," she said. She expertly placed all the necessary equipment on Thunderbird and gave his nose a friendly scratch while securing his bridle.

She stopped at the black door, putting her hat on. "Let's go for a hard ride, boy."

Thunderbird moved his head up and down. She smiled, scratching behind his ear. When she guided him through the gate, she mounted and leaned forward with her body slightly raised and used the pressure of her legs on Thunderbird's flank to get him into a full gallop.

The sun was warm on her face as her hair flew in the wind. When Anna rode at full speed, it gave her a sense of power and control. She pulled the reins back to slow into a trot when she suspected she heard another set of hooves. She looked back, saw nothing, and continued up the hill where she loved to go. She was glad Will was working today so she could clear her head without anyone bothering her.

She dismounted, sat, and stared at the ranch, thinking how much she would miss this spot. As she watched the sun's impressive bright orange and purple sink out of sight, she was torn between her love for Will and the fear of losing her career.

She'd come to Texas for a fresh start, both because she wanted to and because her grandfather had suggested it in his letter. But this wasn't what he'd want for her, being harassed and fearing her workplace. What would've happened if she hadn't been able to escape Dr. Watts in her office? Should she leave her new love and friends behind and return to Missouri?

The sun was almost out of sight when Garrett climbed up the hill. She let out a long sigh, wondering why he was there. She hadn't seen him when she was in the stable, nor his truck in its usual spot when she got home. Then again, she was in no state to notice if anyone was around. She wasn't in the mood to talk to anyone right now.

She jumped up, brushed off her jeans, and slowly turned to face him. "Why are you here?" Her voice was laced with irritation. Her throat tightened at her urge to run like a caged animal. Before he could answer, she walked toward Thunderbird, her mind whirling more confused.

As she opened her stride, Garrett remained steadfast on her heels until he shouted for her, "Anna!" She froze, turning to face him with her eyes downcast.

"Anna, what's wrong?" he asked.

As a sob caught in her throat, she slowly shook her head. "I—I can't talk, Garrett."

"What is it?"

Silent tears trailed down Anna's cheeks as she hugged Garrett. She wanted to tell him what had happened but was still in shock. "I can't tell you," she said, barely audible. Then she pulled away and wiped her eyes. "I'm going back to Missouri after the center opens. I think."

"Listen, I'm not going into the whole story, but I was close to someone who acted like you. The man who was harassing her killed her." Dissatisfaction plowed his brow as he asked, "Is someone bothering you at work?"

Anna took a step back. She couldn't explain it but was afraid to tell him what had happened. She needed to think things through. "It's nothing. I'm fine," she said.

The concern on his face grew as he studied her. "Is everything okay between you and Will?"

As she passed Garrett, she squeezed his shoulder. "Everything is fine."

She mounted Thunderbird and looked at Garrett standing with his thumbs in his pockets. His eyebrows furrowed with concern. "Hey, are you coming?"

He nodded before mounting General and nudged him gently. They rode side by side.

Anna noticed Garrett's creased forehead. "What are you thinking?" she asked.

"When I was in the military, I knew women who had unethical commanders and soldiers harassed." He cleared his throat. "Do you trust me?"

Anna contemplated for a moment. "Although we haven't known each other long, we've spent some time together, and I trust what I know of you."

"Tell me what's going on."

"I can't." She nudged Thunderbird into a trot.

On the ranch, she guided Thunderbird to his stall and groomed him. Garrett came into the stable but cared for General, leaving her to her thoughts.

After finishing, he leaned against the stall and watched her finish. "Would you like some help?"

"Garrett, I'm fine..."

"There's something wrong. You don't have to tell me what's bothering you, but you need to speak to someone about it."

Anna whirled around with tears streaking down her face. "Who?"

She dropped the brush, raced to her cabin, closed the door, and locked it. After some time had passed, she heard the squeak of the swing on the porch. She closed her eyes, knowing it was Garrett. Finally, there was a soft knock on the door.

She swung the door open. "What?" she sighed with exasperation.

Garrett leaned on the doorframe and said, "Thunderbird wanted me to talk to you."

"Did he now?" she asked.

"I told him I would try." He shrugged.

"Do you want a drink?" she asked, heading for the kitchen. "I just poured one."

"Is it going to get rid of what's bothering you?"

At the counter, she drank half a glass of wine. "If it made shit go away, I'd drink all the time."

Gently, Garrett took her glass and the bottle and emptied them down the sink. "Anna, this can become a habit to calm your nerves, to stop hurting, or to stop moving. This doesn't help. It creates problems."

Impatience radiated from her as she crossed her arms tightly over her chest and tapped her foot.

"Please tell me what's going on. I know someone's hurting you. I've seen it in the military. Is it Will?"

Anna stomped her foot at the accusation. "No, Garrett. Will is amazing. That's what makes this so hard," she said.

"Whoever is trying to hurt you is not too powerful to be stopped."

"Garrett, you don't know how it is."

"Sweetie, I worked in a male-dominated field where women are not treated too kindly."

"After the center opens, I think it would be best if I returned to Missouri. I was going to wait until my friend Jenny came to decide, but I've decided now."

"Are you going to tell Will?" Garrett asked.

"I'm so confused, scared, and exhausted," said Anna. "I'm not going to tell him."

His jaw tightened. "Are you asking me to lie if he asks?" he inquired.

"I wouldn't do that."

He gave her a side hug and said, "If you want to talk, I'll listen. We're friends. You can trust me."

"You have grown to be like the big brother I always wished I had. Thank you so much."

Before leaving, Garrett looked back at her and spoke up, "You can always call or text if you want to talk." Then he stepped out the door.

Anna watched him walk to his truck. She prayed he wouldn't tell Will what he suspected. Dr. Watts's threats still rang in her ears. She tossed herself on the couch, exhausted and conflicted. Now she had to decide: would she stay and fight or run home with her tail between her legs?

CHAPTER 43

Anna awoke the following day with a start, her body stiff from a night spent curled up on the couch. She rubbed her aching neck, sending shooting pains down her shoulders. With a deep sigh, she reached for her cell phone and dialed the house supervisor's number to tell them she was "sick." After she hung up, she decided it was time to take a trip to San Antonio and explore the city.

The warm water from the shower helped ease some of the tension in her muscles as she got ready for the drive to San Antonio. She had been wanting to visit there since she arrived in Texas. She just needed a change of scenery to clear her head.

On the hour-and-a-half drive, Anna's thoughts were in disarray. The weight of everything that had happened since she started working at the hospital weighed heavily on her heart, leaving her with a sense of hopelessness. As she pondered the situation with Dr. Watts, it seemed like an unsolvable puzzle and grew more daunting with each passing mile. Amidst the chaos, Anna needed something to focus on, something she could solve. She turned her attention to the budget for the equine center, a problem that could be tackled. She knew Will had no money, and even if they were awarded the grant, it wouldn't come in time to open the center in September. After Will had told her about his lack of funds, Anna had known a fundraiser was necessary. Now, it was just a matter of pride or perhaps a lack of trust in him. She couldn't shake the feeling that there was more to his story than he was letting on.

Anna took in the sights of the cobblestone streets of downtown San Antonio, feeling a sense of freedom. She marveled at the majestic architecture of the Alamo before strolling along the riverwalk. Finally, she went to Historic Market Square, where Sylvia had recommended Mi Tierra, a renowned Mexican restaurant. After settling into a sunny patio table, she ordered grilled chicken fajitas with refried beans, guacamole, and rice. The homemade tortillas were so buttery and flavorful that when she bit into one, she closed her eyes in delight. She savored every bite. The day's warmth filled her with contentment and clarity.

After paying her bill, she strolled around the bustling marketplace before heading back to Cardinal Creek to discuss the equine center budget with Will. Anna held onto hope that he would finally confirm what she already suspected...There's no money. She just wanted to hear it from him. *Will he finally tell me? It's a matter of trust.*

ANNA WALKED the familiar path to Will's house. Her mind was relaxed after spending the day in San Antonio. She needed to get this opening taken care of so she could work on finding a new job in Missouri. It was best to leave before everything she'd worked so hard for was taken from her. It was bad enough that she'd lost her family. The last thing she wanted was to lose her career. Just as Will started making positive changes, she needed to leave because her fears pushed her further away from him.

When she reached Will's, she stood on the porch contemplating returning to her cabin.

He opened the door before she knocked. He was dressed in shorts and a T-shirt that stretched across his chest. His hair was tousled from wearing a hat. His icy-blue eyes danced when he saw her, erasing any doubt. Seeing his face made her feel safe again.

She smiled, her heart melting. "Hi, Cowboy." Her voice was soft and sultry.

"Hey, darlin'. I missed you." He pulled her into his arms, brushing his lips against her ear. "You look tired. Rough day?"

"No. Rough night without you."

"I know what you mean. Try sleeping with Jon." He smiled and shook his head. "Forget what I said."

"I will, but I knew what you meant. Jenny talks in her sleep." Anna giggled.

"Then you understand."

"I do."

They stepped inside. The aroma of freshly baked bread filled the air, and she gasped when she saw the table. A red gingham cloth covered the wood surface, and a fragrant casserole in a Talavera dish was placed in its center. A rustic Italian loaf sat on a cutting board surrounded by matching plates and candles, giving the room a warm glow. Anna was overwhelmed with admiration for Will for going to such lengths to make their dinner so special.

Anna exclaimed in delight. "This looks and smells amazing!" Will pulled out her chair. "I hope you like Italian; I made lasagna. I have wine if you like."

She took her seat and smiled at him. "I love lasagna. Water is fine." Even though Anna wanted a relaxing drink, she knew Garrett was right. Drinking just made things worse.

Will served her a portion of lasagna and took his seat. Anna took a bite and closed her eyes. "This is fabulous."

He leaned in, giving her a warm, inviting kiss. "Thanks, darlin'."

They continued eating in silence. Anna glanced at him as he watched her, causing her chest to tighten. "You look like you have something to say."

"How was work today?" It was as if he was trying to draw a reaction from her like he already knew the answer.

The food in Anna's mouth seemed to grow as she chewed. Her throat was thick, making it difficult to swallow. She washed down her food with a long drink of water. "Uh, it was okay."

"Kati called wondering if you were okay. She heard from the house supervisor that you called in sick today."

Anna's appetite suddenly disappeared, and her food burned in her throat. She wasn't sure how to answer. Should she tell him about Dr. Watts or say she needed a day to herself? The silence loomed between them like a heavy mist. Will's eyebrows drew together in concern as he curled his fingers around hers. "darlin', you sure everything is okay? I didn't see your car at home. Were you sick?"

"Yes, I'm fine," her voice cracked. "Just tired, but not too tired to see you." She took a deep breath and adjusted her smile.

Will squeezed her hand. "I'm happy to see you. Where were you today?" He continued to probe.

Anna set down her fork and looked at him, biting her lower lip. "I wasn't sick. I needed a day away from Cardinal Creek, so I went to San Antonio. I did the tourist thing, then went for a late lunch." She hoped it would end this conversation before the dam broke, releasing a flood of emotions.

Two deep lines of worry appeared between his eyes. "Did something happen yesterday? You didn't text me last night like you normally do."

Her mind raced with excuses for taking off without texting him. She knew he was trying to control his jealousy, but he might be suspicious after the incident with Dr. Watts on Saturday. She swallowed the sob in her throat. "I went for a ride last night, then fell asleep on the couch. I missed my grandfather this morning, so I decided to take the day off and clear my head."

"Why didn't you let me know? I would have gone with you. I want to be there for you when you need someone."

She wished she could tell him everything, but she needed to let it go. It was time to work on making Shelly's dream come true. Then, it would be time to leave him and his wonderful family she had grown to love. "I know. I just wanted to be alone. I'm sorry. It helped a lot. Now we can work on the budget to get the equine center open on schedule."

His gaze softened. "Sure, let's work on the center," he said with a smile. "But let's eat before you hurt my feelings. I worked hard on this," he teased.

They finished their food and cleaned up the dishes together. Will slipped his arms around Anna, placing feather-light kisses along her neck as she washed the dishes.

She laid her head back against him. "Your arms feel so good."

"They feel good around you."

"I'm almost done here. Then we can get started." She dried her hands on the towel and turned to him. "We need to talk about the budget."

Will covered the rest of the lasagna and put it in the refrigerator. "We will."

"Where do you want to work?"

"I'll grab us some water if you want to wait on the couch. I'll be right there."

The conversation at dinner had unnerved Anna. Sitting on the couch with her laptop bag, she took a deep breath. She didn't understand why he played such a cat-and-mouse game about her not working today. Maybe she was reading it wrong like she did everything else. While waiting for Will, she noticed a composition book on the coffee table with "Equine Center Plans" written on the front. Anna picked it up, thinking Will had left it there for them to look at together. He'd finally found Shelly's book. She hesitated, then opened it, paging through the book. She found the structure she'd been looking for, fundraising plans, bids on repairs, and everything she'd struggled with while they wrote the grant.

Anger brewed inside her like a storm. She couldn't believe he would keep this information from her. It was the critical piece they needed to open the equine center in time. She bit her lip as she read what Shelly had written. *Anna, calm down. Let him explain.* She took a deep, cleansing breath and let it out.

Will walked into the room. His shock quickly turned into fury as he stalked across the room, snatching it out of her hands. Anna's eyes flew open wide, and her face flushed. As she seethed with anger and humiliation, she bolted off the couch, pushing past him toward the door. He dropped the book on the table, stringing a long list of expletives, and went after her. She opened the door, and he quickly pushed it closed.

She turned, squaring off with him. "You lied, and now you're pissed at me?" Anna needed something familiar without all the drama Cardinal Creek had caused her. She just needed to have time to grieve. She shook her head. "I can't do this anymore. It's too much. I need to go." A fire roared in her eyes. "It's not always about you, Will. God, you are so selfish." She swallowed her words before she said something she couldn't take back. Her breathing was fast and shallow. She blinked, feeling lightheaded. Anna knew it was time to get her emotions in check before things got out of control.

He cast his eyes downward. "I—I . . ." He raked his fingers through his hair and looked at her with an unspoken pain that was alive and glowing in his eyes. "I was afraid to let anyone see it. It was our thing and all I had left of us." His tone was apologetic.

He leaned against the wall, closed his eyes, and let out a long sigh. "God, Anna, I struggled before you arrived." His voice cracked. "It was the one thing I could give her since . . . she died because of me." His Adam's apple bobbed as he swallowed hard. "I lied to you when I told you I didn't think it was my fault." He laid his head against the wall and looked up. "I can't get past it. It's destroying everyone I love...it's destroying me," he whispered.

Will's face contorted with sorrow, and he crumpled to the floor. His heaving sobs caused her whole body to tense, and she instinctively stepped back. She gazed down at him, trying to get a read on his emotional state, unsure if he would lash out or cry harder.

But she couldn't stay mad at him. The sadness and pain in his eyes were too much to bear. She slowly brushed away the tears streaming down his face. His skin radiated heat beneath her touch, but as she gathered him into her arms, he melted into her embrace, seeking solace and reassurance.

With a gentle hand, Anna stroked his hair and whispered reassurances. At that moment, she knew her love would remain unwavering despite their challenges. "I understand, Will," she whispered.

It was as if he was holding on for dear life as he squeezed her tight. "darlin', I'm sorry, forgive me. I'm trying to change," he uttered.

She stroked his back as he nuzzled her neck. "I forgive you." She kissed his neck and whispered, "I love you."

In a tone of awe and respect, he said, "I don't know what I did to deserve such a kind, loving woman, but I'm grateful to have you in my life." He rose, led her to the living room, and motioned for her to sit on the couch. "It's time I told you the truth."

Anna looked at her watch and realized tomorrow was the anniversary of Shelly's death. Despite her anger at this reaction to her looking at the notebook earlier, she knew it was time to set her anger aside and be there for him now because he needed her love and understanding.

She motioned for him to sit next to her. "Come on, let's talk."

Will sat next to her and buried his head in his hands. "I've had the notebook all along," he confessed. "I couldn't let it go. I'm sorry for causing you so much extra work because I refused to give it up." He took a deep breath before continuing, "It just meant too much to me. And there's no money to open the center."

Anna nodded understanding and reassured him, "I already knew about the money. We'll figure out a way to make it work." She squeezed his hand.

He got up, retrieved the notebook from the table, and handed it to her. "I'm sorry I didn't do this before. I'm sorry for all the lies."

As Will continued his story, Anna thought about how they could have a fundraiser and who she could ask for help. She made a mental list of everyone who had offered to help with a fundraiser: Liz, Kati, and the Quiltin' Bees. Will had stopped talking, and he watched her curiously.

"Are you here with me? You seem a million miles away."

She nodded. "Sorry, I was thinking. What were you saying?"

"Even with what I have in savings, it isn't enough to open in time. There's too much to be done that requires money. How could I have been foolish enough to say yes when I knew it was impossible?"

Anna gave him a sympathetic look. "I understand why you said yes. We'll make this work, I promise. Many people care about you and will help you achieve this dream." She wrapped her fingers around his hand.

"Why would you help me after I lied to you and was an ass to you more than once?"

Anna smiled at him. "Because I love you, Will, more than you know."

His blue eyes shone with emotions as he lightly fingered a loose tendril of her crimson hair on her cheek before gathering her into his arms and claiming her lips in a deep, sensual kiss that caused her neurons to fire into overdrive. Still holding on tightly, he carried her to the bedroom.

Will laid Anna down on the bed. "I'm ready," he said. "Are you?" He walked to the dresser, opened the jewelry box, and took out his wedding band. "I took this off the Saturday night when we went out. I told you I was going to change. It was a silent way of starting. Lying to you was killing me. I was so scared of losing you. This is for us now . . . not just me." He knelt and tenderly held her hand. "You shouldn't have had to go to San Antonio to find peace. That's not going to happen anymore. From now on, I'll be here for you just as you've been there for me."

Will pressed his wedding ring into her hand. "Take this, throw it away. I don't need it anymore."

Anna was silent as she contemplated whether Will's words were sincere or just another empty promise like all the other times. With conviction, she said, "You were going to give me your wedding ring because you don't trust yourself not to put it on again." She shook her head. "It's not the ring. It's the deception of you saying you aren't going to wear it."

Will closed his eyes and sighed. "After all the deception, I don't know how to get you to trust me."

Anna held Will's hand, her heart thumping in her chest. "Have you worn it since Saturday?"

"No."

She placed the ring back into his hand. "That's a start."

He held the ring in his hand, then walked over and placed it into the jewelry box. He lay down next to her, his lips pressed against hers, and then he gently covered her mouth in a soft, sensual kiss. He pulled away and gazed into her eyes. "I love you with all my heart," he murmured.

Anna's heart thundered in her chest as Will awoke the dormant sexuality of her body.

That night, Anna sensed that no one had ever shared this bed but them. He showed physically and emotionally how deeply he cared. Afterward, she lay silently beside him while he slept peacefully. Anna had a sense of fulfillment. She rested her hand on his bare chest as she felt the beat of his heart beneath her touch. When she was away from him, she felt brave enough to end it, but being in his presence made the thought of leaving unbearable. He had trusted her by taking off his ring and bringing her to the bed he'd once shared with Shelly. Maybe he was ready. But was she?

CHAPTER 44

As Will drove to the fire station, his mind buzzed with a mess of static. When he woke up with Anna's head resting on his chest this morning, it oddly brought back memories of the worst day of his life, four years ago. But somehow, being with her helped ease some of the pain before he left for work; they had made love—a coincidence he shrugged off as he tried to focus on the present.

He planned to talk to Chief Erickson so that he could finally take responsibility for his job. He immediately headed toward the chief's office when he got to the firehouse.

At the chief's greeting, he entered and found Luke Erickson seated at his desk with his long legs sprawled out. When Will joined the department, Luke was a new chief and devoted energy mentoring him. He always believed in Will's potential to become a chief someday. But when tragedy struck, and Shelly passed away, Luke went above and beyond to protect and support Will, even when it may not have been the best decision. After Shelly's death, Luke took Will under his wing and helped him through his grief. He understood loss all too well; he had also lost his son several years before, and his wife filed for divorce last year and moved to Austin. Luke knew the pain of grief and could empathize with Will's struggles.

"Good morning, Chief. You have a minute?"

A crease formed on Luke's brow. "How are you doing today?" He motioned for Will to sit down.

"Oddly enough, I'm fine." Will sank into the chair across from him.

Luke raised an eyebrow. "Really?"

"Yes, I've been working on healing." Will lifted his hand to show he wasn't wearing his wedding ring. "I took it off Saturday night." He sucked in a deep breath. "I've been seeing someone."

The beginning of a smile tipped the corners of Luke's mouth. "How long have you been seeing her? What's her name?"

Will smiled. "Her name is Anna. She works with Kati at the hospital. She moved here from Missouri in April, not long after her grandpa died. Kati asked if she could rent one of the cabins and board her horse. As it turns out, we knew each other as teenagers. She went to a roping clinic here in Cardinal Creek. She's been helping me work on opening the equine center." He hoped it would show the chief he was okay to work. "She's a great lady. We've all grown to love her."

Luke stood up and sat on the edge of his desk. "I'm happy for you, Will. But I know you, and you want to tell me something."

Will wiped his sweating palms on his pants and blurted out, "I want to go back on the ambulance."

Luke's eyes widened. "Today? That's not a good idea."

"Luke, I can do this. Jon and I have each other's back." Deep down, Will knew he was right, but he needed to prove to everyone that he was dedicated to Anna.

Luke's voice was thick with emotion. "No matter if you remarry or find someone else, the pain will always be there for you." He placed a hand on Will's shoulder. "You never got therapy for what you saw the night of the accident."

Will took a deep breath and replied, "I know. This is long overdue." It was about time he stopped letting the crew, especially Jon, carry the load of Shelly's accident. Despite working together, he and Jon hadn't spoken much since the night of the campfire. While making amends to people, he owed Jon an apology.

"It's against my better judgment, but you're an experienced paramedic, and we've missed you on the ambulance. You and Jon are great medics," Luke said.

"Thanks, Luke." Will shut the door behind him. Working in the ambulance again gave him chills, but it needed to be done.

ONCE DINNER WAS CLEARED at the firehouse, Will gestured to Jon with a head tilt, motioning for him to follow outside. They grabbed their folding chairs and sat near the truck bay. The sun was setting over Main Street, casting a golden hue over the town. Will's stomach churned with anxiety, praying he could do the job. The chief had been covering for him long enough.

They sat in silence, observing the goings-on of Main Street. Cars drove by, kids laughed on nearby playgrounds, and the smell of sizzling burgers from Saddle Up wafted in the air.

Jon's eyes followed two women in shorts and boots as they entered the bar. "Hot chicks up ahead," he said.

Things had been tense between them recently, and Will's admission that Anna had left all those years ago because he'd been jealous of Jon didn't help. The best part about Jon was his forgiving heart and fierce loyalty as a friend. He always forgave those he loved—except for his parents—but this time seemed different, like it was too much.

Will punched him in the arm. "Dude, I swear that's why Kati won't go out with you."

Jon waved him off. "I don't care anymore."

"Yeah, right," Will scoffed. "At the campfire, you kissed her, danced with her, and held her hand."

A smirk spread across Jon's lips, and he nodded in agreement. "We also made out on your couch."

Will made a face and shook his head. "Dude, my kids sit on that couch."

Jon chuckled, but there was no real humor behind it. "Well, it didn't last long. It's like running up an escalator with her."

Will raised an eyebrow skeptically. "We were good at that."

Jon let out a long sigh in response. "Yeah, I guess."

Will softened his expression. "Hey, are you okay?"

Jon looked at him with a raised eyebrow. "Shouldn't I be asking you that?"

Will gritted his teeth so hard his jaw ached. It was the anniversary of Shelly's death, and while he wanted to remember her, he didn't want to dwell on the horror of that day. He heaved himself up and faced Jon directly. "Everything is fine. Anna is fine." He sighed heavily before continuing. "Come on, man, we have to stop this shit with each other."

Jon lifted himself from the chair and stormed into the truck bay, with Will following closely behind. The fluorescent lights highlighted the dangerous glint in Jon's blue eyes as he loomed over Will. "Stop what? Stop being angry that you abandoned me?"

Will froze in shock, unable to comprehend the intensity of Jon's anger. "Do you blame me? Is that why you're angry?" He finally managed to utter, tears threatening to spill from his eyes.

Jon stepped closer, their noses almost touching. His breath came out in short puffs of heat against Will's face. "No, you moron, I don't blame you. You left me alone to get my sister out of the car. Do you know what that's like? Then you left me after we returned to work, riding around with the chief." He looked away before his gaze returned to Will's face. "She was my family. We only had each other because my parents are so pathetic. They always have been."

He stumbled backward and collapsed onto a nearby bench, putting his hands on his knees and trying to catch his breath. After a few moments, he jumped to his feet again and headed straight for the exit. "I need to get out of here."

Will stood facing Jon, tongue-tied. "I'm sorry, Jon—Anna's right. I've been so wrapped up in my grief that I haven't noticed how much you and Eva were hurting. I even missed that Eva blamed herself for Shelly's death because she was getting ingredients to bake cookies with her when it happened."

Jon clenched his fists, and his face flushed a deep red. "That's bullshit! Did you talk to her about it?"

"Yes, we talked," Will said with relief. "She's doing better now."

"Good . . . poor baby. Take care of her, Will. I don't want her to feel like that. We have to fix it . . . Shelly wouldn't want that."

Will nodded. "I wanted to talk to you about something else. I should have told you before, but I talked to the chief. I'm working with you again, effective today."

Jon smiled and gave Will's arm a friendly punch. "That's great news. I can't believe the chief didn't tell me."

Will met Jon's gaze and said, "I asked him not to. I wanted to tell you myself." He took a deep breath. "I told Anna I love her. I would like to have a future with her if she'll have me, but I wasn't sure how you'd react to me being with another woman besides your sister."

Jon's eyes narrowed in contemplation as he studied Will. "Do you love her?" His voice was laced with skepticism, and his accusation made the air feel heavy between them.

Will glared at him. "What do you mean by that?" he asked, his voice sharp with anger.

Jon narrowed his eyes. "Come on, man. You still wear your ring. Shelly's clothes hang in the closet, and I don't remember you bringing Anna here. You've been living in limbo since she died."

Will held up his hand. "I've finally put it away . . . for good. It's in a special place in Shelly's jewelry box. I'll always love your sister, my wife," he said.

Jon laid a heavy hand on Will's shoulder, a gesture of comfort and understanding in one motion. "If you died in a fire, would you want Shelly to give up on love?"

Will's eyebrows furrowed in thought. "No, I would want her to find someone else if she wanted to."

Jon rubbed both hands over his face. "Man, I know her death was hard for you. It's been hard on all of us." Silence filled the air as Jon stared straight ahead.

Finally, Will spoke again. "Jon, you never talk about removing her body from the car."

Jon raised his hand to signal that he didn't want to discuss it further.

Will respectfully change the subject. "Come on, dude, since she died, you let Kati think you cheated on her. Now you fight to win her back." He paced back and forth heatedly. "Then she makes you angry, and you start talking about picking up girls and taking them home. When she gets pissed, you drink again." His eyes were soft but determined when he spoke again. "Look, man, I know how hard this has been for you too."

Jon had tears trailing down his cheeks. "Will, she was my baby sister! I should have protected her. Every night when I sleep, I see myself recovering her body. It never stops."

Will put his hand on his shoulder. "I understand. I should have protected her or kept her here a little longer. But you protected me from seeing her body. I wish I would have stayed for you."

"Listen, you're like a brother to me. I love your family. I love Kati, but right now, I can't do this. I need to get my shit together if I want to be with Kati, or I need to let her go." Jon wiped his eyes. "If you love Anna, I know Shelly would give her blessing. She lives through Eva, Caden, and the equine center. Shelly will never be forgotten. Caden is right . . . I know my sister, and she likely sent Anna to you."

"You should take some of your advice."

"I need to deal with these demons. Then I'll think about Kati. I don't want to hurt her. I love her that much."

Will knocked his hat off. "Deal with that shit, then. My sister would kill me if she knew I told you, but she's head over heels in love with you."

Jon shoved his shoulder. "Shut up, she didn't say that. She can't stand me."

Will threw a towel at him, walking away. "You'll never know unless you pull it together." He stopped and turned back. "Oh Jon, we aren't like brothers . . . we are brothers, always."

WILL JERKED awake as the shrill sound of the alarm echoed through the firehouse. He glanced at the illuminated face of his watch as he strapped it to his wrist: 0330. Despite knowing this call was for the entire crew, dread coiled in Will's gut like a snake ready to strike. With a heavy sigh, he pulled on his protective gear and trudged to the ambulance, climbing into the passenger seat for the first time in four years. Jon gave him an encouraging slap on the arm before he started the engine and followed the other trucks down the street. As they drove, Will's anxiety grew with every word of radio chatter. When their destination was finally announced—"accident with fatality"—a tightness formed in Will's lungs as he whispered, "Just get through it, Will."

Jon shot Will a concerned look. "Hey, are you doing okay?"

"I'm good, how about you?" Will's stomach churned, and bile rose in his throat as they approached the wreck.

"Fine," Jon replied in a strained voice.

When they pulled up to the scene, the SUV was on its side, and the lights flashed. Will was all too familiar with this scene, yet everything felt like it was in slow motion. The crew had already begun using the jaws of life to cut open the car. Jon parked and got out while Will stayed in his seat, unable to move, frozen with fear.

Jon opened Will's door and grabbed his arm firmly. "Dude, pull your shit together. Let's go!"

Will trudged behind Jon toward the scene of the overturned car. His heart dropped when he noticed a car seat in the back of the vehicle, crushed beneath the roof from the impact. He followed Jon around to the side of the car, where he saw a woman lying across the console, her head bleeding profusely. He made his way to check for her pulse when he spotted a man partially out of the car, eyes wide open.

"Check for a kid, Will," Jon yelled.

Will scrambled to the rear window, looking for any signs of a child inside the car. Relief swept over him when he didn't find a child, a toy, or a diaper bag. "I don't see anything," he choked.

The slightly sweet, pungent scent of fuel filled Will's nostrils, triggering visions of Shelly's accident scene. Bile burned Will's throat. He swallowed hard. His body trembled uncontrollably. All he could think was: *Run!* So he did, fleeing from the scene until he couldn't run any further and bent over to empty the contents of his stomach.

Will stood, his head spinning from all that had happened. He wondered if he could ever do his job again. He wiped his mouth with his sleeve and turned around to see Chief Erikson standing there with an expectant look in his eyes.

"Sorry, Chief," Will mumbled. "I'm going up there in a minute."

"Either pull it together or step aside," the chief commanded. "The people in this car need someone who's fully here."

Another wave of nausea swept over him, and he succumbed to the urge to vomit. When he finished, he looked at the chief, who had been silently watching. Tears streamed down Will's face.

"I think I need some help. I've been a jerk about Jon getting help, but at least he works," Will said.

He stood silently as Jon intently focused on the woman passenger before him. His hands worked diligently, pulling and pushing gauze with finesse as if it were second nature to him. But Will couldn't erase the image of Jon pulling Shelly out of a mangled car and placing her frail body onto the stretcher. A rush of shame flooded him as he moved away from the scene.

The chief placed a robust and comforting hand on Will's shoulder and guided him toward his Suburban. "You can recover from this. You may become the firefighter you once were if you get professional help," he said. Will knew what this meant. He had to get himself back on track before he had any hope for Anna and their future.

Will's throat tightened at the pain of what he'd done to Jon. He choked back a sob. "What about Jon?"

"Unfortunately, he probably won't ask for help until things get bad. If he continues to show up at work sober and can do his job, I can't make him get help. Part of this is my fault. I should have insisted you get help when you couldn't do the job."

Will knew abandoning Jon during the call was his rock bottom. If he didn't get help, there was no way he and Anna could move forward.

He watched the call from the Suburban with a mixture of emotions. He was ashamed of letting down the chief, the crew, and Jon. He was reminded of his failures and inadequacy. Will drove the chief to the firehouse when the scene was cleared. He showered and reported to the chief's office to receive paperwork that declared him unfit for duty and the necessary information to receive therapy. Despite the shame, he was also relieved that he'd finally be able to get treatment. After signing the documents, he searched for Jon, conflicted about his newfound freedom.

He found Jon in the bunkroom, sitting on the bed.

"Hey, I'm so sorry for what happened today on the call," Will said, "I'm taking some time off." He cleared his throat and murmured, "I'm not a good friend."

Jon said something when he started to turn away, but Will wasn't sure if it was directed at him. He cleared his throat and asked Jon to repeat himself.

"We're not friends, Will," Jon said, voice hoarse with emotion. "We're brothers. I'll stop to see you later."

Will looked at Jon, a wave of admiration and love washing over him. "We are indeed brothers. I love ya, Jon."

Jon shook his head and smirked. "Shut up before I throw an axe at you."

Will left the firehouse feeling encouraged that therapy could help him regain his passion for the job he'd loved since he was a child. He was determined to use his treatment plan as part of an ongoing journey to become a better version of himself.

CHAPTER 45

Cathy Watts barged into Anna's office, slamming a piece of paper on her desk. Her eyes sparked with fury. "You need to sign this," she seethed.

Anna picked up the paper and quickly read over it. "I'm not signing this," she declared. "I did call in. I spoke with the house supervisor at about 6 a.m."

Cathy slammed her hand onto the desk, causing Anna to flinch back. "Sign it, Anna," she hissed. "You understand I can ensure you never work in nursing again?" She took another menacing step closer until they were nearly face to face, forcing Anna to step back. "I know what you're doing," Cathy said through gritted teeth. "I know about you and my husband—what you did in the stairwell. Stay away from him, or I'll finish you."

Rage flooded every corner of Anna's mind, making her stand tall and strong. "Do whatever you want, I don't care. All I want is to do my job without any further interruption." Her voice was firm but carried a hint of danger.

Cathy spun on her heels and slammed the door shut as she left the office. The adrenaline seemed to drain immediately, causing Anna to flop into her chair. A chill ran down her spine as she realized this situation was beyond her control. There must be a way to address it since it couldn't be legal. She grabbed her purse, headed to the door, and ducked into an alternate stairway she discovered she could use to exit the hospital. However, when she reached the back entrance, all resolve disappeared with an unexpected horror. Dr. Watts was there kissing one of the OR nurses, and when his eyes met Anna's, terror surged through her body like an electric current. No matter how quickly she ran, Dr. Watts's voice seemed to follow her like an echo calling out her name. Each second felt like an eternity, filled with dizziness and nausea, until she reached the safety of her car.

The drive home was a blur. More than anything, she wanted to go back home to Missouri, away from all the drama with the Watts family, but at the same time, she didn't want to leave Will or his family. It took everything in her to not just keep driving and leave Cardinal Creek forever.

This couldn't go on any longer. She had to tell someone about Dr. Watts's harassment. Who else was he stalking and harassing? She'd seen him kissing an OR nurse. Was it consensual? She had quickly darted out of there and couldn't tell. But it didn't matter. Her interactions with Dr. Watts were harassment, and she couldn't take it anymore. Now, his wife was threatening to ruin her. The air felt suffocating, and she rolled down the window, allowing the cool wind to hit her face.

The stress of opening the equine center was like another weight on her shoulders. She needed funding and was also trying to build a program from the ground up at work. When she pulled up to her cabin, her body ached with exhaustion, and sleep tugged at her consciousness. She made it up the porch steps; her legs were like lead weights.

Anna closed the door, went to her room, and climbed into bed for a long-needed nap. She would worry about the consequences of walking out of her job later. She knew she needed to talk to someone about what was happening at the hospital, but she needed to figure out who.

∽

WHEN ANNA WOKE from her nap a few hours later, she felt refreshed and ready to tackle her mission. She had to speak with Liz, Kati, and Garrett about a fundraiser. She'd decided that she was going to quit her job. Even though her role at the hospital meant a lot, she couldn't see a way out of the situation. It would never get better while Dr. Watts and Cathy still worked there. Now, she just needed to stay focused on getting the equine center funds before deciding whether to stay in Texas or return to Missouri.

With a new purpose in mind, Anna headed toward the stable where Garrett stood leaning against the door, his thumb hooked into the pocket of his jeans. A warm smile spread across his face when he saw her. "Hey there, you here to help me?" he asked.

Anna gave him a friendly side hug before they began gathering the supplies for stall cleaning. "I am, and when we're done, I need to talk to you about something."

Garrett seemed hesitant but asked, "Is it about what we spoke about the other day?"

Setting her jaw and pulling away slightly, Anna answered, "No, it's about the equine center. Do you mind going to Liz's with me so I can talk to you all together?"

Anna began getting their supplies from the tack room to clean the stalls. Garrett observed her, his brow furrowed in curiosity as she passed by, and she raised her voice in irritation, "What?"

He rubbed the back of his neck. "Just making sure you're okay. I'm worried."

She placed the wheelbarrow on the ground and spun around to face Garrett. "Right now, opening the equine center on time is a huge problem. When can you come with me to Liz's house so I can talk to you all together?"

He lightly nudged her shoulder, an easy gesture of friendship. "Sure, let's take care of the horses so we can discuss it."

They did their chores in tandem, Anna tossing hay into each stall while Garrett filled up water buckets. As she fed Thunderbird carrots, Garrett leaned against the stall door, watching her. "No wonder he loves you?" he said with a smirk.

Anna smiled back. "The feeling is mutual."

Chuckling, he scratched behind Thunderbird's ear, "Hey boy, she gives you a lot of love." He lifted his head up and down, "You're a lucky boy." Again, Thunderbird lifted his head up and down.

Anna laughed. "Thunderbird has been my friend for a long time." He turned, nudging her arm. She scratched his muzzle and kissed his cheek.

Garrett grabbed the grooming tote as she fed Thunderbird another carrot. They headed out of the stall and closed the stable door. Garrett seemed hesitant. "Can you tell me a little more before we go to Liz's place?"

Anna explained that she needed help with a fundraiser to open the equine center. As they had suspected, Will required more funds to get work done and operate for several months. She mentioned that he had a notebook with ideas for a fundraiser and other helpful information that could have helped the grant process.

Her frustration was palpable as a heavy sigh escaped her lips. "Now I need to plan a fundraiser to open on time. I should have started planning it when I suspected there was no money."

Garrett closed his eyes, took a deep breath, and slowly exhaled. "I came here to heal from my injuries. I don't want to get involved."

Anna's hopeful request stuck in her throat as she saw the refusal on his face. "I thought you said . . ." her voice trailed off. She bit her lip to hold the tears at bay. "Will you still come with me to talk to Liz and Kati? Maybe we'll figure out if there's anything you can do to help without being involved." Anna held her breath, waiting for Garrett's answer.

Garrett rubbed his hands nervously against his thighs. Anna could see the tension in his body; his muscles were tense, and his jaw was clenched. She knew of his injuries, but he never talked about it. Her hand moved instinctively toward his shoulder, offering a gentle squeeze as a small gesture of support.

Anna started to leave the stable when Garrett touched her arm. "I told you I would help," he said, "I'm sorry . . . I've just been having some rough nights. I promised you my help and will give it. I have contacts who can help."

Anna gave him a side hug in appreciation. "If you need to talk," she said, "I'm here. Let me know if it's too much."

"Making a few phone calls isn't hard." He adjusted his hat. "Something that happened before the military has been haunting my dreams, so I haven't been sleeping."

"I appreciate you."

They walked in silence to her cabin. Anna was enjoying the sun beginning to set; the deep purple, pink, and orange danced away from the sun. Garrett waited on the porch while Anna grabbed her computer. When she stepped onto the porch, her stomach was tied in knots.

Garrett got up from the swing. "You ready?"

She raised an eyebrow. "Not really. I'm nervous." That was an understatement. A lot was riding on the opening of the equine center. She was curious to know if Will even understood the magnitude of help this could create for the community.

"You'll do just fine. Let's hit it." They walked in silence to Liz's cabin. Anna took a deep breath and knocked.

When the door opened, a smile spread across Liz's face. "Come on in. I'm in the kitchen." Anna followed her, noticing she was walking better every day.

"Where's Kati?" Anna inquired.

"She just texted me that she's on her way home." Her eyes narrowed as she looked at Anna. "Is there something wrong?"

Anna blinked rapidly. "Why do you ask?"

Liz motioned to Garrett. "You brought reinforcement."

Anna chuckled. "I need to talk to all of you when Kati arrives. It's about the equine center."

"Y'all want a drink? I have water, wine, soda."

"Water," Garrett and Anna said in unison.

As they sat chatting about the days getting warmer and longer, Kati entered the room. "Hey, what's going on?" Her lips quirked to one side. "What did Will do?"

Anna started to giggle. "Will didn't do anything. I need to talk to you about the equine center."

Kati dropped her bag onto the table with a thud. "Are you feeling better? The house supervisor said you were sick earlier this week."

Anna's stomach tightened as she replied, "I'm fine. I just took a mental health day."

Kati raised an eyebrow and stared into Anna's eyes. "Has Dr. Watts bothered you again?"

Anna's throat constricted from the shock of Kati's words. She couldn't speak, so she opened and closed her mouth a few times before finally squeaking, "I don't know what you are talking about."

Everyone was staring at her intently. A lump formed in her throat as she realized what she had to do: divert the conversation away from the topic that made her uncomfortable. She took a deep breath and exclaimed, "I need to talk to you about the equine center!"

Liz motioned for everyone to sit down. "We'll table the conversation about Dr. Watts . . . but it's not over yet." She raised an eyebrow. "Do you understand, Anna?"

Anna nodded, understanding that there would be more questions later, but now was not the time nor place for them.

She opened her laptop with a trembling hand, and everyone around the table leaned closer to listen. She spoke in a small, panicky voice as she clicked through spreadsheets and documents. They stayed silent as she explained that they needed money to get the equine center functioning. Her gaze landed on Garrett; in her mind, she thought Garrett was the key to helping her. She knew he was an officer in the military stationed in Texas, so he must know people who could help.

Garrett ran his fingers through his hair and leaned forward with hands on his forehead, lost in thought. The silence was heavy between them until Liz finally cleared her throat, breaking it with a single sound. "I have an idea. I need to make some phone calls. I'll be back in about thirty minutes," Garrett said.

"Garrett, thank you." He smiled and nodded at Liz and Kati as he walked out.

Before he exited, Liz yelled, "Just come back in, darlin'. No need to knock."

"Yes, ma'am," he chuckled as he closed the door.

When the door shut, Liz cleared her throat. "Anna, what can we do to help?" She held up her hands. "When did Will tell you all of this?" Her brows drew together in an angry frown.

"Not long ago." Her tone was apologetic. "I told Will I would figure it out, and the only way to do that is to have a fundraiser." She took a long, deep breath. "Will you help?"

Liz slapped the table, causing Anna to jump. "I knew he wasn't telling us something," she said with a strange note.

"Mom, he hasn't been himself since Shelly passed away," Kati said, looking at Anna. "But he's been happier since you arrived, and so have Caden and Eva."

Liz reached over and squeezed Anna's hand. "What can we do?"

"When we had breakfast, we talked about making some quilts to auction, but we would also need things for the silent auction." Anna smiled. "I was thinking of doing a dinner benefit to honor Shelly."

A smile spread across Liz's face. "You bet, darlin'." She clapped her hands. "That's just up our alley."

"I'll talk to the hospital to see if we can sell staff tickets," Kati said.

Liz was beaming. "I hope Will can see the love you have for him."

Anna swallowed hard as she looked at her schedule. "Could we do a breakfast meeting this Saturday?"

"I'll make the arrangements," Liz said.

Anna heard the door open, her pulse began to race, and she felt flush. She hoped it wasn't Will. She sighed in relief when she saw Garrett enter the kitchen.

Garrett sat in the chair next to Anna. "Okay, I need you to call and reserve the Saddle Up for one month from today." He handed her a piece of paper with the phone numbers of people to contact for donations of items and money. "These are buddies of mine who are going to help us."

Anna jumped up, hugging him. "I knew I could count on you."

Over the next half hour, Anna devised a plan, including a spreadsheet with the amount they needed to raise. "Do you think this amount is possible?"

Garrett winked at her. "We'll get the money, Anna, I promise you."

Liz chimed in, "Garrett's right. We can get this done."

As Anna concluded the planning session, Garrett rose to leave. He hugged Anna, mentioning needing her to travel with him for a few donor meetings in San Antonio. Anna offered to combine it with Jenny's visit in a few weeks. Liz was overcome with emotion and thanked Anna for pushing the project forward.

Anna choked back a sob. She had grown to love this family. It was going to be hard to say goodbye after the opening. She was going to miss Eva and Caden. Then she realized that the kids weren't there. "Where are Eva and Caden?"

"They're with Will at dinner. He's been acting strange since his last tour at the firehouse," Liz explained.

Anna wondered if she'd see him tonight. It was strange that he didn't text her and let her know he would be late. Anna reached for her back pocket and rolled her eyes. "I seem to have forgotten my phone in my cabin." She got up, but Kati stopped her.

"Will you please talk to me about what happened with Dr. Watts?"

Oh God, not this again. Fear etched her features as she rubbed her temples. "You didn't tell Will, did you? You know he gets jealous. He'll think I caused this." Her body started to tremble. She made her way toward the door, almost knocking the chair over. "I should go."

Kati touched Anna's shoulder. "I haven't told anyone. Momma is the only one who knows."

"And Garrett," Anna choked. "And JW." She was headed toward the door when she heard Liz's commanding voice, which immediately halted her. She slowly turned to face Liz.

"Come in here and sit."

As Anna headed to her chair, sweat began trickling down her back. She slowly sank into the chair.

After taking a few cleansing breaths, Liz began speaking. "We consider you part of the family." She reached for Anna's hand and squeezed. "You have worked tirelessly on this center, you stepped in when I got hurt, and you love Caden and Eva . . ." She choked back a sob. "What you have done for Will is almost a miracle. You haven't talked about your loss or asked for a shoulder to cry on. Anna, you have a good heart, and we love you for that, but you need to talk about your losses and tell someone what's happening with the doctor."

The air in the room became thick. Anna's heart shuttered, and there was a falling, spinning down feeling. She hung her head. "I can't tell anyone." She slowly raised her chin to Liz. "I'm returning to Missouri after the center is open, but promise me you won't tell Will. I'm going to tell him after the opening."

Liz's hand flew to her mouth. "You can't go. Let us help you."

The tears began to slide down Anna's cheeks like a waterfall. "I want to stay, but the situation is hopeless. Maybe it's fate that I return to my grandparents' farm in Missouri." She hugged Liz and Kati. "I need to go."

She walked back to her cabin, and her heart sank, knowing it was time to start pulling away from them, especially Will. The seed of fear in the bottom of her stomach was beginning to grow. *Could she trust telling them about Dr. Watts without destroying her career?*

CHAPTER 46

With urgency, Will left his house, walking long across the yard to Anna's cabin. The night before, he had spent time with Caden and Eva, reading them stories until they drifted off to sleep. By the time he finished, Anna's cabin was dark, so he'd had a restless night, anxious to talk to her this morning before she went to work. He was finally taking time off for therapy and had made an appointment to see a therapist. He had been coping with Shelly's death with alcohol and enabling Jon's drinking problem instead of being there for his children like he should have been. Shelly's death had affected him more deeply than he realized, and it was time to face that reality. He quickened his pace as he thought about failing to offer his children the emotional support they needed, finally reaching Anna's cabin. A wave of unease washed over Will when he tried to turn the doorknob and found it locked. She always left the door unlocked in the morning. He hesitated before knocking. When Anna opened the door, her eyes were cold as she walked to the kitchen.

Anna leaned against the counter with a cup of coffee, and his lips curved with tenderness as he approached her and gave her a gentle kiss on the cheek. "Hey, darlin', I wanted to see you before you left for work. I need to talk to you."

Anna let out an exasperated sigh. "I don't have time. I've got a ton of stuff I need to do before I go to work."

Will's gaze flickered across her face as he saw the intensity of her emotions. He was torn between providing comfort and giving her space to figure out what was wrong. Ultimately, his desire won; he swept her into his arms, and their lips locked passionately. His kiss spoke louder than any words could express. She shuddered against him before gently pushing away.

Will stepped back, his confusion growing as he watched her face. "What's wrong?" He took a hesitant step closer, desperately needing her to trust him enough to tell him what was going through her mind. His chest ached as she began packing her stuff for work without meeting his gaze. Her tone was cold and distant.

The tension between them was palpable, as if both were realizing the gravity of the situation that neither wanted to acknowledge. Anna let out a long breath as she packed her lunch, and Will froze, confused about what he should do. He ran his fingers through his hair, overwhelmed by the emotions that had stirred during the call that led to his leave from the fire department. He wanted to embrace her and let her know that it would all be all right soon and that he was finally getting the help he needed.

As if sensing him, she stopped packing and turned to face him. "I'm sorry, Cowboy," she said, "I have so much on my mind with organizing the fundraiser."

Will opened his arms, and she stepped into them.

She looked up at him with earnest eyes, her fingers lightly brushing away the words on his lips. "Cowboy, trust me, it's under control. I can do this," she said as she embraced him tightly, her lips pressing hungrily against his in a passionate kiss.

At that moment, Will got lost in the emotions that coursed through his veins, hoping she could feel the intensity of his love. He pulled away slightly, interlacing their fingers and pressing them against his chest.

He whispered, "Anna, I need to tell you something." His heart raced as he attempted to find the words that would convey his commitment to changing for everyone he loved, including her, but the lump in his throat grew.

She tried to pull away, but Will gently placed a hand behind her head and whispered, "Please, I need you to hear me out . . ."

He sucked in a sharp breath and started talking, his voice shaky as he relived the traumatic events of his last call. Anna nodded as he spoke, keeping her eyes on him. He recounted how he and Jon had responded to an ambulance call, but he panicked and left his partner behind. He allowed the terror to wash over him. Tears burned his eyes as they rolled down his face. He opened his eyes before whispering, "I told the chief—"

Anna's face had changed while he spoke, her expression shifting from concern to confusion to anger. She stepped away from him, her lips pursed into a thin line. "Why are you telling me this?" she demanded, interrupting him.

Her sudden outburst took Will aback, but he couldn't help the anger growing inside him. He was confused and hurt that she didn't understand what he was trying to tell her. "Why are you so angry?" he asked, trying to keep the emotion out of his voice.

She bit her bottom lip and stared at him for what felt like an eternity before taking a few steps back with a sigh. "I've been here for months trying to help and support you in your grief, but it's like my grief is all but forgotten," she said, her voice shaking. "I'm working so hard to open the equine center—losing sleep because of it—yet here you are bringing up another problem without thinking of me. It's too much! I need time to grieve. I miss my grandpa! Do you ever think about that? He died just before I moved here," She turned abruptly and stormed off toward her room, slamming the door so violently that Will jumped.

He heard a scraping sound followed by a heavy thud and then muffled, choking sobs from the other side of the closed door. He leaned his head against the door, helpless, as he whispered, "I'm sorry."

Will stood frozen, trying to process what had just happened. He wanted to apologize and explain himself but couldn't find the right words. She was so angry with him, rendering him powerless, and it was as if he'd been struck in the gut. If only he could say the right words, she might have understood why he acted so desperately, but his mouth remained uncooperative.

His hands shook as he walked out of the cabin, knowing he'd lost his chance to explain himself.

By the time he reached the stables, Will's shock had given way to a white-hot fury that pushed him onward as he viciously mucked out the stalls. When he arrived at the next stall, he snarled an icy hello at Garrett before throwing the shovel at the wall and ramming his fist into the wood. In the back of his mind, he knew Anna wasn't his target; it was his guilt for not listening to her when she mentioned the equine center or considering how she was doing whenever they spoke.

Garrett leaned against the stall with his thumbs hooked into his jeans pockets. "Feel better?"

"No," Will said. "Oh my God, she is just so . . ." He hit the wall again. Of course, he had blamed her—what else was new? He turned to Garrett and asked, "Has she talked to you?"

Garrett took a few steps closer. "About you or the equine center?"

Will's shot up an eyebrow. "What do you mean?"

Garrett offered no further explanation; instead, he said, "We need to saddle up and ride so we can talk about this properly."

Will shook his head as he tossed a shovelful of manure into the wheelbarrow, trying to understand what had happened since he and Anna had spent the night together. She seemed so far away, no matter how devoted he was to her. He wanted to show her his commitment, so he'd returned to the ambulance even though fear threatened to paralyze him. He was going to start therapy in a desperate attempt to become a better man . . . for her. But doubt lingered in his mind, whether he could change or if it would be enough for Anna.

When they finished mucking the stalls and feeding the horses, Will's head was spinning with a million questions. What had Anna said to Garrett? Had she decided to leave Cardinal Creek? Had he pushed her too far away?

Garrett and Will saddled their horses, Jake and General, and headed for a ride. They trotted at a slow pace across the field. An uncomfortable silence hung in the air, and it was unbearable.

"Has Anna said anything about me to you?" Will ground out.

Garrett bit his lip like he was holding something back. "Not really . . . just told me something about the equine center opening." He carefully avoided making eye contact with Will.

"So, you know about not having the money to open?" Will said, his voice beginning to strain with frustration.

"All she told me was that she was feeling homesick," Garrett said.

Will's fist clenched, desperately trying to keep his voice calm. "Did she say if she would move back to Missouri?" He swallowed hard, feeling the lump in his throat growing more significant as his words tumbled out. "I just don't know what I did."

"No, she just wants to get the equine center open."

"That's what she told me, too." Will rubbed the back of his neck. "I don't think she understands how much I care about her. I don't want her to leave. Now, she's pushing me away out of nowhere. I don't know what I did."

Garrett reassured Will. "Don't blame yourself. She's preoccupied with work and trying to keep her promise of making the equine center a reality."

As they continued to ride, a wave of guilt swept over Will, and he bowed his head. "But I made such a mess of things by lying to everyone . . ." He sighed as he scrubbed his hand across his face. "I don't know how to fix this." There was a long pause and another sigh before he said, "I'm not sure if this has anything to do with what's going on with Anna, but we went out to eat and had a weird encounter with the doctor who did Momma's surgery. Do you think something's going on between them?"

Garrett sat up straight in his saddle, his eyes narrowed. "What about the doctor?"

Will ran his fingers through his hair, racking his brain for an answer. "He came to our table, and there was this bizarre interaction between them. He grabbed Anna's hand and tried to hold it, but then his wife showed up and gave her this icy stare. You know, if looks could kill . . ." He sighed deeply. "Anna got quiet like she was trying to hide something from me. He invited himself to sit until his wife arrived."

"What did Anna say then?" Garrett inquired.

"She got angry but didn't say much else at all. When Dr. Watts left, she was completely silent." Will's eyebrows furrowed. "It feels like you aren't telling me everything."

Will tightened his reins and leaned back in his saddle, studying Garrett's face for clues. He had a sneaking suspicion Garrett knew something about Dr. Watts and Anna that he wasn't telling him. Will felt a pang of guilt as he realized that maybe Anna hadn't told him because she thought he wouldn't listen or understand.

"She hasn't told me anything, but I have suspicions," Garrett said, his voice heavy with concern. "You know she's always willing to help everyone else but won't ask for help."

"Wait, what are your suspicions? And how much did she tell you?"

"I'll talk to her and let you know, but I don't want to make assumptions. What can I do to help with the equine center?"

Will shook his head. "No, Garrett. How much did she tell you?" He wondered what else Anna hadn't told him. Did she frequently hide stuff from him because he was so emotionally unavailable?

Garrett chuckled. "Very little; she's tight-lipped about a lot. The center won't open on Shelly's birthday if we don't have a fundraiser. Have faith in Anna. She'll make sure the equine center will open. These things have a way of working themselves out."

"Thanks, Garrett. You know I love Anna, but my heart was torn between letting go of Shelly and committing to Anna. It felt like the right thing to do a few days ago, but now I'm unsure."

"Why do you think you need to leave Shelly behind to love Anna?" Garrett asked.

Will hesitated before replying. "No one said I had to, but it wasn't fair to Anna. I told her I'm committed to her."

Garrett shook his head. "You don't have to forget Shelly or erase her from your heart to love someone else. She'll always live in your memories and Caden and Eva, but that doesn't mean you can't open your heart to someone new."

Will's breath hitched in his throat. He'd been struggling to choose between Anna and Shelly, unsure if he could move on with Anna without losing his memories of Shelly. It seemed like an impossible situation, but he realized it wasn't. He tightened his grip on the reins, understanding that he could love Anna without giving up his memories of Shelly.

Garrett continued as he reined his horse back, "It's normal to feel grief and guilt for living without them, but don't stay stuck in that place out of fear of letting go of the past."

"I feel so much guilt and regret," Will said. "I rewind that night countless times, trying to make sense of it. I can still see her arm hanging outside the car at the scene . . ." His gaze caught a single yellow butterfly fluttering around a sunflower basking in the sunlight in the field he and Shelly had been riding in before the accident. Was this a sign? Was Shelly sending him a message? *Maybe it wasn't my fault.*

Garrett's voice brought Will out of his thoughts. "Have you talked to anyone about losing Shelly or what happened at the accident scene?"

Will shook his head. "Just Jon." He glanced at Garrett. "He stayed at the scene to help with recovering her body."

He could still see Jon entering the hospital, tears and dirt staining his face, walking toward him on the fateful night that Shelly died. His parents blamed him for not being able to save Shelly. He remembered how Jon held him close, saying he was sorry he couldn't save her and handing over her phone. He'd seen the text he had sent just before she got into the accident and the beginning of the text that never got sent. Tears threatened Will's eyes as he watched Jon at the funeral, explaining why his parents weren't there for Eva and Caden.

Garrett winced. "That explains why you always want to protect Jon when he drinks. Body recovery is something that is . . . uh, haunting."

Will tilted his head in agreement. "The nightmares have gotten better over the years, but Jon still doesn't sleep much and uses alcohol as a temporary escape when he does."

"I've seen soldiers go down that same path. He needs to talk to someone before it gets worse. It would do you some good, too," Garrett said.

Will gave Jake a nudge to move, and Garrett followed them. "That's what I wanted to tell Anna this morning. I'm taking time off from work to begin therapy. I need to start talking about my feelings instead of just relying on her and putting all my grief and anguish onto her shoulders alongside her grief and worries about the equine center, which also belongs to me. Yet, she never complained until today." He sighed with resignation.

Garrett looked at him with empathy. "Don't beat yourself up over what happened this morning," he said, "I know emotions are running high for both of you." He paused, then continued, "The chief gave you a name for a therapist, right? Let me know if there are any problems scheduling an appointment, and I can refer you to someone."

Will nodded gratefully. "Thank you for listening and being here for me and Anna."

As they rode back together in silence, Will mulled over Garrett's words. Clinging to pain wouldn't bring Shelly back, but creating something that honored her would. It was time for him to focus on becoming a better person, to be the father, son, brother, and someday the husband Anna deserved. He still hoped one day they would be married. In the meantime, he'd work on getting the center open to honor Shelly, not just for himself but also for their kids.

CHAPTER 47

Anna spent the entire week feeling guilty about how harshly she'd reacted to Will. It was like he was everywhere she went, even though she knew it wasn't possible. She wanted to reach out and apologize for her outburst, but the words seemed to get stuck in her throat. Throughout the week, she caught glimpses of him, appearing at home more often than usual, but she pushed away any curiosity, realizing it was none of her business.

Anna felt miserable at work, too, and had to continuously dodge Dr. Watts's accusing gaze on her every time he passed by. As if that wasn't enough, she had to endure constant verbal assaults from Cathy Watts. Each evening, she met with Garrett to help raise money from his contacts in San Antonio. All the upcoming meetings coincided with Jenny's arrival. Garrett was careful not to mention Will's name, and Anna didn't ask.

It was a conflicting time for her, wanting to stay in touch with Will while also preparing herself for their inevitable separation. He'd never want to be with her after she told him she wanted to leave. And maybe that was how it was meant to be. Perhaps they weren't supposed to have a future when there was just so much hurt between them.

During one of their planning meetings, Anna and Garrett secured the Saddle Up as the venue for the fundraiser. They scheduled a meeting with

Kati, Liz, and the Quiltin' Bees to procure donations and set up a silent auction. Liz said the Quiltin' Bees were excellent at obtaining donations for charity events. They also specialized in making quilts tailored for each organization, which could bring large sums of money. Kati said she would sell tickets after speaking to the owner of Saddle Up about some food donations. Between the quilts and the tickets, the event could work.

On Saturday, Garrett and Anna arrived early at the Cattle Trail Café to finalize the meeting agenda. With each passing moment, Anna was increasingly uncomfortable as she sensed Garrett's eyes watching her. She eventually mustered up the courage she needed.

"Garrett, what's going on?" she asked.

"Are you okay?"

Anna let out a long sigh. "I'm just tired. I don't want to talk about Will if that's where this is going." She averted her gaze back to the laptop.

Garrett paused before saying softly, "He notices you're avoiding the stables when he's there."

Surprised, Anna looked up to meet Garrett's gaze. "Really?" Anna debated whether she should ask Garrett why Will had been home more the last week but decided against it.

"Really." His voice was warm and comforting. "He loves you, Anna."

Part of her wanted to be with Will. She wanted to go to him and figure out all their problems and find a way through their grief. But the other part needed a break to work on the fundraiser and have peace. She just needed time.

Would Will ever know how much Anna loved him? Even if they could work through their grief, and even if she stayed, this whole thing with Dr. Watts could end her career. Cardinal Creek was small, with only one hospital. The neighboring towns were too far away, and she wasn't willing to spend over three hours daily on the road to work in San Antonio. She couldn't continue working in palliative care in Cardinal Creek if she quit. It would be better for everyone if she left.

She gave a halfhearted, "I know."

Garrett rose from his seat. "Our guests have arrived. Let's go greet them."

They held each other's gaze for a moment. "Thank you, Garrett."

Liz limped over to Garrett and hugged him. "Thank you for helping Anna with this, Garrett."

"No problem. How's your leg?"

"Getting much better. I have an appointment with Dr. Watts next week."

Anna tensed up hearing his name.

"That's good," Garrett said. "I guess you will be coming back to muck stalls."

She smirked. "Well, I don't know about *that*."

As Anna finished her plan, she felt two little arms wrap around her shoulders, pleasantly surprising her.

Caden hugged her tight and beamed, "Anna! I've missed you."

"I've missed you too." Anna prayed the next question wouldn't be about why she hadn't been to visit.

Eva walked up just in time.

"Hey, Eva, how are you?" Anna asked. Caden stared at her with his head tilted like he had something to say. She smiled; Will did the same thing when he wanted to speak but was trying to choose his words.

He hugged Anna. "Are you mad at Daddy?"

The chatter around the table stopped. Anna looked up. Everyone's eyes were peering at her. She knew this could come up since she avoided the cabin and ranch as much as she could this week. One night, she exited her SUV and saw Will sitting by the campfire ring. She felt his eyes on her as she entered the cabin and closed the door. All she wanted to do was go to him, but it would just delay the pain of her leaving once all this was done.

Anna cleared her throat. "Of course, I'm not mad at him. I've been busy working on this fundraiser."

"I knew it." Eva looked at Caden. "I told you she still likes Daddy. Who does all this work and not like someone, duh."

Kati came over, gathering them and giving Anna an apologetic glance. "Sorry," she mouthed.

The waitress hurried over to take their order and gave them all a few moments of privacy. Anna spread some paper across the table, each adorned with colorful sketches and diagrams. Peggy Sue, Sissy, and Liz had been quilting together since they were kids, blessed with an uncanny ability to create intricate patterns that earned them numerous awards at 4H shows.

Though it was rarely easy to decide who would get the honor of having their quilt sent to someone in need, the Quiltin' Bees knew that providing warmth to those less fortunate brought them all an immeasurable sense of satisfaction.

Both Peggy Sue and Sissy were business owners in Cardinal Creek who believed in giving back to the community. Sissy Hogan owned Cardinal Creek Quilting and opened her shop to plan any fundraising event that needed a place to work. Anna was thankful Sissy had offered her business, supplies, and skills to make this fundraiser a success. Anna's heart soared as the plans began coming together. Now, they just needed to set dates to work on the quilts for donations. She excitedly flipped through three bright quilt sketches intended to be the main auction item. When she saw the design featuring children's drawings, excitement bubbled inside when she stood up and said, "Why not have the kids at the therapy center draw their pictures to incorporate into the quilt?"

Sissy clapped her hands. "I love it. Let's plan to meet next week on Friday in the evening. I'll call the president of the local guild and get some of those ladies to come. We'll do a potluck."

Anna looked at Liz, Sissy, and Kati. "Ladies, does that work for you?"

Anna was thrilled to meet new people since she didn't know many in Cardinal Creek due to her busy schedule at the hospital and ranch. Then her heart sank. *You're leaving, remember? It's probably one of the first and last times you'll see any of them.*

She pasted a smile on her face. "Thank you so much to all of you."

Kati cleared her throat. "Anna, I'll take care of getting tickets printed and sold. I'll sell them at the hospital. I already have permission."

Sissy and Peggy Sue offered to sell them at their stores and talk to other shop owners. Anna couldn't help but have a glimmer of hope that they could make this happen for Will. The group worked together to bring Shelly's dream to life. Anna's heart soared with joy. She knew how difficult it would be to keep this plan a secret from Will, given the small-town grapevine in Cardinal Creek, but she didn't want to involve him yet. She hoped that he would see how much people cared about him when it all came together. Sissy said she would give the stink eye to those who feel it was their responsibility to broadcast the personal business of others to each person they saw.

When they brought her plate to the table, she felt herself head back into a place of hopelessness when it came to having to leave. As she pushed the food around her plate, she got a text.

> Unknown: Anna, this is Jon. I got your number from Kati. You can count on me for the fundraiser. Kati filled me in. I'll talk to the fire chief here about how they can help. Thanks, Anna. This whole thing means a lot.

Garrett leaned in. "Hey, are you okay? Someone bothering you?"

"No, it was Jon offering to get help from the fire department."

"Good. I think we have the entire town covered. I've made other calls, so all the meetings are set up in San Antonio."

Anna stood after the table was cleared. "Garrett is working with some people he served with to help us. We have meetings set up in San Antonio. And my friend Jenny from Missouri is coming to help, too."

"I'm super excited to meet your friend, Anna," Kati said. "I can smell a girls' night."

Anna forced a smile. "Sounds great. I could use some time off."

"Don't push yourself too hard. You look tired," Liz said, her voice filled with concern.

"This is important to Will and the kids. I'll have time to rest after it's done." Anna was having trouble sleeping because she never knew what would happen at work with Dr. Watts and because she missed Will something terrible. She loved the nights when he held her all night.

After everyone had left the restaurant, Liz said, "I'll see you at Sissy's place on Friday. Please don't be a stranger. I've grown quite fond of you."

Anna swallowed hard. "Yes, ma'am."

Liz hugged Anna tight. "We can't thank you enough for what you're doing."

Anna smiled. "I couldn't do it without all of you too."

Liz smiled. "darlin'. I'm here if you need to talk."

She choked back the tears. "Yes, ma'am."

"Stop by and see me sometime this week if you can."

Anna nodded, knowing she'd only stop by if it was about the fundraiser. The plan was to work on the fundraiser at Garrett's as much as possible. She feared that if she saw Will, she'd give in to her need to be with him.

When everyone had left, she couldn't believe how things were coming together. She wondered if Will was doing okay. She missed him and wished she could tell him everything with the equine center would be fine. Anna jumped when Garrett approached and bumped into a nearby chair.

His left eyebrow rose slightly. "Sorry, I didn't mean to startle you."

She smiled. "It's okay. Are you ready?" Anna packed up her stuff and started to get up. Garrett was staring at her with concern written all over his face. She rolled her eyes because she knew what was coming next.

"I'm ready, but before we go . . . Anna, what is going on at work?"

She grabbed her bag and stalked toward the door. Garrett took long strides to catch up as she walked out the door toward the parking lot. Her heart was pumping so hard she thought it would leap from her mouth.

"Anna, stop, please."

She spun around fire in her eyes. "Garrett, we need to get this done so I can leave, okay?"

"Anna, please let me help you. If not me, talk to someone about what's happening."

"How? I'll never win." Her voice was thick with emotion. She stared at him, biting her bottom lip, trying to hold back her tears. The exhaustion from everything was beginning to overwhelm her. Her shoulders fell. Everything except this fundraiser was spinning out of control.

"Can I give you a hug?" Garrett asked, and Anna nodded. He gathered her in his arms. "I'm sorry."

Anna sobbed into his chest. "God, I miss Will," she hiccupped. "I don't want to leave, but I have to, and I think you know why."

He remained quiet, holding her close. Then Anna pulled away. "I need to go. Thank you, Garrett. Please don't tell Will anything."

"I won't promise anything. I want to make it clear that I will not lie to Will for you or lie to you for him. Right now, I have assumptions about what's going on at the hospital because of what Kati said, so I won't say anything to Will if he asks. But if I find out something is happening and he asks me about it, I won't lie. I'll tell you if you ask me about him, and I know something." Garrett ran his fingers through his hair. "I won't play the middleman for you two."

She dried her eyes. "Fair enough." Anna knew putting Garrett in the middle of their problems wasn't fair. "See ya after work tomorrow so we can finalize a few things?"

He nodded. "I'm here if you want to talk."

Anna watched him walk to his truck. If he only knew how much she wanted to tell him everything.

Anna's thoughts were filled with a sense of dread as she made her way back to the ranch. She knew she didn't want to leave Cardinal Creek after the equine center opened, but her work environment was hostile and unsafe. Dr. Watts's advances were getting even more aggressive. It was hard to avoid him at the hospital. She wanted simple things, but the situation with the Wattses made it difficult. She'd even looked up the HR representative last night, intending to tell someone. Still, she was quickly deflated when she remembered that the HR representative, Melanie Cartwright, was friends with Cathy Watts. She'd seen them together eating lunch and laughing on more than one occasion. The situation seemed hopeless.

When she pulled up the cabin, she saw Will sitting on his porch with Jon. He watched as she drove by. He waved with a wistful smile on his face. She waved back. After she put her bag inside, she went to sit outside on the porch. Not long after the door shut, she saw him walk toward the firepit with Jon, carrying a beer. His eyes never left her as he walked across the yard, taking a long sip of his beer. She wanted to sneak off in the middle of the night but had told them she'd help with the equine center. The blood in her veins began to boil. Was he taunting her right now? She abruptly stood, stalked inside, and slammed the door.

CHAPTER 48

As the days ticked by, Anna's nerves began to fray. She hoped they would have more time to prepare everything for the fundraiser. Each night after work, she met up with Garrett. They discussed plans for San Antonio and worked out ways to pull off the fundraiser without a hitch. This evening, they took a break from their work and planned to meet at Saddle Up for food before she headed off to Cardinal Creek Quilting to work on the quilt and silent auction items.

They quietly ate dinner, and she stared at Garrett. Something was going on, but she couldn't quite put her finger on it.

Finally, Garrett said, "Say what you need to say, Anna."

She narrowed her eyes. "Why are we meeting? We've talked about San Antonio several times."

He set the menu down and leaned on the table. "I just wanted to make sure you were okay."

She smiled. "I'm fine. I'm excited about Jenny's visit in a couple of weeks. I'm hoping Kati or Liz will let her borrow one of their horses so we can ride."

"She can borrow mine," Garrett said.

"General is so big, but Jenny is super tall, so maybe that would work."

Anna began to relax as their conversation became light and general. She didn't want to talk about Will or Dr. Watts.

"I haven't seen you much around the stable this week. I miss mucking the stalls with you."

Anna laughed. "I don't miss mucking the stalls. I've been leaving early to prepare stuff for my resignation." She closed her eyes, unsure if she'd told him she was leaving. She'd finally decided to go, but there was still a lingering doubt. Before she could recover from the blunder, the waitress came for their order. Anna ordered a glass of wine. Garrett raised an eyebrow.

She shook her head. "I'm not going to get drunk."

"Call me when you're done at Sissy's place. I'll drive you home."

Anna's neck muscles began to tighten. She wanted to tell him no but handed him her keys anyway. Just as they landed in Garrett's hand, a glass of wine was placed before her. Anna looked up, and there was the ginger cowboy who'd saved her.

"Well, hello Red, how are you?" JW said.

"Hey, JW. This is my friend Garrett. He's helping me plan a fundraiser."

JW reached out to shake Garrett's hand. "Hey, nice to see you again. I met him the other day when he came for a drink."

"You came in for a drink?" Anna asked with an eyebrow raised.

Garrett tapped his fingers on the table. He looked at JW, then at Anna, and back at JW. The three of them looked at each other, waiting for someone to say something. Anything.

A smile spread across JW's face. "Hey, Red. You want a tequila shot?"

Garrett shot him a look.

It suddenly dawned on Anna why Garrett had come there. Anger coursed through her veins. Garrett had come here to speak with JW about what had happened the night she came with Kati. But how did he know? Then she realized that Kati must have told him, and another round of anger coursed through her. She reached over, grabbed her keys, and tried to leave the booth.

JW stepped in front of her. "Sit." His voice was a commanding baritone.

He turned to Garrett. "Sorry, I thought she knew you came in." He took the glass of wine from Anna. "I'm taking this since you took the keys back." He leaned in close. "Don't let that damn temper get the best of you when people are trying to help." He turned on his heels and walked away.

She turned to find Garrett's eyes were gentle and understanding. "What do you know?"

"Kati told me what happened that night. Look, I'm worried about you. I know things can get out of hand with someone like Dr. Watts." His Adam's apple bobbed up and down. He let out a long sigh. "It feels like . . ." He stopped mid-sentence. "I'm sorry, I need to go. I'll explain later. Are you good?"

Anna watched, speechless as Garrett placed the fifty-dollar bill on the table and marched out of the bar. Confused, she shook her head and motioned for the waitress, handing her the money for the ordered appetizers. As soon as she sat down on a stool, JW's gaze locked with hers. His face was intense as he strode toward her.

He placed his hands on the bar and leaned forward. "I know that no one else is going to say this to you, but you need to do something about that fool doctor before you get hurt. Kati and Garrett care about you." Anna glared at him, and a smile spread across his face. "Hey, doll, your fiery, angry eyes don't scare me. I rode bulls for a living."

"You don't even know me, so it's none of your business. I met you once," she said with venom in her tone. "Why do you even care? I'm not your girlfriend." With that, she grabbed her bag and started to walk away.

He grabbed her hand and burst out laughing. "Sister, if you were my girlfriend, I would have broken that guy's legs."

A flush of anger rose inside Anna as she snatched her hand away. "I wish you would have," she said tightly, fighting back tears already pooling in her eyes. "You have no idea how much I despise him." She turned quickly and rushed through the door, gulping in huge breaths of humid summer air as tears streamed down her face. Lately, Anna only had two emotions: fury and overwhelming sadness. As she stubbornly marched toward the quilt shop to focus on happier things, she jumped in surprise to see Will standing on the sidewalk, worry etched into his features.

"Hey, Ginger. What are you doing here?" He handed her his handkerchief. "Are you okay?"

She wiped her eyes. "Do I look okay? Why are you here?"

"I was in town and was heading back to my truck."

"Oh, I need to go." Anna took off toward Cardinal Creek Quilting. Her legs were moving so fast she was almost running.

"Anna, please stop. darlin' please," Will pleaded.

Anna came to a halt and gradually pivoted on her heel. He was standing in front of her, his chest heaving. All she wanted to do was wrap her arms around him and let him hold her. She desperately wanted to confide in him about the chaos at work, but her apprehensions and uncertainties held her back.

"I know I always say this, but I'm genuinely sorry for dumping all my baggage on you the other day. I love you so much, Anna. If you need time to sort through things. I'll be here when you're ready." He gently kissed her lips before wrapping his arms around her and murmuring into her ear, "I love you, baby."

Tears pooled in Anna's eyes when he let her go. "I love you too . . . I do," her voice cracked. All she wanted to do was tell him to come to her cabin later so he could hold her all night. She forced a smile and touched his unshaven cheek. "I like the look."

He smiled and winked. "Thanks."

It was the wink that did it for Anna. She grabbed the front of his shirt and pulled him in. When their lips met, it was like everything had melted away: Dr. Watts, resigning from her job, leaving all the wonderful people she met in Cardinal Creek and the love of her life . . . Will. They were both breathless from the kiss. She smoothed over his protective arms.

"I have to meet the girls. We're doing a sip and sew tonight."

"You what?" He let out a hearty laugh, the first in a while.

She playfully smacked his arm and rolled her eyes. "I'm meeting a multi-generational group of women to sew."

"Oh, you're meeting with Momma and the Hens?"

Anna threw her head back and laughed. It felt so good to laugh. She nodded. "Yeah."

He leaned in and whispered, "If wine is involved, I'll drive you home and tuck you in."

She winked at him before she left. For a moment, everything felt right. Her handsome cowboy drove her crazy. His face had several days of facial hair, giving him a rugged look that she found irresistible. Anna gave him one last wave before she entered Cardinal Creek Quilting.

The quilt shop had an aura that transported her back to Nana's house. In one corner was a vintage Singer treadle machine, like the one in her nana's sewing room. There were bolts and bolts of vintage fabrics. It brought Anna back to when they would attend church picnics with all the gingham and flower prints. She thought of the older church ladies wearing flower dresses and black patent leather handbags. Several quilts that looked to be very old were hanging.

It was time to put on a happy face and get to work. Sissy said all the ladies would work on the children's quilt. She had assignments for everyone.

Liz was sitting at one of the tables. "This reminds me of my grandma," Anna said.

"Most of these quilts are from Sissy's momma and grandma," Liz said as she hugged Anna. "How are you, darlin'? You haven't been around much this week."

Anna choked back the lump in her throat. All the vintage stuff was too much. She had no idea this place would make her miss her nana so much. "I'm sorry. I was busy with Garrett planning everything. We, uh, we have a lot of donations coming from San Antonio, so it's been a lot to um . . ." She shook her head. "A lot to coordinate."

Liz studied her face and took her by the hand. "Come on, darlin'. Let's chat for a minute." She led Anna to a small area decorated with Dallas Cowboys regalia, rodeo photos, and cowboys. A big screen TV was hanging on the wall next to a sign. Anna smiled as she and Liz sat down on the couch. "Husbands' Waiting Room," she read aloud and laughed.

Liz nodded. "I know. It's so Sissy." She leaned in and whispered, "It helps increase sales."

"That's funny."

Anna sat for a long moment, not sure what Liz had to say to her. She had so much she wanted to tell her but was afraid. She likely knew more than she let on. This was more about Will. After all, he was her son.

"I'm going to start by saying that I'm not talking to you because Will is my son. As much as I love him . . . right now, I could throttle him for lying to all of us. I've never met anyone like you. You keep moving forward and helping us no matter what he does." Liz paused, then said, "I have an idea that someone is hurting you at work."

"What?" Anna whispered, stiffening.

"You heard me."

She tried to leave, but Liz looked at her sternly and said, "Sit, Anna."

Anna quickly sat. Liz Deluca wasn't a woman to be disobeyed.

"As I said, you don't have to tell Will, Garrett, or me, but you need to talk to Kati or the hospital."

Anna clenched her jaw to keep her mouth shut. She sat with her fists clenched.

"Sweetie, we want to help you, just like you're helping us. You are not alone. We all love you."

Those words broke the dam within Anna, and her body was flooded with sobs. She sobbed for the loss of her grandparents, for all the loneliness she'd been feeling, for Tony and Emma's betrayal, for the fact that she loved Will so much, and for living in fear of Dr. Watts and his wife. Liz wrapped her arm around her and held her until Anna's sobs reduced to small hiccups, and she finally fell silent.

When the sobs ended, Anna was exhausted. She murmured into Liz's chest, "I miss my grandpa so much. I miss us sitting on the swing drinking lemonade. I miss sewing with my grandma. I don't remember my parents anymore. I want to go home . . . I need something familiar. Everything seems so surreal right now."

Anna felt safe in Liz's arms so she could tell her what she felt. Anna stayed a few minutes more. It had been so long since her grandma had hugged her like that. She barely remembered her mom holding her. That was becoming a distant memory. How many more people was Anna going to lose in her life?

As Anna sat up, Liz gently placed her hand on Anna's knee. "Baby, you're not alone. I know I'm not your momma or your grandma. I could never replace them, but I'm here for you. I'm quite fond of you, not because of my son but because of who you are. Anna, you have something special, and I'm so glad you are in our lives."

At that moment, Anna again doubted her decision to leave Cardinal Creek. Liz hugged her tightly and whispered, "I love you, sweetie."

Anna let out a ragged breath and said, "I love you too."

Liz stood and chirped, "Let's get these ladies moving. We have a lot of stuff to do."

Anna excused herself to the bathroom to wash her face. When she emerged from the restroom, Liz, Peggy, Sue, and Sissy had a group of forty women broken into groups with assigned tasks. There were ten groups of five working on different projects. Anna was proud to be placed in Liz's group and oversaw the children's quilt. Sissy had designed a quilt made up of squares with pictures drawn by kids from Caden's therapy center. Anna smiled as she watched the women work on their projects, laughing and talking about everything from music to men. She couldn't help but smile as she overheard a group of older women discussing the toned butts of rodeo cowboys.

They spent the rest of the evening cutting fabric while others started to sew. Five quilt tops and about half of the children's quilt were completed when the evening ended. Kati had taken Caden to therapy a few times and gathered drawings from the children that would fit in the squares. At least thirty squares were done. The ladies would meet in a few days during the day to work. Sissy assured Anna they would get a lot done during the day. Anna was thrilled to hear that the next meeting would be in a couple of weeks. Jenny would be in town by then. Anna looked forward to merging her Texas and Missouri lives and hoped it could keep her here.

Kati came over and hugged her. "Garrett texted me and told me that you know he talked to JW. I hope you aren't mad at me."

Anna pasted a smile on her face. "I'm not mad. Thanks for your concern." She was thankful for Kati, Garrett, and JW's concern for her. She was just afraid that if she pursued anything, it would ruin her career. She didn't want to go through any legal proceedings. From what she had read, it was her word against his. She hadn't kept records of when he'd approached her, nor did she have any recordings. All she had were witnesses on the night at the bar, but even that case was flimsy. Not to mention, she had other enemies at the hospital who wanted to take her down. She loved nursing—it was part of who she was—but she also had no way to support herself if she quit her job.

"Girl, you're like a sister to me." She took a deep breath. "Have you talked to Will?"

Anna nodded. "I saw him on my way here. We're okay."

They were okay because Anna wanted to be with him. Fear of Dr. Watts was what was holding her back. She feared being dragged through the mud and losing everything she'd worked for. She hugged Kati. "Thank you for being a good friend."

Kati laughed. "No, thank you. Good night, Anna."

Anna hurried to the parking lot and got into her SUV, excited to return to the ranch to see Will. Pulling up to his house, she saw Jon's truck parked there. Her headlights brought Will and Jon into sight on the porch. Anna sat, trying to decide whether she should get out or leave. She put her foot on the brake and shifted into reverse when Will came to her window and opened the door.

She looked at him, breathless. "Hi, Cowboy. Are you busy?"

He shut the door and ran to open the passenger side. Anna's body ached with longing for Will. "What about Jon?"

"Hold on, darlin'." He turned and shouted, "Dude, I'm going with Ginger. See ya later."

Jon laughed. "See ya tomorrow."

Will got into the car and pulled her into a passionate kiss, leaving her breathless. "I would bring you inside, he lamented, rolling his eyes. "But Jon's here."

She smiled. "Oh, I get that." At that moment, every cell in Anna's body was on fire to be with Will.

When she parked in front of her cabin, Will approached the SUV's driver's side. He scooped her into his arms and headed toward the door. "darlin', I'm going to make love to you all night. I promise you I'm working on becoming a better person how you feel matters to me. Please believe that."

"Cowboy, I'm sorry for yelling at you."

"Oh, baby, I deserved it."

She ran her hand down the stubble on his face. It was a look Anna liked on him. "God, I love the beard you're working on."

"You want me to keep it?"

She nodded.

He smiled. "Now kiss me."

He opened the front door, walked in, and kicked it shut. The passion and love filled Anna with hope that she could conquer her fear of Dr. Watts and his wife.

CHAPTER 49

Anna paused at the arena entrance, taking in the scene before her. Will and Caden stood there with the roping dummy between them. She watched as Will patiently demonstrated how to set up his target and loop the lariat, but as Caden missed repeatedly, frustration began to show on his face. Will kneeled, speaking quietly to him with an encouraging hand on his shoulder. A small smile stole Caden's lips as he nodded and slowly tried again. As time passed and Caden missed his target again, she could see his frustration growing, but Will refused to give up. He kneeled again and spoke to him in a calming tone until he nodded and smiled.

Caden wrapped his arms around Will in a tight hug. When the rope finally snagged its target, they both jumped and cheered, fists pumping. Anna smiled as she saw the transformation in their relationship—gone was the confusion that used to fill the space between them whenever they were together.

Will caught sight of her watching and tipped his hat at her. He then turned back to Caden, leaned down to whisper something in his ear, and they held up both hands in the shape of a heart toward her. Emotion welled inside her as she returned the gesture with her hands now over her heart. Anna had a glimmer of hope things could work out and continue to bloom.

A FEW DAYS LATER, Kati entered her office where Anna was at her desk, her gaze fixed on her computer screen. Anna greeted Kati with a warm smile as she became aware of her presence.

"Hey, are you up for some coffee before heading home?" Kati asked.

"Yes, I would love it. Let me grab my purse."

They exited the office, and Anna closed and locked the door. As they walked to their cars, she was quiet. Kati glanced at her and said, "Anna, I need to talk to you, but we need to get away from the hospital."

Anna stopped and looked at her. "What do we need to talk about?" Her mouth suddenly became dry. She knew it would be a conversation about Dr. Watts, but she needed more time to think.

"I talked to Will. He said you all spent some time together the other night, and y'all have been talking, so I thought we should come up with a plan for . . ." She gestured vaguely around them.

Anna's eyes flashed open wide. "Oh God, what does Will know? Did you tell him anything?" She was hit with a wave of nausea.

"No, I haven't told him anything."

Anna rolled her head stiffly to work out the kinks in her shoulders and forced a smile. As much as she didn't want to think about Dr. Watts, she wanted to see everything work out at the hospital. "We need to find something that starts with *death by chocolate* and talk."

Kati nodded in agreement. "If I know Cowgirl Sweets and Treats, they have it." She looped her arm inside Anna's as they walked to their cars.

"Let's find a solution to this. I'll meet ya there." They climbed into their cars and took off. As Anna drove, she was hopeful she and Kati could devise a plan to stop Dr. Watts.

When they entered Cowboy Sweets and Treats, Anna's senses were pleased by the aroma of baked goods and coffee. Her mouth watered as they headed to the counter.

Anna eyed a piece of chocolate cake with chocolate icing. "This will fix everything," she said, pointing to the cake.

They each ordered a chocolate cake and a vanilla latte made with almond milk. As they settled in their seats to enjoy their cake, Kati had a smile on her face.

Anna raised an eyebrow. "Why are you smiling?"

"Well, I heard you and Will made up."

"Oh, you did. Who told you that?"

She shrugged. "Maybe he wasn't a reliable source."

"Who?"

Kati cleared her throat. "Jon."

Anna laughed. "He was there when Will jumped into my SUV. I think he had a view of us making out."

Kati nodded. "He did."

Anna knew the anniversary of Shelly's death was not too long ago. It was the day before Will told her he froze at work. "I noticed he's been spending a lot of time at Will's, but I wasn't sure if it was for Will."

Kati kept quiet for a few minutes. "Jon has had it tough since Shelly died." She rubbed the back of her neck. "He was one of the guys who recovered her body." Kati's voice cracked. She swallowed hard. "I'm not sure if Will ever told you, but Shelly was Jon's sister."

Anna's eyes flew open wide. "No, he never told me. My God."

"He started drinking afterward." Kati's eyes welled with tears. "As you know, he cheated on me."

Anna curled her fingers around Kati's hand. "I'm so sorry. It explains a lot."

She sniffled, wiping her eyes. "That's why Will is so protective of him." Her voice broke. "He didn't have to stay but felt he needed to."

"Wow, I don't know what to say." Anna couldn't imagine how Jon could recover his sister's body like that. It explained why Will had spent so much time taking care of him. A new respect formed for them both. But was it hard for Jon to see her and Will together, to see Will moving on?

Kati continued, "Jon's parents haven't seen Eva and Caden since Shelly died. They also blame Will because they know he texted her, and she was responding to the text when she got into the accident."

There was so much going through Anna's mind right now. It wasn't just grief Will was dealing with, but also guilt. She hoped they both got therapy for their pain. Anger coursed through her veins at Jon's parents for abandoning him, Eva, and Caden when they needed them. She was thankful they had Liz, Jon, Kati, and Will. As much as Will tried, he wasn't always available for Caden and Eva until recently. She wondered what had caused the sudden changes.

"When people die, it seems like they need to find someone or something to blame," Anna said. "The doctor, nurse, first responder, family members, themselves. There's no way to explain why people die other than they do."

"I know, right?" Kati sighed. "In the meantime, Jon lost his sister and his parents. We're the only family he has left. I love him but won't be with him until he gets help."

"I totally get that. It's a horrible situation. I hope he gets help for both of you."

Kati's eyes narrowed, and Anna felt a hand run across her back. She looked over her shoulder, thinking it was Will, but she was shocked to see Dr. Watts standing there. His hand rested on the middle of her back. Anna quickly jerked her body out of the way, scooting her chair over a few inches toward Kati. The feeling of his disgusting hand still lingered.

"Hello, Ms. Deluca and Ms. Samuels. How's your mom?"

Kati stared at Anna wide-eyed, like she was trying to communicate with her, but Anna went numb. She prayed that Kati would do or say something. She wanted to get up and run screaming out of there, but Kati put her hand on her knee under the table, and Anna relaxed a little.

"Uh, she's fine, Dr. Watts."

"Well, that's good. It's almost time for her to graduate from PT."

"Yes, she's getting around really well."

He looked at Anna, who was staring at her coffee, and said with a charming tone, "It was lovely seeing you, Ms. Samuels."

No words could escape her lips. Anna watched as he exited.

She looked back at Kati. "I—I need to go." She grabbed her purse and ran out the door.

"Anna, wait!" Kati called, but Anna kept going.

When she got to her SUV, Dr. Watts was leaning against it. "It looks like we keep bumping into each other. Wonder why that is."

Anna cleared her throat. "Get out of my way."

"I felt your body get warm when I touched you, and now you rushed out to see me."

Blood rose into her ears from anger. *How dare he!* "You're delusional. I want to get as far away from you as possible." Anna's body trembled so much that she couldn't get her key fob out of her purse.

He stepped forward, tucking a piece of hair behind her ear, and she slapped his hand away. "I don't understand why you won't go out with me. After all, I'm a doctor."

"You make me sick," she seethed.

She tried stepping around him, but he grabbed her shoulder, swinging her to face him. He pushed her into the car and slammed his face against hers, kissing her on the lips. Their teeth clattered together. She shoved him away and screamed at the top of her lungs. Footsteps pounded the pavement as Kati was shouting and running toward them.

Dr. Watts hissed in her ear, "This isn't finished." The chocolate cake she had just eaten reached the top of her throat.

When Kati showed up, Dr. Watts smiled. "Ah, Ms. Deluca. Nice to see you."

Kati's eyes narrowed to fiery slits. "What are you doing here?"

"I was just helping Ms. Samuels. She seems to have dropped her bag, and I picked it up for her." His jaw was set tight. "It was nice seeing you both." Then he hurried away.

Anna's hands trembled, and Kati wrapped her arms around her shoulders. "It's okay, Anna. You're safe." She took the key fob from her and pressed the button to unlock the door. "Anna, look at me." Anna slowly looked at her, frozen, unable to move. "Anna, you're safe."

She opened her mouth to speak but had no words. Kati opened the door. "Sit, okay."

Anna heard her commands and did as she was told. Her mind was blank. The only thing she could do right now was go . . . run . . . run. "I gotta go . . . I need to go, Kati."

Kati hugged her and whispered, "You are safe." The more she whispered that she was safe, the more Anna relaxed. Tears burned her eyes. All the hope she had before Dr. Watts showed up had died.

"There's no hope. As much as I love Will and your family . . . I need to leave. When I'm done with the fundraiser, I have to go."

"No, Anna. Please give me some time. I'm begging you," she spoke with quiet but desperate firmness.

She wished she could believe nurses could win against a doctor. Cathy Watts knew what her husband was up to. It seemed like a sick game to them, but it wasn't a game to Anna. It wasn't just her career; it was her life. When she thought the situation couldn't get much worse, it blew up in her face. Anna should go to the police and file a report. Who knew when he'd show up at her house? He could easily get her address. Fear paralyzed her at the thought.

"I can't, I'm sorry. I need to go." Anna closed the door and pulled away. She looked in the rearview mirror. Kati was watching as she drove away.

Her head was spinning. The memory of Dr. Watts's breath on her neck made her skin crawl. When Anna pulled up to her cabin, Will stood by the stable. A smile spread across his face as she parked. When he started for her SUV, her hands began to tremble again. She couldn't face him right now. What was she going to tell him when he asked what was wrong?

Before she got out, she took a deep, cleansing breath, opened the door, and slowly stepped out of the SUV. Will stood in front of her, his smile fading. He tilted his head and looked at her as if he wanted to say something.

The silence put Anna in a state of panic. Sweat beaded across her lip, and then the wave of nausea hit her. She placed her hand over her mouth, sprinted to her cabin, and slammed the door. The chocolate cake and coffee hit the toilet when she reached the bathroom. After she finished, she put a cold washcloth on her face. When she heard the door shut, she came out of the bathroom.

"What's wrong, darlin'?"

"I don't know . . . I don't feel well. It could be contagious. I want to shower and go to bed, if you don't mind. It's probably best I don't hug you if it's contagious. Love you." She went into the bathroom and shut the door.

"Love you too, darlin'."

She knew what she had to do when she heard the door close. She needed to leave. She'd quit her job and return to Missouri. Her phone buzzed—a text from Kati: "You okay? I'm coming over. We need to talk."

Anna's hand hovered over the numbers. She dialed nine, then one, then . . .

She flipped to Kati's text. "I'm fine. Don't come over. I'll talk to you tomorrow. I promise."

She threw her phone onto the soft bathroom rug and vomited into the toilet again. She flushed and sat on the cold tile, trying to catch her breath. She finally had the one man she loved, but she couldn't stay in Cardinal Creek any longer.

CHAPTER 50

The next day, Anna sat in her office contemplating her conversation with Kati, the incident with Dr. Watts, and having to leave a man she loved with all her heart. Her door was locked, and she had even moved the chair in front of it as extra protection. This was what she'd resorted to, cowering in her office like a scared little girl. But she couldn't hide forever. She needed to make a move. Tonight was the night she would tell Will.

Anna needed to use the bathroom, so she grabbed the letter opener and shoved it into her purse as added protection. She needed a weapon, something she could use to defend herself. Dr. Watts wasn't ever going to touch her again. Anna moved the chair out of the way and unlocked the door. She cracked it open and peered out into the hallway. When she thought the coast was clear, she stepped out of her office and was surprised to see Liz and Will standing in the hall.

Oh my God, did Kati tell them what happened? she thought. She'd ignored all thirteen of Kati's text messages. She walked toward them with a painted smile on her face. "Hi, Liz."

Liz smiled. "Hi, honey."

Her gaze went to Will. "Hey, Cowboy," her voice low.

The warmth of his smile echoed in his voice. "Hey, darlin'." He stepped toward her, wrapping his arms around her. "Are you feeling better? I'm surprised to see you here."

She was relieved. He made no signs that he knew what had happened yesterday. "Yes, I'm feeling much better."

"Can I see you tonight?"

"Yes, I need to talk to you," her voice was just above a whisper. "What are y'all doing here?" she asked.

"Momma has an appointment with Dr. Watts." Anna saw Dr. Watts leaning against the wall across the large waiting room. His eyes collided with hers.

Anna stiffened. "Oh, I should get going. You can stop by when I get home." She turned and quickly headed down the hall to the bathroom.

"Anna?" Will called. She turned, looking back. "When Momma's done, I'll stop by your office after I drop her with the Quiltin' Hens."

Liz slapped his shoulder. "William, stop calling us hens!"

Anna couldn't help but chuckle. "That sounds good. See you then."

I need to write my resignation. No, I should talk to Will first. This thing is getting scary.

Anna went back to work at her desk. When there was a knock, Anna stiffened. Then she got up, pushed the chair aside, and unlocked the door. It was Kati, and her face was strained.

"Do you want to tell me why you've been ignoring me? We need to talk about what happened yesterday."

"I . . . yes, come in," Anna squeaked.

"I can't. I have a budget meeting in two minutes. But we'll talk about this when I'm done." Kati's eyes softened. "Anna, this can't go on any longer. We'll come up with a plan. We'll go to HR. I'll be your witness—"

"Okay," Anna said too abruptly. "Yes . . . you're right. I'll be here. Just stop by when you're done."

Kati hugged her and said, "I know you're scared, but we will get through this. You're not alone."

Just as Kati left, Anna's phone rang. She quickly shut the door and picked up her phone on her desk. The door opened again, and Anna turned.

It was Dr. Watts. He shut the door behind him.

He advanced toward her in a predatory manner. "Yes, your friend is right. We should talk about what happened yesterday."

Anna scanned the room for something to defend herself with, but there was nothing. The letter opener was in her purse, sitting on the chair across her desk.

"I need you to leave," she said, and she tried walking around him to go for the door, but he roughly grabbed her arm and pushed her toward the desk. She slammed her tailbone on the edge, sending a bolt of pain up her spine. He leaned in, pressing his weight against her, and kissed her neck.

"Stop, please," she whimpered, pushing back against him, but he was too strong.

"We both know this is what you want." He pulled at her shirt, ripping off the top button, but she was fighting him, so he grabbed the back of her head, forced his mouth on hers, and thrust his tongue into her mouth.

No, no, please, she thought as she tried to fight him off.

The door burst open. Cathy Watts barged in with fire in her eyes. "I knew it. I saw you together yesterday! Seth, I'm tired of this!" She marched over and slapped Anna across the face. The sting of the slap burned her cheek. Then, she squared up with Dr. Watts. "I am so tired of you messing with every hussy who shows you their—"

Dr. Watts slapped his wife across her face. Anna let out a loud gasp. Dr. Watts turned his attention back to Anna with fire in his eye.

"Anna, you are finished!" Cathy screamed. "When I get done with you, they won't allow you to nurse animals." She stormed toward Anna, stopping when she was just inches from her face. "I hope he was worth it."

Anna couldn't steady her erratic pulse. "I have never done anything but ask him to leave me alone."

Dr. Watts ran a finger down Anna's cheek, causing her to shiver. "Come on, baby, tell her the truth. I already told her everything. We have been sneaking around since the first day you came for the interview." He ran his hand down her arm. "Tell her how we satisfy each other's needs."

Before Anna could answer, she heard someone clearing their throat. Her head was spinning when she saw Will staring at her. She opened her mouth to talk, but nothing came out.

Cathy looked at Anna. "I expect you won't be working here by the end of the week." She headed for the door and looked at Will before she left. "She looks innocent, but from what my husband says, when you take her clothes off, she's a . . ."

Cathy darted out of the room sobbing.

Dr. Watts adjusted his pants and shirt and quickly left the room without another word.

Will just stood staring at her. Anna frantically tried to button her shirt, realizing her bra was exposed, but the button was missing. She knew how this looked. The only thing that came to Anna's mouth was the bile from her stomach. The fire in Will's eyes turned to disgust as he turned and walked out without a word. Anna fumbled with her blouse, her hands shaking, her cheeks glistening with tears as she followed him to the door.

"Will . . . I—"

"No," he said, his jaw tight. "I need to drop Momma at . . ." His voice trailed off. Then he disappeared around the corner.

A huddle formed in the hallway, heads together like puzzle pieces. Their accusing stares fixed on her, murmurs mingling and accusations silently swirling like a storm. She quickly shut and locked the door. Her body trembled, leaving her legs unsteady as a newborn foal taking a step. When she reached her chair, she sank into it, dissolving into tears.

Her trembling hands took out a mirror, wondering what Will saw when he looked at her and what he heard Cathy or Dr. Watts say before he walked in. When she looked in the mirror, her lipstick was smeared, and her hair tousled. She lowered her head and closed her eyes. It was no wonder Will walked out. After the way Dr. Watts kept touching her, the words thrown around, and her appearance. It all looked terrible for Anna. The hope she had dissipated like a vapor.

Her trembling hands reached for her phone, and her vision blurred with tears as she searched for JW's number. She could hear his baritone voice: "If you need me, call me. I'll be there."

She dialed his number, and it rang once. *I need to hang up and leave before anything happens. I can get Thunderbird and go.* Second and third ring . . . *I can't leave. It doesn't matter if Will is angry with me.* Fourth ring . . .

She started to press the end button when a breathless baritone voice said, "Hello."

That was all Anna needed to hear to break into an uncontrollable sob. "JW," she hiccupped. "I—I need you. I'm at the hospital." The sobbing continued.

"Anna, text me what floor you are on. Don't try to talk. When I get there, I'll tap on your door. Don't open for anyone but me."

Anna nodded, not realizing he couldn't see her head.

"Before I go, do you need any medical help?"

She hiccupped several times before answering. "No . . . please hurry."

When she ended the call, she texted JW her office location. She sat trembling, praying he would hurry. She looked at herself again in the mirror. She muttered, "No wonder he walked out. It looks like I was enjoying it."

She wiped the smeared lipstick from her face with a tissue. Flashes of Dr. Watts's face filled her mind, the way his disgusting breath smelled, the feel of his grubby hands all over her. Her jaw clenched as she wiped the black eyeliner mixed with tears from her eyes.

When she finished, she shoved the mirror in her purse and smoothed her skirt. She laid her head back on her chair, playing the scene over and over in her head. The look on Will's face—the accusation and disappointment. Alarm and anger rippled through her spine. Who knew how far Dr. Watts would have taken it if his wife hadn't barged in? Would Anna have been able to defend herself? For his amusement, Dr. Watts played sick games with people's lives and careers. *How could Will leave me like that? Damn, his jealousy! He should know better. He should know me enough and trust me.*

Anna heard a light knock on the door, which startled her even though she knew it was likely JW. She got close to the door. "JW, is that you?" she said just above a whisper.

"Yes, it's okay. You're safe."

She threw the door open and fell into his arms, squeezing tight. She didn't even care if Will walked in. JW only cared about helping her, not judging her. As much as Anna loved Will, his willingness to abandon her left her doubting his love for her.

"Hey, it's okay. I called Garrett. We're going to his place."

Anna released him and looked up at him. She never realized how he towered over her. His T-shirt stretched across his chest, and his amber goatee and black hat made him look like he was straight out of the TV show *Yellowstone* and would take someone to the train station if they tried to hurt her. He placed a jacket with a hood around her shoulders and pulled the hood up.

He leaned down and whispered, "Listen, we're going to take the stairs out and go straight to my truck." He winked at her. "People usually don't mess with me."

"I don't doubt that," Anna said with a slight smirk.

"Come on, Red."

True to his word, JW got Anna out of the hospital safely and into his truck. They rode in silence. Anger about the entire incident began to spiral from the pit of Anna's stomach. The more she thought about Will, the angrier she got. She squeezed her hands into fists until her palms stung from digging her fingernails into them. Anna felt a hand curl around hers. She turned to see JW glance at her.

"You want to tell me what happened?"

She shook her head. "Not right now."

"Do I need to call anyone else? Will? Kati?"

"Not Will," she growled. The emotions began brewing like a tornado. The flashes of Will's face and him walking out. She slammed her hands on her legs. "How could he just walk out like that? What if he came back and hurt me? If his wife hadn't walked in, he would have! Oh, God." She began to hyperventilate. "Why me? What did I do?"

Her head began to spin, and sweat was beading on her forehead. She leaned her head back, trying to take deep breaths, and closed her eyes. *Deep breath in, deep breath out, deep breath in, deep breath out.* When she opened her eyes, the truck had stopped moving. JW was facing her in the seat.

Anna's head continued to spin. It was time she got herself under control. "I'm safe. The sky is blue. I'm safe."

JW placed his hand on hers. "Look at me, Red." Anna slowly turned toward him. "None of this was your fault. I have known Deluca for a long time. What he did is nothing new for him." He chuckled. "Jon and I have been friends as long as they have, but Will thought I wanted to date Shelly because he saw me talking to her after they started dating. Essentially, Jon and I haven't been close since then."

"Oh, so being with you wouldn't settle well with him."

He laughed. "Not at all."

She dropped her head back on the seat. "Great. Did you like Shelly?"

He shook his head. "Not like that. She was like a pesky sister," he said. "All Jon and I cared about was riding bulls."

"You know, what I don't understand is how he could think I was sleeping with that disgusting piece of shit while I've been proving myself to him over and over, showing that I love him." She hit her hand on the dash. "God, why can't he believe when people say they love him?"

JW asked, "Did Kati tell you that he and Shelly almost got a divorce a year before she got killed?"

The heavy lashes that shadowed her cheeks flew up. "What? Really? Wait, I think he mentioned it the night he was drunk. Go on."

"I came home from the rodeo circuit and saw Shelly at the grocery store. Will walked up when she was hugging me." JW continued, "He wanted to fight me like we were teenagers. I tried to walk away, but he grabbed my arm. Shelly stepped in at the same time, which led to her getting hit in the nose by Will. I lost my temper and threw him into a shelf, knocking everything off and causing a huge mess."

Anna had her hand over her mouth. "What happened then?"

"Shelly called Kati to come get her. I waited with her. Kati and Jon showed up. Kati threw a bag at Will and told him to go home with Jon because he wasn't welcome at the ranch."

Was Will ever going to change? At the very least, Anna would lose her job or reputation. If Will wouldn't change, nothing was left for her here.

"Well, my life in Cardinal Creek will end soon. At least I have my grandparents' farm to go home to. Hopefully, with my nursing license intact." Anna laughed—a mirthless, hollow laugh. "Want to know the real bullshit, JW? I was going to tell him *everything* after work tonight."

When they pulled up to Garrett's house, JW turned off the engine. "Listen, let's get inside and talk to Garrett, and I think we should get Kati over here."

"I don't want to go to the ranch, but I have nowhere to stay."

"That's why we need to talk to Kati. Do you mind if I call Jon?"

Anna shrugged. "As long as he doesn't tell Will a thing. He lost his right to know anything about me the minute he deserted me."

"Fair enough." JW exited the truck, leaving Anna to figure out how to center herself enough to tell them what had happened. She needed to draw on the strength she found when her mother and father died, Nana and Papa died, and Tony cheated on her.

JW opened the door for her and offered her a hand to get out of the truck. Her legs trembled with each step up the sidewalk to Garrett's door.

She was aware of her disheveled look and red puffy eyes. When Garrett opened the door, she swallowed hard, hoping to numb the pain and stop the sobbing.

"Hey," Anna choked up.

Garrett put an arm around her. "Let's sit," he said. He looked at JW. "Thanks for bringing her here. Come on in and have a seat."

Garrett led her to the couch and sat next to her. "Please tell us what is going on. We want to help you."

"There's a doctor at work who's been harassing me since I started at the hospital," she said, her voice strained. "He told me he'd ruin my career if I reported it. Each encounter got more aggressive. His wife has been threatening me too, saying she'd make sure I would lose my license."

"What happened today?" Garrett asked in a hushed tone.

"He came into my office and attacked me. He slammed me into the desk and tried to get on top of me, and he kissed me and pulled on my clothes. Then his wife walked in, slapped my face, and said she would ensure I never practiced nursing again." She closed her eyes, remembering the look on Will's face, causing her stomach to churn. A shiver racked her body. "Will walked in, and Dr. Watts told him we've been seeing each other this whole time." She felt sick even saying his name. "Then Will walked out, and when I tried to catch him, he just said no and walked away." She choked up, "He . . . he . . . just left me." She fell against Garrett's chest, sobbing. He pulled her close.

After her sobbing subsided, she looked at Garrett and JW's faces. They were flushed with anger.

"Where is the doctor?" Garrett asked.

"I don't know." The scene started playing in Anna's head as she placed her head into her hands. "He just left," her voice shuttered between sobs.

Garrett sat at the table in front of her. "Listen to me. You didn't do anything wrong. I knew something was happening, but I didn't do anything either. I'm sorry for that. I should have intervened."

"Thank you for believing me."

"Of course we do," Garrett and JW said in unison.

"Red, I witnessed him groping you, but you begged me not to tell. After my history with Will, I didn't feel comfortable going to him," JW explained. "I'm to blame."

She shook her head. "I'm so stupid."

"He played on your fears, Anna."

Anna wrung her hands. "I can't go back to the ranch. I have nowhere to go." She jumped up. "I'm alone here, with nowhere to go. I need to go back and get my stuff." She paced back and forth. "Garrett, help me get my horse and stuff so I can go home."

"Hey, hey," he said, leading her back to the couch. "You aren't alone. We'll call Kati and see if she'll stay here with you. I can bunk with JW or stay here if you are okay with that."

JW stood up. "Listen, Garrett's right. He can stay with me."

Anna looked at Garrett. "I don't know if I ever want to go back."

"You don't have to make any decisions about anything tonight. We need to pick up your friend in San Antonio in a few days." Garrett took out his phone. "I'm going to text Kati to bring some stuff for you and see if she'll stay with us tonight."

A short time after Garrett texted Kati, his phone rang, and he excused himself. When the door closed, Anna looked at JW, who was staring at her. She wasn't sure if what she saw in his eyes was pity, anger, or disgust, so she looked away.

"Don't look away."

"You look disgusted with me."

He huffed out a laugh. "Disgusted with you?" He shook his head. "I want to go kick Will's ass. And this time, I don't just want to hoist him into a shelf of canned goods," he fumed.

She glared at him and snapped. "Don't you touch him! Got it!"

He stood. Anna stood and squared up with him. JW looked down at her with amusement in his eyes. "What's so damn funny?" She spit with venom.

"Girl, you love him. Don't you dare run. Trust Garrett and Kati. Got it?"

She narrowed her eyes. "And you?"

He huffed out a laugh. "I'm just a dumb washed-up bull rider who looks mean."

She punched his arm. "You're more than that. Thanks for helping me. I hope you can fix things with Jon."

"That boat sailed, darlin'."

"Don't call me *darlin'*." Anna closed her eyes tight. She was with JW but heard Will. God, she missed him, but he'd made his choice.

He squeezed her shoulder. "I still want to beat his ass. If that guy would have hurt you, I would have done more than that."

Before Anna could say anything, Garrett walked into the room. Relief flooded through her as Garrett explained that Kati was on her way home from work and would be over after dinner. Anna desperately wanted to believe that Garrett and Kati could help, but she couldn't coax any optimism from her cynical mind. She was relieved that JW, Kati, and Garrett had her back.

CHAPTER 51

Will sat in front of the firepit on his patio, turning his phone repeatedly in his hand. Anger had been like a raging fire inside him since he'd walked into Anna's office and heard what Cathy Watts had said about her sleeping with her husband. Anna's hair was tousled, lipstick smeared, and shirt untucked. For God's sake, Dr. Watts's hand was on her ass, and she did nothing but stare at him, blinking.

He knew something wasn't right about Dr. Watts and how he'd acted toward Anna. Will ran his hand through his hair, remembering Dr. Watts at the nurses' station the day of his mother's surgery. Could he be wrong about what he saw? He took out his phone to send Anna a text. After erasing the text six times, he finally sent one.

> Will: Anna, I need to talk to you. Please call me or text me. I'm sorry.

There I go again, saying I'm sorry.

Therapy had been going well for Will regarding the accident and the loss of Shelly, but the jealousy thing had been a little more challenging to crack. Was this part of a jealousy thing? What if Dr. Watts hurt Anna after he left? The thought made him sick. After he'd dropped his mom off at Sissy's, he returned to the hospital to look for Anna. But she was nowhere to be found. He even checked Dr. Watts's office, but it was closed. Frustrated, he waited thirty minutes in the parking lot where her car was parked. Anna's cabin was dark when he got home, and he didn't have the courage to knock.

God, you are such a coward.

After a few hours, when Anna didn't text, Will traded anger with fear. He hoped nothing had happened to her. It would be his fault. How stupid was he? Anna had come home from work upset on multiple occasions. Was he so caught up in his grief that he couldn't see the situation for what it was? *I understand she's angry, but I want to know she's okay.*

He pushed himself out of the chair and stalked to Liz's house. When Will walked in, he did his best to make eye contact with his mom. Kati sat at the dinner table, so he sat across from her and watched as his mom served them dinner.

He kept his hands busy by checking his phone every few minutes. He couldn't understand why Anna wouldn't answer his text.

Will finally made eye contact with his mom. There it was, that look she'd given him since Shelly died. *Will, are you okay? What can I do for you? Nothing, Mom, bring my wife back. Rewind my stupidity with Anna? Don't lie about the funds. Be a better man.*

Sitting down, she looked at Will. "Are you okay, darlin'?"

His brow furrowed. "Have y'all seen Anna?"

"I haven't seen her since the hospital when I was with you."

Kati shook her head. "I haven't seen her since this afternoon. After my meeting, I went by her office, but she wasn't there."

He saw Kati staring at him. Her eyes flashed with outrage. "What, Kati?" He knew that look; it was the one she had when Shelly threw him out for two weeks.

"Have *you* seen her, Will?" she asked in a harsh, raw voice.

He pushed his plate back. "I'm not hungry. Sorry, Momma. I'm gonna do chores."

Kati stood up. "That's right. Run, you coward."

Will stopped. "What did you call me?" *What the hell is she talking about?* "Kati, I'm guessing you're angry about something."

"You bet your ass I'm angry. I have no idea where your head is right now." She flashed him a look of disdain.

He walked toward the kitchen. Her tone infuriated him. "Look, you want to stop talking in riddles and let me know why you're so pissed at me?"

"You know what? You have no right to know why I'm pissed, but I will tell you that if you don't get your shit together, you're going to lose Anna." Kati's lips were thinned with anger. Her phone buzzed, and her eyes widened when she read her text message.

Will took a few deep breaths, hoping to keep his temper in check. It was bad enough that he had no idea where Anna was, but now Kati spoke in angry cryptic riddles. If she knew where Anna was, she needed to tell him so he could try to make things right. The fire in her eyes was like the day she came to get Shelly when his jealousy had gotten the best of him.

"Have you seen or heard from Anna?" He threw his hands up. "Okay, you don't have to tell me, but can you tell me if she's okay?"

"You don't deserve to know anything about her. Stew in your shit, Will." Kati grabbed two overnight bags and her purse. "Momma, I'll be home tomorrow. I'll text you where I am when I get there." She stared at Will until she got to the door, then said, "You lost the right to know anything about Anna when you walked out on her." She turned and walked out the door, slamming it behind her, jolting Will enough to take a step back.

Will's broad shoulders were hunched, and he leaned against the doorframe. Kati's words ran through his head. She was rightfully angry that he'd abandoned Anna when she needed him. His grip on the doorknob tightened as he tried to restrain his anger and fear. Sweat beaded on his forehead as visions of Anna in danger flooded his mind. Guilt and regret weighed on him like lead as he recalled how quickly his assumptions and jealousy had led to this confrontation. He had never been able to shake the insecurities that had haunted him since adolescence, and they'd caused him heartache. The tension from the last few therapy sessions hung over Will when they'd discussed what caused him to react strongly to certain situations. Those discussions hadn't made a dent in his struggles.

"William, you need to . . ."

He turned to her with tears in his eyes. "I need to what, Momma?"

"Nothing, son. I love you."

"I love you too." his voice cracked.

Will stormed out of the house, slammed the door behind him, and ran to the stable. Fear gripped him like a tight fist around his chest, and he needed a moment. His hands shook as he grabbed the pitchfork and started mucking out stalls in a frenzy. With every stab into the straw, he checked his phone for a message from Anna. Each time, when there was none, he felt his frustration mounting. Will leaned on the pitchfork, inhaled deeply, and considered throwing it against the wall, but then he remembered he wasn't a child anymore. He chuckled bitterly to himself, muttering, "Yeah, right."

The silence of the barn surrounded him, accentuating the palpable turmoil in his chest. Will's emotions were like a fireball on the verge of explosion; he had to get himself under control.

Liz stood at the stall where Will worked. "Please talk to me."

He continued working without looking up. "Not now."

"William, what's going on?" Her tone was stern.

He straightened, gazing at her, filled with anguish. He removed his gloves, slapping them on his leg. "Well, I walked into Anna's office, and Dr. Watts had her in a lip-lock, and his wife was talking about how she's been sleeping with him."

A fire blazed in Liz's eyes. "Then what?"

His head lowered, and he kicked at the ground, avoiding eye contact as he continued. "Well, I just walked out." A panicked expression flittered across his handsome features. "Momma, what if I was wrong and it wasn't what it looked like?"

"Oh my God." She slapped his arm. "Damn it. She loves you and would never do anything to hurt you! How could you desert her like that?"

His head whipped up. "I didn't mean to desert her . . . I . . ." He fumbled over his words. "She's shown me nothing but love. How could I be so blind?" Shame flowed through Will like a flood.

"Are you so blinded by jealousy that it clouds your judgment? That girl has been working tirelessly for the equine center, and this is how you repay her. Do you even love her?"

"So much it hurts thinking of never seeing her again." He let out a long sigh. "I don't want to make the same mistakes that I made with Shelly."

"You mean like the incident with JW Walker?"

The year before Shelly died, Will challenged JW Walker to a fight, and JW threw him into a shelf full of canned goods. Shelly let him know she would not tolerate his childish jealousy. He ended up sleeping on Jon's couch for two weeks. Shelly had almost called it quits because of his insecurities.

Dissatisfaction plowed his brow. "Here we go . . . JW Walker. I didn't like the way he looked at Shelly."

Liz gave him a look designed to peel his hide. "Where did your daddy and I go wrong with you? Did we criticize you too much? Was there something we did wrong for you to believe that you're not good enough for someone?" She shook her head. "I remember when Anna came here all those years ago, and you ignored poor Jon because you thought he was flirting with her. And your jealousy ruined Jon's friendship with JW because, for some reason, that boy is fiercely loyal to you."

A stab of guilt lay buried deep in Will's chest. The lump lodged in his throat prevented him from speaking. His parents hadn't done anything to cause his insecurities. It all started with the awkwardness that came with being a teenager. JW and Jon were popular among their peers due to their outgoing personalities, while he felt like a tall, thin outsider. The girls seemed more drawn to the bull riders than the ropers, leaving him in the cold.

As he mulled over his thoughts, they sounded ridiculous. The silence in the stable roared like a freight train. He lifted his head slowly.

"You and Daddy didn't do anything. I never grew out of my teenage insecurities and carried them into adulthood. I guess in some ways I haven't changed since the day Anna left all those years ago." His voice broke. "I cared for her then and want to be with her now. I'll always love Shelly and miss all our time together, but it's like Anna and I have a connection that's. . ." He chuckled. "I can't explain it."

Liz squeezed his shoulder. "You don't need to. I had that with your father. In my day, we called it soul mates." She took his face in her hands. "Talk to her."

"She won't answer my texts or calls. She's gone, and my heart aches."

"I love you, Will, but this stuff needs to stop."

"I just hope she's safe."

"Me too." She shook her head.

"If Kati texts you that Anna is okay, can you tell me at least?"

Liz nodded. "I will. Goodnight." She stopped before she walked out. "Shave your face."

Will scrubbed his hand across his face. "Anna likes it."

She smiled. "Then, by all means, keep it."

After she walked out, he was left with the memory of the night he and Anna spent together. How could he think she had anything less than love for him when she showed him nothing but passion in all parts of their relationship? He needed to figure out how to fix this with her, and he was almost out of time.

CHAPTER 52

Anna absentmindedly moved her salad around her plate as memories and worries of the day accumulated in her mind. Fear rushed through her after the events with Cathy and Dr. Watts. The pain from Will walking out on her and not knowing what to do next was overwhelming. She was grateful for the support she'd received but scared of opening a can of worms at the hospital. There were no witnesses, only Dr. Watts and Cathy, and they were on the same side.

"Are you still working on your salad?" Garrett asked.

She was grateful for the question, which brought normalcy back to the conversation that her spiraling thoughts had disrupted. And, despite her fear, a smile tugged at the corners of her lips as his comforting manner quelled her anxiety.

"I'm sorry, y'all. I was just lost in thought." She handed him her plate.

Anna was startled by a knock at the door. JW glanced at her with an eyebrow raised. "We should do some tequila shots."

Garrett yelled over his shoulder as he headed to the door. "Oh yes, that's *exactly* what she needs."

As soon as he opened the door, Kati stepped inside. Anna ran to her, burying her face in Kati's chest. She held onto her friend tightly, letting all the fear and uncertainty she'd been carrying finally wash away.

"I should have listened to you that day we went for coffee. I—I . . . should have told Will," Her voice quivered with barely concealed terror. A sense of relief pooled beneath Anna's skin when Kati flashed her a reassuring smile. Her friend was the only ray of light left in this dark situation, and Anna couldn't be more thankful for having her by her side.

Kati led her to the couch, and Anna laid her head on Kati's shoulder as she began to speak. "Even though Will is my brother, I don't even want to look at him right now because of what he did."

Anna interrupted, "I don't blame him for walking out. You should have seen how I looked, and Dr. Watts is compelling. Cathy believes I'm sleeping with him." She shivered at the thought of him touching her.

"That's bullshit." Kati and JW said in unison. Anna knew about JW and Will, so there was no reprieve for him.

Garrett, always the diplomat, came from the kitchen drying his hands on a towel. "I know y'all are mad at Will, and I get that, but it's counterproductive to hash that out repeatedly. We need to devise a solution that won't cause Anna further anguish."

Anna chimed in. "I agree with Garrett."

JW stood. "This is where the dumb bull rider exits. I have complete faith in Garrett and Kati to find a solution." He pointed to Anna. "If you need any trash taken out, I'm the guy. I don't know what it is about you, but people are drawn to you. When you feel alone, think of that." He headed to the door. "Good night, y'all. Let me know if you need anything."

When JW closed the door, Anna looked at Kati. "He's a good guy like this one," she said as she pointed to Garrett.

Anna had developed a friendship with Garrett while she lived at the ranch. They spent countless hours working in the stable, sharing occasional lunches and dinners, and raising funds for the equine center. He had a way of being a mediator between her and Will. Over the years, Anna had often wanted an older brother or sister to have the sibling relationship she'd seen so many of her classmates and friends have. Garrett had become that for her over the last couple of months.

Anna knew there would be difficult conversations between her, Kati, and Garrett over the next few days as they tried to figure out what to do about Dr. Watts. She had her heart set on leaving after Will walked out and left her alone, but Kati and Garrett wanted her to fight. As Kati handed her a bag with some clothes for the night, she told Anna that she'd do her best to take care of this thing with Dr. Watts without her name coming into it.

After Garrett went to his room and Kati went to his guest bedroom, Anna lay on the couch, wishing she had the guts to text Will back, but she put her phone in her purse to avoid temptation. There was talk about ensuring Dr. Watts got fired and hopefully lost his license because, according to Kati, Anna wasn't the only one he was harassing. Still, she was the only one on Cathy Watt's radar currently. She was torn between resigning from her job and going home to Missouri and staying to fight for her career, even if she let go of Will.

~

Anna's eyes blinked open groggily. It took a moment for her to realize she was not in her bed. The pain in her back made it clear that this wasn't familiar territory. Taking note of the stillness around her, Anna wondered if Garrett and Kati had left for work already. She glanced at her watch on the table nearby; it was past nine o'clock, and she'd be late for work. After phoning the house supervisor to let them know that she wasn't feeling well, she read Will's message from the night before. She started tapping away a response, only to delete it several times as she wrestled with conflicting emotions. Anna still loved him, but she couldn't get past Will's sudden departure when she had needed him most—the hurt and anger were too fresh.

Anna changed into shorts and a T-shirt after a long hot shower. She tied her tennis shoes, then went to the ranch to pack a bag for her stay with Garrett. When she pulled up to the cabin, she was surprised to see Will sitting on her porch. The rope in her stomach tied itself in a knot. The hope that he was at work just vaporized into the air.

"I can't do this right now," she muttered.

Her emotions were still all over the board, which scared her because that was when horrible things could be said. Right now, she wanted to say awful things to Dr. Watts, but Will didn't deserve *all* her anger. She drew in a deep breath and got out of her SUV, swallowing hard, trying to remove the golf ball in her throat as she walked to the porch.

Will's clear blue eyes connected with hers, and she was sure her weakness for him would allow him to say, "I'm sorry," and it would be done. But it was time for him to know that his behavior was unacceptable. After all, he wasn't a teenager.

"What do you need?" her voice was like ice.

He looked at her intently, then strode to her. "Anna, I should have stayed. I'm sorry."

She pushed past him, opening the door. "It doesn't matter, Will." Before walking inside, she looked at him. "Anything else?"

"Anna, please talk to me. Can I come in, please?"

"It's your house." She opened the screen door so he could come in.

Will's face contorted with anguish. "Anna, it's not like that." He held his hand out to her.

She took his hand, and a sob caught in her throat. "Come in." Her eyes cast downward. When she took Will's hand, she wanted him to hold her and tell her it would be okay.

He pulled her into his arms, "Darlin', are you okay? I was worried about you."

Anna was like putty in Will's hands. This is precisely what she needed yesterday. His love and understanding. His protection from a predator. She took a deep breath, squeezing him tight. "I'm fine. I stayed with Garrett last night."

He kissed her passionately on the lips. Passion was not what she needed right now. They needed to talk about what happened yesterday. She needed to know that he didn't believe Cathy Watts.

Anna pushed him away breathlessly.

"What happened yesterday, Anna? I don't know what I saw, but I saw you with . . . him. And I don't know what to think. I heard what Cathy Watts said. Tell me what happened."

Her anger and hurt could no longer be controlled. Anna couldn't believe what she was hearing. Questions like the ones he just asked screamed *I don't trust you*. "What do you think you saw?" her voice harsh and raw. "You shouldn't need clarification." She stalked toward her room.

He followed with long, purposeful strides.

She grabbed a suitcase from the closet and tossed it onto the bed. Hastily rifling through her drawers, she threw clothes into the bag, then glanced at Will, whose eyes were wide.

"Where are you going?" His voice was thick with anguish.

"Garrett's house. He doesn't accuse me of things. How could you ask such things? Don't you trust me?" She walked into the bathroom and started throwing things into her travel bag. "I've done nothing but show you that I love you." Tears leaked from her eyes as she zipped the bag. "You don't love me if that's what you think of me." Anna trembled as she continued to pack.

He touched her arm, but Anna whirled around. "No. You have no right to touch me."

She fought back tears as she shoved her clothes into the suitcase with a violent thrust, anger churning in her chest. She tried to focus on the task, but her thoughts kept returning to Will's accusatory questions. What would it take for her to give in and forgive him yet again?

With a final sigh, she snapped the suitcase shut and turned to him, her voice unwavering and sharp despite her fragile emotions. "I have nothing else to say. You don't deserve an explanation. And you know what? I don't believe you are sorry because you keep repeating the same mistakes as if you were a child. You know, children are smarter than that. But it doesn't matter anymore. I'm quitting my job. I don't need this from anyone."

Will's face was pale, his breathing shallow. "Was Dr. Watts hurting you?"

"Yeah, you know what? He did hurt me. And you just left me there." Anna threw the words at him like stones. Her level of anger was indeed tipping the meter to explosion. She was breathless with rage. "Do you have any idea what could have happened?"

He stepped toward her.

She held her hands up. "Listen, I need some space. I'm going to stay with Garrett for a few days. And for the record, I'm not sleeping with Garrett, Dr. Watts, JW Walker, or anyone else you want to ask about! Maybe you want to know if I want to be with the cashier at the gas station? Jesus, what makes you so jealous? Are you that insecure with yourself? Look in the mirror, or better yet, at your heart." Anna's face was on fire, and tears burned her eyes.

"I'm so sorry," he muttered.

She growled, "Oh really? Say it again, then slap me because that's what it's like." She placed her hands in front of her as he stepped toward her. "You need to take it down a notch if we ever hope to fix this thing between us."

Anna stood toe-to-toe with Will, poking her finger into his chest as she glared at him. "I dated one person since I was sixteen because I had held on to a strange fantasy of being with you." Although she knew he wasn't to blame for her fixation on their Cowboy and Ginger summer, she knew what jealousy did. "Don't do this. I won't tolerate it."

"darlin', I . . . Please let me explain."

Anna wanted to let him explain, but at this point, she was afraid that if she let him talk, all the anger, humiliation, grief, and pain brewing inside would be taken out on Will, and he didn't deserve all of it.

"No." Anna shook her head. She didn't want to hear his excuses. "You walked in the middle of a man assaulting your girlfriend, and then you walked out because you got jealous." Just the thought made her blood boil and her heart break simultaneously. Anna shoved his chest. "Why? Why would you do that? You're supposed to—" Her voice cracked. "You're supposed to protect me, and you just left me! You left me *with him!*"

Anna collapsed onto the floor, hugging her knees as sobs racked her body. He'd left her. He'd left when she'd needed him most.

He tried to go to her, but she put up her hand. "I know this is your house, but can I have a few minutes? Then I'll go."

He choked back his tears. "Anna, please let me hold you. Please."

She stiffened, standing up straight. "You lost your right to touch me when you walked out on me when I needed you. I don't know if I could ever trust you."

She grabbed her bag, headed toward the door, and turned to look at him. "I need some space." As she walked out the door with a wall of silence between them, she realized coming to the cabin without backup was the wrong move. Her emotions were too raw to be around Will right now.

When she drove away, she watched him in the rearview mirror until the dust in the road blocked her view. Right now, the only thing that came to her mind was to run—pack up and run. But another part of her wanted to run back and listen to what he had to say, then tell him what happened with Dr. Watts.

CHAPTER 53

Will's feet were like lead with every step. His footsteps echoed in the stable as he shuffled to the tack room, amplifying the emptiness that Anna's departure had left behind. It was almost like Shelly had died all over again, except this time, Anna was alive. He stepped into the tack room, letting the heavy door close behind him with a thud. He lingered there momentarily, then flopped onto an old hay bale. His vision blurred as he stared at Thunderbird's grooming tote, wondering if there was anything he could do to win back Anna's trust.

Garrett was startled when he found Will in the tack room, perched on a hay bale, gazing ahead with a vacant expression. "Hey," he said. "What's up? You here today, or do you have to go to therapy?"

Will didn't answer right away. All he could do was stare silently ahead, his chest tight with guilt and shame for not being there when Anna needed him most. The realization that things between them may be irreparable sunk in like an anchor. Slow and steady, it filled him with grief.

"I don't know how to fix this," Will said, tears trailing down his cheeks. "I walked in and saw Anna with Dr. Watts, and then I walked out." He threw his hat across the room and ran his fingers through his hair. "What kind of man does that? I don't deserve to be with her. I seem to hurt everyone I love."

Garrett put his hand on Will's shoulder. "Listen, this is Anna's story to tell, but I will say she was in a scary situation that could have been even more life-changing than it has already been."

"Did he hurt her?" Will questioned.

Garrett shook his head. "She never said she was hurt physically, but emotionally, it's going to take time, support, and most of all, love."

"Why didn't anyone tell me about this? How long have you known?" Will asked.

"I found out when I talked to JW. I met him at the Saddle Up when I went in for a drink, but it was mostly speculation except for one incident, which I said is Anna's story."

Will's head was spinning. How could he have missed the signs? The night they ate at the Saddle Up, Anna was distressed when she saw Dr. Watts. Then there was the time when they went dancing, and Cathy was upset because her husband danced with Anna. Will's stomach was tied in knots as he thought about what she had endured. He should have listened to his gut that first time he saw Dr. Watts massaging a nurse's shoulders when his mom was in the hospital.

He jammed his hands in his pockets. "I should have noticed instead of being so wrapped up in myself. I've lost her... She's going back to Missouri."

"Give her some time." He slapped Will on the shoulder. "Listen, one of my buddies owns a security firm. I have him doing some investigating on Dr. Watts. I'll share the information with Kati so she can take it to hospital administration."

Will picked up his hat, knocking the hay off it. "I hope we can get this creep out of the hospital. To think he had my momma in his operating room." He shivered at the thought. "Thank you, Garrett, for being a good friend to Anna. I'm glad you were there for her last night. I was worried about her."

"I'll take good care of her for a few days. When Jenny gets here, I'll give her a day or two, then I'll let her know she needs to come back." He gave him a friendly shoulder push, "She loves you. She's just hurt, very hurt."

He kicked at the dirt, gazing downward. "I know. Will you tell her I'm sorry and I love her?"

Garrett walked toward the door and looked back. "Anna has a great heart. She cares about your family and is very committed to opening the equine center. I assure you if she decides she's leaving, it won't be until after it's open. If she comes back to you, hold onto her. She's an amazing woman and should be cherished." As he walked out, he added, "Remember, I'm going to San Antonio tomorrow so I won't be in. I'm taking Anna to pick up Jenny from the airport."

"I'll be here. Besides, Momma is anxious to help since she's been given the green light to do whatever she wants." Will stood at the door of the stable, looking at Anna's cabin with a hole burning in his heart.

Garrett turned before getting in his truck. "My goal is to get her to come home by Saturday. I'll use my charm and wit," he said, trying to lighten the mood.

Will chuckled. "You do that." *Please bring her home for me.*

WILL SPENT the rest of the day mending fences, assessing what needed to be done in the lodge and arena, and determining what equipment was necessary for the equine center. Concentrating when he worked on things for the equine center was hard—all the times he and Anna had run into Dr. Watts played in his mind as he searched for what he'd missed. Every time they ran into him, Anna became quiet and withdrawn. Shame coursed through Will's body over missing the signs.

It was time for him to get this whole jealousy thing under control. Anna was right. He was a man now and needed to stop the petty, jealous games.

He remembered when he saw JW hugging Shelly; he'd gone after him because he always thought JW was flirting with her. Shelly assured him that JW was like an older brother. But his problem cost Jon and Shelly their friendships with JW.

The most despicable thing he'd done was walk out on Anna. He shivered at the thought of what could have happened.

Despair struck him when he realized there may be no repairing what he'd done to Anna. It was time to examine why he had always thought so little of himself—that he could be easily traded in. After all, Shelly had been faithful to him since they started dating. She was a good mother and a devoted wife up until the day she died. Anna had been tirelessly helping his family since her first day in

Cardinal Creek despite still grieving a loss that occurred a few months ago. He frequently turned to her with his problems, and she comforted him. The entire time she'd been working at the hospital, she was being harassed, but he missed it all. Maybe insecurity wasn't his problem; perhaps he was nothing but selfish.

As the bright orange sun began to sink, the sky turned from blue to magenta, then dark purple. When the sun finally slipped away for the night, Will walked to his mother's house. It was time to talk to Kati about what happened. He needed to know why she'd kept it a secret from him.

When he arrived at Liz's, he walked in, ready to talk or go to war with Kati. As he entered the kitchen, Caden and Eva hugged him. "Hey, guys. Did you have a good day?"

"Yeah," they said, jumping up and down.

"Do you smell cookies?" Eva asked.

Will closed his eyes and took in a deep breath. He pasted a smile across his lips. "I do." He needed to ensure the kids didn't know what was happening with Anna. So, he needed to fake it until he made it. Will looked around. "Where's Grandma?"

"She went to her room. She'll be back in a sec," Caden said. "We're having spaghetti for dinner."

Will ruffled his hair. "I thought I smelled garlic."

Will shifted in his seat, the rough fabric of his jeans scraped against his palms to dry his sweaty palms. He had been waiting for Liz's return for what felt like an eternity. He sprang to his feet and approached her when she entered the room. What he needed right now was no judgment or anger for his mistakes. He needed to hug someone because things may not be okay no matter what he did.

"Hey, y'all, go watch TV until dinner is ready. Aunt Kati will be home very soon," Liz said to Caden and Eva.

When the kids had gone to the living room, Liz directed Will to a chair. "Sit. What's going on?" She spoke in a gentle tone.

Will leaned forward, putting his face in his hands. "She's gone. I don't think I can fix this." He lifted his head to look at Liz. His chest had a vicelike pressure on it as he tried to speak. "Did you know that Dr. Watts was harassing Anna?"

Liz let out a long breath. "I just found out a couple of days ago. You have to understand that these things are sensitive. Anna was the one being harassed. Don't forget that."

"How did I miss it?"

Liz sighed. "What's done is done. You can't go back and change the past. I didn't know either until recently, but I suspected something was happening. The fear in her eyes told me everything I needed to know."

Will shook his head. "I saw her, and we got into a fight. I'm so stupid. I asked her if Cathy Watts was telling the truth," he said in a suffocated whisper.

Liz shot out of her chair. "Really, Will? Why would you ask her that?"

"I don't know, Momma. I didn't know what was going on! I just saw Dr. Watts on top of her, and Cathy was screaming about her husband being unfaithful. I didn't know what to think! But Anna let me have it. Then she told me she needed a break and didn't think it could be fixed."

"I don't blame her for leaving you," Liz said with her arms across her chest. "I know you don't want to hear anger and disappointment, but that's all I feel right now." She took a long, deep breath.

Will looked at her, his eyes growing wet, tears blurring his vision. "I think I should let her go. She deserves someone better than me. Garrett and JW protected her, but I walked away. You and Kati believed her, but she didn't trust me enough to talk to me," he said in a choked voice as tears streamed down his face.

A hand gripped his shoulder as he silently cried. After a few minutes, Liz shook him. "No matter how upset I am with you, I love you and want you to fix this with Anna. But one thing you need to fix is *you*. So many people love you, but you don't love yourself, which is beyond me."

He looked at her, his eyes red and puffy. "I was a tall, lanky teenager." It sounded so silly when he said it. "Girls just . . . flocked to Jon and JW. They are both outgoing and persistent flirts. Girls loved that, not the super skinny awkward guy who never knew what to say." Will never understood how Jon and JW could charm people. It wasn't in Will's nature. No matter how hard he had tried in high school—before Anna and Shelly—no girl had taken an interest in him. Not when Jon and JW were around. He'd never been picked, superficial as it might've sounded. The constant rejections stung, reminding him that he preferred riding horses and roping to trying to charm someone.

She stared at him and burst out laughing. "The kind of girls that like guys like that, minus Kati, who can get past Jon's bullshit, aren't like Shelly and Anna. They see you. Were you able to find things to talk about with Anna when you met her the first time and then now? How about Shelly? Were you able to talk to her?"

"Well, uh . . . Momma, why was that so funny?" he asked.

"Think about the first time you met Anna and Shelly."

"We talked about everything. We had a lot in common." It was like an ah-ha moment for Will. He closed his eyes and remembered how Anna had always looked at him. When they danced, she never looked around. It was like they were the only people in the room. Shelly was the same. Always quality women who saw him, no bells and whistles, just him.

A smile spread across Liz's face. "Looks like it hit you. Your daddy and I always loved you and saw you for the person you are. You have a family that loves you. Shelly loved you, and Anna loves you. Don't you think you should learn to love yourself?"

The door closed, and the kids in the living room erupted into cheers for Aunt Kati coming home. Then, they ran into the kitchen, announcing it was time to eat. When Kati walked into the kitchen, Will was ready for her to tear into him, but she walked across the room and hugged him. "How are you doing?" she whispered in his ear.

"I messed this one up."

She took him by the shoulders. "I should have told you about Anna, but we were in a bad situation. I'm staying with her at Garrett's place."

Will cleared his throat. "How did JW get involved in all of this?"

Kati tilted her head, narrowing her eyes. "Anna and I went out with the girls one night, and JW was working the bar at Saddle Up. He helped when Dr. Watts grabbed Anna. He drove us home that night because we were both a little intoxicated. Anna begged us not to tell you. I don't know what happened, just that Anna was drunk. Dr. Watts was there, and they'd gotten into some scuffle near the bathroom. But I didn't see anything, and JW threw him out. I asked JW to give her his number so she could call him if she needed help. That's the short version."

"I'm glad he was there to help. I owe him an apology, and Jon too, for having him choose between me and JW."

Kati looked at Liz with her mouth open. "Momma, did aliens abduct Will?"

"Leave it to you to lighten the mood." Will gave her a friendly shove. "Is there anything I can do to help?"

Kati let out a long breath. "Right now, I think the best thing to do is to keep going to therapy. Spend time with the kids. Garrett and I are going to help get Anna home after Jenny comes. She'll be busy as she gets things ready for the grand opening. Most of all, you can support her. She's been through a lot."

Will was intrigued about how she kept planning without knowing where he'd get the money. "How does she plan to pull this off with no money?"

The beginning of a smile tipped the corners of her mouth. "Big brother, you have no idea how amazing Anna is and what that woman can accomplish." She winked at him. "No more questions, and trust us. Just get better."

Liz set a pot of spaghetti on the table, then a tray of garlic cheese bread. "Come on, kids, let's eat, but first, wash your hands."

As the kids headed to the bathroom, Will looked at Liz and Kati. "It was my fault Shelly died." The shock on their faces was nothing compared to the turbulence flowing through him. "I know the kids will be here any minute. So, I needed to let you know. I texted her. She read it and tried to text back. That was when she hit the truck." Will heard the kids coming up the hall and spooned spaghetti onto their plates. Then he looked at Kati and his mom. "Can we table this until after we eat?"

They nodded.

Will pushed his food around his plate as they attempted to keep dinner as normal as possible. He wasn't sure what possessed him to blurt out what he did right before they ate. Caden and Eva could have heard him. The guilt had been bothering him constantly since the night Jon handed him Shelly's phone with the text message staring at him. He looked at his mother watching him from across the table, and she winked at him. Relief washed through Will as he ate a few more bites. He could always count on Kati to lighten the mood. When she looked at him, she raised an eyebrow. "What?"

Kati gestured toward Will's face. "What's with the dark, brooding cowboy look? You know, like the guy on Yellowstone?" She tapped her finger against her lips. "Rip Wheeler."

He scrubbed his hand across his face. "Like it?"

"Not really, not to dampen the mood. Did Anna?"

Will nodded. He could still feel her hands running down his face the last night they spent together. As the kids finished eating, Will cleared the plates and loaded them into the dishwasher while Kati and Liz wiped down the table and put cookies on it.

Kati came alongside and put her arm around Will. "You aren't responsible for when someone answers a text. We both know that was an issue we all had with her, especially when the kids were in the car. It was an accident."

"But I knew she always looked. I should have waited. She . . . she was pregnant. I lost my wife *and* child." His voice broke. He leaned both hands on the sink and let the tears flow.

Liz came alongside him while Kati stood on the other. "Why didn't you tell us about the baby?"

"Losing her was painful enough. The only other person who knows is Jon."

Kati closed her eyes. "He's been a good friend to you, which explains a lot."

Will looked at Kati. "He's more than a friend. He's a brother. He's protected me in more ways than one. I need to make amends with him too. He loves you, Kati. He never cheated on you."

Kati's eyes flew open. "What? Why are you confessing all this tonight?"

"So, I can get my head straight and fix things with Anna. I've been going to therapy. I'm not working because the chief put me on leave so I can get my head on straight." He swallowed hard. "And about Jon . . . He made me swear I wouldn't tell you, but he's suffered enough and there have been enough secrets."

Will side-eyed his mother, wondering what she was thinking because she was so quiet. "What is it, Momma?"

She opened her mouth to talk, then closed it again. "Shelly chose to read that text and respond. I'm not sure why you carried this burden and the loss of your child all this time, but I'm glad you're starting to talk. It was a big step to let it all out like you did. I'm proud of you." Her chest started to heave, and tears filled her eyes. "It hadn't been too long since we lost your daddy, then Shelly died. Well, that's a lot of blows at one time. You did the best you could. Keep going to therapy and working through it."

The weight on Will's back seemed to lift when he admitted he thought it was his fault Shelly and the baby died. The therapist had told him the same thing his mother and Kati told him, but he needed to hear it from them. He put his arms around them. "Thank you for loving me." The loss of his wife and child was tragic, but he was learning not to carry the guilt. He was a work in progress.

Liz looked at him. "Will, there's more to love than you know, but you'll learn."

Kati kissed his cheek as she grabbed her bag. "I'm gonna sit with Anna and do my best to get her home soon. I love you."

He hugged her and whispered, "I love you too, and thank you."

Will walked Kati to her car, feeling less despair than before he talked to them. He would do everything he could to support Anna, starting with making amends with Jon and JW.

CHAPTER 54

Anna spent most of the day struggling to return to the ranch to get all her stuff and run as fast as she could from Cardinal Creek, not saying a thing to anyone. Her plans sounded completely sane in her head. She would drive back to the ranch, pack up all her stuff, load Thunderbird into the trailer, and take off. She'd get a new phone number the first chance she got so they couldn't reach her again. Then she would spend the rest of her life forgetting she ever came here.

Then there were questions about those people she had come to care about. How would it affect Caden and Eva? The equine center opening would happen with or without her because capable people were working on the fundraiser.

Then she thought about Kati. She couldn't just leave without saying goodbye. Could she walk away from Will again without looking back and have no regrets? That was the one she doubted the most. He seemed genuinely sorry, but he had said it many times before, and it meant nothing. He needed help from the demons chasing him, ruining the love she knew was in his heart. She wanted to forgive and return to him, but could she ever trust that he wouldn't walk away when she needed him?

After picking up her phone and setting it down a million times, she texted Jenny. She needed some clarification and validation. One of the things Anna loved about Jenny was her ability to speak her mind tactfully.

> **Anna:** I'm excited to see you tomorrow. This is Garrett's number. Call or text him. I'm going to turn my phone off.

> **Jenny:** I'm so excited. I don't know if I'm gonna sleep. Are there any cute guys?

> **Anna:** Well, maybe a few. Why do you ask?

> **Jenny:** Well, because I'm single and coming to a place where I don't know one person. I may snag a decent guy and move to Texas. Oh, hey, why are you giving me Garrett's number? Where are you?

> **Anna:** I'm at Garrett's house. I'll explain when I see you.

> **Jenny:** Uh, why are you staying at Garrett's? Isn't he your friend?

> **Anna:** Yes, he's my friend. Kati is staying here too.

> **Jenny:** Easier to plan the fundraiser?

> **Anna:** Something like that.

> **Jenny:** Why do I smell BS?

> **Anna:** Really, things are fine.

> **Jenny:** Things okay with Will?

> **Anna:** Why do you ask? Can you see my face?

> **Jenny:** Really, we're playing that game? Angry emoji: We were nine when we met. This isn't how you answer. Are things okay with Will?

Anna frowned and set the phone down, not wanting to answer, but Jenny would call if she didn't answer. Her voice would give it away.

> **Anna:** Will and I are having some issues. We'll talk tomorrow. Can you bring Nana's photo album?

> **Jenny:** I'll give you a pass until tomorrow. Is the album in the same place?

> **Anna:** Yep, one constant was Nana's house.

> **Jenny:** That's the truth. Now remember I'm coming on the prowl . . . Lol.

> **Anna:** Well, Garrett and JW are single. Take your pick. Lol.

> **Jenny:** Lol, well, thank you. Don't be late tomorrow.

> **Anna:** Garrett is very punctual.

> **Jenny:** See ya tomorrow.

It was important for Anna to wait until Jenny got here to tell her everything. She needed to talk to her in person. Since they were young, she'd always had a unique way of grounding Anna. She smiled, thinking of Jenny throwing her arms around her after her parents' funeral, telling her that she would always be there as her best friend. Jenny's dark, curly hair in pigtails. She smiled. "Tell me anything, and we can fix it. When we can't, we listen." Then she'd held up a pinky. "Pinky promise?" She nodded and linked pinkies with her.

Anna needed some distance between her and Will while she worked through what happened at the hospital. She spent the rest of the afternoon working on the stops she and Garrett needed to make in San Antonio for donations. She reviewed everything that needed to be done for the fundraiser and checked off completed things. Everything was coming together.

The sound of a truck pulling up to the curb caused Anna's chest to tighten. A cloud of worry hung over her. She prayed it wasn't Will and Dr. Watts hadn't figured out where she was staying. She slowly headed toward the window and was relieved when she saw Garrett.

"Hey, are you okay?" Garrett asked as he stepped inside.

There was a thin smile on her lips. "Yeah, just working on the fundraiser."

He raised an eyebrow as he hung his hat by the door. "Anything happen today?"

Anna shook her head as she pretended to look at her computer. She wondered if he had talked to Will. If he'd spoken to him, he should tell her.

Garrett sat in the chair across from Anna and set a bottle of tequila on the table. He put two shot glasses on the table, the entire time staring at her. Exhaustion from the turmoil of the last couple of days left Anna feeling as scattered as leaves in the wind. She shut her laptop and made eye contact with Garrett. "Do you have something to say, or are we doing shots?" Her tone sounded more irritated than she intended.

"Do you need a drink?" he asked.

"No, I don't need a drink. Do you?"

He shrugged. "Maybe."

Garrett was acting strange, and she wondered if something was wrong. He didn't usually act like this. If anything, he was the voice of reason. "Did something happen today?" Anna asked.

He leisurely stretched his long legs. "Funny you should ask, but I talked to Will. Do you want to tell me what happened? Are you okay?"

The conversation with Will at the cabin kept playing back in Anna's mind, but she wanted to focus on the fundraiser, so she put it out of her thoughts. Unlike his usual self, she could sense the strain on Garrett's face. She wondered if everything was beginning to take a toll on him. "I'm okay . . . given the circumstances."

Garrett opened the bottle, poured two shots, and drank one. "You want one?"

Anna stared at him. "No, thanks."

He drank the second shot, stood up, and took the bottle to the kitchen. When he came back, he sat on the couch. "I talked to Will today. I told him that Dr. Watts was hurting you, but it was your story to tell." He threw his hands up with a sigh. "The thing with Dr. Watts is hitting too close to home for me. I'm just glad you're here and safe. You'll need to return to your cabin in a few days."

It took everything in Anna not to get angry with Garrett for telling Will anything, but he said he would tell him if Will asked. It stood to reason he would ask Garrett what was going on. She let out a long sigh. "Are you saying I can't stay here?"

"No, you two need to talk. He's sorry for what he said . . . the regret he felt was in his eyes. He loves you."

"Sometimes love isn't enough until you conquer some horrible flaws."

He clamped his jaw tight and stared at her. Anna could see the anger brewing inside him. It was apparent Will was sorry before she left the ranch, but how many times was he going to say he was sorry and keep doing the same things over and over?

He opened his mouth to speak, then stopped. He threw his hands up. "Love isn't conditional on someone fixing their flaws."

"I know that. I'm planning on going back by the end of the week."

"Fair enough."

"You sure you're okay?"

Garrett nodded and said, "I'm gonna shower and change."

He went to his room and shut the door. Anna was left with his words about love and knew that her love for Will was unwavering, so she wondered if there was any point in listening to his apologies again. But she'd felt alone and abandoned when he left. Something that had crept up in her life since her parents died.

While Garrett showered, she ordered pizza from Brick Oven Pizza. The nice part of living in town was pizza delivery. Ordering dinner for Garrett was the least she could do for all he'd done for her. She went to the refrigerator and got two cans of soda, paper plates, and napkins. The pizza delivery arrived at the door when Garrett returned to the living room.

Anna sat on the floor before the table and opened the box of cheesy pepperoni pizza. She placed a slice on a plate and handed it to Garrett, watching him with a curious eye. His eyes were a little red and puffy. Had he been crying? She got herself a piece of pizza and took a bite. "I know I've asked you this, but you haven't answered. What's wrong?"

"This is too much."

"I don't want to be a problem."

"Not you, the Dr. Watts thing. I don't want to talk about it other than I lost someone close to me after a similar incident. I had just graduated from college." He cleared his throat. "Needless to say, that's part of why I chose the military. I promise you, Dr. Watts won't hurt you again."

Anna placed a hand on his forearm. "I'm sorry." There wasn't anything else to say. She respected that he didn't want to elaborate on who he had lost.

He smiled and touched her hair. "You remind me of her. I want to tell you more, but I don't think I can now."

"I respect that. I'm here for you when you're ready or need to talk."

There was a knock at the door as they were finishing dinner. While Garrett answered the door, Anna took the pizza box and plates to the trash. When she came back, she saw Kati and smiled. "You're finally here." She hugged her. "How are you?"

Garrett shrugged. "Wow, I didn't get that kind of greeting."

Anna swatted at him. "Stop. We got pizza."

Garrett wiggled his eyebrows at Kati. "She bought me dinner."

Kati laughed as she dropped down into the chair. "You won't believe my conversation with Will at dinner."

Anna's stomach churned. A wave of guilt washed over her for running away from their argument rather than trying to work it out. No matter how hard she tried, she could not ignore that her tendency to run away from her problems needed to be addressed. She sat in the chair across from Kati and Garrett, prepared to listen with an open heart.

"So, tell us," Anna said.

"Well, he told us that he thought it was his fault that Shelly died, and Momma and I were floored. He told us he felt responsible because he had texted Shelly, and she was trying to answer the text when she had the accident."

Anna nodded. "This has been something he's talked about many times," she said in a choked voice. "I told him he needs to talk to someone."

Kati put a hand up. "We'll get there." She continued. "Then he admitted that he feels inferior to so many people because of how he felt when he was younger. When he saw Jon talking to you at the camp all those years ago, he got jealous. He was awkward around girls and lacked self-esteem; he carried those feelings throughout his life. He was the same way with Shelly."

Anna sat in shock as she listened to Kati. How was it possible that Will felt that way all this time? She never thought of him as awkward since the day she met him.

Kati put her hands up again. "I'm not done yet. So, have y'all noticed the Rip Wheeler look going with on him?"

A smile spread across Anna's face. "Yes, I did."

"Well, well, look who still likes my brother."

"I love him still. I'm just hurt," Anna said.

"Well, the chief put him on leave. He's been going to therapy working through Shelly's death, the loss of the baby Shelly was carrying, Daddy's death, and his jealousy issues. The guy confessed everything, including that Jon never cheated on me and loves me." She wiped her brow. "That's it."

Anna put up her hands. "Wait, Shelly was pregnant?" This was too much for her. No wonder he'd been a mess. That was a huge burden to carry.

"Jon didn't cheat on me. Will knew it, but Jon made him swear not to tell. Will didn't want to tell us about the baby because we were hurting enough. So, he carried it alone."

"Wow." Anna looked at Garrett. "Did you know any of this?"

Garrett shook his head, stood up, and placed his hands in the pockets of his shorts. "I'm going to go to bed. We have a long day tomorrow. Good night."

Anna gave him a side hug. "Good night."

"I think I'm going to turn in, too," Kati said. "You think you'll come home soon, Anna?"

"I do. The only thing we need to solve is Dr. Watts."

Before Garrett headed to his room, he said, "Kati and I have that under control. You worry about the fundraiser."

"We want you to stay. All of us," Kati said.

"I know. Night, y'all."

Anna heard the door shut to Garrett's room and the guest room.

The shock of everything Kati had told her had hit her with full force. Will had carried such a heavy burden after Shelly died. That was enough to take a toll on anyone. She shook her head when she thought of his low opinion of himself. She never saw anyone but her handsome cowboy, who always had enough to say.

She lay on the couch, grabbed her phone, and opened a text message to Will. Deep down, she wanted to text him to say she was proud of him and loved him. On the fourth time she typed it, she finally pressed send.

> Anna: I'm proud of you. I do love you.

She put the phone on the table, hoping she didn't open a can of worms. He deserved at least a crumb to continue progressing in therapy. Indeed, he was trying to change, and everyone deserved a second chance.

CHAPTER 55

Anna rolled her window down and felt the early morning warmth. Garrett stared ahead in the driver's seat with tired eyes hidden beneath his aviator sunglasses. They rode in silence, deep in thought, for the entire two-hour drive to the San Antonio Airport. Anna watched the orange sun emerge from beyond an endless landscape of rolling hills and remembered why she found this state so beautiful. They turned off the highway and parked outside the airport terminal as her excitement grew. After months of separation, Jenny—her best friend since childhood—was coming to visit.

"You haven't spoken since you got up."

She laughed. "I thought you wanted the quiet."

He gave her a friendly nudge. "No, I thought you wanted to be left alone." Anna noticed his eyes gleamed as he looked ahead.

She turned to see what had his attention. Coming toward baggage claim was Jenny, wearing a pink summer dress and waving enthusiastically with an enormous smile. She ran to meet her, almost losing her balance in haste. When they came together, Anna gasped with relief; it seemed like forever since she left for Cardinal Creek. This was the longest they'd ever gone without being able to share a hug. Smiles spread across their faces, and Anna couldn't believe how good it felt to be reunited with her best friend.

"Oh my God, it is so good to see you," Jenny said.

Anna noticed Garrett's gaze lingering on Jenny when their hug was complete. They walked arm and arm toward him. "Garrett, this is Jenny."

Garrett held out his hand. "Nice to meet you," he said with a strange note.

A grin spread across Jenny's face as she shook his hand. "Hi, nice to meet you."

"I can get your luggage if you like," he said.

She shrugged. "If you like. It's black with a bright pink ribbon and Hello Kitty stickers."

He looked at Anna and raised an eyebrow. "Hello Kitty?"

"Yes," Anna giggled, "since I can remember."

"Okay, a black bag with Hello Kitty. Y'all catch up while I get it."

When he took off for the baggage claim, Anna looked at Jenny. "I think he's smitten."

She waved a hand at her. "Nah, he's just being nice."

"Didn't you see how he looked at you?"

"Like I had a third head because I like Hello Kitty." She threw an arm around Anna. "Tell me what's going on with you. It looks like you haven't slept for a week."

What is wrong? How about what isn't wrong? Anna wasn't prepared to discuss this at the airport, but she could give her the short version. "Okay, I argued with Will, so we're staying with Garrett."

"Did y'all break up?"

"No, but I'll tell you about the rest in the truck." The tightness in her chest returned as she talked to Jenny. Everything with Dr. Watts started flooding back and made her stomach sour. His hands on her, the heat of his breath, him touching her . . .

"Anna." Jenny stood in front of her, waving a hand in her face. "You okay?"

The sound of Jenny's voice brought Anna back to the present. "Uh yeah. Oh, look, there's Garrett."

As Garrett walked toward them, Jenny leaned in and whispered, "What are two things that don't go together? A big cowboy like him pulling my bag with Hello Kitty on it."

They erupted into a fit of giggles. Leave it to Jenny to break the tension.

She held her hand out to Garrett. "I'll take my bag. Sorry you had to put up with the stickers, but it was easy to find."

A smile spread across Garrett's face. "It was indeed. I can take it. I'm fine."

"You are a gentleman."

They headed toward the exit to take care of some business for the fundraiser. Garrett had two stops scheduled to pick up stuff. Then they could head back to Cardinal Creek to prepare for another night of working with the Quiltin' Bees. Anna was excited to introduce Jenny to Liz, Kati, and the extraordinary ladies she'd met.

Garrett pulled into the first stop. It looked like a big security firm in downtown San Antonio. "I'll grab what I'm supposed to get for the fundraiser and talk to a friend for a minute. Y'all catch up." He winked, giving them a wide grin as he got out. "I'll be back."

As soon as the door closed, Jenny climbed into the front seat. "Okay, I need to know what's going on. You look exhausted, and your texts seemed off to me. Why are you staying with Garrett instead of at your cabin?"

There was a long silence before Anna answered. "Do you remember me telling you about the doctor at the hospital who was giving me the creeps?"

"Yeah."

"Well, things are really out of hand, and he was trying to . . ." Anna's throat tightened as she started to explain. Jenny put her hand on Anna's shoulder and squeezed. "Long story short, he's been harassing me since I started at the hospital. It all blew up a few days ago when he tried to force himself on me. His wife walked in and accused me of sleeping with him, and she slapped me. Then Will walked in, and the doctor made it look like I was a willing participant. Will just walked out and left me there. Since that time, Will admitted a lot of stuff to Kati about his wife's death and that he's getting therapy, but it's all very complicated."

Jenny gasped in horror. "Thank God you're okay."

Anna wiped the tears. "I was so scared . . . I still am. Then I was angry that Will left because I think Dr. Watts was going to . . . well, you know." Anna shivered at the idea of him taking more of her than he already had. He'd already humiliated her by making it look like she wanted him. Her blood boiled every time she replayed the scene in her head.

Jenny was quiet for a minute and just held Anna's hand. "Can I ask a question? Please don't get mad."

She quirked her eyebrow. "What?" There was fear cropping up inside Anna. Was Jenny going to question whether she asked for it or not? Anna couldn't think of one time she led Dr. Watts on.

"Why didn't you tell anyone?"

Before Anna could answer, the truck door opened, causing Anna to jump and scream. She covered her mouth and began to cry. "I'm sorry. I'm sorry."

Jenny hugged her. "It's okay." She moved over so Garrett could climb in. "Is there enough room for me to sit up here?"

He looked from Anna to Jenny. "Yes, here's the seatbelt."

Jenny and Anna buckled up. Garrett opened an envelope, taking the papers out. Anna watched the redness creep from his neck to his face as he read the documents. He sat shaking his head. "What the fu—" He looked at Anna. "Are you okay to read this right now? Looks like you're upset."

"Let me see them first," Jenny said, holding out her hand.

Garrett raised an eyebrow. "Why don't you ask Anna if it's okay, then I will."

She slowly turned her head toward him. "Excuse me?"

"This concerns Anna, so if she wants you to see them, she should say it's okay."

Jenny bit her bottom lip before responding. "Anna, would you like me to look at them first?" she said through clenched teeth.

"Garrett, it's okay."

He held the envelope in Jenny's direction, and she snatched it from his hand. Anna elbowed her in the ribs and whispered, "Stop."

She let out a long growl. "He's kind of rude."

He leaned toward Jenny. "I'm hard of hearing, not deaf. I can hear you."

"Oh my God, stop you two," Anna yelled. The stress was getting to her. She didn't need the two people she depended on right now to be her rock to bicker and drive her up the wall.

"Sorry," they muttered together.

When Garrett pulled out of the parking lot, Jenny started reading the report Garrett gave her. "Oh my God. What does this mean?"

"It means Anna is lucky someone walked in on them. The last woman didn't fare well. For some reason, she dropped the charges and disappeared after refusing to testify. Not long after that, Dr. Watts and his wife resigned from the hospital."

Anna began to tremble all over. "What happened to her?" She held her hand out for the papers. There was part of Anna that wanted to know exactly what he did and another part of her that didn't.

"No, I'm not going to let you read this," Jenny said, wrapping an arm around her. "Thank God his wife walked in."

"Because she knew what he'd had done and knew he would do it again," Anna choked.

"We have enough to get rid of him. Plus, some other women have also come to Kati," Garrett said.

He stopped at a large financial investment company and returned with an envelope. Anna gave him a quizzical look. "What's that? More bad news?"

Garrett grinned and said, "Nope, good news. But you'll have to wait until the night of the fundraiser."

They rode the rest of the way back to Cardinal Creek in silence, each lost in their thoughts. Anna wondered if presenting this information to the hospital would help her case. She noticed Jenny rested her leg against Garrett's leg. Jenny stared straight ahead. Garrett made a couple of side glances. Anna wondered what was happening between them but had other things to consider. She felt the fire of rage slowly builds in her chest, tightening its grip with every breath. Her thoughts raced through what had happened with Dr. Watts and how some people enjoyed manipulating innocent victims. Tears of anger rose in her eyes, and she clenched her fists so hard that her knuckles turned white. *No one should have to endure this kind of treatment*, she thought. She laid her head on Jenny's shoulder and decided it was in the past, but she was no longer a naïve woman for men to take advantage of. And she vowed to protect other women from predators.

WHEN THEY RETURNED from San Antonio, Garrett left for the ranch to feed the horses and do evening work for Will. Anna and Jenny grabbed some dinner at the Saddle Up before making their way to Cardinal Creek Quilting, where they would spend the evening working on completing the children's quilt and sorting things for both the silent and live auctions. As they shared a platter of nachos with beef brisket and a sweet tea, Anna looked over the plans for the fundraiser. Most of the things that needed to be done had been checked off. She just needed to find out how many tickets had been sold and see when the band planned to arrive the night of the fundraiser. Jenny had been quiet since they returned from San Antonio, which left Anna wondering if she was okay. Anna continued to look at the planner, aimlessly thinking about the events of the last week. She hadn't been to work since the incident, calling in sick every day, which gave Kati enough time to help her with all the issues with Dr. Watts. All Kati told her was that she and Garrett were trying to get as many witnesses as possible without her having to come forward. Kati thought she had been through enough.

She raised her eyes to find Jenny staring at her. "What's wrong? You've been quiet."

"Could ask you the same thing."

"I was terrified. To answer the question you asked in the truck. Dr. Watts and his wife threatened my nursing career. I didn't know what to do."

Jenny wrapped her fingers around Anna's hand. "I'm at a loss for words. It's difficult to comprehend you having to go through all this alone. Do you want to come home?"

Anna shrugged. "I'm torn between resigning and returning to the farm. Part of me wants to fight while the other part is so paralyzed with fear that running seems to be the only option."

"Do you love Will?"

"I do, but sometimes that isn't enough, especially when you're against a guy like Dr. Watts. What if Will doesn't want anything to do with me?"

"My guess is he wants to be with you."

Anna thought for a minute. That was true, and she didn't have many doubts about her and Will. She had a lot of doubts about her career and what would happen with Dr. Watts's situation.

Anna pasted on a smile. "You'll like the ladies from the quilt shop. They're so nice and funny. You should hear their stories. They also really like to help the awesome community. It's a nice mix of multiple generations."

"Sounds kind of like home at the coffee shop," Jenny said, smiling.

"We should head out. Let me pay the check." Anna paid the bill and grabbed a to-go bag filled with appetizers. "These ladies love to drink wine and eat."

Jenny looped her arm in Anna's. "Sounds like my kind of women."

They laughed as they exited the restaurant and headed toward the quilt shop. Just then, she saw Will, Eva, and Caden heading to the Cattle Drive Café. She watched as he interacted with Caden, who was smiling and appeared to be telling Will a story. Will held his hand, listened intently, and smiled as Caden talked. He was dressed in a pair of black Wranglers, and his muscles rippled under his navy T-shirt, which quickened her pulse. The black Stetson with the dark beard that was almost filled in gave him a sexy, mysterious look.

Jenny elbowed her, interrupting her ogling. "Is that him?"

Anna slowly nodded. "And his kids."

She crossed her arms across her chest. "Anna, he's . . . wow."

Again, Anna was overcome by a sick yearning to be with him. While Will held the door open for the kids, he caught her gaze, and when their eyes locked, every skin cell tingled, every neuron fired. She offered a small smile and waved. He placed his hand on his heart and then blew her a kiss. Anna touched her cheek. He looked at her for a few seconds, then entered the restaurant. It took everything Anna had not to run to him, but she needed to get inside to finish things for the fundraiser.

Anna knew she had to put everything on the back burner and concentrate on the tasks. There was so much to look at when they entered the quilt shop. Anna loved the vintage fabric and sewing machines at Cardinal Creek Quilting. There were even several Singer Featherweight machines for sale. It was a legendary American sewing machine and was highly desirable among collectors. The quilt shop created a warmth for Anna that reminded her of the loving home she grew up in with her grandparents. Jenny leaned in and whispered, "It's like being at your nana's house, isn't it?"

Anna nodded, holding back the tears. "I feel at home here. I don't want to leave."

"Then don't," Jenny said.

"Let's take this food to the table, and I'll introduce you." Anna walked to the food table, filled with fresh fruit, cookies, wine, and various appetizers. She took the appetizers out of the bag and opened them.

While arranging the food, Liz walked beside her, placed an arm around her shoulders, and squeezed tight. "Honey, are you okay? I've been so worried about you."

A raw, primitive grief overwhelmed her when her eyes met Liz. She opened her mouth to speak but stopped. Liz took her by the hand and led her to the husband's waiting room. The overwhelming need to be held must have been apparent in Anna's appearance. She wasn't sure how Liz knew what she needed, but her simple question had triggered a flood of emotions she had been holding in. The new information she'd learned this week had her mind reeling. *The simple answer is that I'm not okay. Dr. Watts is worse than I could have imagined, and Will abandoned me, but I can forgive that . . . eventually.*

Anna sat staring ahead. "My friend Jenny . . ."

"Oh, honey, Sissy took that little firecracker under her wing. Now talk to me."

A sob caught in Anna's throat. "Do you hate me? I swear I wasn't doing anything with Dr. Watts."

"I could never hate you, Anna. I'm so sorry you had to go through that with that bastard doctor. I was disappointed in Will when I found out that he left you. He has a big heart, but that doesn't mean he was right to walk out on you. He knows that too. He would have never forgiven himself if something even more terrible had happened to you. I know he loves you, and he's making some changes. I can see it in how he is with the kids. You need to know he believes you and is sorry he walked out."

"I know. I saw him earlier walking with the kids. I was touched by the way he was interacting with Caden. He's been working hard to communicate better with him . . . I saw that last week when they were in the arena. He was teaching Caden to rope."

"Do you think you're ready to see him?" Liz asked.

After seeing him before entering the quilt shop, she knew it was time. Anna replied. "Absolutely."

Liz took her by the hand, and they exited the store. As they turned the corner off the main street, Anna saw Will leaning against his truck. Her face lit up as Eva and Caden ran to her and wrapped their arms around her waist. She leaned down and hugged them tight.

She whispered to them, "I missed y'all."

They both kissed her cheek. Eva said, "We're going with Nana for a minute. Be right back. Keep Daddy company."

Anna nodded as Liz took the kids up the block. She stood staring at Will. The space between them seemed like a million miles. She saw the heartrending tenderness of his gaze as soon as he smiled and walked toward her with his classic swagger, making her stomach flip a thousand times.

"You have no reason to believe me after the way I acted, and I know I've hurt you deeply, but I promise I'll become the man you deserve. And I'll spend the rest of my days on God's green earth, making it up to you." He gathered her into his arms and held her tightly.

Locked in Will's embrace, she felt his lips touch her like a whisper. It was a kiss that her tired soul melted into. Anna had missed him every minute they had been apart.

He lifted her chin to meet his icy-blue eyes. "I hope you come back to the ranch soon. It's okay if you still need time. I'm going to therapy and spending some much-needed time with the kids. I'm here if you want to talk, but it's important that I fix myself before you and I become us."

Anna smiled. "I'm so proud of you." She placed her hand on his heart. "I see you, Cowboy—your heart and your soul. The rest is just gift wrap." She placed a hand on his cheek. "I love you with all my heart." When she finished, she knew the next thing she would say would stab his heart. "As much as I love you, I need to make sure that things are resolved with the Dr. Watts situation. I can't stay in Cardinal Creek if it's not resolved. I wouldn't feel safe."

Will pulled her into his arms and rested his chin on her head. "Then I guess we'll move to Missouri with you. I'll sell the ranch."

The world seemed to stop. He couldn't be serious. She stepped back. "What?"

"I'll sell the ranch, and we can move to Missouri. We can figure out all the equine stuff. If you need to leave because of Dr. Watts, we will. I want you to be safe and in my arms."

Anna was speechless. That offer . . . well, that meant a lot to her. "I promise I won't be ignoring you the next week or so. I'm just working on a project to make you very happy."

He held her hands and pulled her close. "darlin', nothing could make me any happier than having you with me."

She looked at him and smiled. "I love you. And I like the beard."

Taking her hand, he guided it to his face. "I missed your touch." He leaned in and kissed her neck. "I miss you so much."

She whispered, "I'm coming home tomorrow. Maybe I'll sneak over to your house."

A low moan escaped him. "I'll leave the door unlocked." He took her by the hand. "I should get you back."

As they walked to the quilt shop, Anna's heart soared. No matter the outcome with Dr. Watts, she knew deep in her soul that Will meant what he said, that he'd make a considerable change in his and his family's lives for her. That spoke volumes. She loved him with all her heart, and she would learn to forgive him. They could grow and learn together. Now, she needed to prove to him that she could raise the money for the equine center. She couldn't wait to see his face the night of the fundraiser.

CHAPTER 56

$\mathcal{A}$nna pulled up to the cabin and stepped out of the car. Will couldn't peel his gaze off the woman he loved and had almost lost. The burden of guilt weighed heavily on Will's shoulders. It would take a lifetime to make it up to her. Anna waved as she broke into an open, friendly smile, then laced her arm through Jenny's and walked toward him. Nervous, Will wondered how much Jenny knew about what a jerk he'd been to Anna.

"Hey," she said, leaning in and kissing his cheek. "This is my best friend. Jenny, this is Will."

Jenny stuck out her hand. "Hi, Will. It's nice to meet you finally."

"Same here, Jenny. Welcome to our home."

Jenny looked around. "It's lovely. Anna says you have some beautiful horses."

"If y'all want to ride, she can ride any of the horses here."

Anna laced her arm around Will's waist. "Thank you for that. We do want to go riding."

"I'll grab your stuff and put it in the cabin, then I'd better get back to work. I'll be taking off for the afternoon in a bit. I can catch up with you later." He winked at her, causing Jenny to giggle.

Anna swatted at her. "Stop."

Will kissed her on the cheek before he grabbed their bags and took them inside her cabin. They were sitting on the swing talking when Will walked back outside. He loved seeing how relaxed Anna was with Jenny around. It would be better for her if he sold everything and moved to Missouri with her. He would figure it all out for Momma and the kids. He loved Anna too much and would do anything for her.

When the screen door shut, Jenny jumped up. "I think I'll go change so we can go riding."

Will sat beside Anna, putting his arm around her. "Sneak over tonight. I want to hold you for a while," he whispered in her ear.

She nodded. "Just hold me?"

"That's it, baby." He kissed her head. "I'm gonna finish up some chores. Enjoy your day."

~

WILL NERVOUSLY RAN his fingers through his hair as he watched Jon and JW enter Saddle Up. He recognized the familiar way they laughed together, filling the bar with their energy, and for a moment, he felt a pang of regret. Even after years of not talking, the energy was still the same. He had always envied how these two friends seemed to fit in everywhere, how they quickly attracted people while he slinked into the shadows. He'd always felt he wasn't good enough because he was quiet. He now realized that not every woman preferred that in a man. Women like Anna and Shelly liked his calm, gentle nature, as Anna called it.

Will felt himself shrinking away from them as they approached. Jon waved at him, but JW's expression was still unreadable. He stood up when they reached the table, uncertain what would happen next. JW eyed him warily, crossing his arms over his chest. But after Jon broke the awkward silence with a joke about the rodeo circuit, JW reluctantly joined in the laughter, and Will breathed a sigh of relief.

Will held out his hand, and JW grasped it. "Thank you for what you did to protect Anna. Please sit." They took their seats. The bar was unusually crowded for a weekday afternoon. The mellow tone of George Strait's music filled the space, pulling everyone into its rhythm. Something shifted in Will's chest when the opening notes of "Cross My Heart" filled the air. He could almost feel Anna's presence beside him. At that moment, the tension evaporated.

Will cleared his throat. "First, I would like to apologize to both of you for the last twenty years. I made unfair demands to Jon about being your friend. I guess we can grow old but not grow up. I'm truly sorry for ruining your friendship." He looked at Jon. "Brother, you have been the best friend anyone could ask for, but I've sucked as a friend to you. I would understand if you—"

Jon held up a hand. "Will, don't finish that sentence. I accept your apology and hate to say it, but you're stuck with my sorry ass." He pointed to JW. "This guy, I wouldn't blame him if he told me to get screwed after how I treated him. I chose fire over bulls and you over him."

JW looked at them. "I hate to interrupt the bromance here, but Will, I accept your apology. I will say one thing: if you ever—and I mean *ever*—do what you did to Anna again, I will beat your ass. I'll never forget the terror on her face when I picked her up from her office. That . . ." He stopped and let out a sigh. "Garrett found out that scumbag doctor raped at least two women. They ended up refusing to testify and disappeared. Both cases were dismissed, and he and his wife moved on."

Will couldn't believe what he was hearing. The word *rape* kept ringing in his ear like a loud bell. He swallowed hard. "Oh God."

JW leaned in with both hands on the table. "So that you understand, he intended to rape her that day. He could have come back and attacked her after you left her. It makes me sick to think that could have happened to her or any other woman."

Will took a long draw on his beer. A knot tightened in his stomach. "Do you know if anyone has seen him at the hospital?" He asked, trying to steady his voice.

Jon shrugged. "Why?"

"Because Anna is at the ranch with Jenny. He wouldn't go there, would he?" The sound of Will's heart was beating in his ears.

JW shook his head. "I spoke with Kati. He and his wife have been laying low and haven't been seen, so it's not likely, but I'll text Garrett to see if he could go hang out at the ranch until you get home."

"JW, I don't know how to thank you for everything you've done for Anna. I promise my days of jealousy are over. I'm sorry for the past too."

JW nodded. "It's in the past. Maybe I can get Jon to get back to riding bulls."

"Not a chance," Jon said. "Aren't you broken?"

"Never. I'm in the gym, ready to go back next season."

Jon shook his head. "You're crazy."

JW laughed. "Like running into a burning building is sane."

"He has a point, Jon." Will laughed.

Jon got up. "This calls for a round of tequila."

Drinking with these guys didn't seem like a good idea to Will, but he needed to blow off some steam. He sent a text to Anna and Kati.

> Will: We may need you ladies for a ride tonight. We're at Saddle Up.

> Kati: Emoji with wide-open eyes.

> Anna: Should we get the puke bucket? Lol

> Kati: Oh no way, they're on their own.

> Will: Who's going to pick us up?

> Kati: All of us. Call us when you're ready.

Will sent a text to just Kati.

> Will: Is Anna safe on the ranch? Where is Watts?

> Kati: He's been reported to the administration and medical board. We're almost done. He shouldn't bother Anna again.

> Will: I know what he did. I'm sorry, Kati.

> Kati: I know you are. And I forgive you and love you, big bro. Thanks for telling me about Jon, btw.

Jon set down three tequila shots for each of them. "Okay, guys, one's for the past we're leaving behind, one's for the present where you can fix the past, and one's for the future where we aren't supposed to make the same mistake twice."

They each slammed them—one, two, three—then Will ordered a round of beers. They drank and talked about their high school rodeo days. The thing that clouded their friendship disappeared with an apology. He looked at Jon, laughing with JW. He knew he was blessed to have Jon as a friend and a brother. It was essential for Will not to get too drunk because he wanted to spend some time with Anna, so they ordered one last round of beers, and he texted Kati to get them.

> Will: Come to get us, crazy bastards. Can we give JW a ride home?

> Kati: Sure, but he texted Garrett already.

> Will: How do you know?

> Kati: He's on guard duty.

> Will: He's there?

> Kati: Yeah, we're all coming.

> Will: Make sure everything's locked up.

> Kati: Yes, dear. Lol, we're on our way.

JW leaned back in his chair, discussing his time on the rodeo circuit: his wins and ankle injury. Jon and Will shared stories about their jobs as firefighters. As they shared stories, laughs sprinkled in between, Will decided to buy another round of tequila shots. They clinked glasses and enjoyed one last round before venturing outside the bar into the warm night air.

Will stepped out of the bar, and his gaze was drawn to a figure—Anna's bright red shock of hair held his attention as she sauntered toward him. She smiled when she reached him, and his calloused hand moved to her face, cradling it as he looked into her eyes, then leaned forward to kiss her with an enthusiasm he'd never felt before. "I love you, baby. Let's go home." For the first time in a long time, Will's soul was free.

CHAPTER 57

On the morning of the fundraiser, Anna woke up early to review everything that needed to be done. It amazed her that they had kept the event's details a secret. Kati had reported that they'd sold out of the tickets, which raised $10,000. There were items for both the silent auction and the live auction. A few single guys from the fire department had even volunteered to be auctioned for a date with a firefighter. Anna shook her head, smiling. Jon had offered to organize the entire event. Her heart soared at his offer and the community's love put into this event for Will.

She grabbed carrots from the refrigerator and headed to the barn. Her plan was to help Will with the morning feeding and then ask him if they could all get together for dinner at Saddle Up for Jenny's last night in town. The thought of having enough money for Will to finish what he needed to open the equine center warmed her insides, and it was a time to celebrate.

She grabbed the wheelbarrow to muck the stalls when she entered the stable. She put in her AirPods and played her George Strait playlist.

Thunderbird hit his hoof on the ground, causing Anna to smile. "I'm coming there first." She pulled carrots out of her pocket. "Look what I have." He whinnied and released a big gusty blow from his nose. Anna smiled, scratched his cheek, and held her hand out with a carrot.

Thunderbird moved his head up and down and nickered toward the stable entrance. Anna turned to see Will approaching her. His blue eyes met her emerald-green ones, and her cheeks burned hot scarlet. This was the moment they had been working toward since she found out there was no money. Tonight, she would show Will how loved he was by so many.

He increased his stride until he reached her, and she was in his arms in one forward motion. "Mornin', darlin'," he whispered.

The touch of his lips on hers was like a shockwave throughout her entire body. "Wow, good morning."

Thunderbird nudged Will's shoulder, causing them to laugh. Will took a carrot from Anna and fed it to the mischievous horse.

"I want to take Jenny out since it's her last night in town. I invited Jon, Kati, Garrett, Liz, and others for dinner at Saddle Up." She wrapped her arms around his waist. "I thought we could dance."

"Of course, darlin'," he murmured, kissing her neck.

"Great, we should hurry and get done. I need to go shopping."

He slapped her backside. "Take off. You and Jenny, go have fun."

It took everything Anna had to contain her excitement. It was time for her to get an outfit, finish the final touches at Saddle Up, and do a few last-minute things for tonight. She threw her arms around his neck. "I love you. Jon is going to bring you tonight. Jenny and I are going to, ya know, do girl things and meet you there with Kati."

Will raised an eyebrow. "Is Momma coming with Kati?"

"She's going with the Hens," she yelled as she hurried out of the barn. It was time for her to exit quickly before he figured everything out; she could tell he was getting suspicious. Anna rushed to the cabin, eager for her and Jenny to get new outfits before their spa appointment. The door to the cabin opened just as Anna reached the porch. Jenny walked out with their purses. "Alright, let's hit the road."

JENNY AND ANNA spent the day enjoying each other's company and preparing for the fundraiser. Anna wanted to make sure she looked nice for Will. She tried not to let the whole thing with Dr. Watts hover like a cloud over her head while she and Jenny enjoyed shopping at Diamond Saddle Boutique, getting pedicures, and having lunch at Cowgirl Sweets and Treats.

Anxiety squeezed Anna's chest every time she thought about the fate of her job on Monday. The worst part was that Jenny was leaving, and she loved having her best friend here as a support. The hospital board would be issuing a verdict on Dr. Watts's alleged sexual harassment violations. *Alleged . . . ha!* Cathy Watts was also under investigation for using her position of authority to harass nurses.

Whenever Anna heard the name Watts, her body tensed up, a wave of nausea rolled through her, and she felt like she was going to be ill. She did her best to push all that aside while focusing on the fundraiser. Tonight was for Will and his family to realize Shelly's dream of an equine therapy center. The best part was that it would be opened on Shelly's birthday.

The afternoon flew by for Anna and Jenny. After finishing their pedicures, they returned to the ranch to prepare for tonight's event. They were going to Saddle Up early to ensure everything was ready. They were supposed to meet Liz and her gang at five.

When Anna returned to the ranch, she saw Will walking away from Liz's cabin. Their gazes locked, and butterflies fluttered in her stomach. He waved at her and smiled. She smiled back, continuing up the road to her cabin.

"Girl, you've got it bad, and so does he," Jenny said.

"I do, I suppose."

Anna took extra care with her preparation for the evening, selecting the sweet-smelling vanilla cinnamon soap that Will loved. She carefully applied her makeup and hair product, taking time to ensure that her wavy copper locks lay across her shoulders dramatically. Then, she slid into a beautiful cream-colored lace dress that hung off one shoulder and flared out at the waist. She wore a turquoise-and-silver belt and brown boots with bright turquoise accents to complete the look. Finally, she lined and painted her lips with a deep wine shade of lipstick.

Jenny looked her up and down when she entered the room. "Woo-hoo, you look gorgeous."

Anna flushed. "Stop it." She did a double take in Jenny's direction. "Wow, so do you."

Jenny admired herself in the mirror, fingering the intricate silver barrette with a turquoise stone embedded in the center. Her light chestnut curls cascaded down her back and framed her face against the brown spaghetti-strapped dress that hit just above her knee and boasted small turquoise patterns. She paired it with a short denim jacket and brown boots, making her legs appear longer.

"Thanks. Do ya think Garrett will notice?" she teased.

Anna narrowed her eyes. "Do you like him?"

She shrugged. "He's nice enough, but something about him seems . . . I don't know, sad, maybe."

"What makes you say that?"

"Forget it, just a vibe."

Anna was curious why Jenny got that vibe from Garrett. She hadn't told Jenny about his time in the military or that he'd shared that he was also grieving someone. When it was time to leave for Saddle up Anna smiled at their reflections in the mirror.

She looked at Jenny. "It's show time. Let's go."

∼

ANNA PULLED into the parking lot of Saddle Up and parked. A whirlwind of emotions coursed through Anna when they got to the entrance. Anna knew she would have to talk, but talking in front of people tied her stomach in knots. A ball of worry and foreboding twisted in her gut like a fist, trying to bury itself in her rib cage. She just wanted everything to be perfect. The ball of worry was replaced with butterflies in anticipation of seeing Will's face when he walked in and saw what they had done.

Jenny suddenly stopped before they reached the entrance. "The ladies have a huge surprise for you," she said. Anna was confused but also excited. Jenny placed a hand over Anna's eyes as they entered. "You ready?" she whispered.

Anna nodded. "Yes."

When Jenny removed her hand, Anna saw Maggie standing right before her.

Tears immediately sprang to her eyes as Maggie wrapped her in her arms. "God, it's good to see you." She stepped back and dabbed Anna's eyes. "We're gonna mess up our makeup."

Anna laughed. "I don't care. It's so good to see you."

"Oh honey, it looks great here, and these ladies are great. I stayed with Sissy last night. I'm the newest Bee!"

"Or hens, as Will calls them," Anna said. They both laughed. "Let's go see what's happening."

Saddle Up had transformed into the perfect place for the fundraiser. Each ticket included dinner and drinks donated by Saddle Up, and a local band offered to play free. Anna liked that they sang a whole bunch of George Strait songs, not as good as *the king*, but his songs, nevertheless. A flicker of a smile passed across Anna's lips in anticipation as she unveiled the children's quilt. It had been made from colorful blocks of fabric, each decorated with a drawing from the children who attended the autism therapy center. As Anna admired the intricate details and vivid colors, Sissy mentioned that this charity quilt could raise upwards of fifteen thousand dollars. Anna felt a sense of pride when Sissy shared they had named it Rising Stars in honor of the children who would benefit from the equine center.

She felt a tap on her shoulder. When she turned around, she saw Kati.

"Hey," Anna said. "You made it!"

Kati nodded. "I was supposed to leave work early today, but the hospital administrator called me into the office."

Anna's stomach dropped. "What?"

"It's good news," Kati said with a relieved laugh. "They fired both Dr. Watts and Cathy Watts. They want you to come back and continue the awesome work you've been doing. The hospital administrator even had letters from patients and their families thanking you for your help. The program is a huge success."

The news was slowly sinking in. If Dr. Watts and his wife were gone, she could stay in Cardinal Creek. She could stay with Will and keep doing the job she loved. A smile slowly spread across Anna's face. "Oh my gosh, you did it."

"And I have huge news!" Kati said. "Are you ready?"

"What more could there possibly be?" Anna asked with a laugh.

She jumped up and down with glee. "They asked me to take Cathy Watts's place. The administrator felt that anyone who would go to great lengths to protect a group of nurses should lead them."

Anna threw her arms around Kati. "I couldn't agree more. Thank you, Kati. Thank you so much. I'll never forget what you did for me."

"Let's go share the news. Then get this party started! Jon texted that they're on their way."

CHAPTER 58

"Why are you knocking?" Will said as he opened the door to see Jon standing there with a goofy grin.

Jon shrugged. "I better get used to that. When you marry Anna, I don't need to walk in and see her naked."

Will rolled his eyes. "Dude, shut up. I have no idea why I'm so nervous."

Anna had been gone so much this week, and he suddenly became uncertain about everything. Had she changed her mind about being with him? But no, that would be wild. She'd been fine earlier this morning when she came to the stable to help.

As he climbed into Jon's truck, Will's stomach was tied in knots. He was both excited to see Anna and anxious about finding out whether Dr. Watts would get fired. Then, the added threat that he would show up somewhere and hurt Anna lingered in his mind. He closed his eyes and summoned a deep breath, holding it in and slowly letting it out.

Without thinking, he said, "If they don't fire Dr. Watts, I'm moving to Missouri with Anna. I love her too much not to."

"Trust your sister, Will. She's worked tirelessly on this since he attacked Anna," Jon said.

Relief flowed through Will. Undoubtedly, he would leave Cardinal

Creek to be with Anna, but he didn't want to. He would only stay if it was safe for Anna, and he hoped it would be. He needed to trust Kati.

Jon pulled into the parking lot. Will looked around, wondering why it was so crowded. When they got out, Jon clasped his shoulder. "Let's do this. I think I'm going to ask your sister on a date."

"Go for it. Just take it easy on the drinking."

Jon opened the door for Will. "Yes, Father. I'll keep it to a six-pack."

Will laughed as he entered. He did a double take when he saw a banner stretched across the stage that read, "Fundraiser for the Shelly Deluca Equine Therapy Center."

He turned to Jon, his breath catching in his lungs. "What is this?" His voice broke.

Tears filled his eyes to the brim until they spilled over and ran down his cheeks. He looked around until he found Anna talking to Jenny, the hens, and his mother. He walked over and stopped in front of her. When their eyes met, a warmth flowed inside him. The words he needed to express, everything he felt, were nowhere to be found.

He swept her into his arms. "I love you," he whispered in her ear. "How did you do all of this?"

"With a lot of help."

He took her face in his hands and looked into her eyes. "You are amazing." First, he kissed the tip of her nose and then her soft mouth. He stepped back and looked at her. "darlin', you look radiant."

She leaned in. "I need to tell you something before we get started. Can we sneak off for a minute?"

He nodded and led her outside. The knot in Will's stomach returned. He just knew he would end up having to go to Missouri. *The important thing is that Anna is safe.* That was the mantra Will used until they were somewhere private.

Anna turned to him and took his hands. "We don't have to wait until Monday. Kati told me they fired Dr. Watts." She threw her arms open. "I don't have to leave. They're pleased with the program I've been building."

Will grabbed her and hugged her, lifting her off the ground. "I can't believe it. You must be ecstatic."

"Kati said the administration received letters from family and patients about the care they've been receiving and how much it has helped. That's what fulfills me, helping others."

"Oh wow. After this, we'll celebrate." A wave of relief washed over Will. He and Anna could start their life in Cardinal Creek with Dr. Watts out of the picture. He gazed into her eyes; he knew that being with her was all that mattered. Anything was possible with her by his side.

"Jenny's mom, Maggie, is here too." She took him by the hand. "We better get inside. You won't believe the best part of the news, but Kati should tell you that."

People began to arrive, and food and drinks were abundant. Will recognized many of the faces as community members he'd known for most of his life. His surprise came when JW Walker entered with his father, James, one of the area's biggest landowners. Until recently, there hadn't been much affection between the two, but things had changed after Will apologized to him. They shake hands and exchange greetings. Will put an arm around Anna and introduced her to James.

"Well, this is the woman who persuaded me to donate," James said before handing her a check. "Will, you have yourself a keeper! She knows a lot about horses and how they can help people with more than autism." With that, he excused himself to mingle with others.

Anna was giddy as she stood beside him. "What is it, love?" Will asked. She showed him the check, and he whistled between his teeth.

"This is just the beginning. We'll start a live auction after Garrett and I present two more checks. Others are bidding on items for the silent auctions," Anna explained.

As Anna continued explaining the evening's events, the band started playing "Carrying Your Love with Me" by George Strait. She held her hand out to Will and said, "We have to dance before it gets too wild. I requested this as the first song."

He took her hand, and they headed for the dance floor. He pulled her close; the earlier knot in his stomach slipped away, and butterflies took over. Since his dad and Shelly's deaths had left him with an empty soul, he had merely been living from day to day. Therapy had brought him closer to Caden and rekindled their relationship. He was deeply touched by the love and support he received from family and friends, whom he'd hurt or ignored since Shelly's death. Anna had always been there, giving of herself even when she needed comforting.

During the dance, Anna whispered, "Please never think you aren't enough. You've always been enough for me. Just the right amount of everything. There's only one William Deluca; he's the man I love and always have."

Will let out a long breath, choking back his emotions. He hoped he could say something, but the emotion clogged his throat. "Thank you. I'm so . . ." He cleared his throat. "I'm . . . so overcome with emotion, but I can say one thing. I love you always. You're an amazing woman."

When the song ended, Anna took Will to meet with Garrett and the auctioneer. The rest of the evening was a whirlwind until it was time to present the money. Anna and Garrett brought Will to the stage and presented him with two checks totaling eight hundred thousand dollars. Will stared at the checks in amazement.

"I can't believe all of this. I'm in awe." Will stood looking out at the crowd. There was a deep swell of emotion as he saw the smiling faces, overwhelmed by the words *loved* and *good enough*.

Anna announced, "Besides these two checks, I would like to thank Mr. James Walker for his generous donation of two hundred thousand dollars. Now, we will begin with the live auction."

The family gathered to watch the live auction as Will walked around the table to hug everyone who helped. He squeezed his momma extra hard. "Thank you." She smiled at him and squeezed his hand.

Garrett, Will, and Anna went to the front to close the event. Garrett thanked everyone for coming, and Anna announced that they'd raised one hundred thousand dollars from ticket sales, donations, and the live auction. It was surreal when Will heard the total raised so far had surpassed a million dollars. When Anna handed him the microphone, he thought of all their support and couldn't believe how many people cared without him noticing.

"Wow, what an amazing evening," Will said, exhaling into the microphone. "Thank you to everyone who organized this fundraiser, the donors, and my family for believing in me. Thanks to Anna and Garrett, who made a small idea work."

As they exited the stage, Will's legs were shaking, but his hand was steady as he squeezed Anna's hand.

The band started playing "Cross My Heart" by George Strait. Will pulled Anna to the dance floor and held her tightly. "Thank you for everything. Seriously, Anna, this wouldn't have been possible without you."

"I guess I am pretty awesome, aren't I?" she teased, gazing up at him with those beautiful eyes.

"darlin', you have no idea."

She laughed. "Well, it's time to prepare everything for the grand opening in two months. The work never ends."

Will leaned down, kissed her, and whispered, "Anything is possible as long as you're by my side."

EPILOGUE

Two months later

Since the fundraiser, a whirlwind of work went into getting the equine center opened on time. Will continued his therapy visits while rejoining the fire department, fully fit for duty. He was delighted that Anna was reinstated as Director of Palliative Care, and he was proud of her and Kati for standing up against workplace harassment.

With his anxiety at bay, he carried on with shifts in the ambulance and hospital visits. Overseeing renovations with Anna's help, they worked hard to have a successful launch day. Additionally, Jenny and Maggie came to lend their assistance and returned for the grand opening. Watching everything come together made Will blissfully happy and fully alive.

Will stared at himself in the mirror. Sweat trickled down his neck, and his pulse was racing. His starched sky-blue button-up shirt and dark Wranglers were pristinely pressed. He opened the black velvet case, revealing a vintage pear emerald ring with rose gold twig leaf floral setting, diamond and emerald accents shimmering in the light. His hands trembled as he placed the box into his front pocket. Taking a deep breath, Will stepped out of the room and headed toward the grand opening, hoping and praying that Anna would say yes. He smiled as he realized the night may end much better than he had imagined.

He was pleased with the restored rustic appeal when he entered the newly decorated lodge dining hall. The dining hall had large, sturdy tables with turquoise-and-brown couches, chairs, and cowhide rugs. The walls were decorated with rustic steel stars and old rodeo pictures they had acquired. Will smiled at the accomplishments that resulted from the fundraiser.

When Anna entered, Will gasped at the sight. She wore jeans that clung to her curves, a bleached-out blue button-down, a brown T-shirt, brown boots with turquoise accents, and a Stetson. He quickly embraced and kissed her softly, inhaling her sweet scent.

"Hey, darlin'," he said huskily, "you look beautiful."

"Cowboy, you look great and smell even better," she said playfully before kissing his neck.

"darlin', you better stop, or we won't get to breakfast," he teased.

"Wouldn't that be awful?" Her silky voice held a challenge.

Will smiled coyly. "Not at all, but we have an opening, and I think we need . . ." He could almost read her mind, or was it just the lustful sparkle in her eyes that sent chills down his spine?

She giggled. "You are so right."

Liz stepped out of the kitchen in her Kiss the Cook apron, beaming. "Breakfast is ready!" she exclaimed.

Everyone moved to their seats as the delicious smells reached their noses—scrambled eggs, bacon and sausage, pancakes, and biscuits smothered in gravy. Will surveyed the table, filled with his closest friends and family who had supported him through the turbulent past four years. He was overwhelmed by the thoughtfulness of this moment. His family had forgiven him for past mistakes, and Anna had worked tirelessly to ensure Shelly's memory lived through this center. It was a day of grace and peace, and he could hardly believe it.

Will kissed Anna. "You are why this day is happening."

"It's very much a community effort. They prove love never dies."

When the ranch gates opened to let those invited to the grand opening inside, beads of sweat popped out on Will's forehead. Anna squeezed his hand like she sensed he was nervous, or maybe it was the sweat beading on his lip and brow.

"Cowboy, it's okay. We're in this together," Anna said.

Will chuckled. "How did you know?"

"Your eyes are like saucers."

He furrowed his brow. "No, they aren't."

"Now that you're relaxed, let's have fun. Look around this place. Maybe we can dance." She wiggled her eyebrows.

He gently held her face in his calloused hand. "Ginger, you're right. Let's have fun."

Will surveyed the property in awe. Three cabins had been renovated, and Anna's team of Liz, Kati, and the Quiltin' Bees had brightened the exteriors with colorful potted plants. There was a wooden dance floor surrounded by gingham-draped tables adorned with Mason jars filled with wildflowers that seemed to have sprouted from nowhere in the Texas heat, and vintage lights twinkled from the trees like stars. In addition, Garrett, Jon, and JW had built new fences for the arena, while Jenny had taken on setting up activities for children.

Will hoped he could convince Jenny to manage the physical therapy department. Every time Anna spoke about her friend, she lit up, and Jenny joining their team would make them both happy. Will loved the sparkle in Anna's eyes when they all worked together.

The smell of slow-cooked brisket and sweet, smoky baked beans wafted around the picnic tables as friends and family gathered for the equine center grand opening. Will stood apart from the crowd, admiring a golden orange sunset on the horizon. He uttered a silent thanks to whatever forces may have been at work in helping make the grand opening a reality. The particular force had arrived from out of town, and he knew it was Shelly's handiwork.

THE SUN SANK BEHIND the hills, its golden rays fading as sparkling stars illuminated the night sky. Will watched the glimmering lights cast their magical glow onto the dance floor, where he planned to ask Anna to marry him—a fitting finale to a beautiful day.

Will nervously marched into the lodge in search of Liz, who was helping Eva and Caden get ready for the big moment.

He paused when he heard Jenny's voice calling out his name. She arrived at his side and gave him an encouraging smile. "We're ready. I've got your back, Will. I'll get her to the dance floor." Her warm eyes met his, and she gave him a reassuring touch. "Hey, she loves you. Don't be nervous."

Will nodded silently, and Jenny rushed off full of purpose.

Liz arrived, her face beaming with joy as she held Eva's and Caden's hands. "You ready?"

"More than you know," he said.

Eva had a tight grip on a bundle of roses wrapped in white paper.

Will's heart raced with anticipation. "Y'all ready?"

Caden nodded eagerly, his short brown hair combed back neatly and boots polished until they shone. He put a reassuring hand on Will's shoulder. "We got this, Daddy. Right, Eva?"

Eva stepped forward in her crisp new denim jeans and a tan T-shirt with horses galloping across the front. On top of her head was a brown straw hat with a turquoise-and-silver medallion pinned to it. She glanced up at Will with a warm smile, her presence enough to ease his nerves. "Daddy, what do you think of my outfit? Nana got it for me."

Will smiled at Eva. "Eva, you are beautiful as always."

The trio then moved toward the dance floor, Will taking their hands in each of his own to steady himself against the thundering beat inside his chest. Caden and Eva gave him strength, and they both had carefree smiles. As soon as Will saw Anna, everyone else faded away.

She smiled. "Hey, Cowboy, I was looking for you."

"You were?" he said. "I was looking for you too." Their gazes locked.

Caden grabbed Anna's hand excitedly. "And Dad was looking for us. Don't we look nice? I took a bath!"

Anna laughed as she looked down at him. "You look handsome." She hugged him sweetly before gazing at Will as if they shared a secret bond.

Eva handed Anna roses and explained shyly that they were for helping them so much. Tears glistened in Anna's eyes as she thanked them both, pausing to remark how beautiful Eva looked in her special outfit. Will could only stare in silent admiration, wondering what he'd done in life to deserve her kind heart.

Anna was talking with Eva and Caden when she realized the group was standing around them. "Is everything okay?" she asked Will.

He went down on one knee. "It's more than okay. darlin', I would love it if you would become my wife." Waiting for her answer, the air seemed to be sucked out of Will's lungs. *Please let her say yes.*

Tears trickled down Anna's cheeks, and her hand went over her mouth. She gave Will a slow nod. "Yes," she whispered.

He stood, took her in his arms, picked her up, and twirled her around. "I love you," he said.

"I love you too," Anna said. Then she looked at their family and friends. "I need to borrow Will for ten minutes, then ya'll better cue up some King George so I can dance with"—she motioned to Will—"this guy."

Anna grabbed Will's hand and pulled him into a shadowy alcove. Two chairs faced a field, and she pointed to one of them. "Sit," she said as she sat beside him. A couple of seconds later, Anna turned to Will with a cupcake on her lap, and a single flickering candle illuminated her face. "Look up at the stars. There are a billion of them, I think. One of them is Shelly. Wish her a happy birthday."

Will closed his eyes and blew out the candle, silently wishing that someday he'd get married and have a baby with Anna.

"What did you wish for?" Anna asked when he opened his eyes.

With a teasing smile, Will replied, "A baby!" before quickly adding that he was only joking.

"That wouldn't be so bad," she said, poking his side. "And we'd have fun making it."

Laughter bubbled between them as the familiar notes of George Strait's "Carrying Your Love with Me" began to play. Without hesitation, Will grabbed her hand and pulled Anna onto the dance floor, where they swayed under an impossibly starry sky.

The End

Follow Jon and Kati's love story in *Their Mended Hearts*.

ACKNOWLEDGMENTS

I have to be thankful for many things in my life, but the love and support of my husband have been a blessing. As I counted my blessings, I have eight, including five children, a fabulous son-in-law, and two amazing grandkids.

When I wanted to give up, my husband always encouraged me. I am truly blessed to have such a wonderful man in my life.

To the rest of my family and friends, thank you for your love and support on this journey.

Since the dedication is so short, I want to acknowledge the people who got me here. My grandparents had an unwavering belief in me. Losing both of them broke my heart. I treasure the memories, and they continue to live in my heart.

Thank you to Danika Bloom for being such a great teacher.

This book is dedicated to those who have lost loved ones. May they find comfort in Will and Anna's story. Grief is an individual journey and will be different for all who have experienced it.

This is the short list of people I have lost that touched my life. Some played a minor role because they died when I was young; others played a significant role. My grandparents played the most significant role in my life. They were my anchors. Losing an anchor in life can be devastating. I have learned the more you love, the greater the loss. Imagine this life without that kind of love.

Oliver Cole 1922-2002
Lily Cole 1923-2006
John Rodriguez 1935-1968
Sheila Rodriguez 1946-2020

The Cole Brothers and their wives
Dorthea Rodriguez (Dottie) 1956-1972
Sofia Hernandez 1947-2023

Gone but never forgotten.

ABOUT THE AUTHOR

My journey as a romance author is deeply rooted in my personal experiences of love, loss, and resilience. The profound impact of the losses I have endured, including the passing of my grandparents and my mother, has shaped my perspective on life and love.

My love story is one of healing and finding joy after heartache, and it mirrors the themes I explore in my novels.

As a survivor of grief and a believer in the power of love, I channel my experiences into crafting stories that resonate with the complexities and triumphs of the human heart. My writing is a testament to the idea that love can emerge from the most unexpected places, offering hope and healing.

Made in the USA
Middletown, DE
31 May 2024